TRIUMPH TO TRAGEDY

Book Four

The Clash of Pétion and Christophe

DANIEL J.D. BAYARD

In Collaboration with Jean-Bernard Bayard

Cover by Carl Craig

Illustrations by Dian Triyasa

L&D Publishing

Daniel J.D. Bayard

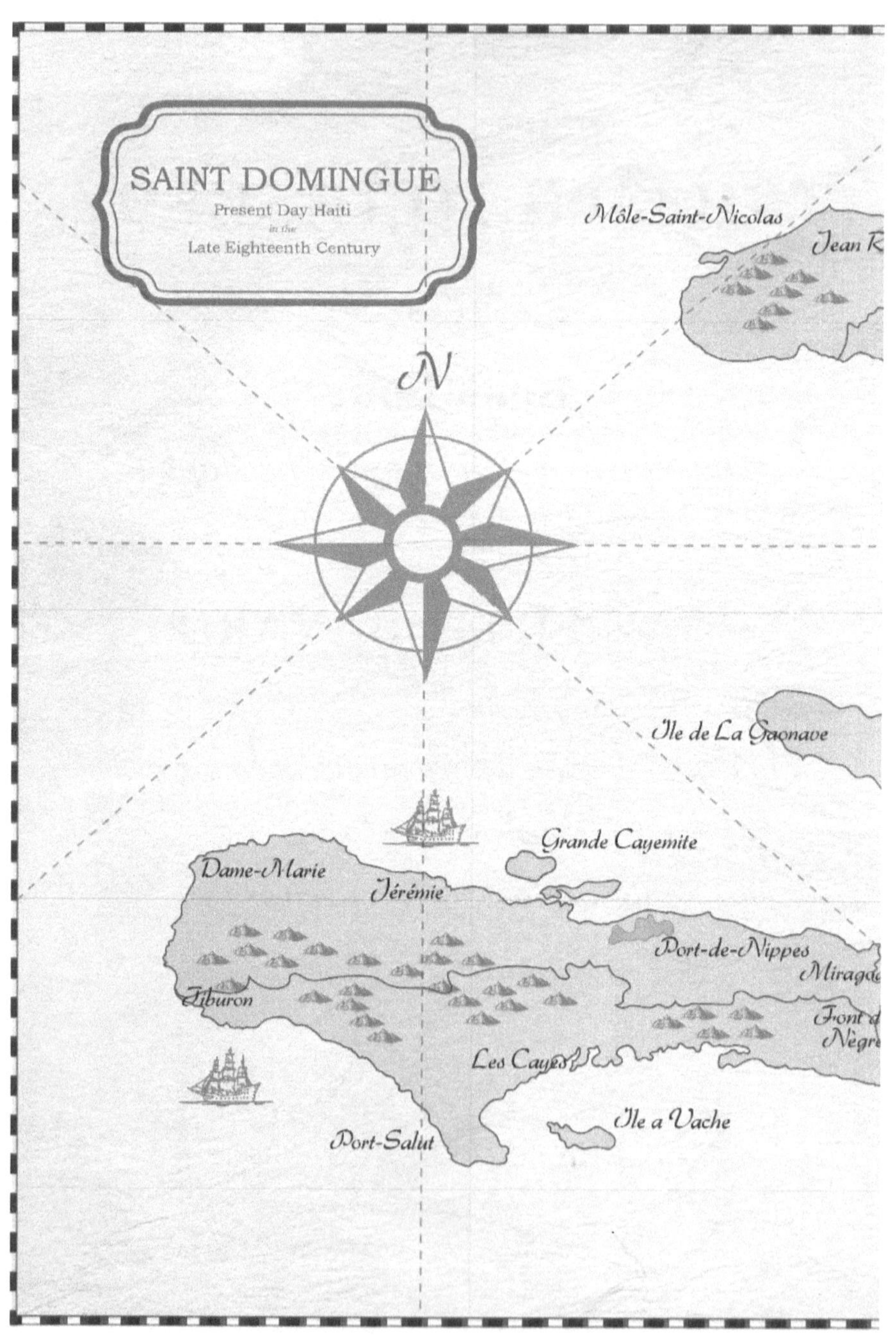

La Tortue
Port-de-Paix
'abel
LaBorgne
Cap Français
Fort Liberte
Fort Dauphin
Limbé
Acul Plaine du Nord
Gros Morne
Terrier Rouge
Plaisance
Dondon
Ouanaminthe Dajabon
Enmery
Marmelade
Gonaïves
Saint Raphael
La Croix
Ravine à Couleuvre
Estêr
Hinché
La Crête à Pierrot
Verrettes
Petit Riviére
Banica
Saint Marc
Artibonite Valley
Cote Espanol
Mirebalais
Elias Pina
Arcahaie
Sources Puantes
Croix des Bouquets
Port-au-Prince
(Port Républicain)
Léogane
Plaine de Cul de Sac
Grand-Goâve
Petit-Goâve
Jacmel
Bahoruco

Daniel J.D. Bayard

Triumph To Tragedy
Book Four

First Edition

First Printing, 2024
L&D Publishing

Email: Author@TriumphToTragedy.com

Paperback ISBN: 978-1-961297-24-1
Hardcover ISBN: 978-1-961297-23-4
eBook ISBN: 978-1-961297-25-8

www.TriumphToTragedy.com

Dedicated to the strong women in my life:
My loving wife Lily
My sisters Marie-Denise and Mica

With Wonderful Memories:
Mom, Dad and Jackie

To my children;
Laura, Daniel III, Phillippe and Brock

And my Grandchildren;
Bianca, Calista, Daniel IV, Andre, Julien, and Adrian

Parental Discretion Warning

ADULT SEXUAL CONTENT
GRAPHIC VIOLENCE
Not suited for young readers under 18.

For Young Adults under 18 years of age, refer to:

**TRIUMPH TO TRAGEDY
YOUNG ADULT SERIES**

The Cover Artist

Carl Craig

Style
"Symbolic Expressionism"

"My Passion Lies in The Challenge of Capturing the Beauty, the Delicacy and the Fragility of the Human Expression"

Born in Ayiti, moved to New York with his family at the age of 15. He served honorably in the U.S. Air Force for more than 5 years. He pursued a Bachelor of Science Degree in Finance and International Business at Florida International University. After a successful career in the financial markets for 16 years, Carl ended his vocation on "Wall Street" and decided to apply his experience and acumen in international consulting.

Despite his successes in the financial markets and as an international consultant, Carl has chosen to walk away from all the power and structure to satisfy his thirst for creativity by unleashing his talent in the arts: painting, photography, and music.

As a self-taught artist, he brilliantly and skillfully projects the inspiration he finds in his models. Since 2008, his work has been constantly displayed on the local and international markets. In 2015 and 2016 Carl was the semi-finalist in the yearly national contest organized by the Bombay Sapphire, The Artisans Series.

Carl is internationally celebrated and has exhibited his works in Mexico by special invitation from Ayisyen Ambassador in Mexico City. His artworks have also been shown in Cayenne (formerly French Guyana) again, by special invitation of the General Consulate, including many more. Carl's admirers consider him as one of the best Portrait artists of our generation. His critics revere him as the Ayisyen artist who captures the "Sensuality of the Ayisyen Woman" like no other. Using Fine Arts By Carl platform, he supports local not-for-profit organizations with the "Philanthropy Through the Arts" program.

La Force ne fait pas l'Union

By Carl Craig

"La Force ne fait pas l'Union," evokes a profound historical reflection on the fragile unity that followed Haiti's hard-won independence. The painting's narrative highlights the division between two key figures, General Henri Christophe and General Alexandre Pétion, whose differing visions for the new nation set the stage for conflict rather than cohesion. Despite their shared victory over colonial oppression, their inability to unite in governance is a central theme.

The painting captures the somber mood of a young nation at a crossroads, using dark, muted tones to symbolize the uncertainty and disillusionment that shadowed Haiti's early years of independence. The conflicting leadership styles of Christophe, the self-proclaimed king, and Pétion, the mulatto president, reflect their divergent influences from the European military cultures of that era.

The significant influence of women, such as Marie-Madeleine "Joute" Lachenais and Marie-Louise Coidavid, are also notable. These women, who played crucial roles during the independence struggle, continued to wield their power of influence, guiding and supporting their respective leaders. The piercing look in their eyes is a confirmation of the warrior mentality that dominates their being.

The Citadelle Laferrière, the largest fortress in the Western Hemisphere, remains an enduring symbol of Haitian liberty and resistance. It stands as a guardian over the nation's hard-won freedom from slavery. It represents the enduring spirit of liberty.

Despite internal divisions and shattered dreams of unity, this cornerstone continues to prevail.

Overall, the painting serves as a poignant reminder of the complex and often tumultuous path of newly independent nations, where the fight for freedom does not always guarantee unity or peace.

La Force ne fait pas l'Union – Oil on Canvas painting – 18" x 24"
www.fineartsbycarl.com
Editing by Marie-Donald Manigat-Craig

Daniel J.D. Bayard

TABLE OF CONTENTS

Daniel J.D. Bayard

PREFACE

The date was January 1st, 1804, and the beginning of a new era for the island of Ayiti, where the spelling would later change to Haiti. After 13 years of constant turmoil and war sparked by the first insurrection led by Vincent Oge and Jean-Baptiste Chavannes in 1790, in the precursor French colony of Saint Domingue, the island was finally on the brink of freedom. Oge's motivations were rooted in gaining voting rights for the Gens de Couleur, while Chavannes fought for true abolition and the liberation of all slaves. However, their revolution would ultimately fail and cost them their lives. In his final moments, Chavannes called for all slaves to rise and fight for their freedom.

No one can say for certain if this call to arms was the defining moment that sparked the Ayisyen Revolution, but it cannot be denied that August of 1791 ushered in a pivotal event. The sound of drums filled the air as voices chanted and danced around ceremonial fires, igniting a fire within the hearts of those who had been enslaved. A voodoo ceremony led by Oungan Boukman and Mambo Priestess Cecile Fatiman empowered 80,000 slaves from the Plaine du Nord to rise against their oppressors. This was only the beginning of a long and bloody battle for freedom and independence that would shape the history of Ayiti forever.

Over thirteen tumultuous years, the land underwent a series of unprecedented events that would forever shape its destiny. A fierce internal revolution with the French led to an invasion and subsequent expulsion of British and Spanish forces. This was followed by a brutal civil war, and finally an invasion by Napoleon Bonaparte in an attempt to re-enslave the people of African descent who had fought so fiercely for their freedom.

Amidst this chaotic chain of events, emerged a quartet of founding fathers: Toussaint Louverture, who never sought complete independence from France but instead desired an autonomous colony that could govern itself and freely trade with any nation. He rose to become head of the military and Governor General of the colony, leading his army against Napoleon's General Charles Leclerc's occupation forces until he was ultimately captured and put to death in a French prison.

After Louverture's death, Jean-Jacques Dessalines took up the mantle and assembled a mighty army of 40,000 men and women organized into divisions. They successfully defeated the French army and declared Ayiti a free nation. Dessalines was joined by two other notable generals and also considered as founding fathers, Henry Christophe and Alexandre Pétion.

As the years passed, the Bayard family deftly navigated their personal lives, business endeavors, and the ever-shifting political landscape. In a world where death and destruction loomed at every turn, they not only survived but thrived, determined to carve out their success despite all odds. Their days were filled with calculated risks and strategic moves, each one bringing them closer to their ultimate goal of prosperity in a time of chaos.

Book Four opens on New Year's Day, in three different cities - Cap Français, Gonaives, and Port Républicain - where our main characters and principal protagonist begin to navigate their way through the aftermath of liberation in their newly named country, Ayiti. As they strive to establish stability and peace in their homeland, they will soon realize that this may be even more challenging than fighting for their freedom.

Our story begins here.

Author's Note:

Before continuing, I highly recommend if you haven't done so already, reading Triumph To Tragedy Books One, Two, and Three. By doing so, you will have a deeper understanding of the characters and events that have led up to this moment.

.

Daniel J.D. Bayard

Daniel J.D. Bayard

BOOK FOUR

The Clash of Pétion and Christophe

1804 - 1820

Ayiti
Present-Day Republic of Haiti

Ay-ti
'Land of Mountains'
Indigenous Taíno-Arawak name
for the entire island of Hispaniola

"From Our Ashes We Will Rise Again!"

… Henry Christophe

"Land for Each Family.
Because in many, we are one. United We Are Strong"

… Alexandre Petion

Daniel J.D. Bayard

One

JEAN & MARIE'S FIRST DAY IN THE NEW ERA

Cap Français
January 1, 1804

An anxious rooster was the first thing that registered into Jean-Baptiste's consciousness, crowing in the distance to announce the dawning of a new day, a new year, and as Jean cleared his senses from that lullaby world between asleep and awake, he suddenly realized that it was also the dawning of a new era.

He looked to his left at Marie, still dozing, wondering what her mind was dreaming of. A smile crossed her lips and he thanked God once more for bringing this woman to him so many years ago. They would be married thirty years, this coming September, and she was still as beautiful and desirable to him as the day they had met, though he knew her so much better now.

He turned on his left side, cropped his head up with his elbow, and decided to enjoy a few moments before the household would awaken and the New Year, the new era, and the new country would begin its first day.

In the past thirty years, they had built an incredible business and life together, encompassing a shipping company, an import and export business, a luxury hotel, and birthed the pride and joy of their lives, Jean-Baptiste Junior. They had also known their share of hardship and strife; the destruction and rebuilding of their hotel, the constant turmoil and interruption to their business, and their survival from the wars with the Spanish, the British, the internal civil war, and of course the expulsion of the French. The dangers of his military service and battles in the American Revolution were now a distant memory so long ago.

And here she was and had remained the steady and known quantity in his life. She had never wavered, was constantly the optimist, and was consistent in her devotion. He was grateful for her saving him from internal destruction as a result of the battering administered by Jean-Jacques Dessalines, now the General and Supreme Commander of the Revolutionary Army - L'Armée Indigéne as they are now called. All of this strife had worked to bring them closer, and bond them tighter, as the calling of death can certainly enlighten one's thoughts to what is most important.

Marie brought her arms high above her head in a stretch, arching her back which pointed her breasts upward, exposing her nipples through the sheer garment. It aroused Jean as she turned her body towards his and instinctively opened her eyes. "How long have you been staring at me, husband?" was her first sentence in this new era.

"Long enough," answered Jean.

"Long enough for what?" she countered, a smile forming on her lips.

"Long enough to know you are the most beautiful woman in the world and grateful that you are all mine," Jean answered.

"I've been dreaming of you," Marie offered, with a seductive smile on her lips.

"Is that so," Jean replied, easily and willingly taking the bait to her seductive game of words. "Was it a good dream?" Jean ventured.

"Oh yes," Marie responded, now biting her lower lip and looking deep into his eyes. "But I awoke and interrupted the finale," Marie said, knowing Jean would realize in an instant what exactly she meant.

"Jean moved towards her, and placed his lips gently on hers, as together they rolled into position, her willingly spreading her legs and he gently entering her, her wetness confirming the truth of what indeed she had been dreaming of.

Together they sought the familiar rhythm of love, each knowing what pleased their partner and without hesitation providing it.

When they had both climaxed into exhaustion, Marie cuddled into his arms, relishing the feeling of safety and stability that Jean had, and always would provide. They lay in silence until the familiar three knocks on the door announced the arrival of Odicelle, their trusted server, with her tray of just brewed coffee, cups, sugar, warm milk, and glasses filled with fresh water. "Bonjour Monsieur et Madame," she announced with a singing voice, always on time, usually at 6:00 am, but Jean and Marie had given the staff the morning off due to last night's celebrations and ordered them to report at 11 am instead.

"Bonjour Odicelle," they both answered.

"And how does the New Year arrive for you?" asked Jean.

"Oh, so well, Monsieur Jean. We have a new country made possible by Général Dessalines who assembled a great army and kicked our oppressors off of our island! My children can now live without fear of being enslaved, as I once was," Odicelle said with excitement. "General Dessalines is great and will protect us from white slave masters. He will keep us safe and," she suddenly stopped and caught herself as Marie gave Odicelle a stern look as if to say STOP!

Odicelle had ventured into forbidden territory. The name Dessalines was taboo to be spoken in this house. Dessalines had almost killed her employer and Odicelle knew that, but in her exuberance, she had forgotten that incident in Jérémie that had almost terminated Jean's life four years ago, and possibly her employment today.

"Forgive me Monsieur Jean. I wasn't thinking. Please forgive me. Look what I have done on the first day of this New Year. I have caused you pain. I am such an idiot. I do not deserve your kindness, Monsieur et Madame. Cast me away. I am of no good to you. Of no good to anyone. I do not deserve your kindness. I am shamed and…"

Marie raised her hand, the familiar gesture that everyone understood to immediately stop talking, to stop walking, to stop fighting, to stop arguing, or to stop whatever Marie wanted stopped at the time. Everyone called it "The Hand" as if the gesture was a personage all of its own. A personality that no one messed with. The Hand was supreme. The Hand was direct. The Hand was final. You did as The Hand commanded. Odicelle obeyed The Hand as she knew its consequences. No further words were needed. The Hand had spoken.

"You are forgiven," Marie gently stated to Odicelle, with The Hand still in its commanding position, as she looked at Jean, knowing that the pain of those memories endured still today. She reached out for him, but he lay there motionless as Odicelle poured a cup of coffee for them both through the awkward silence that pursued.

Jean seemed to have gone back in time. He would be fragile today, Marie thought. Général Jean-Jacques Dessalines had prevailed. He had taken over when Toussaint Louverture had fallen. Toussaint had been arrested by the French in a diabolical ploy, shipped to France, and murdered in jail. Dessalines had assembled a great army of 40,000 men and women and in a matter of months had vanquished Napoleon's French army from the shores of Saint Domingue, now of Ayiti, the new nation as it is now called.

There was no longer the colony of Saint Domingue, but a new country that had risen from the ashes of colonialism, of slavery, of oppression. The new country of Ayiti, wherein Jean's nemesis now reigned supreme – Jean-Jacques Dessalines – General and supreme commander of the Armée Indigéne.

Jean had his eyes closed and transported back four years during the end of the Civil War when twenty five soldiers entered the Bayard plantation. He could see workers in the fields tending to the crops. Their commander had his men assemble them all in the front of the house. "I am seeking the criminal named Alexandre Pétion and anyone in his association. Has anyone seen this man or any of his accomplices around here?" barked the commander."

The laborers looked at each other and shook their heads. Jean had come out of the house and approached the commander who was on horseback, surrounded by other soldiers on horses as well.

"Welcome to our property Commander. How may I be of assistance?" he remembered saying to him.

Visibly upset, the commander had turned and looked directly at him, eyes cutting into him, he dismounted from his horse, and walked towards Jean at the sanded clearing in front of the house. "Who are you?" he had barked.

"My name is Jean-Baptiste Hippolyte Bayard, Captain of the Chasseurs Volontaires de St. Domingue, retired. And you are sir?" Jean had politely responded to not get the reputed wrath of the Général.

"My name is Jean-Jacques Dessalines, Général and Supreme Commander of the Southern Colonial Army. Where is the rest of the family of this house?"

"They are not here General. They left town a few days ago," replied Jean.

"Are you the Bayard with the ships?" Dessalines had asked.

"Yes, I am Général"

"Did you provide safe passage to that scum and rebel Alexandre Pétion and his men? Think wisely before you answer that question as it may be your last if it is not the complete truth," Dessalines said.

"I did not provide, General. I sold passage to the man and several men with him. I was paid as any other passenger would pay me. That is my business, to provide transportation of people and cargo" Jean said.

Dessalines's forehead had begun to contort in a wicked frown and his lower lip tightened until Jean could see his teeth clenched behind it. Suddenly and without warning, Dessalines had raised his arm and swiftly thrown a punch which struck Jean on the right side of his face with a massive blow prosecuted from the huge fist.

Jean was caught off guard and knocked back in shock. As he was steadying himself, another crushing blow had hit Jean on the left side of his face. Jean's first instinct was to lash back out and fight, but he knew he would be killed instantly by either the Général or his men. He had the comfort of knowing that the families were in the newly constructed bunker a kilometer away and well-hidden, so as not to be found.

"You have robbed me of the satisfaction of killing Pétion and his men myself, you piece of shit," as he dealt another crushing facial blow to Jean's forehead. Then suddenly, as if an animal was unleashed, Dessalines had tightened both arms as his hands formed fists. He looked up at the sky and had let out one huge primal yell of frustration which had been building inside of him during the yearlong military campaign - the Civil War named the War of Knives, as he realized he had lost his prey and Jean had been the reason for it. Jean had now become the target of his unleashed anger and his rage.

Jean's body had received blow after blow after blow until he could no longer stand and had fallen to the ground. He then endured the pain of Dessalines' boots kicking him everywhere as he went into a fetal position to try and stay alive through the savage beating which seemed like an eternity until he could smell the stench of thick dark yellow dehydrated urine coming out of Dessalines' body and onto him.

It was the ultimate humiliation. Jean had sunken to the lowest level of existence in his entire life as the acidic urine stung the open bloody wounds on his face and neck. But that was nowhere near to the pain it had prosecuted to his heart, his pride, and his will to live. It was the last thing he remembered as his desire to remain conscience left him and his instinct to give in had overcome him. His eyes had gone dark as he passed out into unconsciousness.

He had been lost in a sort of half-life for months, with nothing that any doctor could understand until Marie had saved him, and nurtured him back to health and to life. The pain of that incident still haunts him to this day.

Jean was now bathed in sweat. He had once again lived the pain of that day back in Jérémie of 1800. It had taken him years to repulse it, but today it had come back to him as vividly as if it were yesterday. It wasn't only due to Odicelle's remarks of the General but of the unknowns of land to be now ruled by the brutality of such a man. Jean had seen the true nature of Jean-Jacques Dessalines.

"Jean, Jean!" he could hear Marie saying in a distant fog. They were now alone in the room, Odicelle having been dismissed by Marie for some time now. "You did it again," Marie said as she wrapped her hands around his head. "It's been quite some time since you had your last episode like this."

Jean composed himself and he and Marie came down the steps, holding hands and smiling in anticipation of a wonderful day together. It was a Sunday and the entire town was in preparation for the grand celebration of not only ringing in the New Year but also the new country. The staff; Pierre the coachman, Reynaud, the house boy, Odicelle, the server, and Yolande the cook, were all assembled at the bottom of the steps. Each was given a hug as was their custom every January first.

Odicelle was at first shy and apprehensive when she approached Jean and began to speak an apology for her words upstairs before Jean put a finger on his lips in an order of silence, smiled, and gave her a huge affectionate hug.

"We will depart right after our late morning petit-déjeuner," Jean said to Pierre. Have the coach brought around at one." Jean and Marie entered the dining room where the food had already been spread on the table for them; cooked smoked herrings smothered with onions, hard-boiled eggs, plantains, yuka, tomatoes, avocados, and of course, Yolande's fresh baked bread accompanied by fresh churned butter.

Jean and Marie feasted as they drank the rich blend of Jérémie's coffee, fresh from his family's plantation. Reynaud had gone to town to fetch a new edition of Cap Français' favorite newspaper, Le Nouveliste's first edition for the New Year, proclaiming story after story of bravery, dedication, perseverance, and victory by the Armée Indigéne - the Indigenous Army of Ayiti.

After the meal, scanning the papers, and leisurely lounging in the sitting room, Marie announced that it was time for her to get ready for the day's celebration. "I'm going to take my bath, Jean," exclaimed Marie. "I would have you join me, but that would make us extremely late for the festivities, and it is important that we are there for them all,"

"You enjoy teasing me way too much, mon amour," Jean smiled back. "Go, I will see you when ready to leave."

Marie Bayard's fingers traced the delicate embroidery of her gown as she and her husband, Jean, alighted from their carriage amidst the pulsating heart of Cap Français. The air was thick with the scent of ripening mangoes from nearby stalls, mingling with the salty tang of the sea that skirted the bustling port town. Laughter and chatter rose above the clamor, a rhapsody of celebration and triumph that marked this momentous day – the commemoration of Ayiti's independence.

Jean adjusted the cuff of his crisp linen jacket, his eyes reflecting the vibrant hues of blue and red that adorned the streets and the people who filled them. The colors of freedom unfurled on every banner and in every heart, flapping like wings eager to soar in the newly claimed sky. They walked hand in hand, Marie's thumb caressing the back of his hand, sending a cascade of shivers along his spine despite the tropical heat. Her presence was an intoxicating blend of strength and sensuality, a reminder of their shared past and intertwined future.

"Mon amour," Marie whispered, leaning close enough for her moist lips to graze his earlobe, "look at what we have contributed to all this." She gestured subtly toward the throngs of well-dressed citizens making their way to the ceremonies. Her words were not merely meant for him; they carried weight for their employees too, who managed their affairs with precision, helping to build a company that performed with excellence. Their ships were part of the lifeblood of the island, importing clothing, dried fish, hardware, arms, and a host of raw materials to manufacture much of the life of the colony, now the new country.

"Indeed," Jean replied, pride evident in his voice as they passed by a group of fellow merchants, some of whom owed their prosperity to the ventures the Bayards had established. "Our shipping routes have not only brought wealth but also ideas, foreign exchange, and the export of goods that foster growth."

"Ahh, les Bayards!" exclaimed a portly man with a boisterous laugh, clapping Jean on the shoulder. "Your ships sail as if blessed by Agwe himself, and your hotel," he continued, casting an admiring glance toward Marie, "is the crown of Cap Français."

"Monsieur Deschamps. Hotel de la Couronne thrives because of our commitment to excellence," Marie interjected warmly, her gaze sweeping across the faces before them. "We are honored to serve as a gathering place for the finest minds and the most fervent hearts of our nation. You are an exemplary example of what I speak. I trust you have received your invitation for this evening's celebration?"

Their conversation flowed as smoothly as the aged rum that Ayiti exported, a testament to their expertise and the impact they'd had on the local economy and the people who shaped it. Snippets of exchange highlighted how the Bayard businesses had flourished, providing employment and fostering trade connections that extended far beyond the island's azure coasts.

"Your acumen has indeed set a high bar," another merchant, Louis LaPlace, agreed, nodding in respect. "And tonight," he added with a knowing smile, "we expect nothing less than grandeur at your soirée. Lucette is already at the coiffure in anticipation of a wonderful evening."

"Every detail is accounted for," Jean assured him, though his thoughts danced around the intricacies yet to unfold. "It will be a night worthy of our nation's birth."

As Marie and Jean moved through the crowd, the tapestry of sounds enveloped them: the rhythmic beat of drums, the murmur of anticipation, the rustle of silk and brocade, interspersed with the scent of perfumed sweat and drying rum. Each step they took was a silent testament to their resilience, the hopes they harbored for their country's nascent journey.

The exuberance of the gathering swelled as they drew closer to the square where the ceremonies would commence. Here, amid the cobblestone streets where blood once flowed, joy now sprang forth like the lush greenery that blanketed the hillsides after heavy rains.

Marie squeezed Jean's hand, her eyes alight with the reflection of their hard-won freedom. He felt the promise of her touch, the subtle play of her affections that spurred him forward, weaving their aspirations with the destiny of the land they loved.

Jean's gaze wandered over the crowds, taking in the vibrant tapestry of faces that represented the heart and soul of Ayiti. He caught the eyes of a fellow homme de couleur, an old acquaintance from the days of fervent whispers and secret meetings conspiring against the French, now replaced by hopeful conversations spoken aloud. They shared a nod of mutual recognition that transcended words—a silent acknowledgment of their shared heritage and the strength it had lent them.

"Look at how far we have all come, Jean," Marie whispered, her voice tinged with pride as she leaned closer to him. Her hand rested on his arm, her touch both comforting and empowering. "Our Henry must be proud. As proud as we are of him", she said, referring to Henry Christophe, the great revolutionary general, but most importantly considered family and near brother to Jean.

"Indeed," Jean replied, his chest swelling with pride. "Henry's resolve is etched into every city he has fought. And so is Alexandre Pétion—his vision for a republic resonates with the very spirit of our son."

"Jean-Junior carries that same spark," Marie said, her eyes gleaming with maternal affection and admiration. "The same fire that drives men like Henry and Pétion to shape nations. It is quite interesting that fate has placed Junior as the bond between Henry and Alexandre, though I wish those two would forge a better relationship."

As they mingled through the gathering, the couple engaged in earnest discourse with other leaders of the community, their voices a blend of nostalgia for the struggles past and anticipation for the future to be forged.

"Freedom has been hard-won," Jean stated, locking eyes with a cluster of attendees who nodded in solemn agreement. "But it is the foundation upon which we must build. We stand here today because we dared to dream of a world where the color of one's skin does not determine one's destiny – or freedom."

Marie's hand tightened around Jean's, her thumb still tracing small circles on the back of his hand—a gesture that spoke volumes of their shared bond.

"Yet, we must tread carefully," she added, her voice carrying the weight of experience. "With independence comes great responsibility. Our nation is young, its soil still tender from revolution's plow. We must help nurture it, guide it towards prosperity."

"And we shall," Jean affirmed, meeting her gaze with quiet determination. "We will face challenges, yes, but we do so together. As a people united by freedom's call, as entrepreneurs who bear the torch of progress, and as parents who wish to leave a legacy of hope for Jean-Junior and all children of this island."

Their conversation was punctuated by the distant sounds of the ceremonial drums that echoed the heartbeat of a country reborn. With each beat, their cautious optimism grew stronger, woven into the very air that buzzed with the promise of tomorrow—an Ayiti just born, to remain resilient, and filled with boundless potential.

As the echoes of past struggles subtly permeated the revelry, Marie Bayard allowed herself a moment of reflection. She gazed across the throng of faces at Cap Français, each one a mosaic tile in the grand portrait of a free country. The air was redolent with the aroma of spiced meats; beef, goat, and chicken over flavorful charcoal, mingling with the aroma of robust coffee brewing, and the molasses scent of newly fermented dark rum, a testament to the island's bounty and its people's zest. But as her eyes met those of her husband, there passed between them an unspoken remembrance of a time far less jubilant. She understood.

"Jérémie," she whispered, almost inaudibly amidst the cacophony of celebration. "It seems like a lifetime ago."

Jean nodded solemnly, the shared memories etching lines of resolve on his otherwise smooth brow. "Those were days of uncertainty, Marie. When our businesses were but fragile seedlings in a storm-ravaged field, and trust was a currency more precious than gold."

"Where we bartered for peace with our words and wits alone," she added.

"Yes," he said, his arm wrapped protectively around her waist. "We may not have fought with guns or swords, but our battles were no less fierce. We navigated through treacherous waters, steering our ventures with steady hands while the tempest of revolution raged around us."

"Yet here we stand," Marie reaffirmed, her gaze lifting to meet the vibrant horizon, "stronger for the trials, unyielding as the mahogany trees that grace our hills."

Their exchange was interrupted by the uneasy shuffling of feet nearby. A group of former slaveholders, their stark white skin and attire standing out against the colorful garments of the Ayisyen populace, moved cautiously among the celebrants. Their once imperious gazes were now downcast, lips pressed into thin lines that betrayed their disquiet.

Marie watched them with an analytical eye, noting the subtle clutching of hands, the nervous glances over shoulders, and the stiffness in their posture. "They are like ghosts lost in broad daylight," she murmured to Jean, whose own observations mirrored hers.

"Phantoms of a bygone era," Jean agreed, his diplomatic instincts attuned to the undercurrents flowing through the crowd.

"They know the world they once commanded has irrevocably changed. Freedom has taken root, and it will not be uprooted by them."

"Nor should it be," Marie added firmly, the fire of determination alighting within her. "But let us not forget the delicacy of this moment, my love. For them and us, it is a dance upon the tightrope of a new reality. I admire their courage for venturing out here today without the spyglass of the future in their hands."

"True," Jean concurred, his eyes scanning the sea of faces, black, brown, light-skinned, and white, "the birth of our nation will not be without its labor pains."

Together, they stood amidst the festivities, emblems of resilience and hope, their hearts tethered to the past but their sights set firmly on the future. They understood that the road ahead would be paved with challenges, but it was one they were ready to walk—side by side, step by step, towards the promise of a new nation.

Marie's fingers once again traced the delicate embroidery of her dress, a gesture betraying her impatience for the ceremonies to commence. She caught Jean's eye, and in that silent exchange, a universe of emotions swirled—pride, anticipation, and an undercurrent of trepidation for the tapestry of tomorrows yet to be woven.

"Today marks the beginning," Jean whispered, his voice barely rising above the hum of conversations around them. The city of Cap Français teemed with life, a mosaic of faces reflecting the dawn of liberty. "Do you feel it, Marie? The pulse of a nation finding its heartbeat."

Marie nodded, her gaze flitting across the vibrant crowd, where the air was thick with the scent of blooming flamboyant, the savory aroma of street vendors' fare, and the sound of vendors shouting their food and merchandise for sale. The colors around them seemed brighter as if the very essence of freedom had imbued the world with more vivid hues.

"Children will read about this day," she said, her words mingling with the laughter of youngsters weaving through the crowd, their innocence untouched by the scars of history. "They will know what it cost—and what it brought us."

The distant sound of drums rolled towards them, heralding the start of the official ceremonies. A collective breath seemed to be held and then released as people craned their necks, eager to witness the military parade that would assert Ayiti's sovereignty. Soldiers marched by, their uniforms crisp, the sun gleaming off brass buttons and polished bayonets. It was a display of discipline and might, but within their ranks, Marie discerned something deeper: a quiet dignity born from the ashes of subjugation.

"Look at them, Jean," she murmured, pride swelling within her chest. "From laborers in chains to guardians of their destinies. What a transformation."

Jean's hand found hers, squeezing gently, an anchor in the tide of jubilation. Music began to swell—a symphony of drums, horns, and strings intertwining to create an anthem for the ages. Children danced alongside the parade, their joyous movements painting the air with hope.

And then came the speeches, voices ringing out over the crowd, each word a testament to the trials overcome and the victories achieved. Phrases like "liberty" and "brotherhood" cascaded from the speakers' lips, not as mere rhetoric but as sacred vows spoken before the altar of the future.

"May our unity endure as the mountains," one orator proclaimed, gesturing to the imposing peaks that cradled the city in their embrace. "And may our spirits soar as the malfini – the hawk, never again to be caged."

As the ceremony reached its zenith, the pomp and circumstance were more than tradition; they were the manifestation of dreams long deferred now taking flight. Flags unfurled, snapping in the breeze that swept through the square, while the crowd erupted into cheers, their voices a chorus of triumph.

Marie and Jean stood, shoulder to shoulder, absorbing the reverberations of change. They knew the road ahead would wind through valleys of uncertainty, but on this day, under the bright afternoon Caribbean sky, they allowed themselves the luxury of simply being present—at this moment, at the precipice of possibility.

Later that evening, under the soft glow of oil lamps and crystal chandeliers, the grand ballroom of Hôtel de la Couronne pulsed with the rhythm of a nation reborn. The air was thick with the scent of jasmine carried in from the gardens and the heady fragrance of French perfumes mingling with the local vetiver, as 500 guests moved through the space with a grace that belied the gravity of the day's events and dancers overflowed from the dancefloor.

"Madame Bayard, your vision for this evening is unparalleled," a familiar merchant gushed, his eyes wide as they scanned the expanse of marble floors and silk-draped tables laden with exotic fruits and spiced meats.

"Merci, Monsieur Dupont," Marie replied, her voice a melodious hum that seamlessly blended with the strains of the orchestra's violins. "It is but a reflection of the Ayiti we envision—prosperous, united, and free."

Jean Bayard, ever the consummate host, navigated the sea of guests with an ease born from years of shaping outcomes in rooms just like this one. With a warm handshake here and a knowing nod there, he engaged with a blend of charm and candor that had become his trademark.

"Indeed, Jean, your trading ventures have set the standard," commented a well-dressed government official, swirling a glass of aged dark rum in his hand.

"Only by standing on the shoulders of giants like Toussaint," Jean replied, tipping his glass to acknowledge the legacy of the leaders who had paved their path to freedom. "Our prosperity now must be the foundation for our children's future—an Ayiti where opportunity knows no color."

As the room swelled with conversations of commerce and governance, the couple wove through dialogues laced with both optimism and apprehension. The weight of expectation hung heavily upon them, but they bore it with a dignified resolve, understanding that each word exchanged was another brick in the construction of their fledgling society.

"Marie, do you remember the days of '99?" whispered a somber-faced man in a corner huddle, his eyes reflecting the flicker of candlelight. "Fear choked the streets of Cap Français back then."

"Those were times that tested our mettle," Marie responded softly, her gaze steadfast. "But look at us now, gathering not in fear, but in celebration. Our resilience has been our greatest ally."

At the most strategic moment of the evening, Jean signaled the orchestra to pause as his staff of waiters clinked spoon handles to crystal glassware as the ceremonial signal for attention. The murmur of voices ebbing away as all eyes turned toward him. He stood beside Marie, their hands lightly touching—a silent testament to their shared journey.

"Mesdames et Messieurs," Jean began, his voice commanding yet tinged with emotion, "Tonight, we stand on hallowed ground. Ground soaked with the blood and sweat of those who refused to bow before the yoke of oppression," he began, as he nodded to Marie who proclaimed, "Today, we celebrated our independence, but tonight, we toast to our future," her voice resonating with a strength that commanded the room.

" À notre Ayiti," Jean firmly said, as he raised his glass in a toast and Marie followed. "May she flourish in peace, and may her children never know the chains of bondage!"

Glasses raised high, and a chorus of assents rose to meet the vaulted ceiling. The clink of crystal rang out like a bell tolling the advent of a new era—an era birthed from the ashes of the old.

"À notre Ayiti!" they proclaimed in unison, and for a moment, the divisions of the past dissolved into the unity of the present—a unity hard-won yet deeply cherished – whether he be black, white, or mulatto.

The orchestra swelled once more, the music a vibrant tapestry weaving together threads of freedom, resilience, and hope,

Jean & Marie toast the New Year and the new country at their hotel's plush Casino de la Couronne during the celebration on January 1st in Cap Français.

encapsulating the spirit of a people who had dared to dream and, in dreaming, had forged their destiny.

Andre, his younger brother, approached with Joseph Bunel, Toussaint Louverture's trade envoy to the United States in 1798. Bunel had negotiated with the John Adams administration for the resumption of trade to the island during America's Quasi-War with France. His counterpart, U.S. Secretary of State under Adams, Tim Pickering, had ushered legislation in Congress untying President John Adam's hands and allowing him to trade with the colony, albeit to the ire of France. What had passed in Congress was dubbed "Toussaint's Clause" in the American press which touted the enormous trade benefits for both the United States and Toussaint's colony of Saint Domingue. Before long, over a thousand merchant ships were plying the waters between Saint Domingue and American ports with more ships being built each month.

A tripartite agreement with Britain had ensued and things were going great, until the U.S. Presidential election and the defeat of John Adams by Thomas Jefferson in the 1800 heated elections in November of that year. Upon taking office in 1801, Jefferson had unwound all of Adams' favorable trade policies with Toussaint, recalled his naval vessels and diplomats, and cozied up to France, endorsing France's re-enslavement of the black citizens of the colony. Being a Southern planter, Jefferson understood the allure to American slaves of a black-governed colony just a few hundred kilometers from his southern shores. At the behest of his Southern planter class, Jefferson chose to side with the French and slavery over expanded slave freedom in the United States.

Bunel then joined the resistance and began working with the Bayard brothers, Andre and Jean, to run military contraband and guns to the colony. Andre dealt with arms dealers, Jean provided the transportation on his sailing vessels, and Bunel facilitated payment from sympathetic financiers and Dessalines' army.

"Nice party, my brother," Andre said as he gave a big hug to his older brother.

"When did you guys get in?" asked Jean.

"We just got here this afternoon, checked in a couple of hours ago, cleaned up and here we are," answered Bunel who also hugged Jean. Jean was the person who had enticed Bunel to join Toussaint years ago. Since then, Bunel had become Toussaint's go-to man; trade envoy, army paymaster, and many other things to be trusted with, especially when cash was involved.

"Come, let's get a table," Jean said as he nodded to the head waiter of the restaurant, who efficiently approached four men and women at a nearby table, and whispered into the ear of one of the men who looked over at Jean, Andre, and Bunel as they approached.

The man stood, fully knowing the power of the person he was talking to, "Monsieur Bayard, a lovely party. The table is yours, of course," the man said.

"Maurice is setting you up a corner in the casino with a bottle of my finest champagne and all you can order to eat. Apologies for the disruption," Jean concluded.

The trio took over the table as waiters cleared the glasses from the two couples, changed the tablecloth, and brought a bottle of the finest refined rum in the house.

"Report," Jean said to Andre. 'What is the current state of affairs with regards to the new Ayiti with this Jefferson administration?"

"They have tolerated the contraband trade because it boosts the U.S. Treasury quite a great deal. Our allies, Tim Pickering, ex-Secretary of State under John Adams, and Dr. Stevens have attempted to rally government support since Jefferson got elected, but the new Secretary of State Madison had already begun to unwind all Adams' friendly trade stances towards Saint Domingue within a week of taking office. No friend there," replied Andre.

"You've been through quite a great deal," Jean said, looking at his friend Bunel.

"No kidding. You know that my wife and I were arrested by Rochambeau, and shipped to France under virtual house arrest.

"Yes, for not renouncing the Ayisyen revolution and financing their expedition, of what I understand," Jean said.

"We were lucky to pay for forged documents and sneak out of France and flee to Philadelphia. Marie and I have done well there, opening up a mercantile house for exports to the West Indies.

"Accounting for half of the arms benefitting the Armée Indigéne," Andre said.

"On your sailing vessels, Jean. We have done well together," Bunel responded.

"And what of our friend, Dr. Stevens, and his lovely wife Hester?"

"Discredited by the Jefferson administration. The man who made the U.S. Government and citizens millions of dollars, making Americans rich, was denied even a cent from the United States government resulting in his duties as a trade envoy in Saint Domingue.

"So sad," Andre said.

"He sued the government and with the help of ex-Secretary of State Pickering, finally convinced Jefferson to open the government's wallet and hand him a few coins this past year," reported Bunel.

"Where are they now?" asked Jean.

"They went back home to St. Croix. Hester's family owns Gallows Bay and other plantations on the island. Dr. Stevens is back to being what he always wanted, a doctor."

"There was no better friend to this island or Toussaint Louverture than Dr. Stevens," Jean added as he took his glass and raised it in a toast.

"Bunel raised his glass and added, "Nor a better friend to I," added Bunel.

"Just then, Marie approached the table and all three men stood in respect as Jean held a chair for her to be seated.

"Andre took her extended hand and gave it a respectful kiss as Joseph Bunel bowed his salute. Marie sat, "I hope this conversation revolves around the return of my two ships; the Laura and Le Matin," Marie stated with a firm voice.

Andre looked at Jean and Bunel lowered his gaze to the sniffer of rum before him. A server approached and placed a glass of

Benedictine in front of Marie. She raised it and pronounced, "A Ayiti."

The others followed suit.

"Well?" she asked. I have been trying to get information from my husband here who has been quite illusive of the location of our ships, and her crews."

"That subject was next on our agenda, Marie. Your timing is impeccable. Joseph and I have just arrived but hours ago aboard your vessel Marcelle."

"Well then, let Jean and I hear it for the first time together," Marie said as she sipped at her Benedictine.

Bunel looked at Andre and began, "Both vessels left Philadelphia on August 12th, 1803. They were carrying a total of 12.000 rifles, two tons of ammunition and powder, concealed with a few tons of dried cod."

"And what happened?" asked Marie.

"That is where it gets confusing. All arrangements were made with all of our contacts up and down the eastern coast, Authorities had been paid, and the navy officers were on board, they still hate the French for sinking all those vessels years ago, and those ships should have landed here at Cap in mid-September."

"So, what went wrong?" asked Jean.

"Ricardo Desbardes," Bunel instantly answered.

"Desbardes? Desbardes the French spy?" asked Jean.

"Yes. He worked for French consul Philippe de Létombe to destabilize the trade policies of the Adams administration and is now teamed up with Louis-André Pichon, the new French consul to the U.S. They are instruments, I'm afraid, to destabilize the new Dessalines government and the new country." Bunel said.

"What has he to do with our ships?" asked Marie.

"Pinchon gained power from his favorable negotiations for the Louisiana Purchase with Jefferson. Call it a payback by Jefferson to seize our ships. They currently lie at anchor in Charleston with their crews as prisoners on board. A political game of chess," Andre added. "And we…"

Before he could continue, Marie put up "The Hand" to cut him off and said "Enough of this talk tonight. This is a celebration. I want to dance with my husband tonight. You three will think of the way you will return our ships, and our sailors, to rejoin their families. But tonight…"

Jean had already stood as did Andre and Bunel as Jean extended his hand to his wife with a slight bow. She took his hand and turned to Andre and Bunel. "Enough planning and conspiring tonight. Go, find a partner, and enjoy. Tomorrow is another day."

As the last strains of music from the orchestra faded into the night, a hush settled over Hôtel de la Couronne. The celebration had reached its zenith, leaving behind an air thick with the perfume of hope and the subtle undertone of fine rum. Marie Bayard's gaze swept across the grand ballroom, where the glitterati of Cap Français still lingered, their voices a soft murmur against the backdrop of opulence.

Beside her, Jean stood in quiet contemplation, his eyes reflecting the candlelight that danced upon the walls, casting long shadows that seemed to whisper of days past and those yet to unfold. Together, they moved toward the balcony overlooking the city, the cool Caribbean breeze of January offering a gentle reprieve from the fervor inside, yet finding streets still filled with reverie, from every cafe, food stand, and open bar.

"Look at them all," Marie whispered, her voice barely rising above the wind. "A nation born. And we...we are part of this tapestry, Jean."

Jean's hand found hers, their fingers intertwining as they observed the jubilant throng below. "We've woven our thread, mon amour, through commerce and community. Our legacy is not just what we build for ourselves, but what we leave for Ayiti."

Their shared silence was one of reflection, each lost in the gravity of the day's events—a day that marked both an ending and a beginning. The weight of responsibility pressed upon them, yet within it lay the buoyancy of possibility.

"Marie, do you remember Jérémie? Jean asked, his eyes distant. "The way the sun set over the fields like it was setting fire to the horizon?"

"I do." Marie nodded, her curls catching the light. "Our hometown, the place we first met, it seems a lifetime ago, yet here we are, standing on the precipice of a future we could only imagine then."

"Imagination," Jean mused, "fueled by resilience. That's what brought us here. That's what will carry us forward – our love for each other, for each other always."

Marie hummed in agreement, allowing the memory to envelop her—the hardships endured, the sacrifices made—all leading to this singular point in time.

A shadow approached them, materializing into the form of an elderly man whose skin bore the intricate etchings of a life spent under the unforgiving sun. His eyes locked with theirs, an unspoken understanding passing between them. It was Bayon de Libertad, that old wise French man who ran the Breda plantation, easily in his eighties, who had once freed Toussaint Louverture from bondage, set him up in business, and became Toussaint's lifelong confident, almost a father figure.

"Madame, Monsieur Bayard," he said, his voice rich with the timbre of experience. "Your toast this evening, it moved me greatly."

"Thank you," Marie replied, her smile genuine. "Your presence honors us, Monsieur Libertad."

Bayon de Libertad had also been instrumental, at the behest of Toussaint, in luring the white planters back to the colony years ago to reignite commercial plantations. Success had been mixed with some whites adhering to the new paid labor system and others wanting to maintain the system of slavery through a series of ministrations designed to keep the blacks in servitude. Many had cooperated with the French invasion and looked forward to the reinstitution of slavery. They both knew that Libertad wasn't like that, but he was labeled a conspirator for his association with them.

"Freedom is a costly jewel," he spoke, his gaze sweeping over the cityscape. "One that I never thought I'd live to see in my lifetime here."

"Nor did we," Jean added solemnly. "But it is ours now—to cherish, to protect."

"Indeed," Libertad nodded, his eyes glistening. "May we be worthy custodians of its brilliance? The most important question is can we bring all our factions together? Black, white, mulatto? That will be the key and my doubts are to whether our Supreme Commander, General Dessalines can do so." With a respectful dip of his head, the man retreated into the shadows from whence he came, leaving Marie and Jean to ponder his words.

"Every soul tonight carries with them a story of survival," Marie said, her voice a tender caress against the night. "Our hotel, our businesses—they are more than mere enterprise. They are sanctuaries for those stories, pillars for the lives built upon them."

"Sanctuaries," Jean echoed, feeling the truth of it resonate deep within his chest.

As the clock tower in the distance chimed the midnight hour, Marie and Jean turned back to face the remnants of the celebration. Their hearts were filled not just with determination but also with a sense of kinship with every individual who had fought, suffered, and triumphed in the name of freedom.

"Let us go," Jean suggested, holding out his arm for Marie. "There is much to be done, and we shall do it side by side, for our family, our new country, and our people."

"Oui, mon amour," Marie agreed, accepting his arm. "Together, always."

And with steps measured by the beating of their unified heart, Marie and Jean Bayard reentered the fading revelry, their spirits undaunted by the road ahead, and their resolve as unyielding as the spirit of the land they called home.

As the final notes of a rousing Creole ballad faded into the warm night, Marie and Jean stood on the balcony of Hôtel de la Couronne, gazing out over Cap Français. The city was alight with the glow of torches and lanterns that flickered like a thousand stars come to rest upon the earth, mirroring the constellations above. The scent of grilled meat and ripening fruit mingled with the salty tang of the sea, wafting up from the streets where vendors still hawked their wares to the lingering celebrants well into the night as servers from the hotel cleaned up after yet another successful affair hosted by the Bayards.

Two

DESSALINES AND HIS FIRST DAY

Gonaïves
January 1, 1804

The vibrant sounds of celebration filled the air in Gonaïves. The streets teemed with joyous crowds, their faces painted with the colors of Ayiti's new flag as they danced to the rhythmic beats of drums and waved their arms exuberantly in a carnival of color and pageantry. Laughter rang out, blending harmoniously with the rhythmic beat of drums, bamboo horns, and conch shells which had become the trumpets of the revolution. The atmosphere was electric, a palpable energy pulsing through the throngs of people celebrating their newfound independence.

In the corner of a busy small watering hole, a maroon named Diédoné sat with Ricardo Desbardes, the French spy who now had to deal with the realities of a free new nation they now call Ayiti. Diédoné had been an ally and devoted follower of Lamour Desrances before his death at the hands of Dessalines.

Desrances was born in Africa and brought to Saint-Domingue as a slave who had shortly afterward escaped for the mountains to join the maroon bands. He had mixed loyalties throughout his lifetime. At the time of the Civil War of Knives, Desrances was loyal to André Rigaud in his battle against Toussaint Louverture and was one of the few black officers in the predominantly mulatto Rigaud-loyal army. After Rigaud's defeat by Louverture, Desrances accumulated power and mobilized the maroon warriors in the mountains surrounding Port-au-Prince and Saint Marc. After the Leclerc invasion, he later changed his loyalty to the French under Général Pampile de Lacroix to fight against Dessalines' forces, defeating Dessalines' army at the outskirts of Port-au-Prince and forcing his retreat, a victory that finally convinced Toussaint to surrender to the French and seek retirement before his arrest, deportation, imprisonment, and subsequent death in France. Dessalines had made good on his word to kill Desrances last July.

"What is it you speak of here," Diédoné spat towards Desbardes. You French are finished, caput, defeated. Put your tail under your stinking asses and just disappear."

"You are mistaken, my great général. We have only just begun," responded Desbardes.

"What are you talking about?" asked Diédoné with a smile on his face. "Are you delusional about your situation here?"

"Dessalines clings to a fragile alliance with his army. It is no secret that he does not enjoy the loyalty of its entirety," Desbardes accurately stated. "And you are not on his good list either, Diédoné. I need not remind you of that."

"I am fully aware of this. But my strength is in the mountains and there I will live out my life comfortably as long as Dessalines is in power."

"Help us expedite that timeframe, Diédoné. You have no love for him and he would kill you given the chance. He will hunt you down in the mountains, and be it months or years, he will find you and you will be killed," Desbardes said matter of factly.

"So what? Dessalines is now the supreme commander. He defeated your French army and it is only a matter of time before you are caught and hanged as a spy yourself."

A young server girl, no more than 15 arrived with a refillable bottle of native rum and two wooden goblets and set them down with a pitcher of water. "Anything to eat Monsieurs?

"Give us an order of that, what they have," Desbardes said, pointing to the adjacent table with a platter overflowing with several fried whole fish, fried potato slices, and carrots cooked over charcoal. As the girl scurried off, he turned back to Diédoné.

"Help us sow seeds of doubt within his ranks. Dessalines strives for trust. Let us sow distrust within his corps of Générals. Have them doubt him and each other. Over time, the fabric of his command will begin to disintegrate."

"Who is 'Us'," asked Diédoné.

"We French. We are not finished here. An unstable Ayiti will show signs of opportunity to exploit. Plus, after all, don't you have a score to settle with Dessalines for your murdered commander, Lamour Desrances?"

"Tell me more," Diédoné inquired as crowds of people began to enter the café.

"Let's put it this way, we have soldiers strategically stationed on the Spanish side of the island and loyal French armed planters within this new state itself. As I said, we are not finished here," Desbardes said with a smile as he picked up his goblet of rum.

Across town, amidst the jubilant crowd, a figure emerged onto the stage, commanding an immediate hush that rippled throughout the city. Jean-Jacques Dessalines, the formidable leader of the Ayisyen Revolution, stood tall and proud. His dark eyes surveyed the sea of faces before him, his presence radiating strength and determination. Though he bore the scars of battles past, there was an undeniable air of authority and respect that surrounded him.

The forty-six-year-old Dessalines was born a slave in the colony of Saint-Domingue on the Duclos plantation. He worked there until he was about 30 years old in the harsh sugarcane fields as a laborer. He demonstrated an ability towards leadership and rose to the rank of Commandeur, or slave foreman.

Still enslaved he was sold and bought by an affranchi, a slave freed during his lifetime, with the last name of Dessalines who assigned his own surname to Jean-Jacques. From then on he was called Jean-Jacques Dessalines. He worked for that master for about three years and kept this name after he gained his freedom during the slave uprising of 1791.

When the uprising began, it spread across the Plaine-du-Nord. This was an area of very large sugar cane plantations where the mass of enslaved Africans lived and worked. Mortality was so high that French colonial planters continued to import more captured people from Africa during the eighteenth century. Dessalines received his early military training from a female Dohemian warrior whose name was Victoria Montou or to him, simply Aunt Toya, his closest thing to a living relative and a confidant throughout his lifetime.

Though he had attained a life that fared much better than his fellow slave, Dessalines still carried the scars of slavery on his body; the welts of the whip and scars of the shackles. But the harshest of his scars lay underneath where no one was the wiser; the damage to his soul.

"Me Zanmi – *My People*," Dessalines began, his voice resonating across the gathered masses. "Today we stand as a free and independent state! We have dared to be free. Let us dare to be so by ourselves and for ourselves."

Cheers erupted from the crowd, "Let us swear to fight to the last breath for the independence of our country," Dessalines continued, as the crowd once again cheered in a frenzy.

"Some will have you believe that I am cruel. Others, that I am a monster, and still others that I possess the skills of a butcher. What do I care for the judgment of posterity, provided I save you and my fellow countryman?" Dessalines roared to the enlightenment of the crowd.

"I have avenged all of the Americas!" Dessalines declared, linking the revolution of his enslaved black people to the decimation of the indigenous peoples of Hispaniola, and all colonies within the larger scope of the Americas at large, as a shared battle against European conquest, colonialism, and subjugation. "This battle, I am afraid, will continue as long as I am alive to fight it," he roared to the delight of the crowd.

Surrounding Dessalines stood his most trusted black Générals: Christophe, Charéron, Boisrond, Capois, Gabart, Daut, François, Férou, Cangé, Ambroise, Herne, Brave, Yayou, and Roux. Among the mulatto officers were Clerveaux, Bonnet, Bazelais, Vernet, Romain, and Guérin. Conspicuously absent were Pétion and Boyer, who would celebrate in Port-au-Prince as they were uninvited by Dessalines to Gonaïves. The scars of the civil war of 1799 had not yet healed, even though they had set their differences aside during the revolution against the French for a common cause.

As the applause continued, Dessalines allowed himself a small, satisfied smile. However, beneath his triumphant exterior, a whirlwind of thoughts churned within him. He knew all too well the challenges that lay ahead for him on the international scene, and the delicate balance of power he would need to maintain among his Générals, the remaining French white population, the mulattos still bitter from the civil war, and a freed population of slaves not motivated to return to a system of commercialized farming. Yet, in this moment of celebration, the people hailed him as their hero, a savior who had led them to victory against the French oppressors.

"Viv Libète!, Viv Ayiti!, Viv Desalin!" the people chanted, their voices swelling with pride and adoration. The sound washed over Dessalines like a wave, filling him with both awe and humility. For it was not just his strength that had brought them to this day, but the resilience and determination of every man, woman, and child who had fought alongside him for freedom.

"Viv Libète!, Viv Ayiti! Dessalines roared back, raising his fists in solidarity with the people who had entrusted him with their future as their Governor General.

And so, as the music resumed and the dancing continued. Marie-Claire Heureuse Félicité Bonheur Dessalines joined her husband on the stage, united by a common hope for a brighter tomorrow.

Her appearance contrasted his own, with a lighter complexion and a composed demeanor. She hid her hair with a blue turban wrap that highlighted her smooth facial features. Her eyes were a huge dark brown, her lips full, and her skin was void of any imperfections.

She wore a bright yellow dress that hid her small breasts that hung high on her chest, pressing on the tight garment.

Together, they lifted their arms to the sky, holding hands, to the roar of the crowd. But beneath the surface of the festivities, a lingering sense of uncertainty and anticipation hinted at the challenges still to come.

As Dessalines stood on the stage, Marie-Claire could see that he was basking in the adulation of his people. Their cries of joy and gratitude washed over him like a warm tropical breeze, but she also knew that there was a storm brewing within him. The price of freedom weighed heavily on his broad shoulders, and they both knew that the battle for Ayiti's soul had only just begun.

"Viv Libète!, Viv Ayiti!, Viv Viv Desalin!" many again shouted, voices cracking with emotion. "Viv Libète!, Viv Ayiti!, Viv Viv Desalin!"

Yet even as he accepted their praise, he could not help but feel a gnawing sense of responsibility. For it was up to him to lead these people into an uncertain future - one where the specter of French occupation hung over them like a dark cloud, and the scars of centuries of cruelty still festered beneath the surface.

"Général," called Henry Christophe, approaching Dessalines from behind. "The people adore you."

"Oui, it appears so" Dessalines answered, his brow furrowing. "But appearances can be deceiving and we must not forget that our enemies still lurk in the shadows, and others who not dare show their faces in the bright of day. We have won our freedom, but now we must fight to keep our mental freedom."

Christophe nodded solemnly, his expression betraying a hint of doubt. "You speak the truth, Général. But some fear your methods may be too harsh. They worry that your iron grip will choke the very freedom we fought so hard to obtain."

"Is that what you think, Christophe?" Dessalines asked, his eyes narrowing. "Or is that what Pétion would have you believe?"

"Pétion has his own concerns," Christophe admitted. "But I cannot deny that my loyalty lies with Ayiti and its people first. I have seen firsthand the lengths to which you will go to secure our independence, and while I respect your dedication, I also fear the consequences of your actions."

"Freedom comes at a cost," Dessalines countered, his tone hardening. "Never forget it or what I will do whenever I feel it necessary to protect our people and ensure that Ayiti remains free of tyranny."

"Even if it means becoming a tyrant yourself?" Christophe challenged, raising his face to look into Dessalines' eyes.

"Enough!" Dessalines snapped. "I have made my choices, and I will not waver in the face of adversity. If you cannot stand by me, then say so now and be done with it, and I will be done with you."

"Général," Christophe began, his voice softening. "You know that I have and would follow you into the fires of hell itself if need be. But some question whether we can truly forge a new future for Ayiti while clinging to the ways of the past. To constant war."

"Then let them question," Dessalines declared, his fiery gaze sweeping over the assembled crowd. "For I will continue to fight for our freedom, no matter the cost."

As the cheers of the people swelled once more, Dessalines could only hope that his resolve would be enough to guide Ayiti through the stormy seas that lay ahead. As he stood there, a beacon of strength and determination, he knew that the spirit of the Ayisyen people would never be broken – no matter the challenges they faced. However, can it be channeled into the productivity required to run a country this size and maintain an economy? Only time will tell.

The celebratory atmosphere in Gonaïves continued to swell, reaching a feverish pitch as the sun dipped below the horizon. Amidst the throngs of jubilant revelers, Marie-Claire stood by her husband's side, her unwavering support and keen intellect evident in every word she spoke and action she took.

"Jean-Jacques," she murmured softly, her voice barely audible above the din of the crowd, "you have achieved something truly extraordinary today. But you must remember that these people need more than just freedom from France; they need guidance and understanding as they heal from the wounds of the past."

Dessalines nodded thoughtfully, his brow furrowing as he considered his wife's words. Though he sometimes found her compassion puzzling, he respected her opinion and often deferred to her wisdom. "You are right, as always, my love," he replied. "I will do everything in my power to lead our people forward – not only as their Général but as their shepherd as well."

Meanwhile, Général Henry Christophe surveyed the scene from a distance, his eyes narrowing as he assessed the loyalties of the various Générals in attendance. The absence of Pétion weighed heavily on his mind, though there was no love lost between them. Henry had witnessed the violent nature of mulattos in battle and had lost many comrades to Pétion's fighters. But he could not shake the feeling that some of the men surrounding him might be tempted to break ranks with Dessalines.

"Can we truly trust all of them?" Christophe wondered, his gaze lingering on each face in turn, especially the mulattos. He was no stranger to Dessalines' capacity for cruelty – he had witnessed it firsthand during the revolution and the War of Knives prior – and he worried about the future of Ayiti under such a ruthless leader. Would his desire for vengeance against the French and the white slaveholding class ultimately overpower the need for unity and stability?

As he mulled over these concerns, Christophe couldn't help but feel a pang of envy towards his wife Marie-Claire. She was the only one to possess an innate ability to calm Dessalines' tempestuous nature and temper his rage with her kindness and empathy as no man ever could. Christophe knew that he could never hope to achieve such a balance, but he vowed to do everything in his power to protect Ayiti from the potentially disastrous consequences of unchecked anger and in the process, protect Dessalines from even himself.

"Only time will tell if we can truly overcome the shadows of our past," he mused, his eyes never leaving the sea of faces before him.

"But one thing is certain: we must remain vigilant and united if we are to succeed."

"Do you speak the truth?" Diédoné challenged Desbardes. "That the American president wants this country unstable?"

"Absolutely. I have it under the best of authority," replied Desbardes.

"But why would this be so? If he is an intelligent man, he can surely see the advantage of dealing with Dessalines to dominate trade and harness the production of this land to his citizen's benefit," Diédoné reasoned.

"You would think so, wouldn't you?" Desbardes answered. "However, he deals on both sides. He sides with the merchants who want to expand trade here and with his southern class of American slave masters who want to ensure that Dessalines does not export freedom north to their lands. An army in chaos can serve both purposes."

"And France?"

"The same. France has reinstituted slavery in the French West Indies. Containment of this uprising is paramount to that success."

"But it is I that has the most to lose. I have nothing to gain here." protested Diédoné. "I do not seek to own slaves and have no desire to be a farmer."

"You have everything to gain. Build your power, recruit your maroons, and destabilize Dessalines. Keep him constantly on his toes and his people will eventually turn on him. We, in turn, will do our part as well," answered Diédoné. "France will reward you for your loyalty, Diédoné"

"Then what? What is left for me then?"

"There is opportunity in destabilization. You will very quickly find that out," Desbardes concluded.

Across town, the vibrant atmosphere of the Gonaïves square was a sharp contrast to the heavy thoughts lurking in the minds of Dessalines, Christophe, and the other Généraux. As they stood on the parade viewing stand, their eyes scanned the jubilant crowd, searching for any hint of treachery or danger. The people's cheers and laughter seemed at odds with the unspoken fear that France could return and attempt to reclaim their former colony, or that the United States might refuse to recognize Ayiti's hard-won independence. Or that the fragile detente with Britain may evaporate at any time.

"Général Dessalines," whispered Général François, leaning in close to his leader so as not to be overheard by the celebrating masses. "I have heard whispers of unease from the American and British merchants who linger at our shores. They are willing to trade with us, but there is hesitation – they worry that doing business with us may provoke France on the seas and place their ships in jeopardy."

Dessalines furrowed his brow, his dark eyes flashing with anger. Yet he knew that the support of these foreign traders was crucial to Ayiti's survival. He forced a tight smile onto his face, careful not to let his true emotions show. "We must tread carefully, my friend," he advised, lowering his voice to match François'. "Our freedom is still new, and it will take time for the world to accept our place within it."

Christophe watched the exchange from the corner of his eye, fighting back a surge of anxiety. His mind raced with thoughts of betrayal, and he found himself wondering which of his fellow Généraux might turn against them. What if Pétion, who was absent from the festivities, had already made a deal with the French, or the British? Or worse, what if his own candor and honesty placed him in suspicion of disloyalty towards Dessalines?

He tried to shake off the paranoia, focusing instead on the powerful display of military strength before him. Rows of uniformed soldiers marched in perfect formation, their weapons gleaming in the

Victory parade in the city of Gonaïves as Governor General, Jean-Jacques Dessalines, and his general look on.

sunlight as they saluted their commander-in-chief. The sight filled Christophe with a sense of pride and determination – surely this disciplined army could stand against any threat, be it foreign or domestic.

Then came the Polish Legion, or what was left of them. Nearly 800 white-skinned Polish troops marched in the street, their commanders mounted on their large steeds brought over from Europe during the Leclerc invasion. Dessalines remembered the day that they had surrendered to him, their commander, Général Władysław Franciszek Jabłonowski, was a proud soldier, a Polish mulatto of all things, and a brilliant fighter unfortunately lost to La fyèv Jòn– Yellow Fever. He would honor his legacy by allowing his soldiers, those who wanted to remain, to be integrated as citizens in his new country. The first white black citizens of Ayiti, Dessalines mused.

"Look at them, Général Christophe," said Dessalines, his gaze fixed on the soldiers below. "These men are our brothers, our sons, and our future. We must never forget the sacrifices they have made to secure our freedom."

Christophe nodded solemnly, knowing that those same sacrifices weighed heavily on his conscience. As he looked out over the sea of faces, cheering and chanting for a brighter future, he silently vowed to do everything in his power to protect his people from the shadows of their past.

"Yes, Général," he replied, his voice steady despite the storm of emotions raging within him. "We have come too far to falter now. Together, we will forge a new Ayiti – one free from the chains of oppression and the specter of fear."

As the military parade continued, the Générals exchanged quiet words of reassurance, their spirits buoyed by the resilience and hope on display before them. Though uncertainty still hung in the air like a thick fog, they knew that they were not alone in their struggle. For every challenge that lay ahead, there was a courageous heart ready to face it head-on, fueled by the unyielding desire for freedom and justice.

The sun dipped low in the sky, casting a golden glow over the city of Gonaïves as the celebrations reached a crescendo. The rhythmic drumbeats and lilting melodies of traditional Creole music filled the air, providing an electrifying accompaniment to the fervor of the crowd. As Jean-Jacques Dessalines stepped forward to address his people, the cheers reached a deafening volume, a testament to the esteem in which he was held.

"Frè-m ak Sè-m yo - *My brothers and sisters*" Dessalines bellowed, his voice resonating with passion and conviction. "Today, we stand united in our struggle for freedom and justice, no longer shackled by the chains of oppression."

The crowd erupted in applause, their faces alight with pride and determination. "Viv Libète!, Viv Ayiti!, Viv Viv Desalin!" they again chanted, their voices melding together in a powerful chorus of hope.

"However," Dessalines continued, his eyes sweeping across the sea of faces before him, "we must not be complacent in our victory. The enemies of liberty still lurk in the shadows, waiting for a moment of weakness to strike us down."

A murmur rippled through the crowd, a mixture of concern and defiance. "We will fight!" a man shouted from the throng, his fist raised in solidarity. "For Dessalines and for Ayiti!"

"Oui," agreed a woman nearby, her eyes shining with unshed tears. "We have come too far to surrender our freedom now."

Dessalines nodded, his heart swelling with pride at the resilience of his people. "Together, we must remain vigilant against those who would see us enslaved once more. We must forge our new Ayiti, one that is strong and independent, able to withstand the storms that seek to tear us apart."

"Kouraj, zanmi m yo!" he roared, his voice rising above the din. "*Courage, my friends.* For we are the children of slaves who have risen against our captors, and we will never again submit to tyranny!"

"Kouraj! Kouraj!" the crowd echoed, their voices ringing through the streets of Gonaïves like a clarion call to arms. As

Dessalines looked out over the sea of determined faces, he understood that the struggle for Ayiti's future had only just begun.

The sun dipped low in the sky over the streets of Gonaïves while music and laughter filled the air as people of all ages and backgrounds came together to celebrate their newfound freedom. Men, women, and children danced in the streets, their bodies swaying to the rhythm of the drums and the melody of the traditional Ayisyen tunes.

Across town, inside the darkening café, the two outliers still schemed and scorned the excitement of the celebrations. "Look at them," Desbardes nodded to Diédoné. "Adults acting like children waiting to be led. And they think Dessalines is the one to lead them."

"Dessalines did vanquish you Frenchmen, you must give him that credit," Diédoné responded as he polished off the final remnants of the potatoes left on the plate that both men had feasted on.

"I bid you adieu, mon Général," Desbardes said as he stood and gulped the remaining rum from his wooden goblet. "We will be in touch. We have much work to do and we shall soon begin. On your end, start to get your maroons in the mountains ready. I will reach out through our normal channels."

Before Diédoné could utter another word, Desbardes had vanished through the crowded restaurant. The skills of a spy, Diédoné thought.

As the celebration continued late into the evening, Dessalines stood on a balcony overlooking the festivities, lost in thought. He couldn't help but feel a sense of unease, despite the triumphant atmosphere that surrounded him. The people were united in their desire for freedom, but would that unity hold once the adrenaline of victory faded and the harsh realities of nation-building set in?

"Jean-Jacques," a sweet and familiar voice called out from behind him. He turned to find Marie-Claire approaching, her dark eyes filled with concern. "You should join the celebration. The people need to see you, to know that you stand with them."

Dessalines hesitated, his thoughts still clouded by doubt. "I know my place is among them, but I cannot shake this feeling that our struggles are far from over and we are just beginning a new chapter."

"Perhaps they are," Marie-Claire admitted, placing a gentle hand on his arm. "But we must also take time to celebrate our victories and to remember what it is we're fighting for. We have come so far, Jean-Jacques, and there is still much to be done. But for tonight, let us stand together and rejoice in our unity. It is also your duty to do so."

With a deep breath, Dessalines nodded and allowed himself to be led back into the heart of the celebration. He looked out over the sea of faces – mostly black, with a sparse attendance by mulattos, and a few white Polish officers. They were the children of slaves and former slave masters, of farmers and merchants, soldiers and scholars. And yet, for one shining moment, they stood united as one people, bound together by their shared hopes and dreams for a brighter future.

"Viv Libète!, Viv Ayiti!, Viv Viv Desalin!" a voice cried out again, and soon the chant was taken up by others, spreading through the crowd like wildfire; "Viv Libète!, Viv Ayiti!, Viv Viv Desalin!"

"Viv Ayiti! Viv libète!" Dessalines echoed, his voice strong and clear, giving the people what they needed as they roared their approval, their cheers ringing through the night air like the pealing of church bells.

And as the sun began to set on the first day of Ayiti's independence, Dessalines couldn't help but wonder what challenges lay ahead for his beloved country. Would they find a way to heal the wounds of the past and forge a new path forward? Or would the ghosts of their history continue to haunt them, threatening to tear apart the fragile bonds that held them together?

Only time will tell.

As the evening shadows deepened, the official reception had moved to the government house where Dessalines stood alone for a moment on the balcony of the grand reception hall. The air was heavy with the scent of tropical flowers and the lingering smoke of celebratory gunfire. Closing his eyes, he allowed himself a brief respite from the festivities, a moment to reflect on the long journey that had brought him to this point. Images from his past flickered through his mind – the cruel lash of the whip, the taste of saltwater mixed with sweat as he labored in the cane fields, and the cries of his comrades as they fell on the battlefield. "Every drop of blood shed," he whispered to himself, "every tear, every scar, every sacrifice... it has all led to this day."

He clenched his fists, determination steeling his resolve. He would not allow those sacrifices to be in vain. Ayiti's independence must be protected at all costs, even if it means making difficult decisions along the way.

The sound of raised voices cut through Dessalines' reverie, drawing him back to the present. Inside the hall, a heated argument had broken out between the black Générals Charéron, Boisrond, Gabart, and the mulatto Générals Clerveaux, Bonnet, and Guérin. The topic of contention: the necessity of the Civil War that had raged five years ago. Though these Générals had fought together in unison during this past year, they were still bound by the chains of past differences, and animosities never healed. Worsening the differences was the subject of color, of race. The mulattos, Dessaalines thought, still believed themselves one step superior to the blacks. They were white lovers and would never change.

"Enough!" Dessalines bellowed, striding back into the hall. The arguing Générals fell silent, their faces a mix of embarrassment and defiance. "This is not the time nor the place for such arguments."

"Forgive us, Général Dessalines," Clerveaux said, his voice tight. "But we cannot stand idly by while our contributions to this revolution are belittled simply because we are not black."

Dessalines scanned the room, his gaze settling on Christophe, who stood nearby, observing the scene with a furrowed brow. Dessalines knew that Christophe was not entirely comfortable with his methods, but they needed each other to keep the new state safe from internal and external threats, he thought, as he walked over to him.

"Christophe," he said in a low voice, drawing him aside. "I need your loyalty. Swear it to me, and me alone."

Christophe hesitated, his eyes flicking back to the arguing Générals before meeting Dessalines' unwavering gaze. "Dessalines I swear my loyalty to you," he finally replied, his voice strained with the weight of the promise. "But I am also tormented by the fractures I see among our highest officers."

"Then we must work together to mend those fractures," Dessalines said, his tone resolute. "Our unity is our strength, and we cannot allow petty arguments or past grievances to weaken us. L'union fait la force – *unity is strength*."

"Do you promise to adhere to that yourself, Mon Général?

As the two leaders exchanged solemn nods, the reception hall echoed with tense whispers and uneasy glances. The festivities continued, but beneath the surface, uncertainty and tension simmered. Dessalines knew that the challenges awaiting were far from over, and that only through steadfast determination and military strength would they secure a lasting peace.

As the evening wore on, the formal reception thrived with laughter and lively discussions. Dessalines watched the animated crowd from a distance, his thoughts clouded by the recent events. The music, once a source of joy, now seemed to taunt him with its frivolity.

"Jean-Jacques," called a soft voice behind him, gently pulling him from his pence. He turned to find Marie-Claire, his beloved wife, standing by his side, her eyes filled with understanding. "You are troubled, my love."

Dessalines hesitated, reluctant to burden her with his worries. But as he looked into her compassionate gaze, his resolve crumbled before her, like it could never for any other human being. "I fear for our unity, Marie-Claire. The disagreements among our Générals... the lingering scars of the past... my fear that the French whites will conspire to once again enslave us, it weighs heavily on me."

Marie-Claire took his hand, her touch a soothing balm to his unease. "These tensions are not new, Jean-Jacques. You cannot expect them to be resolved overnight. But you have brought us this far. With your leadership and determination, there is hope for healing."

"Is it enough?" he asked, his voice wavering with vulnerability. "Can we truly overcome these divisions and build a brighter future for our new country?"

"Only time will tell," she replied softly, her gaze never leaving his. "But I believe in you, in us. We must stand together and face whatever challenges lie ahead."

Dessalines felt a warmth spread through him, a renewed strength drawn from the unwavering faith and intelligence of the woman before him. She believed in him and gave him the strength he needed. At that moment, amidst the uncertainty and tension that surrounded them, he knew that their bond was unbreakable – a beacon of hope in the darkness.

"Thank you, Marie-Claire," he murmured, pressing a tender kiss to her forehead. "Your support means more to me than you will ever know."

"Then dance with me. Let the people see the other side of my great husband. They are afraid of you, you know," she whispered, her words finding a nerve within his need to be accepted. Some think you are a monster. They do not know you as I do. Show them some of that other side. The soft side of you so often reveal to me.

Dessalines closed his eyes and thought back to the atrocities of war, the necessity for those atrocities. If his woman knew what he had done, what he had sacrificed of his soul for this day, would she still speak like this? Speak so softly and kindly to him still?

She took his large hand and had it lift hers as they walked to the bulging dance floor. Everyone parted the way to let the first couple through. They were their promise and the guardians of their future.

As Marie-Claire and Jean-Jacques Dessalines swayed to the music, he forgot everything else. For in their love and devotion, they found the strength to face whatever fate had in store – united in their quest for a brighter tomorrow.

Daniel J.D. Bayard

Three

PÉTION IN THE SOUTH

Port-Républicain
January 1, 1804

The sun bore down upon the jubilant throngs that packed the streets of Port-Républicain, its glare reflected off the white buildings and into the eyes of the revelers. The air was thick with the scent of roasting meats; goat, pork, chicken, conch mixed with sweet cane juice, punctuated by the rhythmic cacophony of drums and the lilting melodies of flutes. It was a day of culmination, the city itself pulsing with the heartbeat of liberty—the first inauguration day in 1804.

Amidst this tapestry of celebration, an imposing figure emerged, his presence like a lodestone drawing gazes and stirring the already electric atmosphere. Alexandre Pétion, astride a chestnut mare, the animal dancing knowingly to the pleasure of the crowd, prancing through the confetti-strewn cobblestones, radiated the charisma that had marked his ascent to prominence. His brilliant uniform, adorned with the trappings of his rank; medals, epaulets, and ribbons, caught the sunlight, the epaulets winking like stars coming down to join the festivities.

Beside him rode Jean-Pierre Boyer, younger by five years but no less formidable in his own right and a near-perfect twin to his mentor, his demeanor that of unwavering support and respect. They were flanked by an entourage of the most loyal officers, each distinguished by their resolve and the shared trials that had forged them in the crucible of revolution. The crowd erupted in cheers as they recognized the leaders among them, voices lifting in adulation for the men who had helped birth their nation from the chains of oppression. Pétion had inherited the region's mantle of power from André Rigaud who had disgraced himself amongst the French for not explicitly following orders and had systematically been arrested and deported before their defeat.

"Liberté! Liberté!" The chant wove through the throng, a reverberating affirmation of the hard-won freedom they celebrated. Some from the threat of being re-enslaved, others from the constant abuse and racism inflicted on them by French authorities since they were gens de couleurs; free mulattos, and blacks. The French would ransack their businesses for food, clothing, and equipment - providing worthless government vouchers that they knew would never see the day of payment but forced by law to be accepted.

Pétion acknowledged the masses with a practiced ease, his smile wide and genuine, and his hand rising to give a subtle yet gracious wave. His gaze, however, held an introspective glint, betraying the weight of the responsibility he shouldered on this historic day. He knew the eyes of the world were upon Ayiti, scrutinizing the nascent country's every move, awaiting signs of promise but predicting precursors of failure.

"Today," he mused silently, "we stand as a beacon to all those still languishing in shackles. Today, we are the harbinger of hope for Cuba and all of the Spanish Americas, Jamaica, and the British colonies, Martinique, Guadeloupe and the other French colonies, and of course the Southern United States where half a million African slaves languished in servitude with the hope that they too could also find this freedom, as Ayiti now enjoyed to their south."

As the procession navigated the heart of the city, children darted forward to present garlands of vibrant tropical flowers, their laughter ringing out like chimes amidst the festivities. Pétion graciously accepted these tokens, his heart swelling at the sight of such uninhibited joy—the kind that could only flourish under the auspices of freedom. Catholic nuns led children's choirs in song on almost every street corner, and priests from every congregation in the city and surrounding villages, blessed the processions with incense and prayer as it passed.

"Général Pétion!" called out a voice from the crowd. A young woman with a baby in one arm and a toddler clinging to her mother's dress, her face alight with pride, extended her hand towards him, a simple gesture that encompassed centuries of dreams now realized. Pétion leaned from the saddle, his fingertips brushing hers in a fleeting yet poignant connection.

"Pour l'avenir! – *For the Future!* My husband fought with you but perished, mon Général. He would be proud of this day" she exclaimed, her words echoing the aspirations of all who had fought, suffered, and triumphed.

Pétion stopped the procession, fully realizing the depth of the moment and taking the opportunity to orchestrate his next moves. He ceremoniously dismounted and approached the woman. He looked into her eyes and smiled as she smiled back, basting in the glory of his presence. Pétion placed his hand on her cheek and brought her in for a hug, turned to the crowd and shouted "Pour l'avenir,"

The crowd echoed back, imbued with the gravity of the moment. For the future—a future where resilience would be rewarded, where hope would be the cornerstone upon which they would rebuild their shattered world.

Pétion remounted his mare, the reins being held by an assistant and the procession continued, winding its way toward the square where Pétion would address the city. As he rode forth, the reflection in his eyes was not of the sun-drenched streets or the fluttering flags of independence, but of a people unbroken, a land fertile with potential, and the delicate strands of unity that he was determined to weave into an enduring fabric of peace.

"Today, we are architects of our destiny," Pétion proclaimed as he dismounted in the square, his baritone voice rising above the cacophony, vibrant and sure. "No longer shall we be shackled by the chains of oppression. Our resilience has carved this path, and it is with hope that we shall pave it."

The crowd erupted in a chorus of affirmation, a sea of hands reaching toward him as if to draw strength from his very presence. Pétion moved among them, his touch a benediction, his smile a shared secret of brighter days to come. Each handshake, each nod, was a covenant of mutual endeavor, a silent pact forged in the crucible of shared struggle.

"Liberty!" someone shouted, the word cascading through the masses like a sacred mantra. "Resilience! Hope!"

Pétion's heart swelled with the resonance of those words, a symphony of triumph that drowned out the lingering whispers of past enmities and future uncertainties. This was his hour, their hour, and nothing could diminish the incandescent glory of a people reborn.

Pétion felt the mantle of leadership settle upon his shoulders like a mantle woven from the very spirit of the land. And amidst the symphony of celebration, the future unfurled before them, a canvas vast and uncharted, teeming with possibility. The southern and western regions would become his reign, and he swore to protect it with his life.

But amidst the euphoria of the moment, Pétion couldn't entirely silence the bitter memories of his complicated relationship with Dessalines, whom he imagined reigning over similar festivities in Gonaïves. They had been on opposing sides during a bloody and bitter civil war - the War of Knives it was called, nearly five years earlier. Their ideologies clashed like fire and ice, similar to the cold and disciplined sword blades of that war. Their skin color and background are an everlasting bone of contention. He was the son of rich parents, one being a white Frenchman and Dessalines born into slavery. Dessalines could never reconcile these differences.

Yet, they had come together during the revolution to vanquish the French, a testament to the strength of their shared cause. But, despite this uneasy alliance, tensions still simmered between them, an undercurrent of mistrust that threatened to erode the fragile foundation of their newfound nation. Pétion's animosity was further fueled by his exclusion from the formation of Ayiti's first constitution, a snub he couldn't easily forgive after joining Dessalines and willingly fighting alongside him.

At first, he had felt insulted, shamed, and discarded. However, to maintain an air of solidarity, Dessalines had named Pétion the military Commander General of the Western Department which encompassed all territories in the South-central region, linking the North and the Tiburon - or Southern Peninsula.

His counterpart, General Nicolas Geffrard, was named the commander of the Southern Peninsula and was based out of Les Cayes. Geffrard commanded an army of 1,500 men, about half the size of Pétion's army in strength. Most of this army had been that of General Louis-Jacques Beauvais, who in 1799 had refused to side with either Rigaud or Toussaint in the civil War of Knives and instead had boarded a ship for France to seek direction on what to do. Mysteriously, his ship had sunk and he never made it there.

Dessalines had grown a liking to Geffrard, the dark Mulatto as he was called, who after the War of Knives swore allegiance to him. Geffrard was one of the mulattos invited to draft and sign the Declaration of Independence.

Pétion and Geffrard had a good relationship, with Pétion even assisting Geffrard by negotiating a safe passage agreement with the powerful Maroon leader Lamour Desrances who controlled the territories in the mountains from Port-Républicain to Saint-Marc, while Desrances was still alive before Dessalines had him killed.

However, Pétion commanded the respect of the South - from Port-Républicain through the entire Southern peninsula to his west; Jacmel, Jérémie, Les Cayes, and the rest of the mulatto strongholds. This was past Rigaudin territory, the phrase coined for the followers of André Rigaud during his failed attempt to secede from the French colony that was quashed by Toussaint Louverture's army in a stunning victory and show of force on behalf of France. But, that was before the French defeat. Much had and may still change.

Lost in thought, Pétion barely noticed when Jean-Baptiste Bayard Junior approached him, a smile playing on his lips as he clapped his friend on the shoulder.

"Look at you, my friend," Bayard said, his eyes gleaming with pride. "The people adore you, and rightly so. You have given them hope for a brighter future."

Pétion returned the smile, grateful for his friend's unwavering support. Their bond was strong, anchored by a shared vision for the future of Ayiti and their collaborative efforts in shaping the new nation. They had weathered countless storms together, their friendship forged in the fires of adversity.

Pétion—who was 5 years his elder, had met Junior while he was studying in Paris when Pétion had addressed the university students about *gens de couleur* in the French Military and opportunities for advancement. Like Junior, Pétion was a Mulatto— born to a wealthy white French father, Pascal Sabès, and Ursula, a free mulatto woman, and designated "Quadroon" in the French caste system. He'd been sent to France at the age of 18 to study at the Military Academy of Paris and began his military service immediately following the completion of his academics.

Though Pétion was born with the surname of Sabès, he adopted the Pétion surname out of admiration for the Mayor of Paris from 1791-1792 named Jérôme Pétion de Villeneuve. The mayor made a lasting impression on the young man as he was a staunch abolitionist and extremely vocal about his opposition to slavery.

After the lecture, Junior had invited Pétion to an outdoor Parisian café, frequented by many of his university student friends, for coffee. They spent hours sharing their experiences in Saint-Domingue and France; quickly becoming friends. Pétion hailed from the western capital of *Port-Républicain* while Jean-Baptiste Junior had arrived from *Le Cap* in the north.

The two vowed to keep in touch as best they could while in France and back at home, which they did over the years.

"Well, one thing is certain, mon général. You were right about we mulattos advancing in the military. You are living proof of that!" laughed Junior to Pétion.

"Pétion thought back to that speech years back and smiled at Junior for remembering it.

Junior had to juggle an interesting dynamic between his friend, Alexandre Pétion, and Henry Christophe, considered nothing short of a brother to his father, Jean-Baptiste. The two believed in much of the same principles, anti-slavery and all, but the divisions between black and mulatto ran deep. Blacks considered mulattos an extension of the whites and mulattos considered blacks a remembrance of the past enslavement of their ancestors before gaining freedom.

It was on Christophe's behest that Junior had convinced his friend Alexandre to defect from the French army last year, a major career-changing move, and meet with Christophe and Dessalines to form an alliance which led to the creation of the revolutionary army dubbed L'Arrmée Indigene. The rest had led them to this glorious day.

"Jean, I've been meaning to speak with you about something important," Pétion said, his tone growing serious. "You know how much I value your counsel."

And I, yours, Alexandre," answered Jean. "What's on your mind?"

"I believe it is time for you to consider entering politics yourself. With me leading our military forces and you in the political sphere, we can build a stronger foundation for Ayiti. I need people that I can trust in positions of power. Those I know to be true to our cause."

Bayard's gaze held Pétion's, "But what of Dessalines? He has been named the Governor Général, meaning the supreme leader." Junior said, considering his words carefully. "You cannot change things unless you get his permission, even in the South."

"I fear that his ambition will only worsen, my young friend," Pétion replied. There are already rumors that he plans on seizing the title 'Governor Général for Life', God forbid. That destroys any sort of constitutional government like that of the United States," Pétion complained. "The people will not stand for it. Ayiti is too diverse, too spread out, for one man's tyrannical rule. That is why you must be ready. Dessalines will not last long if he makes a power play like that. Too many powerful people will resist. It will be a major miscalculation on his part."

"I have it under good authority, my Uncle André as a matter of fact, that a strong military government is the recommendation of one of the founders of the United States, Alexander Hamilton himself. He does not believe that a population raised as slaves can comprehend anything other than a feudal law system controlled by a strong military," answered Junior.

"Yes, I have heard that as well, and he may be right, but you would need the right supreme leader. I am not so sure that Jean-Jacques Dessalines can be the chosen one," Pétion replied. "However, what do you think of my idea of you being instrumental in the political world, and an ally to me?"

"It is an honor to be thought of so highly by you, Alexandre. I will give it serious thought, but only if you promise to guide me along the way, and most importantly, out of the way of Dessalines."

"I owe your father Jean-Baptiste a debt of gratitude, you know. The last time I saw him, I was but a fragment of my current self. Starved, beaten, shamed, running to save my life and that of my men."

"Yes, he had told me that," Junior answered, lowering his head in the sorrow of what it had cost his father, almost his life.

"He saved me and nearly 30 of my men. Gave us safe passage out of Dessalines path, but at a terrible personal cost to himself. A savage beating by the butcher himself," Pétion said. "I owe your father my life, and when I see him once again, I will certainly tell him so. I also understand from you that General Christophe is considered almost a brother to your father?"

"Yes. They go way back to when Henry was but a boy lost in the army during the American Revolution. It is my father who swayed me to have both of you meet and come to an agreement to join Dessalines and wage war against the French. Why?" asked Junior.

"Christophe will be key to balance the power of Dessalines, to curb his appetite for violence," responded Pétion. "I believe Christophe can be reasoned with."

"Is it true that Dessalines mass executed noncombatants - men, women, and even children, at the town near the fort at Crete a Pierrot during the war?" asked Junior.

"My God, a scene I will never forget. I, and Boyer, arrived a near week later as they were burying the last of the victims. All with their throats slit, eyes staring motionless at the sky. They had to bury them in shifts of only one hour at a time as the soldiers would fall ill from the stench of the rotting flesh and the gruesome sites."

"And this is the man that now rules supreme," Junior said as he shook his head in disbelief at what he was hearing and now realized it was fact and not rumor.

"Many say it was Dessalines form of psychological warfare. If so, he's a diabolical genius because it was most effective," concluded Pétion. "But, no more. Today is a joyous day. Let us make it so. As for your question, of course, I will guide you as best I can," Pétion replied, clasping Junior Bayard's hand in a firm grip. "Together, we will forge a path to greatness for our beloved country, no matter what obstacles lay in our way."

As they continued to celebrate the dawning of a new era, Pétion couldn't shake the lingering concerns for his safety. The War of Knives had left deep scars, and rival factions within Ayiti still posed potential threats. He knew that Dessalines still harbored resentment, but he would not let fear dictate his actions. He would stand strong against adversity, and Dessalines, if it came to that. But how many other disciples of Dessalines should he fear that lay in wait?

The sun dipped low in the sky, casting a warm golden glow across Port-Républicain as the inauguration day celebrations reached their climax. Pétion stood backstage, taking a moment to savor the anticipation that hummed through the air like electricity. He could feel the weight of history bearing down on him, pressing him forward to seize this moment and make it his own.

"Alexandre," called Jean-Pierre Boyer from the wings, gesturing for him to take the stage. "It is time."

With Jean-Pierre Boyer by his side, offering unwavering support and assistance, Pétion knew he could weather any storm. Together, they would navigate the treacherous waters of politics and power, guided by their shared ideals and an unshakable belief in the resilience and hope of the people of the West and South.

With a deep breath, Pétion strode out onto the stage and relished the warm afternoon sun upon him and the cheers of the crowd, his eyes sweeping over the vast sea of people who had come to bear witness to this pivotal moment in Ayiti's history. As he took his place behind the podium, he felt an irresistible surge of pride and purpose, steeled by the conviction that he was standing on the cusp of greatness.

"Mes chère frères et soeurs – *My dear brothers and sisters,*" he began, his voice resonating with authority and passion, "today marks not only the birth of our nation but the beginning of a new era. We have been shackled by tyranny, enslaved by prejudice, and hobbled by fear for far too long. But now, we are free. Free to forge our destiny, to build a future of peace, prosperity, and unity."

The crowd roared its approval, their faces upturned in a sea of rapturous adoration. Pétion let the cheers wash over him, relishing the taste of victory and recognition that came with each wave of applause. With a flourish, he removed a cheroot cigar from his pocket, the signature of his persona, lighting it with a practiced hand and taking a deep draw, letting the rich smoke envelop him like a shroud of success. His other hand clutched a glass of dark, rich, and refined southern rum, its cognac quality and warmth spreading through him, fueling his speech.

The crowd went wild with enthusiasm as an army of servers began circulating through the crowd with lesser-grade rum, pouring a small amount to anyone who asked or raised a goblet for it. It was as if Pétion was in the intimacy of his home, flanked by thousands of people, and informally laughing, joking, drinking, and smoking in informal style with all of them.

"He is one of us!" they exclaimed, basking in his affection and attention.

"Make no mistake, my friends," Pétion continued, his voice rising above the din, "the challenges we face are great. But together, we are stronger than any obstacle that stands in our way. We are the children of revolution, the heirs to a legacy of courage and sacrifice. And as long as we stand united, there is nothing we cannot achieve."

"Let us join hands, my brothers and sisters," Pétion cried, his voice soaring to a crescendo, "and together, we will build the entire state of Ayiti into a nation worthy of our dreams!"

The crowd erupted into thunderous applause once more, their fervor matched only by the intensity of Pétion's convictions. As he looked out over the sea of faces, he raised his goblet and saw not just the people of Ayiti, but the embodiment of resilience and hope. They were a living testament to the indomitable spirit that had propelled them to victory against all odds. "Au sud et à l'ouest!" he yelled - to the South and West! "Au sud et à l'ouest!" the crowd cheered as they raised their glasses in unison, and even those who pretended they had one, chanted "Au sud et à l'ouest!, Au sud et à l'ouest!, Au sud et à l'ouest!!".

As the final echoes of his speech faded into the gathering dusk, the cheers of the crowd surged like a tidal wave, buoying him up on a current of adulation and awe. He stepped back from the podium as the band began to play, his heart swelling with pride, knowing that he had captured the hearts and minds of his people. He could feel it. And yes, it felt good. He vowed at that moment that he would not let Dessalines or anyone else steal victory from the people of the south and the west, his people, and his mulatto brothers in arms. He would fight to protect them, protect them all, from tyranny.

For Alexandre Pétion, the future was a boundless horizon, ripe with promise and possibility. On stage, he stood ready to stride boldly into the unknown, guided by the unshakable belief that together, they could forge a brighter tomorrow, with or without Jean-Jacques Dessalines in it.

The last vestiges of sunlight ebbed away, bathing the streets of Port-Républicain in a warm, golden glow. As the revelries continued around him, Pétion savored a moment of respite amid the chaos, his fingers deftly rolling a cheroot cigar between them. The pungent aroma of tobacco filled his nostrils as he took a long, slow draw, allowing the rich smoke to languidly coil around his tongue before exhaling a cloud of satisfaction.

The festivities of the day had subsided and the beginning of the evening's celebrations was about to get underway. He was grateful to have bathed, perfumed, and adorned a brilliant new uniform for the evening's celebratory ball at the ornate government house to be hosted by Mayor Paul Jean.

He exited the entrance of the Hotel Excelsior of Port-Républicain. Awaiting was his honor guard of mounted soldiers, a dozen in front and a dozen in the rear of an ornate carriage, equally shining in their brilliant uniforms, all invited to accompany him as representatives of the army at the grand ball.

The procession wound through the wide streets of the city that were lined with patrons hoping to get a glimpse of Pétion as he headed toward the government house. The procession made a turn on Rue Bois de Chene, proceeded a couple of blocks, and stopped at No. 27, the home of the cousin of his Mistress Concubine, Marie-Madeleine Lachenais, affectionately known as Joute.

As a military man, Pétion didn't believe in marriage as an option for a warrior. In colonial times, the designation of a woman as a man's Concubine was very much accepted as the closest relationship to a wife. Just like in marriage, concubines were recognized sexual partners of a man and were expected to bear children for him.

Joute was from Arcahaie, a commune along Ayiti's western coast. They had met a few years back at a government reception in Arcahaie. She was not yet 26 and Pétion 34. She was well accustomed to power and influence as the daughter of Marie Thérèse Fabre, a socialite in Arcahaie and the powerful French colonel de Lachenais. While in Port-Républicain, she would always stay with her cousin Regine Auguste.

The house butler opened the door and Regine began to descend the steps, followed by Marie-Madeleine. Pétion exited the carriage, approached Regine, and kissed her hand, exclaiming how beautiful she looked.

He then turned the intensity of his attention to Joute, who gripped his affection like no other woman could. He was mesmerized, almost in a trance-like state in her presence ever since they had met a little over a year ago. She commanded his attention without ever asking for it. Her facial features were of a delicate mulâtresse; dark eyes, dark straight hair, and a beautiful café-au-lait complexion. Her nose was slender, inherited from her white French father, but her lips were that of her mother's; large, puffy, and what Pétion thought, the most comfortable kissable lips of any woman. Her body was slender with her dress hugging her breasts as he hoped he could do.

Joute basked in his affections, knowing full well the power she held over him as he helped both ladies into the carriage. She knew and had come to terms with the fact, that she could never be his wife. For this trade-off, she was committed to one day be even more than that, to newly define the term of concubine and expanding the power it could yield over a military man of such importance.

The procession proceeded rapidly and with formality to the government house as carriages parted to make way for Pétion's procession. The night was cool and perfect, devoid of insects and heat. As they approached the government house, soldiers sprang to attention down the long road leading to the sprawling building. Jean-Pierre Boyer, now a Général, had ordered soldiers to be at attention during the arrival of Pétion with their sabers pointed in the air for pomp and ceremonial respect.

When the carriage stopped in front of the huge government building, adorned with newly minted flags of the country, Pétion exited as the crowd cheered in jubilation, held back by soldiers from charging the carriage for a closer look at Pétion.

"Général Pétion," Jean-Pierre Boyer hailed, approaching with the confident stride of a seasoned soldier. Beside him walked Jean Bayard Junior in a sparkling green suit, his youthful visage alight with the fire of conviction. "A remarkable speech, sir. You've

General Pétion arrives at the celebration at Government House in Port Républicain the evening of January 1st and is greeted by Jean-Baptiste Bayard Junior and Jean-Pierre Boyer as Joute looks on from inside the carriage.

inspired us all, officers, soldiers, and citizens alike, today at the square," Boyer announced.

"Thank you, Jean-Pierre, Pétion replied, inclining his head in acknowledgment. "But it's not just my words that inspire—it's the spirit of our people. Our Gens de Couleur, both black and mulatto, have shown time and again that they are more than capable of shaping the destiny of this nation, and their contributions must not be forgotten."

"Yes," Bayard Junior chimed in, his gaze sweeping across the jubilant throngs. "Their courage and resilience during the revolution have paved the way for the Ayiti we now strive to build."

"Yet there remains work to be done," Boyer noted, a shadow passing over his features. "Our brothers and sisters in the Northern department may still harbor reservations about the role of us mulattos in the new government. We must continue to prove our worth and earn their trust."

Pétion nodded pensively, his brow furrowing as he considered the task ahead. It would not be an easy one, but he was no stranger to adversity. "We'll break down those barriers, just as we've overcome every other obstacles in our path," he vowed, his voice resolute. "We are all Ayisyen, united by our shared history and our common dreams."

"Forgive me for broaching the subject, sir, but there's another matter that concerns us," Bayard Junior interjected hesitantly. "Your safety. The war of knives may be over, but the threat remains – rival factions still hunger for power, and we fear they may target you."

"Bayard speaks the truth," Boyer added, his eyes narrowing. "Dessalines has not forgotten your escape during the siege of Jacmel. He sought to kill you then, just as he nearly killed Junior's father, and we worry he may yet harbor that desire."

"Your concern is duly noted," Pétion acknowledged, his expression taut as he weighed the risks. He knew all too well the treachery that lurked in the shadows, the specter of betrayal ever-present in these uncertain times. But he would not let fear deter him from his mission. "I appreciate your vigilance, my friends. But we must not allow the darkness of the past to overshadow the brightness of our future. We've come too far to turn back now."

"Of course, Général Pétion" Boyer assented, his loyalty unwavering. "But know that we stand by your side, ready to defend you and the ideals we all hold dear."

"Thank you," Pétion murmured, his heart swelling with gratitude for the steadfast support of his comrades. They were more than just allies—they were brothers-in-arms, bound by the indelible ties of shared struggle and sacrifice.

"Alexandre," he heard Joute call from the carriage. "I hate to break up the boy's club reunion, but we have a ball to attend, no?"

"Forgive me, my love. You know how boys get when they speak of the military. I am now yours," Pétion said as he turned towards the carriage. Joute exited first and Bayard helped Regine, who he handed over to Boyer to escort her behind the Général and Joute to the ball.

"And where is that lovely wife of yours, Jean?" Joute asked of Junior.

"Marie Victoire Georges and Jean-Baptiste Junior had begun their relationship over ten years ago in 1793 when they both attended catholic school in Cap Français together. He was 18 and she 17. They had married seven years later in 1800, during the height of the revolution in a small ceremony at the same school cathedral downtown, followed by a lavish family dinner at Hotel La Couronne with less than a hundred guests in attendance.

His parents had grown affectionate to Marie Victoire, with Marie even finding it comical, chiding Junior that his mother and his new bride shared the same name and that would be somewhat confusing in a crowd.

"She will be arriving shortly, Mademoiselle Lachenais," responded Junior. She is in one of those many carriages back there."

"Alexandre, you should have had her ride with us. She should not be waiting in a hot carriage in this long line here, Joute said with authority, almost scolding Pétion. "You should have planned better, Alexandre."

"As usual, your counsel is wise, mon amour. Next time we have a revolution, I will make sure that happens."

"Really Alexandre. You enjoy toying with me," Joute said. "Jean-Junior, isn't Marie blessed with child soon?"

"Yes, Mademoiselle. We expect our child in the summer," answered Junior.

"Call me Joute. You are too much of a friend to my general to be so formal."

"Yes, Mademoiselle," Junior answered with a respectful bow of his head as Pétion led her away, but looked back at Junior and winked.

Junior smiled and impatiently turned his head towards the approaching carriages, one after one stopping to unload their passengers and driving off. The men and women exiting the carriages were of the elite of Port-Républicain; businessmen, politicians, women of fashion, high-level government workers, and other elites. But Marie Victoire was nowhere in sight.

Junior kept his vigilance and scanned the carriages winding down the government house road as far as the eye could see. He became increasingly impatient until he mounted his stallion and galloped his way down the procession in search of his fiancé's carriage. Finally, he spotted Marie Victoire, somewhere around the twentieth carriage in line, and approached it. He tied his horse to the rear of the carriage and hopped in.

"JJ, I am so happy you found me. We have been in line for nearly an hour since turning into Government House Road. What a jam!" she protested. "But you are a sight for sore eyes indeed!"

Junior looked at his wife and smiled. Her beauty was infinitely more radiant since being blessed with child. Her skin was soft with tiny freckles dotting her petite nose. Her hair was in a bun with jewelry shaped like stars adorning it, and her waist was beginning to show the signs of pregnancy.

Junior couldn't resist taking his head and planting it into her belly. He sniffed long and hard like a dog in a playful gesture of immaturity.

"JJ! What are you doing?" she cried. "What if the coachman sees you?"

"I am simply acting like an animal and enjoying the scent of my unborn child in your womb, my love."

"You are contemptable, Jean-Baptiste Bayard, Junior!"

"And you are most beautiful, Marie Victoire-Bayard."

Marie then took her arms and wrapped them around her husband's head, as he sought her neck and kissed it, exposing his tongue to her warm flesh.

"JJ! If you do not stop this playful jesting, I will not accompany you to the ball! And, this is one you will not steer me from!" said Marie firmly.

"It seems everyone who is anyone has a ticket to this party. I am told over 2,000 have reserved. Are you sure you are up for this?" Jean-Junior asked.

"To admit that I missed probably the largest social event of the century JJ? Really? I don't think so. What would your mother think of me?"

"And our baby?" asked Jean-Junior, alluding to the slight bulge that had begun to grow in his wife's belly. She was now a good three months along.

"He or she will sway with us when we dance. You do know that you will be dancing quite a bit this evening. Forget the military stuff and your military friends tonight, because this evening, you are all mine," she ordered, pouting her lip in her orchestrated demonstration of affection.

"I am all yours, my love. Now, tell me everything about your day. How was it?" asked Jean-Junior.

"Well, to begin with, the coiffure was inundated with customers, even though I had an appointment, and…"

Pétion's eyes took in the jubilant celebration now unfolding in the huge government house building of Port-Républicain. The air thrummed with the rhythm of drums, carrying the weight of history and the hope for a brighter future. It was more than just a moment of joy; it was a testament to the resilience of the Ayisyen people and the possibilities that lay ahead for their newly-born nation.

"Alexandre," came the gentle voice of Pétion's woman, as she approached him from behind, just having disengaged in conversation with a group of friends. Her touch was warm on his arm, grounding him amidst the whirlwind of emotions. "This is our victory, too."

Pétion turned to her, his serious expression softening into a small smile. "Indeed, my love," he replied, his tone reflecting a deep understanding of the historical significance of the day. "And it is our responsibility to ensure that the struggle of our people does not go in vain."

"Your leadership has brought us this far," Joute said, her eyes shining with pride. "I have no doubt it will guide us through whatever challenges come our way."

"Thank you, Joute," Pétion murmured, touched by her unwavering faith in him. "But I cannot do it alone. Your wisdom and counsel have been invaluable to me, and I know that together, we can shape a better future for Ayiti, and in particular, our Western and Southern Regions."

Joute's cheeks flushed at the compliment, but her gaze held Pétion's unflinchingly. "There is still much work to be done," she acknowledged, her voice steady and resolute. "But I will stand by your side through it all, Alexandre."

Pétion knew that to be true. Though he loved this woman immensely, he understood and accepted her huge ambition. He was quite clear that she would play a decisive role in his future decisions, whether he liked it or not. "Then let us face it together," Pétion declared, drawing her close and pressing a tender kiss to her forehead. "For the sake of our people and the generations to come."

As they stood there, their silhouettes bathed in the golden light of candles, Pétion felt a renewed sense of purpose. The road ahead would be long and fraught with obstacles, but with Joute by his side and the support of the Ayisyen people, particularly those of this region behind him, he was confident that they could overcome anything.

"Let this day be remembered as the dawn of a new era," Pétion whispered, his voice barely audible over the din of the celebrations. "The day we fought for our freedom and began to write our destiny."

"History will remember you fondly, Alexandre Pétion," Joute vowed, her eyes alight with determination. "They will name towns and streets throughout the country after you. Your name will be remembered for eternity. And it will remember us – all of us – as the architects of a nation built on hope, resilience, and unity."

With their gazes locked and hearts swelling with anticipation, they turned back to the festivities, ready to embrace the challenges and triumphs that the future held for their beloved new country.

The lingering warmth in the air seemed to embrace Pétion as he stood on the second-floor balcony of the sprawling government house building, taking in the sights and sounds of the city far beyond that had come alive, mixed with the jubilation and the people in the huge grand hall within the building that danced and sang, their voices rising like a symphony as they celebrated a brighter future under Pétion's leadership in the region. He looked out to see the carriages still arriving for as far as the eye could see.

Mayor Paul Jean had weathered his administration through the occupation of the French, the mayhem of war, and now the conquest by his fellow countrymen, called Ayisyen. He understood well that Alexandre Pétion would be crowned the leader of the South and West, no matter what Dessalines thought or could do about it. He had the backing and trust of the people, whereas Dessalines was remembered as the butcher who tore through the south, hunting down Pétion, and doing a lot of killing in the process.

"Général Pétion", Mayor Jean said as he approached Pétion. "You have truly livened up this town. The citizens love you and I must say, are putting a lot of pressure on you to keep them safe and successful. Port-Républicain is your city, and I am your servant."

"You have maintained an incredible administration, Mayor, throughout all the challenges of the past few years. I know well that it was not an easy task. I, and my army, are at your service to help rebuild the region and restore our prosperity. I look forward to our full collaboration," Pétion added.

A well-dressed assistant of the mayor arrived and whispered in the mayor's ear. Mayor Jean then looked up at Pétion and said, "It is my time to address our guests, I am told. Would you like to be with me as I do so?"

"My work was completed during the day, I do not want our citizens to tire of my voice. This is your building and your party tonight. I am but your appreciative guest and plan to enjoy your dance melodies with my fiancé," Pétion added.

"Alexandre," Joute called from behind him, her voice soft yet filled with excitement. "Come, my love. We must join our people and share in their happiness. Do you mind if I steal our beloved general away, Mr. Mayor?"

"It is a woman's prerogative to do just that. I must attend to more formal matters. Enjoy your evening." said the mayor as he turned to address the crowd.

"I am all yours," Pétion surrendered, offering her a supportive smile as he took her hand, feeling her fingers intertwine with his own.

There were so many guests in attendance that the celebration encompassed both the upstairs ballroom and the first-floor grand foyer, each with a separate orchestra. Descending the stairs, they emerged into the throng of revelers, their hearts swelling with pride as they caught sight of the Gens de Couleur, their faces alight with joy and determination. It was clear that they too had embraced the promise of a united Ayiti, where every man, woman, and child would be free, regardless of their skin color.

"Look at them, Alexandre," Joute whispered, her eyes brimming with tears. "This is your legacy – a nation born through unity, strength, and resilience."

"Ours, my dear," Pétion corrected gently, squeezing her hand as they wove their way through the crowd. "It is a future we will build together, side by side."

As they moved among the people, Pétion found himself drawn into the fervor of the celebration. A group of musicians struck up a lively tune, and he felt the irresistible pull of the music tugging at his soul. With a grin, he turned to Joute, his chest swelling with anticipation.

"Would you honor me with a dance, my love?" he asked, his voice barely audible above the din. "I am simply a citizen this evening. I am leaving all of the heavy lifting of diplomacy to my friend the Mayor."

"Nothing would please me more," Joute replied, her eyes shining with affection as she allowed Pétion to lead her into the heart of the festivities.

As they danced, their bodies moving in harmony with the rhythm of the music, Pétion's thoughts turned inward. The road ahead was fraught with uncertainty and danger, but he knew that he could face these challenges with courage and conviction, bolstered by the support of Joute, Jean-Pierre Boyer, Jean Bayard Junior, and his loyal officers.

"Remember this moment, my love," Pétion whispered into Joute's ear as they swayed together. "This is the dawn of a new era – the birth of a nation where hope and resilience will guide us toward a brighter future."

"Forever etched in our hearts," Joute agreed, her voice filled with emotion. "Together, we shall make history."

Their words hung in the air like a promise unspoken, carried away on the winds of change that swept through Port-Républicain that fateful day. And as the celebrations continued late into the night, echoing the hopes and dreams of a people on the cusp of a new beginning, Pétion couldn't help but feel a renewed sense of purpose, fueled by the unity of the Gens de Couleur and the unwavering faith of those who believed in him.

"May our journey be one of progress and change," he murmured, his gaze locked with Joute's as the moon could be seen beyond the horizon, illuminating the night like a celebratory torch until dawn, the dawning of a new chapter in their new country.

Four

CONSPIRACY DIPLOMACY

Washington, D.C.
January 1804

In the dimly lit office of Thomas Jefferson, the late afternoon sun cast a golden glow on the wooden furniture and leather-bound books that lined the walls. The air was thick with the scent of rich leather, ink, and parchment, and the tense atmosphere was almost palpable. A heavy oak desk stood as a barrier between two powerful men: President Thomas Jefferson, a tall, imposing figure with a shock of red hair, and French Ambassador Jean-Pierre Pinchon, dressed impeccably in his tailored French suit, complete with a powdered wig.

Secretary of State James Madison, a smaller man but no less formidable, sat to one side, pensively observing the interplay between these key players in the unfolding history of international intrigue.

"Mr. Pinchon," Jefferson began, his voice measured and cautious, "it has come to our attention that France has not yet relinquished its interest in the former colony of Saint-Domingue."

Pinchon's eyes narrowed, betraying a flicker of discomfort despite his diplomatic training. "Your Excellency, I assure you that France is aware of the recent changes in the colony." He paused, choosing his words carefully. "Nonetheless, we have certain concerns regarding the stability of the entire region."

Jefferson leaned back in his chair, steepling his fingers as he studied the Frenchman. He knew that behind Pinchon's carefully composed façade lay a hidden agenda. With a subtle nod to Madison, who shared his suspicions, he decided to press the issue further.

"Indeed, Ambassador, stability is a concern for us all," he said, his tone cool and detached. "However, let us not forget that Saint-Domingue is now a free country, governed by those who have fought long and hard for their independence, as we had done here in the United States in the past."

A brief silence followed, charged with unspoken tension before Madison spoke up. "France must surely recognize the implications of interfering with a now sovereign nation," he said, his voice tinged with a quiet warning.

"Of course, gentlemen," Pinchon replied, the ghost of a smile playing at the corner of his lips. "We have no intention of meddling in the affairs of independent nations. However, we do believe it is in our mutual interest to ensure that this new government remains... shall we say, contained and cooperative."

At this, Jefferson's gaze sharpened, and he exchanged a knowing glance with Madison. They were both aware of the implications of a black-led nation near the southern slaveholding states of their own country, and the potential impact on their interests. Especially now, when newly minted, black-skinned sailors, once slaves and now free, continuously arrived at the southern ports bragging of their newly freed status and country. Confident loud-mouthed black boys with money in their pockets putting wild ideas in the minds of American slaves working the docks.

"Your concerns are duly noted, Ambassador," Jefferson said, expertly masking his true feelings behind a veneer of diplomacy. "We shall certainly take them into consideration as we move forward." Jefferson also knew that France would not easily let go of its former colony, especially given the lucrative trade it had, and could provide.

US President Thomas Jefferson sits behind his desk as he speaks with French Ambassador Jean-Pierre Pinchon across from him and Secretary of State, James Madison at right.

"Indeed," Madison added, his eyes never leaving Pinchon's face. "However, let us not lose sight of our ultimate goal: a stable, prosperous future for all parties involved in the Atlantic trade."

As the three men continued their delicate dance of words and veiled intentions in this game of politics and intrigue, they each played their part with skill and cunning, concealing their true motivations beneath layers of inscrutable diplomacy. For in the end; power, ambition, and survival would always trump ideals - even those as noble as freedom, resilience, and hope.

Outside, the distant hum of horse-drawn carriages and murmured conversations somehow filtered through the closed window, an attempt to keep the cold out and the warm within. The sun cast a warm glow on the thick parchment of maps and reports that lay strewn across Thomas Jefferson's desk, illuminating the delicate lines and carefully inked words.

"Let me make myself perfectly clear, Ambassador Pinchon," Jefferson said, his voice steady and measured as he glanced up from a map of Saint-Domingue. "The people of what is now called Ayiti, have fought and bled for their freedom, and they have earned it, wouldn't you agree?"

"Their insurrection continues to be debated and the conclusion unclear, President Jefferson," Pinchon replied, his fingers drumming nervously on the armrest of his chair. "And France has not yet relinquished its claim on the island. There are, shall I say... matters still to be settled."

"Ah, matters," Secretary of State James Madison mused, his eyes narrowing as he studied the Frenchman's face. "I trust you understand, Ambassador, that the United States will not condone any interference in the affairs of a sovereign nation in this region where it jeopardizes our country's interests."

"Of course, Mr. Secretary," Pinchon replied, attempting to maintain an air of diplomatic composure. "We simply wish to ensure the stability of the region and protect our mutual interests, including our colonies in Martinique, Guadeloupe, and elsewhere."

"Speaking of interests," Jefferson interjected, allowing himself a small smile at the unease that flickered across the French ambassador's countenance. "We recently received word of a rather... shall we say, an intriguing plot involving French operatives on the island."

Pinchon hesitated before responding, his discomfort now palpable. "Yes, well, those plans were... necessary precautions, given the volatile situation in the colony."

"Precautions?" Madison echoed, feigning surprise as he exchanged a wry glance with Jefferson. "To pit the founding generals against one another and sow discord within the fledgling government so early in its infancy?"

"Such measures were deemed essential to safeguard French interests, including lives and property," Pinchon insisted defensively, beads of sweat forming on his brow.

"Is that so?" Jefferson mused, his gaze locked onto Pinchon's face as if attempting to divine the man's true intentions. The wheels of his mind turned rapidly, considering the implications of this new information and how best to leverage it for the benefit of his nation. "Furthermore, we have reason to believe that several French soldiers chose to remain on the island after the official withdrawal."

"Indeed, President Jefferson," Pinchon confirmed, a note of desperation creeping into his voice. "Those soldiers remained for various reasons. Some could not arrive at debarkation points, others have interests on the island, mistresses, and children even. However, they could prove invaluable in maintaining order and stability in the future, should the need arise."

"Interesting," Jefferson murmured thoughtfully, his eyes drifting back to the map before him. He pondered the balance of power between their nations and the delicate game of diplomacy they played. "Rest assured, Ambassador," Jefferson finally said, his voice carrying the weight of unspoken promises and veiled threats. "We shall consider your words carefully."

Pinchon studied the contours of Thomas Jefferson's face as he leaned back in his chair, fingers tented below his chin. His eyes flicked between the French Ambassador and Secretary of State James Madison, taking careful measure of their reactions to the unfolding intrigue.

"Your revelations, Ambassador Pinchon, are both captivating and puzzling, albeit somewhat worrisome," Jefferson said, his tone betraying a hint of satisfaction. "A black-led country of your former French slaves so close to our own... It raises concerns for the stability of our southern states, shall I say."

Madison nodded gravely, the lines on his forehead deepening. "Indeed, President Jefferson. We must be cautious in dealing with Dessalines and his new government," Pinchon offered.

"Caution is wise, gentlemen," Jefferson agreed, a sly smile playing at the corners of his mouth. "But again, we cannot overlook the lucrative trade opportunities that remain in Ayiti. We will not interfere with your plots, but neither shall we cut ties entirely."

At this, Pinchon straightened his shoulders, a small frown forming on his face. "I understand, President Jefferson. But might I suggest an embargo? Perhaps it would allow us to weaken Dessalines' position while maintaining our respective interests."

"An embargo?" Jefferson repeated, his expression contemplative. He glanced at Madison, who seemed equally pensive. In his mind, Jefferson weighed the potential benefits against the risks, weighing the fragile balance of power and alliances. "How can we trade with an embargoed country?"

Pinchon pressed on, desperation simmering beneath his diplomatic facade. "If you could help persuade the British to follow suit, it would greatly impact Dessalines' ability to maintain control. Between us and the Spanish, whom I am confident we can sway, we could isolate the new country and diminish its threat."

We shall consider it," the President finally conceded. "But we make no promises."

Jefferson studied Pinchon for a moment, the sunlight now casting shadows that danced across the room, mirroring the delicate dance of diplomacy they were engaged in. He thought of Dessalines, that fierce and relentless leader who had fought tooth and nail for his people's freedom. Some called him a butcher, and others a military genius. Jefferson understood that this call to freedom if nurtured, might spread to the enslaved masses in the United States. "Tell me what you know of this man, Jean-Jacques Dessalines," inquired Jefferson of Pinchon.

Jean Jacques Dessalines is somewhere in his mid-forties in age. He was a slave and, in the rebellion of 1791, declared himself free and joined the previous leader, Toussaint Louverture. They first fought for the Spanish, then made a volte-face and switched to our side when the French revolutionary government emancipated all slaves in the French colonies in 1794," Pinchon began.

"I bet you Frenchmen regret that decision today," interjected Madison with a disapproving puckering of his lips.

Pinchon glanced at Madison and decided that he wouldn't give him the satisfaction of acknowledging the comment and continued, "He rose to the rank of general under Louverture, and he along with other favored generals acquired control of several plantations."

"A black African with riches equal to some of our white plantation owners here," added Madison again.

"He loyally followed Louverture, suppressing dissident groups among the insurgents, executing white, black, and mulatto prisoners and even civilians on some occasions, and his destruction of roads, water sources, and cities in a scorched-earth strategy ordered by Toussaint to hinder the French army under Victoire Emmanuel Leclerc, earned him a reputation for brutality.

"It was a war, wasn't it Mr. Ambassador?" asked Jefferson.

"Some will argue that Mr. President. After Toussaint saw his misguidance and submitted to the French authorities under General Leclerc, Dessalines then served Leclerc, and later Rochambeau to disarm the population and hunt down renegade rebel units," Pinchon reported. "In the fall of 1802, however, Dessalines and other Saint-Dominguen officers deserted us and began to rebuild their rebel forces."

"I was under the impression that you tricked Louverture, arrested him, sailed him to France, locked him up, and executed him," Madison said, quite matter-of-fact. "They were not too happy with that and the fact they uncovered your plans to reinstitute slavery in all the French colonies."

Pinchon, unable to contain his composure, raised his voice and said "Mr. Secretary. President Jefferson asked me for an assessment of Dessalines. Not my commentary towards the decisions of the French government."

"That's enough. You have reviewed the same information I am already privy to. You call this man a brutal savage, but his letter indicates a certain skill at diplomacy," Jefferson stated, as he pulled out the letter and extended it for Pinchon to read.

Headquarters, Frère plantation,
Cul-de-Sac plain
23 June 1803

Mister President,

The American schooner The Federal, under Captain Nehemiah Barr, forced by our patrol boats to enter the port of Petit-Goâve, provides me the honor of informing you of the events that have occurred on our unfortunate island since the arrival of the French and the revolution caused in France by the tyranny of their oppressive government.

The people of Saint-Domingue, tired of paying with our blood the price of our blind allegiance to a mother country that cuts her children's throats, and following the example of the wisest nations, have thrown off the yoke of tyranny and sworn to expel the torturers.

Our countryside is already purged of their sight. A few cities are still under their domination but have nothing further to offer to their avid rapacity.

Commerce with the United States, Mister President, offers a market for the huge harvests we have in storage and the even more abundant ones that are now growing. Your country's shippers are calling for it. Your nation's long-standing relations with Saint-

Domingue are evidence of the loyalty and good faith that await your ships in our ports.

The return of the schooner The Federal will prove to your country our current disposition.

Please be sure, Mister President, of the eagerness with which I will exert all my authority for the safety of the United States ships and the benefits they will reap from trading with us.

Accept, Mister President, the expression of my highest consideration.

Dessalines

"The man is a scoundrel," Pinchon said after reading Dessalines' letter.

"Scoundrel, Mr. Ambassador? He did return a valuable ship to us, complete with its cargo intact, the crew had been well fed and taken care of, including the provision of whores with what I have been informed, and he is offering us lucrative trade considerations and safe ports for American vessels," Madison mused. "If he is a scoundrel, he's my type of scoundrel indeed."

The sunlight filtering through the half-drawn curtains continued to cast a warm, golden glow on the mahogany desk, upon which lay the letter from Dessalines that Jefferson had yet to respond.

Changing the subject, Pinchon sighed, "Mon Dieu, If only we did not have to contend with that troublesome Adams, Saint-Domingue might still be firmly within French control."

Jefferson leaned back in his chair, steepling his fingers as he nodded in agreement. "Indeed, Ambassador. Our past president had a willingness to recognize the colony as an almost independent country and broker trade agreements with Toussaint Louverture without French approval. It was, shall we say, most disconcerting."

Madison chimed in, his voice laced with disdain. "Luckily, the election of 1800 turned in our favor, putting an end to Adams' reckless maneuverings."

"Oui," Pinchon concurred, his eyes narrowing shrewdly. "And now that you are President, Monsieur Jefferson, I am confident that we can work together to ensure that Saint-Domingue, or the island you now call Ayiti, does not become a destabilizing force in this hemisphere."

Jefferson's brow furrowed as he considered the implications of this alliance. As a slave owner himself, he understood all too well the precarious balance that held the southern states together – and the threat that a black-led nation posed to the status quo. He glanced at the letter on his desk from Dessalines, a reminder of the resilience and hope that had propelled those people toward freedom and his request to befriend the United States with full diplomatic overtures of cooperation and security.

"Of course, Ambassador," Jefferson finally replied, his voice betraying a hint of reluctance. "But let us not forget that our trade with Ayiti remains lucrative, and it is in our best interest to maintain those ties."

"Ah, yes." Pinchon paused, a sly smile playing on his lips. "But if you can persuade the British to join us in embargoing Ayiti, and I can assure you that the Spanish will follow suit, we may be able to have our cake and eat it too."

"An interesting proposition," Madison mused, his eyes narrowing thoughtfully. "We must tread carefully, however, lest we inadvertently create a rallying point for the oppressed masses of our nation."

"Indeed," Jefferson concurred, the weight of the decision heavy upon him. As the sun dipped below the horizon, casting the room into shadow, the three men contemplated the delicate balance between freedom and control, hope and despair, and the inexorable march of history that waited for no man. These parlays would not end today, as much needed to be planned for and coordinated to move forward.

Northwest Coast of Ayiti

Ricardo Desbardes paced back and forth in the room, his eyes flickering with a dangerous glint. The former French soldiers gathered around him, their faces hardened by the years of conflict and betrayal they had endured. Some of them sat with their mistresses; creole, and black women who held onto their arms, whispering words of support. They were located on the outskirts of Mole Saint-Nicolas.

"Do you have arms?" Desbardes finally asked, his voice a low murmur that echoed in the cramped space.

One of the ex-soldiers stepped forward, his jaw set in determination. "We have some, but we need more. Our resources are limited," he admitted, his gaze unwavering.

Desbardes nodded slowly, his mind already calculating the possibilities. "And can you gather enough support to build a small army? Can you inspire others to join our cause?"

The men exchanged uneasy glances before one of them spoke up, his voice rough with emotion. "It's not easy. Many fear retribution from Dessalines, while others remain loyal to the cause of Dessalines. It did not help that General Rochambeau was so brutal, so evil, towards the end of the campaign. He has instilled fear in their hearts that all French are like this."

Desbardes leaned against the wall, a deep furrow creasing his brow as he pondered their predicament. The memories of Rochambeau's atrocities flashed through his mind, igniting a fierce determination within him. "We must show them that not all Frenchmen are cut from the same cloth," he declared, his voice resolute.

The room fell silent, the weight of their mission settling upon them like a heavy shroud. Desbardes turned to face his comrades, his gaze unwavering. "You may be few in number, but there are others that will join us, and they are many, scattered around the island."

"And who are these 'others' scattered around the island?" asked one of the soldiers.

"Plantation owners, white overseers, and others," Desbardes responded. "They will join us so we can return to the old ways."

In the mountains overlooking Saint-Marc

Diédoné Lespwa had become one of the most trusted and respected members of Lamour Derances and the Maroon community in the mountains overlooking Saint-Marc. His experiences had shaped him into a fierce warrior, skilled in guerilla tactics and survival in the harsh wilderness. But it was his unwavering determination and burning desire for freedom that had set him apart and had motivated Lamour Desrances to make him his number two and future successor.

Derances, the revered leader of their Maroon group, had taught Diédoné and the rest of them the value of unity and careful planning. Together, they raided plantations not only for food and tools but also to liberate enslaved family members and friends, striking fear into the hearts of their colonial oppressors.

Now, with Desbardes standing before him, arrogance oozing from every pore, Diédoné felt a surge of righteous anger but had no choice but to join forces with the French spy to combat their common enemy, Jean-Jacques Dessalines.

Diédone Lespwa approached Desbardes, his eyes burning with a mixture of hope and vengeance. He had seen too much suffering at the hands of the French, his spirit hardened by years of slavery and abuse. The sight of Lamour Derances leading the Maroons had ignited a flame within him—a flicker of defiance against the oppressors who had stolen his freedom and dignity.

Among the rugged terrain of the mountains overlooking Saint-Marc, Diédone had found solace in the camaraderie of fellow runaway slaves. Together, they forged a community built on resilience and unity, their spirits unbroken despite the hardships they faced. They toiled the land and hunted for sustenance.

As he looked out at the vast expanse before him, Diédone felt a sense of purpose stirring deep within his soul. He looked at the French spy with suspicion in his eyes. He had never trusted the French like Lamour Derances had. But who could blame him? He had been enslaved, beaten, and brutalized by the evil French slave masters ever since he had arrived in Saint-Domingue from Africa when he was but a boy, a little over 10 years old.

He had been forced into a sentence of hard labor, seven days per week, 15 hours per day, in the sugar cane fields for over fifteen years until he had run away to the mountains to seek out the legend of the Maroons and a leader named Lamour Derances.

Desbardes was now here and wanted Diédoné to find workers who were close to Dessalines' Generals and pay them to inflict poisons that would eventually kill them over some time.

"Find those closest to Dessalines' most trusted generals," he insisted, Desbardes staring sharp and unyielding. "Pay them enough to ensure their loyalty, but not too much to arouse suspicion. It must appear as though they are acting in your best interest, and not that of the French, to avenge the killer of their leader, and convince them that Dessalines is a mere extension of colonial rule."

Diédoné absorbed the implications of this task, his eyes narrowing with understanding. "And what of these poisons you speak of? What are they and how are we to administer them without raising alarm?"

Desbardes' lips curled into a sinister grin. "You are a cunning man and from what I understand connected to those who practice voodoo and this form of skullduggery with plants, herbs, and whatever else. You will figure it out.

"Why," asked Diédoné, confused as to this strange request. "Dessalines has beaten your army. Your French comrades have sailed away back to Europe."

"That is but a ploy. We are still here and on the eastern side with the Spanish. We will have our day once more."

"Dessalines is strong. His army is strong. You are dreaming," Diédoné spat back.

"We will destabilize Dessalines' army. We need to cut off the head that makes it work by making them have fewer leaders," barked Desbardes.

"I can only do that in my region here with the southern and western leaders," replied Diédoné.

"Do not trouble yourself with concerns about the rest of the island. I have a multitude of others who will join in this task," Desbardes confidently declared. "There are many who do not stand with Dessalines and they will play a crucial role in bringing about a new revolution." His voice was filled with conviction and determination, echoing through the room like a rallying cry for change.

Desbardes rose to leave as Diédoné surveyed him. Could he trust this man to spearhead the destruction of the murderer of his beloved Lamour Desrance? He did not know, but he had no choice.

Samana, Northern Coast of Hispaniola

"Quien va alla - *who goes there?"* yelled a Spaniard with an old, faded, Spanish colonial uniform, tattered from years of wear.

"Soy francés. Llévame con tu comandante - *I am French. Take me to your commander,"* replied Desbardes to the retired soldier.

"Ricardo Desbardes," said the French soldier who returned with the Spaniard. "My superiors informed me that you would soon be here. I had thought you for dead when the savages next door revolted."

"And here I am," replied Desbardes. "Give me a rundown on your strengths here."

Desbardes listened attentively as the French Captain outlined their resources and strategies for a potential assault on Ayiti. His mind raced with possibilities, knowing that this information could be crucial in destabilizing the Ayisyen government. As he absorbed every detail, his eyes flickered with a dangerous gleam, a mixture of ambition and ruthlessness that had guided him through many treacherous situations in the past.

After the Captain finished his report, Desbardes nodded thoughtfully. "We have a solid foundation here to work from. It's clear that France is not giving up on Saint-Domingue just yet," he remarked, his voice laced with determination.

Turning to the Captain, he issued his orders with a steely resolve. "We will bide our time, strengthen our position, and await the perfect moment to strike. Divide and conquer will be our tactic in weakening Dessalines' hold on power. Continue to recruit from this side of the island to build an army from retired Spanish Colonial soldiers."

Washington D.C.

The French ambassador Pinchon had long departed, and Madison and Jefferson continued their play on different scenarios for this new country of Ayiti.

The gentle tap of Thomas Jefferson's pen on the polished wooden desk was the only sound in the dimly lit room. He and his Secretary of State were deep in thought, their faces shadowed in the flickering candlelight.

Madison's voice broke the silence. "You know, Mr. President, there's a line we must tread carefully here. We cannot appear to be interfering in the affairs of a sovereign nation, even one with questionable practices. Our commerce with Ayiti is immense and one that our merchants highly value. Their commodity prices also help to keep ours stable here at home, though our southern planters wished there was less of it to decrease competition for sugar."

Jefferson nodded, a furrow appearing between his brows. "But we cannot support their independence outright. Our Southern states are still heavily invested in the slave trade, and any support we give may cause a rift politically. We will hold on recognizing this new emancipated country and lobby to get the Federalists on board with our policies.

"What of this letter from Dessalines? It has been on your desk for several months now. Do you plan on responding?" asked Madison.

"I cannot respond to the head of a nation that the United States does not yet recognize now, can I?" Jefferson's tone was firm, a hint of reluctance evident in his voice. He picked up the letter from Dessalines, its edges worn from the countless times he had read and reread its contents.

Madison eyed Jefferson thoughtfully before speaking, "Perhaps a strategic delay in responding could serve our interests better. It would not do for us to appear too eager or too dismissive towards Dessalines."

Jefferson considered Madison's words, his gaze fixed on the flickering candle flame that danced in the dimly lit room. "You may be right, James. A delicate dance indeed we must perform in these turbulent times."

"And what of the French?" asked Madison. "It seems that our ambassador has some machinations in store for the Dessalines government," stated Madison.

Jefferson's expression darkened, a shadow of concern passing over his features. "The French have always been cunning in their pursuits. Pinchon's revelations are troubling, but we must maintain a careful balance. As much as we may not always see eye to eye with our French friends, dealing directly with Dessalines could set a dangerous precedent for our own nation's future."

Madison nodded in agreement, the weight of their decisions heavy on his mind. "Perhaps a show of neutrality while subtly supporting stability within the region could serve our interests best."

Jefferson leaned back in his chair, fingers steepled in deep contemplation. "We must navigate these treacherous waters with caution. Our actions now will ripple through history." As he spoke, a flicker of resolve ignited in his eyes, a determination to steer the course of events toward a favorable outcome for the United States.

"This new country of Ayiti must no longer be beholden to the European colonial powers in this Atlantic region"," stated Jefferson. "However, on the other hand, we cannot support a black-run country of former slaves in such proximity. This new country is a paradox indeed."

Madison nodded in agreement with Jefferson's assessment of the delicate situation. "Mr. President, it is a conundrum we must navigate with utmost care. The implications of our actions on this young nation will echo through the annals of history."

Jefferson's gaze lingered on the flickering candle flame, his mind weighed down by the gravity of their decisions. "The balance between ideals and practicality is a precarious one. We must protect our interests while treading lightly in the affairs of others."

As the shadows lengthened in the room, an air of tension hung heavy between the two men. The future of Ayiti lay in the balance, caught between the machinations of European powers and the vested interests of the United States.

Madison cleared his throat, breaking the solemn silence that enveloped them. "Shall I draft a response to Dessalines' letter from my office, as Secretary of State, instead of you, Mr. President? A carefully worded acknowledgment of receipt, perhaps?"

Jefferson considered for a moment the words uttered by Madison. Then he thought of the overall picture and the complexity of it all. Here, these brave souls had fought for freedom, just as he had done so in America against the British Empire of Europe. However, they were black, and we are white. The line is too harsh a reality.

"No, James. History may judge us harshly, but today's realities require us to at times bury our moral compass. Let us keep Dessalines waiting a while longer," Jefferson said, his voice tinged with regret but resolute in his decision. As the candlelight flickered, casting shadows on the walls, a heavy silence settled over the room once more.

Madison nodded in understanding, knowing the delicate dance they were performing on the stage of international politics. "As you wish, Mr. President. We shall proceed with caution in our dealings with this new Ayiti."

With a heavy heart, Jefferson tucked away Dessalines' letter, a weighty reminder of the complexities and contradictions they faced. The future of Ayiti remained uncertain, hanging in a precarious balance between freedom and the harsh realities of power dynamics.

And so, in the quiet of that dimly lit room in Washington D.C., decisions were made that would shape the course of history for both Ayiti and the United States. The echoes of past revolutions and struggles reverberated through the corridors of power, promising a sleepless night ahead for these two powerful men.

Five

THE ULTIMATE SACRIFICE

Marchand
April 1804

A warm breeze wafted through the open windows of Dessalines' home in Marchand, carrying with it the sweet scent of tropical flowers and the distant murmur of the bustling marketplace. Inside, Jean-Jacques Dessalines sat at a solid mahogany table, his brow furrowed as he reviewed documents detailing the progress of the revolution. Marie-Claire, his wife, stood nearby, observing him with concern.

"Jean-Jacques," she said softly, breaking the silence. "You've been working tirelessly for days. You need to rest."

Dessalines sighed, rubbing his temples. "I cannot afford to rest, Marie-Claire. Not while there is an economy to rebuild and enemies that conspire against us."

As if on cue, General Geffrard burst into the room, his face flushed with urgency. "My apologies for the intrusion, but I bring news of great importance. There is a plot afoot to destabilize our government, and it has already begun to take root among certain factions."

Dessalines' eyes flashed with anger. "Who dares to threaten our hard-won freedom?"

"Many French planters, rich Creoles, and their accomplices," Geffrard replied grimly. "They seek to undermine your authority and sow discord among our people. I urge you to be on guard, for they will stop at nothing to see their plan come to fruition."

"Traitors!" Dessalines roared, slamming his fist on the table. "I will kill every last one of them and make an example of their treachery!"

"Jean-Jacques, please," Marie-Claire whispered, placing a calming hand on his shoulder. "Do not let your rage consume you. There must be another way to deal with them, one that does not involve mass killings."

"Marie-Claire, do you not understand the gravity of this situation?" he growled, shaking off her touch. "These are the same people who enslaved us, tortured us, and stole our very lives for their profit! And now they dare to undermine the freedom we have fought and bled for? No, I cannot let this stand."

"Jean-Jacques," she implored, her voice pleading yet firm, "you are a leader, and your actions will define how history remembers you. You must be careful not to become the very monster you fought to destroy."

Dessalines stared at his wife, his chest heaving with suppressed fury. He knew she was right; Marie-Claire had always been the one who could temper his wrath with reason. And yet, the thought of those who would tear apart his work and sacrifice filled him with a rage that threatened to consume him whole.

"Very well," he conceded, his voice tight with barely restrained anger. "I will consider other options. But know this: if it becomes clear that blood must be shed to protect our people and our freedom, I will not hesitate to do what must be done."

"Thank you, Jean-Jacques," Marie-Claire murmured, her eyes full of concern for the man she loved and the future they were forging together. "May your decisions be guided by wisdom and compassion, even in these darkest of times."

Geffrard looked on, attempting to keep his composure. He had never seen Dessalines so docile before.

The sun dipped low in the sky, staining the horizon with blood-red hues as Jean-Jacques Dessalines stood at the edge of a cliff overlooking the city of Jacmel. The wind whipped through his hair, carrying with it the scent of salt and burning wood from the fires below. He could feel the tension in the air, palpable even from this distance, as the soldiers awaited his arrival. They knew what was coming, but they did not know if the general would dare to carry it out.

"Général," Geffrard called from behind him, his voice cautious yet firm. "The time has come. The army needs your decision and your orders, mon Général."

Dessalines turned to face his general, his eyes dark with determination. "Very well," he replied, his voice steady despite the turmoil within him. "I have given much thought to my wife's words, and I cannot ignore her wisdom. But neither can I ignore the threat posed by these traitors who continue to plot against us and fan the flames of resistance."

"Then what shall we do?" Geffrard asked, his brow furrowed in concern, but not wanting to suggest the path forward himself.

"First, we will visit each city where the French white planters and their cohorts are known to reside," Dessalines declared, his voice rising with conviction. "We will demand that they cease their treachery and swear their loyalty to Ayiti. If they refuse, or if they are found to be hiding others who have plotted against our nation, then they will face the consequences."

"What consequences do you suggest, Général?" Geffrard pushed, forcing Dessalines to sound out the plan without him being burdened with suggesting the fate of those accused of treason.

"Death," Dessalines firmly stated, his gaze unwavering. "But only for those who have shown themselves to be enemies of the state. We must not allow our quest for justice to blind us to the possibility of redemption."

"Death?" Geffrard inquired, his voice barely above a whisper, seeking once again verbal confirmation of the draconian orders.

"Yes. You heard me correctly. Death to those who have plotted against our country."

"Understood," General Geffrard nodded solemnly.

Throughout April, Dessalines traveled from city to city, his heart heavy with the knowledge of what must be done. As he approached each town, word spread like wildfire, and the air became thick with anticipation. The people were torn between fear and loyalty, their eyes darting between Dessalines and the conspiratorial French white planters who dwelled among them.

"Are you certain this is the only way?" a local commander asked, as they stood outside a grand plantation house in Leogane. Dessalines orders, in most towns, had been ignored until he would arrive there himself to reissue the order.

The sun had barely risen, casting long shadows over the silent grounds. "They were given ample opportunity to join us," Dessalines murmured, his eyes scanning the horizon for signs of resistance. "Negotiation, diplomacy, even bribery. None have worked. These men will not abandon their treachery unless they are forced to face the consequences of their actions."

"Then let us begin," the commander responded, steeling himself for the task ahead.

As they entered each plantation, Dessalines demanded that the owners and their associates swear their loyalty to Ayiti. Some complied immediately, their voices trembling with fear as they pledged themselves to the new nation. Others hesitated, their faces pale as they weighed the cost of defiance. And still, others refused outright, their eyes burning with hatred as they spat curses upon the soil.

"Enough!" Dessalines roared, his fury igniting like a wildfire within him towards those who had hesitated or refused. "You have made your choice. Now you shall pay the price."

And so, the executions began. At first, they were swift and brutal, carried out by Dessalines' most trusted men. But as word spread of the fate awaiting those who defied him, resistance grew, and the killings became more difficult, with pockets of armed resistance throughout the island.

On the cobblestone streets of Port Républicain, the city had never been so quiet, as if each inhabitant held their breath in anticipation of what was to come. Dessalines rode through the desolate streets, his jaw clenched and his eyes narrowed in grim determination.

Alexandre Pétion was away from the city, visiting General Geffrard in Les Cayes to petition him to reason with Dessalines concerning the executions.

Mayor Paul Jean approached Dessalines and said "General Dessalines, you cannot possibly execute your orders here in Port Républicain!"

"Mind your tongue, Mr. Mayor. My orders are firm. All traitors will pay for their involvement in the destabilization of our country," Dessalines barked back.

"This is barbaric and counterproductive," protested Jean.

"It is necessary," Dessalines growled back. "You do not have the luxury of interfering with my directives," he warned, his gaze never leaving the mayor's face. "But you do have the luxury to stand aside and not participate. You are not a man of the sword."

Paul Jean trembled, but his resolve remained strong. "You mistake me for a man who will watch as my people in this great city are slaughtered without protest. I will not stand by and allow this to happen."

Dessalines' expression hardened, his fingers tightening around the reins of his horse. "You underestimate me, Monsieur Mayor. I have seen people like you before. You speak bravely, but when the time comes to act, crumble like dry leaves in the wind."

The tension between them hung in the air like a thick fog, dense and impenetrable.

A soldier arrived and interrupted the showdown and called out from the shadows, his voice quavering with fear, "General Dessalines, we have done as you ordered. Most of those who plotted against you have met their end."

"Most?" Dessalines snapped, dismounting his horse and approaching the man. "I ordered the execution of all traitors, not just 'most' of them!"

"Sir," the man stammered, "we did our best, but some could not be found. We believe they may have fled the city."

"Then find them!" Dessalines barked, his impatience boiling over into rage. "I will not rest until every last one of them is brought to justice!"

As he spoke, crowds began to gather in the streets—their faces a mixture of fear, curiosity, and defiance. Dessalines stood before them, a lone figure of authority amid the chaos that threatened to consume the city.

"Listen to me, people of Port Républicain!" he shouted, his voice carrying over the murmurs of the crowd. "For too long, we have suffered under the yoke of oppression! Men like Rochambeau and Leclerc have committed atrocities against us, and now it is time for them to pay the ultimate price!"

He paused, allowing the weight of his words to sink in. "I have ordered the execution of all white planters and their co-conspirators who have conspired against us. This is not a decision I take lightly, but it must be made to ensure our survival. I ask each of you, especially those of mixed race, to join me in carrying out this necessary task. Let us show the world that we stand together to no longer tolerate their treachery!"

As Dessalines spoke, a wave of emotion swept over the crowd. Some nodded in agreement, while others exchanged apprehensive glances. The city seemed to hold its breath as it waited for what would come next.

"Begin," Dessalines commanded, his voice cold and unyielding.

The streets of Port Républicain erupted in violence as mobs descended upon the remaining conspirators. Screams rang out through the night, accompanied by the sickening sound of steel meeting flesh. Dessalines watched it all unfold, his heart heavy with the weight of his actions, yet determined in his pursuit of justice.

"General Dessalines," a voice called from the shadows as he prepared to leave the city. "We have received word that similar executions are being carried out in Cap-Français."

"Good," Dessalines responded, his voice devoid of emotion and pleased his orders were being followed.

The air was heavy with the scent of blood and smoke as Dessalines stood atop the steps of the city's cathedral, surveying the scene before him. His eyes were drawn to the bodies that littered the streets—French men and women, some barely more than children, who had been torn from their hiding places and killed without mercy. Their pale faces seemed to stare accusingly at him through the gathering darkness.

"General," called a voice from behind as a man galloped toward him. It was his secretary, Louis Boisrond-Tonnerre, a man whose passion for the cause matched Dessalines' own. "We have located all traitors in the countryside but a few of the French planters and their men have fled here and are hiding in this city. They will be hunted down and dealt with."

"Good," Dessalines replied, though his heart was heavy with the weight of so many lives extinguished. "Let it be known that any white person who will help us build Ayiti is welcomed and granted amnesty. This includes educators, apothecaries, physicians, and others who were non-slaveholding. Of course, our Polish brothers who fought with us, as well as our German friends who never participated in the slave trade, are spared as well."

"Amnesty, sir?" Tonnerre's eyes narrowed, and he hesitated. "But you pledged to kill every white man who soils the land of freedom with his sacrilegious presence."

"Enough!" Dessalines snapped, cutting him off. "I am well aware of what I said. But we cannot build our future on a foundation of unbridled hatred and violence. There must be room for mercy, even in this time of war, especially since they were not part of the conspiracy."

"Very well, General," Tonnerre acquiesced, though his dissatisfaction was evident. "I shall spread the word."

As the news of amnesty reached those still in hiding, a handful of survivors emerged, trembling and tear-streaked. Among them were several Polish, their hands raised to show they meant no harm. Dessalines looked upon them thoughtfully, remembering the sacrifices they had made in support of Ayiti's struggle for independence.

"Your bravery has not gone unnoticed," he told them, his voice softening as it rarely did. "You have renounced your allegiance to France and stood with us in our fight for freedom. For this, I grant you Ayisyen citizenship. You are the 'White Negroes of Europe,' and we welcome you with open arms."

"Thank you, General," one of the Poles replied, his eyes shining with gratitude. "We pledge our loyalty to you, Ayiti, and its people."

As the newly minted Ayisyen citizens were led away to safety, Dessalines turned his attention back to the grim task at hand. He watched as the remaining French were escorted from their hiding places—some were smuggled out to sea under cover of darkness to escape, while others were not so fortunate. Despite his decree of amnesty, many innocents met their end at the hands of his vengeful soldiers.

"Is this what freedom looks like?" Dessalines wondered aloud, his gaze fixed on the carnage that surrounded him. "Or is it merely a new form of tyranny?"

"Freedom, sir," Tonnerre responded solemnly, "is a thing won through blood and fire. Our enemies sought to enslave us, and we have repaid them in kind. I once told you that for our declaration of independence, we should have had the skin of a white man for parchment, his skull for an inkwell, his blood for ink, and a bayonet for a pen!"

Dessalines looked at Tonnerre and said nothing. Feeling the weight of his decisions pressing down upon him, he watched as his soldiers dragged another group of captives from a nearby building: men and women alike, trembling with fear. The soldiers hesitated, glancing back at Dessalines for confirmation.

"Kill them," he ordered quietly, though his heart screamed in protest. "Leave none alive."

"Except those who agree to marry non-white men," Tonnerre reminded him, his tone cautious. "You wished to spare those who would integrate, did you not?"

"Very well." Dessalines nodded, hoping that some small mercy might ease the burden of guilt he carried. "If they choose to unite with us, let them live."

He turned away as the executions continued, unable to bear witness any longer. The sounds of stabbing, beheading, and disemboweling echoed through the air, punctuated by screams that would haunt him for the rest of his days.

"Is this the price we must pay for freedom?" Dessalines wondered, his thoughts heavy with sorrow. "Must we become monsters to survive?"

"Perhaps not," Tonnerre replied, his gaze distant as he too struggled with the harsh realities of their struggle. "But it is the price we must pay to ensure that our enemies do not return, or if they remain, do not rise against us again."

"Then let us pray that it is enough," Dessalines murmured, his eyes filled with a cold determination that left no room for doubt. "For I will see Ayiti free or die trying."

As nightfall neared, Dessalines stood on a balcony overlooking the city's main thoroughfare, his hands gripping the railing tightly as he surveyed the harrowing scene below. The cries of men and women pierced the air, mingling with the merciless laughter of soldiers carrying out their orders. Among them was Jean Zombi, a mulatto soldier known for his meanness, brutality, and lack of empathy, whose actions caused even Dessalines to shudder.

"General, you must see this," Tonnerre said, his voice barely above a whisper.

Dessalines turned his gaze to where his advisor pointed, his eyes widening as he beheld the spectacle unfolding before him. There, in the middle of the street, Jean Zombi had apprehended a white man who was attempting to run away, stripping him naked before dragging him by the hair towards the stairs of the Government House.

"Have mercy!" the man pleaded, his voice choked with panic. "Please, I beg you!"

"Mercy?" Zombi scoffed, his tone cold and cruel. "Did your kind show us mercy when they whipped our backs and sold our children?"

With a swift, brutal motion, Zombi plunged a dagger into the man's chest, twisting it with a sickening crunch. Blood poured from the wound as the man's body shook violently in the throes of death, staining the steps crimson as the man's life ceased to exist. The crowd gasped in horror while Dessalines clenched his jaw, his heart pounding in his chest.

"Enough!" he bellowed, his voice thundering through the square. "This is not how I ordered this to proceed! This is not a show and we do not butcher our enemies like animals!"

Jean Zombi sneered up at Dessalines, unrepentant. "But general, they are animals. They deserve no better." Zombi yelled, defiant towards the general and unbeknown to him that his name would forever be linked to the half-dead creatures that lurked in the mountains due to his actions on this day. They would forever be named Zombies in his memory.

"Even animals deserve a swift and merciful death," Dessalines countered, his voice heavy with sorrow and disgust. "We must not lose ourselves in the process of claiming our freedom."

"General," Tonnerre murmured, placing a hand on his arm. "Perhaps it is best if we retire for now. There is nothing more to be done today."

Dessalines nodded, his eyes never leaving the scene below as he struggled to reconcile the violence of their revolution with the hope for a brighter future. "However, I am leaving for Marchand immediately. Your men have concluded their orders. Break out a supply of rum and allow them to drink themselves into oblivion to block out these scenes they were forced to partake in today.

Alexandre Pétion arrived the following morning as the sun began to rise over the streets of Port Républicain. The scent of smoke and spilled blood clung to the air as Pétion surveyed the carnage before him. Corpses lay scattered like broken dolls, their once-pristine clothing now stained red as soldiers continued to load bodies onto wagons, and hauling them off to the burn pits at the outskirts of the city.

"Was this truly necessary?" Pétion asked Mayor Jean, who stood at his side. "Must they have slaughtered them all?"

"General," the Mayor answered, his voice steady despite the horrors surrounding them, "They chose their targets based on three criteria: complicity towards insurrection, skin color, and vocation. The French most of all as enemies."

"Even the petits blancs?" Pétion questioned, gesturing towards the bodies of several lower-class Frenchmen strewn across the cobblestone street. "They held no power over us."

"Power or not, they said they still bore allegiance to France," the Mayor replied, his gaze unwavering. "Their orders were clear—break the eggs, take out the yoke, and eat the white."

Pétion clenched his fists in anguish as the realization settled upon him: the price of so-called freedom had been high indeed.

In the mountains above, the echo of distant drums could be heard. Alexandre Pétion turned to face the Mayor, his brow furrowed in thought.

"We must tread carefully, my friend," he warned, his voice barely above a whisper. "With each death, we sow the seeds of resentment and vengeance around the world. There will be no peace until we learn to coexist with those who have wronged us."

Mayor Jean nodded solemnly, his gaze fixed on the lifeless forms that littered the ground. "I fear you are right, mon Général," he admitted.

Marie-Claire was surprised when the horsemen arrived at her home in Marchand. Leading them was her husband, who rapidly dismounted from his mare, Galipot.

She hurried to the room where she had hidden two white French families awaiting a way to travel from the inland town to the coastal city of Gonaives where she had arranged passage for them on a small schooner.

"Be very quiet, the General has returned!" Marie-Claire announced to the group as the door burst open and her husband unexpectedly entered.

"I did not expect you home so soon, Jean-Jacques" she announced as she turned to face him.

"I can very well see that, Marie-Claire. What is the meaning of this?"

"Jean-Jacques. Please spare these people," she stated as she stared towards him.

Dessalines did not respond to the urgency in her voice, but instead, he calmly walked up to the families and looked them over with a stern gaze. The parents, who were huddled together with their children, tried not to tremble as their hopes for an escape to freedom were suddenly dashed.

Marie-Claire Heureuse Félicité Dessalines stands in front of her husband, protecting an accused family of French collaborators.

Marie-Claire stepped forward, placing herself between Dessalines and the families. "Jean-Jacques," she said, her voice barely above a whisper, "you cannot do this. They have done nothing to harm us or our fight for independence."

Dessalines' eyes met hers, and for a moment, she saw a flicker of the man she loved. But then it was gone, replaced by the hardened face of the leader he had become.

"I am sorry, Marie-Claire," he said, his voice cold and distant. "We cannot afford to be merciful in these times. We must protect our own, even if it means sacrificing those who pose no threat."

Marie-Claire's heart sank as she realized the depth of the sacrifices that had to be made in the name of freedom. She knew it would be difficult to change her husband's mind, but she could not bear to see these innocent families left to the mercy of his wrath.

With a heavy heart, she wrapped her arms around the families and whispered words of comfort and courage, assuring them that she would continue to plead their case for mercy to her husband.

Dessalines watched as Marie-Claire comforted the families, his heart heavy with the burden of his decisions. He knew that he had become a different man since the revolution began, but he also believed that the sacrifices they made were essential for the survival of their nation.

As they were led out of the room, Dessalines turned his attention back to Marie-Claire, his expression softening slightly as he took her hand in his.

"My love," he began, his voice barely above a whisper, "Tell me of your plans of escape for these people."

As Marie-Claire began to share her plan of escape for the families, Dessalines listened carefully, his expression growing more thoughtful with each detail. He knew that giving these families a chance at freedom would risk upsetting the delicate balance he was trying to maintain within his new nation.

But at the same time, he couldn't help but feel a pang of guilt for the innocent lives that had been destroyed in the name of their fight for independence and the pleas of his wife, whom he loved, respected, and cherished.

As they stood there, in the dimly lit room, their hands entwined, Marie-Claire could see the struggle in her husband's eyes as tears rolled down her cheeks. She knew that he was torn between his love for her and his duty to their nation.

Just then, Dessalines turned to her and said "I will allow them passage to Gonaives. But you must promise me something," he added, his voice stern.

"Anything, my husband. What would you ask of me?"

I ask that you will not involve yourself or our family in any further acts of defiance against the government. For your safety and that of our people, I must ask for your cooperation, Marie-Claire. Can you do this?"

Marie-Claire nodded, knowing that she had to make a difficult decision. "I promise," she whispered, her voice full of determination.

As they left the room, Dessalines' eyes scanned the horizon, his mind grappling with the weight of the decisions he had made. He called his most trusted captain and gave orders to escort the families by wagon to the docks, providing letters of safe passage with his signature.

When they finally reached the docks of Gonaives, a small schooner was waiting for their journey to safety. As the ship sailed away from the harbor, the wind carried with it the sound of hope, renewal, and a promise of a brighter future for them. They huddled in prayer at the good fortune of knowing the wife of the General, Marie-Claire Heureuse Félicité Dessalines.

Back in Port Républicain, Alexandre Pétion stood by the bay, watching the sunset over the ocean. He had never been more conflicted in his life. He knew that Dessalines' actions appeared necessary to maintain stability, but the cost was too high. He couldn't shake the feeling that they were losing their humanity in their pursuit of freedom.

"General Pétion," a voice called out behind him. He turned to see Mayor Paul Jean approaching. "It has been a tough day, my friend. I have loaded the last of the French whites condemned to death that I had hidden in the cathedral. They are on that ship there, at least near 200 of them."

Pétion nodded, but he couldn't help feeling a sense of despair as he watched the ship leave the harbor, carrying innocent lives to an unknown future.

In the days that followed, Pétion found himself increasingly distant from Dessalines' administration. He couldn't reconcile his principles with the violence that had become a part of their daily lives. He longed for a time when they could live in peace and coexist with those who had once oppressed them without resorting to such extreme measures.

The village clearing was bustling with activity, but at its center sat Diédoné Lespwa, a formidable figure flanked by two of his most trusted lieutenants. His piercing gaze fell upon Ricardo Desbardes, the French spy who had cautiously arrived to assure Diédoné that the so-called plan to destabilize the hated army of Dessalines was intact. Each of the lieutenants seated next to their commander brandished a cutlass in their hand, the metal glinting menacingly in the sunlight.

As they rhythmically lifted and brought down their swords onto a dry tree branch, slicing through it effortlessly, Desbardes could feel his heart pounding with fear but he did his best to hide it. It was clear that this display was intended to unnerve him, sending a chilling message of what would happen if he betrayed or went against Diédoné's orders. The tension in the air was palpable, as all eyes were on Desbardes, waiting for his next move.

"You seem to have a different viewpoint on what constitutes success than I do," Diédoné said as he looked directly at Desbardes.

"Consider this a minor setback yes, but also a step forward," Desbardes replied.

"Explain this to me, Blanc," Diédoné spat.

"Dessalines found out about the organized plot, probably from a spy in one of the French planter's homes or some idiot mouthing off at a local watering hole. I do not know how he found out, but he did," Desbardes stated.

Diédoné's expression darkened as he considered Desbardes' words. "So, what do you suggest we do now?" he asked, a sense of urgency creeping into his tone.

Desbardes paused for a moment, weighing his options. "We cannot afford any missteps. We need to regroup and reassess our strategy. Dessalines may have thwarted this plot, but there are other ways to weaken his hold on power," he said thoughtfully. "How goes it with your plants into his generals' households?"

"This will take some time," replied Diédoné. "A worker cannot just drop in and be trusted to get that close and comfortable to these men of power. They are not stupid, you know."

"I came here to re-emphasize to continue and not stop. You must infiltrate so we can weaken him from the head. As his generals get killed, he will become untrusting of them all and may end up killing some of them himself," Desbardes said with a smile.

"What of the killings of all your accomplices?" Diédoné asked.

"The cruel reality of over 3,000 executions have occurred, yes. Their deaths will not be in vain," Desbardes replied with a steely determination. "As we speak, agents in every important foreign city are unleashing information, and disinformation, to newspapers, emphasizing that Dessalines is a savage who slaughtered these innocent people simply for being of the wrong color; white," he continued, his voice filled with conviction.

"What good will that do? How can it possibly help us?" Diédoné questioned.

"If a white man were to kill 3,000 blacks like you and your men here, it would not even make it onto a single page of a newspaper. According to the whites, your lives are not worth the ink. But if a single white person is killed by a black, ah, now that is newsworthy. The Americans, British, French, and Spanish will not only devour the story but their politicians will use it as an excuse to retaliate against Dessalines."

Diédoné turned to Desbardes and let out a bitter laugh. "You whites are truly cunning creatures. It's no wonder you kept us enslaved for centuries. You are the devils we have always known you to be."

A cloud of tension seemed to hang in the air in the White House, casting a somber pall over the office as Thomas Jefferson leaned back in his chair, fingers steepled beneath his chin.

On the table before him lay scattered news reports detailing the horrors unfolding in Ayiti – grim accounts of bloodshed and savagery that left even the most hardened souls shaken. The French ambassador, Pinchon, paced impatiently near the window, while James Madison sat stiffly across from Jefferson, his face etched with concern.

"Mr. President," Pinchon began, unable to mask the urgency in his voice, "the situation in Ayiti grows direr by the day. Dessalines has shown himself to be a tyrant, a savage who will stop at nothing to secure his power. You cannot allow such a threat to fester at your doorstep."

Jefferson studied the man for a moment, taking note of the desperation simmering beneath his genteel façade. He knew well enough that France had much to lose should a free, independent Ayiti emerge from this chaos. And yet, he could not deny the truth in Pinchon's words – the violence and brutality consuming the island nation were a far cry from the ideals of liberty and justice he had fought so passionately to uphold here in the United States.

"Or perhaps," Pinchon interjected, his voice dripping with disdain, "it is simply proof that these so-called 'niggers' are incapable of self-governance and unworthy of the liberties we hold dear. We must embargo them"

"An embargo, you say," Jefferson finally replied, weighing each word carefully. "You believe that by isolating Ayiti, we can contain the danger it poses to the region and perhaps even hasten its descent into anarchy?"

"Oui, Mr. President," Pinchon responded fervently. "With international trade cut off, Dessalines will find himself bereft of resources and support. I believe that the seeds of his own ruin will have been sown, and we will be given the chance to forge their destiny anew."

Madison's brow furrowed as he considered the proposal, his thoughts a tempest of uncertainty and unease. "But what of the ordinary people there, those who have no hand in Dessalines' reign of terror? Would we not be condemning them to suffer needlessly under the yoke of his tyranny?"

"Unfortunately," Pinchon replied somberly, "it seems that there is no alternative. The situation has grown far beyond our control. Innocent French citizens have been mercilessly murdered. Desperate times call for desperate measures. We must act swiftly and decisively if we are to prevent this contagion from spreading to your American shores."

Jefferson let out a weary sigh, feeling the weight of his office pressing down upon him like a leaden mantle. He had always believed in the fundamental equality and dignity of man, but now he found himself faced with the grim reality that some would use their newfound power as a license for cruelty and carnage. As much as it pained him to admit, it seemed that Pinchon's plan was the only viable option left.

"Very well," he said at last, his voice heavy with resignation. "I shall lobby those most powerful in Congress to impose an embargo on Ayiti. May God grant us the wisdom to navigate these treacherous waters and guide us towards a brighter, more equitable future."

Six

END OF AN ERA

Bréda Plantation - Plaine du Nord
May 1804

Général Henry Christophe kicked his mare once more, harder this time, to make the beast increase its speed as he turned down the long winding drive towards the Bréda Plantation with a dozen horsemen in tow. He always marveled at the coconut trees lining both sides of the drive that not only provided visual beauty but a harvest that the plantation reaped year after year.

He had gotten word that Jean-Jacques Dessalines had arrived in the Northern region and his first destination was the Bréda Plantation to confront Bayon de Libertad, one of the whites he considered responsible for the plots against his administration.

As Christophe entered the property, he could see soldiers milling about and spotted the abandoned horses of Dessalines' honor guard, still restless he presumed, after a long and labored gallop. He concluded that they must have just arrived minutes before. He entered the grand maison in time to see Dessalines interrogating the staff as to the whereabouts of its principal resident, Bayon de Libertad.

Unbeknownst to Bayon, who strolled through his magnificent garden on the grounds of Bréda, Dessalines would soon find him. This was his sanctuary, his heaven, his domain. As the scent of tropical flowers wafted through the air, he couldn't help but feel a sense of peace and contentment. The birds sang their sweet melodies, and the butterflies fluttered about, seemingly unaware of the chaos that was unfolding just a stone's throw away.

The Plaine du Nord, southwest of the bustling city of Cap Français, was Bayon's haven. Isolated from the commotion and noise of the city, yet close enough to indulge in its occasional pleasures. For 65 years, this land had been his home. He had come to revere its rich soil and bountiful plantation. Here, everything grew larger and more vibrant. A dozen mangos could feed a village, avocados that could satisfy the hunger of a table of guests, breadfruit trees bearing fruit as big as a man's head, and Bougainvillea, Crotons, and Hibiscus bursting in size with vibrant colors and intoxicating scents.

Here, in his expansive garden, he had become a mad scientist of sorts, experimenting with mixing seeds to create unimaginable hybrids. His fingers were stained with the colors of his favorite flowers, but also the success of his cash crops of sugar and coffee as he thought of what would comprise the makeup of his next generation of seeds for the following year's crop.

The peaceful atmosphere of the gardens shattered loudly as Général Jean-Jacques Dessalines and Henry Christophe marched towards Bayon with a dozen armed men in tow, their boots thundering the ground and swords clanging a menacing opera of death. "What is the meaning of this?" Bayon demanded.

"You are charged with conspiracy to commit treason against the government, Bayon de Libertad!" Dessalines snarled, his face twisted with rage. "I have saved your arrest warrant for last, as Christophe failed to serve it."

Bayon's heart raced as he sized up the situation. Facing two powerful Générals and their armed soldiers, he knew he was in grave danger. But he refused to cower before them.

"Ah, Général Christophe," Bayon said with a small smile as he turned to only address Christophe. "It is always a pleasure. How goes that fine Hotel de la Couronne?"

"Be careful, old man," Dessalines warned, his voice low and menacing. "These are serious charges and I am not in the mood to be toyed with."

Bayon scoffed at the accusation. "You accuse me of treason? But on what evidence?"

"These planters you recruited, the Emigres, that have returned here," Dessalines replied coldly. "They conspired to overthrow my government thanks to your involvement. You brought them back to Saint Domingue, now our country of Ayiti. Their actions are in your hands."

"I take no responsibility for grown men, mon Général," Bayon shot back defiantly.

Dessalines' grip on his sword tightened as he glared at Bayon. "These planters have been dealt with swiftly across the island, and mercilessly...except for you. For some reason, Christophe here has shown you mercy and has left you untouched." The Général's words dripped with disdain and disgust.

Bayon locked eyes with Dessalines, unflinching in his defiance. "I hold no regrets for enlisting the Emigres to aid Toussaint Louverture in rebuilding the farming industry, even though for some reason you may now see me as a traitor. I recruited these planters for their expertise in managing commercial farms under the orders of our Governor Général, Toussaint Louverture. He understood their value and contributions well."

"You speak Louverture's name as if he were a hero, Bayon. But I know the truth. He was a lover of whites and of the French, like you," Dessalines growled, spitting out the words with venom. "I am outlawing any mention of the name Toussaint Louverture, to preserve the honor of our cause."

"Toussaint Louverture was a great leader, Général Dessalines. You were once his loyal follower, his protege even. How could you turn your back on him now?" Bayon retorted.

Dessalines' voice boomed through the air, "The mere mention of his name will be met with death. I clawed my way to victory against the French despite his treacherous presence. And now, you will pay for your crimes," he snarled, unsheathing his sword with a deadly glint in his eye.

Christophe's protests fell on deaf ears as Dessalines swiftly approached Bayon, murder in his heart. "You may join your hero in the afterlife, Bayon de Libertad," he sneered before slitting Bayon's throat with a single swift motion.

Bayon could feel the warmth of blood on his chest and realized his lifeblood was spilling onto the ground as he felt a sudden sense of detachment from his body. From above, he watched as Dessalines and Christophe stood frozen in time, locked in an eternal battle for power and revenge. Was this the moment before death where one's life was said to flash before their eyes?

In a dreamlike state, Bayon saw fragments of his past fly by until a vivid memory emerged: his arrival to Saint Domingue in 1739. Disembarking from the schooner Yolande, he had been overcome with awe at the beauty of Cap Francais, a city that even surpassed Paris in its magnificence, the richest colony on earth.

As he strolled down the bustling boulevard, his leather bag in hand and a sense of excitement bubbling in his chest, he immediately fell head over heels for the city. Its vibrant energy pulsed through the streets, mingling with the rich scents of exotic spices, roasting coffee, and freshly baked bread. The melodic chatter of multiple languages filled his ears, creating a symphony of sound that he had never experienced before.

He had grown up in Nantes, a small town in western France where jobs were scarce and money was a constant struggle. This new city would become his home. He had seen an advertisement in the local paper of Nantes for white workers needed on plantations in Saint Domingue. The idea of managing a workforce of slaves intrigued him, as he had never met one before. As he marveled at the black men walking through town, he couldn't help but wonder what made their skin so dark; it was a question born out of naivety and ignorance.

In the blink of an eye, a runaway carriage hurtled towards him at breakneck speed, careening wildly as two Negro figures raced behind it. His heart pounding in his chest, Bayon's senses were heightened as he took in the chaotic scene before him. A middle-aged white man ran after the men and carriage, his face etched with terror and determination as he desperately tried to catch up to the out-of-control vehicle.

Through blurred vision, Bayon noticed two young girls, no more than ten years old, clinging to each other in fear inside the carriage. Their screams echoed through the street as they bounced around inside, their delicate bodies no match for the rough ride. With quick reflexes, Bayon rushed to aid the man in stopping the carriage before anyone got hurt.

As the stampeding horses charged towards him, his mind raced with fear and urgency. Without hesitation, he lunged for the nearest reins as the hooves thundered closer. The wild animals sprayed dirt and debris in their wake, but he managed to grab hold of one and pull himself up onto the back of a galloping steed. With a death grip on the reins, he expertly yanked them hard to slow the panicked horses to a sudden stop, narrowly avoiding being trampled in the process. His heart pounded in his chest as he looked back at the chaos and destruction he had just narrowly escaped from.

As he dismounted the horse, his heart raced with anticipation and anxiety. With a firm grip, he flung open the carriage door and a tiny figure leaped into his embrace, clinging to his neck with desperate sobs. The older child emerged from the carriage, her arms immediately wrapping around his waist in a desperate attempt to feel safe and express gratitude.

In a matter of seconds, the two Negroes who had been relentlessly pursuing the carriage finally caught up to them, gasping for breath with the white man several seconds behind. The girls scrambled out of Libertad's protective embrace and darted toward their father, tears streaming down their faces. The two men beg for forgiveness of the white man knowing that their carelessness could have caused a tragedy with the runaway horses.

After the chaos settled and the white man and his daughters regained their composure, he approached Bayon with open arms. "I cannot imagine what would have happened if God had not put you in the path of my children. You are a true savior," he exclaimed gratefully, "An angel sent to them for sure!"

Bayon simply shrugged and replied, "I was just in the right place at the right time, sir."

"Forgive me, I did not properly introduce myself. I am Charles Bréda, the Count of Noah."

Bayon bowed his head in respect, taking in the grandeur of the man before him. "It is an honor to meet you, Count Bréda. My name is François Antoine Bayon de Libertat."

"You are skilled with horses," Monsieur Libertat," Bréda observed, eyeing Bayon's muscular frame and confident stance. He continued curiously, "Observing your suitcase by your side, you seem new to town. Or do you always carry your belongings with you while on a stroll?"

Bayon chuckled heartily and explained, "Yes, I am indeed new to this place. I just arrived by schooner, the Yolande there." He gestured towards the impressive ship tied to the wharf. "My home is Nantes. I am currently seeking a suitable hotel. Could you perhaps recommend one?"

"Nonsense," Bréda reassured with a warm smile. "You must stay with us. My uncle, Pantaléon de Bréda Jr., a Grands Blanc, is an absentee landowner, owns a sprawling plantation here on the island that I manage, and we would be delighted to have you as our esteemed guest until you find your footing in Saint Domingue."

Bayon's eyes widened in surprise and gratitude. "I cannot accept such generosity from someone I have only just met," he protested.

"Nonsense," Bréda insisted firmly. "Consider it my heartfelt gift of gratitude for saving my daughters from a possible disaster today."

"Sir, the saving of your daughters requires no payment or kindness on your part," he answered humbly. "I did it not knowing who you were or that I would receive any reward for it."

"That is exactly why you are invited, young man," Bréda stated firmly. "I will not take no for an answer." He then turned to one of the black men nearby and called out, "Tiland, take this man's bag and show him to the wagon. Finish loading the supplies and I will see you back at Bréda." Turning back to Bayon, he continued with an air of authority, "I must get my girls home. They are distressed by today's events and my wife will be furious with me. I have much explaining to do. I will see you tonight for dinner. Tiland will have someone show you to your accommodations." With a nod, Bréda walked away, confident that Bayon would accept his invitation.

Charles Bréda's plantation was a paradise for Bayon, filled with an opulent mansion and lavish stables. But Bayon knew he couldn't rely on someone else's riches forever. He needed to make his way and leave his mark on the world. Despite indulging in all the luxuries of the plantation for a week, he mustered the courage to thank Bréda and announce his plans to depart and find work in the city.

But Bréda had other ideas. "You will work here," he declared.

Bayon was taken aback. "Doing what, may I ask? You have been too kind already. Please don't feel the need to create a job for me."

Bréda's eyes twinkled with determination. "You are good with horses, as I have witnessed. You will be in charge of the stables and begin there. I have many fine stallions that need training and I always wanted to breed horses for sale. We will discuss compensation in the morning."

Overwhelmed by Bréda's generosity, Bayon stayed on at the plantation, becoming an integral part of its management. He began in the stables but soon was schooled about industrial farming and overseeing the vast expanse of land that stretched out before him.

A year had gone by and on a blissful Sunday afternoon, Bréda excitedly announced that he had received an invitation to the grand celebration at the opulent plantation of Antoine Simone, a Grands Blanc known for his immense wealth and fortune. With great enthusiasm, Bréda invited Bayon to join him and his family on this exclusive occasion.

As they arrived, Bayon was taken aback by the extravagant display of wealth and luxury that greeted them. Golden chandeliers sparkled in the sunlight, and marble statues stood tall amidst immaculate gardens and the air was thick with the sweet scent of freshly cut flowers.

The decadent feast, the exquisite music of a string quartet, and the refined guests all exuded an air of opulence at Antoine Simone's plantation. But as the afternoon wore on, Monsieur Simone revealed his true sadistic nature by inviting his guests to a barbaric "sporting event" in the back gardens.

The manicured lawns and perfectly trimmed shrubs served as a stark contrast to the grotesque display of six slaves buried up to their necks in the ground while piles of rocks nearby hinted at the gruesome game about to take place.

With a sickening smile, Antoine announced that these "targets" were for their entertainment. The guests were encouraged to throw rocks at the slaves' heads, earning points for each hit and a bonus if they killed one of the helpless victims. The winner would win a prize he announced.

As Antoine Simone threw the first rock that struck its target with a sickening thud, the darkness of human depravity settled over the plantation like a thick fog with some guests in horror, but many amused.

"This is madness," Charles Bréda's heart pounded as he stepped out of the safety of the crowd and approached Simone. He knew the consequences of speaking out against a plantation owner, especially one as ruthless as Simone. But seeing the brutal treatment of the slaves, he couldn't stay silent.

"Ah, Charles Bréda, the Count of Noah, has no stomach for standing up to the injustice of these slaves robbing me of a day's labor. They are lazy," Simone sneered at him, making sure the rest of the crowd could hear.

Bréda took a deep breath and summoned all his courage. "These are human beings, not mere property. Release them at once and follow the laws stated in the Code Noir!"

Simone burst into laughter at Bréda's words. "The Code Noir? That outdated and meaningless document? We make our laws here in

Saint Domingue. If you can't handle it, then perhaps you should take your leave, my dear Count, and sail away back to the metropole."

"Unearth these men, Simone," Bréda bellowed, his voice echoing through the crowd like a drumbeat. Every eye turned to him, their faces a mix of fear and awe.

Simone's lips curled into a sneer as he replied, "Unless you are willing to purchase these worthless savages before we begin our games, you are in no position to order me to do anything concerning them."

Bréda's jaw clenched as he forced himself to remain calm. "So be it. What is their price?"

"Twenty-five percent profit of what I paid, which I can show you in my ledgers," Simone spat out, his words dripping with contempt.

Some in the crowd gasped at Simone's gall while others laughed as if it were a joke. But Bréda knew there was nothing funny about this situation. "But before you have the opportunity to depart with them, you must provide your letter of credit as well as besting me in a Duel d'Escrime - *dual by the sword*," Simone announced, his eyes glinting with malice.

The murmurs in the crowd grew louder as they realized the stakes of this challenge. Bréda could feel the weight of their expectations on his shoulders, but he refused to back down. "Agreed," he responded firmly. "As the challenged party, I choose the French foil as weapon of choice."

As Bayon returned with the children from escorting them through the gardens, chaos erupted around them. Catherine, Charles Bréda's wife, ran to his side and tried desperately to reason with her husband, but his honor was on display for all to see. He knew that Antoine Simone was a master swordsman, but he could hold his own - having once competed on the fencing team at his university.

"And how will the winner be determined, my faithful Count?" Simone asked, a wicked grin spreading across his face.

"First blood," Bréda declared to the gasps and shocked exclamations from the crowd as a servant produced two swords of impeccable quality. The tension in the air was palpable as the two men faced off, their swords gleaming in the sunlight. This fight would determine not only the fate of these slaves but also Bréda's honor and reputation.

Simone wasted no time as he prematurely launched himself towards Bréda, his eyes blazing with a fierce determination to end this fight quickly to his advantage. With lightning speed, he swung his sword at Bréda's head, aiming to strike a fatal blow.

But Bréda was not an easy target. With expert skill and agility, he parried each of Simone's strikes, surprising even himself as he held his own against the ferocious onslaught. The two warriors clashed with such intensity and skill that it seemed like hours had passed in mere moments.

Meanwhile, Bayon and Bréda's wife watched on in terror, their hearts pounding in their chests as they prayed for his safety. The crowd around them roared with excitement, caught up in the adrenaline-fueled spectacle unfolding before them.

As they battled across the gardens, racing up and down staircases, leaping over obstacles, their swords clashed and danced in deadly harmony. The scorching sun beat down on them, intensifying the already brutal heat of their physical exertion, evidenced by sweat splashing off their faces.

It was a battle of wills and strength, neither willing to back down or give up until one of them would shed their opponent's blood. The spectators held their breath as they watched the intense struggle between these two skilled warriors.

Bayon's heart was pounding in his chest as he watched his newfound mentor engage in a fierce battle with Simone. The clash of swords echoed through the air, sending shivers down Bayon's spine. He could see the determination and fear in Bréda's eyes and felt a surge of worry for the older man.

And then, in a flash of steel, it was over. Bréda's sword sliced through the air with such force that it caught Simone off guard, expertly leaving a shallow gash on his cheek and cutting open his shirt to reveal a trail of crimson blood running down his chest.

Antoine Simone and Charles Bréda battle in front of guests during a Duel d'Escrime as Catherine, Bréda's wife, along with their children and Bayon de Libertad watch the dangerous spectacle.

Bayon couldn't believe what he was seeing - Bréda had emerged victorious, but at what cost? His mentor's body trembled with adrenaline and exhaustion, yet there was a glint of triumph in his eyes. It was a sight that would be etched into Bayon's mind forever, a reminder of the brutal reality of Saint Domingue, as the crowd politely applauded.

Bréda turned to Bayon as Simone stood still, his hand on his injured cheek and not believing what had just happened, unaccustomed to loss. "Have these men unearthed, provide a letter of credit for twenty-five percent over his ledger entry for each as a purchase price. I am taking my wife and children away from this demonic place."

Without another word to Antoine Simone, Bréda took one last look at him and turned his back as the crowd parted to allow him, and his wife and children through. Bayon de Libertad did as instructed.

That evening, Bayon stormed through the gates of the Bréda Plantation, his eyes blazing with determination. He had one goal in mind: find Hypolite, the Commandeur of the slaves and a man he had come to respect deeply.

Bréda had introduced him as a prince from the Allada Kingdom of Africa, known as Gaou Guinou to his people. And on this plantation, his role was crucial. Hypolite, the Christian name given to him on arrival to Saint Domingue, commanded great respect and reverence from the slave population with his regal demeanor and wise leadership. He settled disputes, maintained discipline, and fostered harmony among the oppressed population. Without fail, overseers were required to consult with Hypolite before inflicting any punishment upon a slave, making brutality a rare occurrence here. As Bayon sought out Hypolite, he couldn't help but feel confident about the presence of this strong and just leader on their plantation.

The six slaves rescued were more than grateful. They were in a terrible condition; malnourished, signs of recent beatings and whippings, and insect bites from having been buried in the dirt for so long. Hypolite was well experienced with herb medicine and over several days brought the men back into shape, grateful to be working at the Bréda plantation, albeit in the sunbaked gruesome fields of sugarcane.

Bayon's mind suddenly flashed forward to 1743, four years after he had arrived in Saint Domingue. Hypolite had coupled with a woman by the given name of Pauline and he witnessed their firstborn, a son, whom they named François Dominique Toussaint, followed by four more children; two boys and two girls.

His mind then flashed to 1745, when Charles Bréda departed with his wife and teenage daughters back to France, confidently promoting him to be in charge of the Bréda Plantation as its Général manager and how thrilled he was. Bréda had designated Hypolite as head of the workforce and made Bayon promise that he would collaborate with Hypolite and never give slaves any maltreatment unless ordered by Hypolite to do so.

The journey was moving rapidly in this strange dream as he witnessed Toussaint growing up and developing great skills in natural medicine, eventually becoming a veterinarian, and the health caregiver for the slaves on the plantation. His medical knowledge was attributed to a familiarity with the folk medicine of his father, the African plantation slaves, as well as other Creole communities. He also learned formal techniques found in the hospitals founded by the Jesuits where Bayon allowed him freedom to volunteer.

Toussaint had proved bright and extremely disciplined, hardening himself physically by becoming a superb equestrian and horse trainer. He could hear Toussaint speaking *Fon*, the language of the Allada people, *Kréyòl* the language of Saint-Domingue, and rudimentary French which he was taught by his godfather on the property, a trusted slave named Pierre Baptiste.

Bayon was so moved as he saw Toussaint become an avid reader, achieving fluency in the colonial languages of the time which would become indispensable for Toussaint to later write letters that would demonstrate a moderate familiarity with Epictetus, the Stoic philosopher who had lived as a slave and his future public speeches showed a familiarity with Machiavelli and enlightenment thinker Abbé Raynal, a French critic of slavery.

Bayon saw himself watching as Toussaint received his degree of theological education from the Jesuit and Capuchin missionaries through his church attendance and devout Catholicism. His gentle demeanor warmed Bayon's heart through time as he grew much affection for him.

Toussaint had become attached to the plantation and developed guts when he would stand firm against members of the *Petits-Blancs* who worked there as hired help. They would attempt to bully him, call him Fatra Baton – *feable stick*. He would engage in fights with them or any others who threatened the people or assets of the Bréda plantation, considering himself a Bréda family member. Bayon smiled as his dream visualized Toussaint throwing the plantation attorney Bergé off a Bréda plantation horse when he attempted to take it outside the bounds of the property without permission after a meeting one afternoon.

Bayon arrived at the vision of his wedding day, marrying his sweetheart Solange and witnessing the birth of his children and how Toussaint became a trusted part of his circle of trust. He watched many scenes play out of how he had developed so much confidence in Toussaint that he entrusted the young man as a coachman for his wife and children. Toussaint had rightly earned and been granted the honor of *"Liberté de Savanne"* (freedom of plantation restriction). With letters of passage signed by Bayon, he was allowed to leave the borders of the plantation without fear of retribution.

This life dream flashing before his eyes moved rapidly in the split second when he saw Toussaint as a man in his early thirties. He was proud of himself and Toussaint on the day he emancipated him in 1776, the year of the American Revolution, and honored that Toussaint remained loyal to him his entire life.

Bayon was then transported to the violent slave uprising of 1791 on the night of the raid and riots of the slaves. Were it not for Toussaint and the other loyal slaves, he and his family would have certainly perished. Toussaint and the others had saved their lives by protecting them from injury and death from the marauding slaves.

Bayon saw the good times and the sad times, like the weddings of his two daughters, their departure with their husbands to France, and the death of his wife, the love of his life.

Bayon witnessed his love and respect for Toussaint as he helped him rise from a slave to plantation owner, then as Général of the army that vanquished the Spanish and the British, and eventually as head of the colony and the French Colonial Army, as Governor-Général.

When Toussaint was revitalizing the economy, he had asked him to assist in enticing the Blanc planters to return to Saint Domingue after the slave revolution from New Orleans, Jamaica, Cuba, and other lands they had fled to. They trusted him and he was happy to vouch for Toussaint's integrity and promises to keep them safe. They had arrived, a few at first, but then hundreds to re-open their plantations, jump-start the economy, provide employment for the people, and taxes for the government.

He has lived a good life he thought, and he now understood that it was over for him at the ripe age of eighty-four. He had just witnessed the memories of a good life pass before his eyes. What more can an old man ask for, he thought? A life well lived, a conscience well preserved, and friends that included black, mulatto, and white.

He suddenly looked back at the present, the living; Dessalines, Christophe, and the soldiers, still frozen in his moment of death where his body had not yet hit the floor.

They were, actually Dessalines was, looking to him to be sacrificed to atone for the sins of those whom he had brought back, those Grands Blanc who the island had so desperately needed. But naively, he did recognize that some were also cruel.

In essence, he even agreed with Jean-Jacques Dessalines. He had to be sacrificed for the greater good of a long-term understanding that slavery, abuse, and coercion could no longer be tolerated in this land of the free and must be punished.

He looked away and saw a bright light with many people walking towards it. The majority were women and children with a small proportion of happy men. As he walked towards the light, he felt a warm presence approach him. "I have been waiting for you, Bayon de Libertad, my dear old friend."

Bayon looked at the presence as it became clearer in vision. "Toussaint!" he exclaimed.

"Yes, my friend. I have come to take you home. Our chapter here is complete but it is just beginning over there," as Toussaint's soft voice pointed towards the distance where he could make out a figure coming into view, and directing the dead. It was the mythical Voodoo God, Baron Samedi, the gatekeeper of the after-world. He would point his baton to the right for some to enter the bright light as he did for Bayon, and to the left for others who would continue towards the darkness. He felt relieved to be directed to the sun.

They walked towards that magnificent ray of sunshine and he looked at the damned who it seemed could not see it, men he recognized as evil and cruel men who had abused their privileges. Among those damned, he could make out Antoine Simone, still branded by the scar given him so long ago by Charles Bréda, the Count of Noah. Would they be damned in hell or remain in this land and curse it for eternity from their graves? The answer he did not know. All he knew was that the light was warm and welcoming as he continued to walk towards it with his great friend, Toussaint Louverture.

It was the reward for a life well lived and his kindness and contributions to the land and its people. At that moment, his body went lifeless as it continued towards the ground and ceased to exist as his spirit disappeared through the warmth of the bright light.

As the body of Bayon de Libertad landed hard on the ground with a thud, Christophe looked at Dessalines and said "Why? Did it please you to kill an old man?"

"Watch your tone, Général," Dessalines said as he looked sternly at Christophe. "Your insubordination will no longer be tolerated after we leave this property today."

Seven

THE RESCUE OF LE MATIN
& THE LAURA

Savannah, Georgia
July 1804

The sun dipped low in the sky, casting a warm golden hue over Savannah's cobblestone streets as Jean-Baptiste Bayard, his brother Andre, and Dr. Edward Stevens settled into their chairs at an outdoor table of a modest restaurant. The sounds of laughter and clinking glasses filled the air, providing a stark contrast to the idle ships looming in the distance at the Savannah docks.

"Ah, Jean," Dr. Stevens sighed, swirling the amber liquid in his glass, "I can scarcely believe it's been months since the seizure of the Laura and Le Matin." He shook his head, his expression a mixture of anger and regret. "Those poor souls still held prisoner on board..."

"Regretable," Jean responded, his voice heavy with concern. His eyes strayed to the docks once more, haunted by the knowledge that his ships were so close yet remained just out of reach. "Their families suffer greatly, and every day I feel the weight of my inability to set them free."

Andre sat quietly, his brow furrowed as he picked at the fraying edge of the tablecloth. He too felt the sting of helplessness that came from knowing their ships, filled with supplies once desperately needed for Dessalines' army, lay useless within their sight. At least the war has been won, but the sailors aboard are certainly desperate to get home.

"I have tried every diplomatic channel; the naval administration, the mayor of Savannah, the Georgia legislature, the state department, even the inspector general, though I knew that was fruitless, and I cannot get these ships released," Andre listed frustrated.

"Is there truly nothing else we can do, Ed?" Jean asked, desperation creeping into his voice.

"Perhaps not all is lost," Ed Stevens said, forcing himself to sound more optimistic than he felt. "We have our connections, our allies. We must remain steadfast," said Stevens, his voice low and urgent. "I have made some inquiries among my connections in the past Adams administration. I believe there are certain naval officers at the dock who might be sympathetic and willing to assist in, shall we say, 'liberating' your ships."

Jean's heart skipped a beat, hope flaring briefly within him. "At what cost?" he asked cautiously, his gaze never leaving Dr. Stevens.

"Three hundred silver dollars," Dr. Stevens replied, his expression grim. "One hundred for each officer, and one hundred more for their accomplices."

Andre exhaled sharply, his eyes widening in disbelief. "That is an exorbitant sum," he protested. "We do not have that kind of money on hand."

"Then we shall find a way to raise it," Jean declared, determination igniting within him like a fire. "For our people, no price is too high."

With a frustrated sigh, Dr. Stevens shook his head as he contemplated the daunting task ahead. The weight of the situation seemed to press down on him like a heavy fog, making it hard to think clearly. "If it were not for the obstinacy of Thomas Jefferson," he muttered bitterly, "this would not be necessary."

His voice carried a hint of anger and disappointment as he spoke about the influential figure. "He is thoroughly controlled by the slave-holding members of his party," Dr. Stevens continued, his frustration evident in his tone. "But what am I thinking, he is a slaveholder himself!" The bitterness dripped from his words as he thought about the hypocrisy of those in power.

"I've heard you're getting put through the mill with trying to collect your compensation from this administration," Jean offered Stevens.

"Yes, President Adams had promised me compensation for my years in Ayiti – Saint Domingue, as it was called then – but the current administration refuses to honor that commitment."

Jean furrowed his brow, his thoughts turning to the complex web of politics that connected their new country to the great powers of the world. He understood all too well the sway that men like Thomas Jefferson held throughout Ayiti's future.

"President Adams was a wise man, willing to recognize our independence and partner with Toussaint Louverture," Jean said quietly, his voice tinged with regret. "But Jefferson, and his lackeys, like Madison, cling to their slaves fearing what our revolution might inspire here in their country."

"Yes," Dr. Stevens agreed, his eyes dark with a mix of anger and sorrow. "And so they do everything in their power to undermine your country, to ensure that you remain shackled by chains both literal and metaphorical."

Jean contemplated the weight of the decisions that lay before him and his brother Andre. The warmth and comfort of the restaurant seemed almost incongruous to the gravity of their situation. As he took a slow sip of his ale, he pondered over Dr. Stevens' words once more.

"Timothy Pickering," Dr. Stevens mused, looking into the distance as if seeing something beyond the confines of the room. "He was the Secretary of State under Adams, and I believe he may still hold some influence in these matters."

"Pickering?" Andre asked, his brow furrowed with curiosity. "You think he could help us?"

Dr. Stevens hesitated, then nodded. "There's a chance. He was sympathetic to our cause during his tenure, and I've maintained correspondence with him since. But there are no guarantees in politics."

Jean studied the doctor's face, trying to gauge the sincerity of his words. In this world of diplomacy and intrigue, trust was a rare commodity. Yet, Dr. Stevens had proven himself time and again as a friend of him and the island. "Let us proceed both diplomatically and if that doesn't work, steal our ships back."

"You are determined, Jean," replied Stevens.

"Marie will kill me if I don't get her ships back, and more importantly, the men who sail them!"

"No kidding," replied Andre. "She expects us to pull out all stops to get what she wants!"

A week later, Andre and Jean found themselves back in the same quaint restaurant, just a stone's throw away from the bustling docks. The two ships, *Laura* and *Le Matin,* loomed in the distance, their masts reaching high into the sky. As they sat down to lunch, they couldn't help but notice the flurry of activity on the docks - sailors hustling about, loading and unloading cargo from other ships. But upon closer inspection, they realized that all of these sailors were white - not a single of their black sailors could be seen among them. The only Negros at the docks were slaves.

"Jean, where are all of our black sailors?" Andre asked curiously.

"I was wondering the same thing," Jean replied, taking a sip of his ale. "It doesn't seem right."

Andre nodded in agreement. "Maybe Bunel will have some insight when he arrives."

Their longtime friend, Joseph Bunel, a white Frenchman married to a black Ayisyen Creole named Marie Fanchette Estève, was an abolitionist and loyal supporter of the island. He managed a thriving plantation in Plaine du Nord and also ran an import/export business. Known for his unwavering integrity and character, Bunel had been appointed by Toussaint Louverture himself as trade envoy between Saint Domingue and the United States, back in 1798, successfully negotiating a resumption of trade after an embargo imposed by the US against all French colonies.

Bunel had been warmly received by Secretary of State Timothy Pickering and even dined with President Adams to solidify their agreement. Upon returning to Saint Domingue with his diplomatic partner, Dr. Stevens, to implement the new trade policies, Bunel played a crucial role in benefiting both parties.

But during the revolution, Bunel's principles led to trouble when he refused to denounce the rebels and withheld financial support from France. Arrested by General Leclerc himself, he had been deported to France before making his escape to Philadelphia. There, he had aided Dessalines in procuring and exporting arms, transported by Bayard's vessels, against U.S. laws that prohibited assistance to the rebels of Saint Domingue during the war.

It was Bunel who had been the last to speak with Captain Marbot of the *Laura* and Captain Lafontaine of the *Le Matin* on the fateful morning they set sail from Philadelphia harbor, destined for Saint-Domingue. Their course had taken them southeast past Wilmington and through the channel of Cape May before reaching the open waters of the Atlantic. From there, they headed south towards the Caribbean.

But their journey never reached its intended destination. The two ships were intercepted by the American Navy's Saratoga and Mercury, boarded, and seized along with their crew and cargo - including contraband guns and ammunition. This action was taken under orders from Jefferson himself, who had sided with France instead of supporting Dessalines' rebel forces.

The two men stood enthusiastically as their comrades entered the restaurant, embracing each other tightly with a sense of brotherhood forged through bloodshed and hardship. They sat down in unison, the air thick with tension and worry.

As Andre signaled for another ale for Bunel, he lowered his voice to a whisper. "Ed gave me information on the naval officers and I've met with them to solidify our mission. But there's a major problem."

Joseph's face darkened as he spoke, his words heavy with gravity. "Fourteen black sailors from Le Matin and seven from the Laura have been sold into slavery."

Jean's eyes widened in shock. "No...that can't be true."

"It is," confirmed Bunel. "And it gets worse. They're being held on three separate plantations - Wormsloe, Owens, and Harper - all half a day's ride from each other outside of Savannah."

"This is a nightmare," Jean muttered, running a hand through his hair in frustration. "We should have seen this coming after nine months of their capture."

"And the worst part?" Bunel asked grimly. "They were sold for $250 each. That's over $5,000 total, albeit a fraction of their marketable value here."

Jean's jaw dropped in disbelief. "These are free citizens of Ayiti. How dare they still sell human beings like property? After all, it is 1804, damn it!"

"We don't have time to worry about that now," Andre interjected. "We need to figure out how to get them back."

"But we don't have that kind of money," Jean said, feeling defeated.

Bunel shook his head sadly. "I'm at a loss too."

Jean's mood suddenly shifted from frustration to excitement, his eyes brightening. "Wait! I have an idea," he stated eagerly. "Our Captains, Marbot and Lafontaine, are seasoned and resourceful. They must have already familiarized themselves with the city. We need to arrange a meeting with them."

Bunel's expression relaxed, a hint of hope shining in his eyes. "I can make that happen with the officers on our side," he replied.

"What exactly do you have in mind, my brother?" Andre asked with a playful grin. "I know you too well, Jean. That look on your face means your mind is working overtime."

"Joseph, please arrange the meeting as soon as possible," Jean ordered confidently. The three men's moods had transformed from frustration to anticipation as Joseph stood. "I'll be in touch."

The sun was setting on the coastal town as Jean, Andre, and Bunel made their way to the designated meeting spot. The salty air filled their nostrils as they approached a small tavern bustling with sailors. A warm glow emanated from inside and the sound of lively chatter could be heard from the outside.

As they entered, Jean's eyes scanned the room until he spotted Captain Marbot and Captain Lafontaine sitting in a secluded corner, deep in conversation. With a sense of relief, Jean greeted them warmly and introduced his companion Joseph Bunel. The two captains already knew Andre from their hometown.

"Jean, you are a sight for sore eyes," Marbot exclaimed with a hint of disbelief. "I can't believe it's been nearly ten months since we were apprehended."

"We thought you had forgotten us," Lafontaine added with a wry smile.

"Yeah, I did, but Marie hasn't!" Jean quipped, causing everyone to burst into laughter and easing the tension that lingered among them.

"Have you been well treated?" Andre asked.

"We are officers and get along well with our counterparts here. They give us freedom to roam and we vow not to escape," Marbot stated. "It works for both parties."

After some catching up and lighthearted banter, Jean cut straight to the point. "We need to take our ships and get out of here," he said earnestly, lowering his voice for added secrecy.

"They have us guarded day and night," Marbot sighed.

"We've arranged for a relaxation of the guards on the night of our choosing. However, no one is to be harmed - that must be made clear," Bunel interjected sternly.

"But we are not leaving without ALL of our crew," Jean stated firmly.

"They've sold twenty-one of our sailors into slavery," Lafontaine interjected with anger in his voice. "All the blacks and mulattos."

"That is what we will discuss tonight," Jean declared. "Slaves, no matter where they come from, all originate from Africa."

"We are well aware of this fact," Lafontaine replied.

"And within every group, there is always a leader. Just like back in Africa, there is always an elder or a designated leader who guides the tribe. Here in Savannah, it cannot be any different than in Ayiti or Africa," Jean explained with conviction.

"His name is Jeremiah," Marbot interjected without pause. "I do not know his original African name."

"How did you come to know of this man?" Jean inquired.

"The slaves working the docks speak of him," Marbot revealed. "They hold him in high regard and he often visits them. He has the freedom to leave his plantation because he serves as a judge for slave relations - a sort of peacemaker."

"Then we must arrange a meeting with this Jeremiah," Jean said determinedly.

"I can make that happen. We will signal you when we do," Marbot stated.

In just three days, they would meet again, this time at a run-down stable on the outskirts of town. Jeremiah was a pariah in the eyes of white society, never permitted to step foot in any respectable establishment. But he didn't care. He knew the truth about the two captured vessels and their daring mission to smuggle arms for Dessalines' army - a legend among the slaves, a glimmer of hope for freedom from the cruel shackles of slavery. And now, he stood face to face with Jean, determined to bring his brothers home.

"I need your help," Jean said, his voice heavy with urgency.

Jeremiah's eyebrows furrowed in confusion. "Why do you care about these black people? Are they your property?"

Jean's eyes blazed with righteous anger. "In Ayiti, we have no slavery. We fought for freedom for all people on our island."

Jeremiah's jaw dropped in disbelief. "So, it is true that such a place exists in this Atlantic world where Africans are truly free. Our slave masters have continuously told us that it is a lie created to deceive us."

"But it does exist," Jean insisted. "And you can be a part of it too. Help us rescue our comrades and join us on our journey to this land of liberation."

With adrenaline coursing through his veins and a fierce determination burning within him, Jeremiah knew that this was his only chance at true freedom - not just for himself, but for his family and friends who suffered alongside him. "Count me in," he declared boldly, meeting Marbot's skeptical gaze head-on. "But my family must be freed as well."

Marbot exchanged a wary glance with Lafontaine before turning to Jean, who looked equally unsure. "How many are we talking about?" he asked cautiously.

"Fifty," Jeremiah replied without hesitation, his eyes blazing with fierce conviction.

Jean's eyebrows shot up in surprise, and Andre and Bunet let out a sigh. "That is no small feat," Jean remarked, his tone serious.

Jeremiah met their doubtful expressions with steely resolve. "I know it won't be easy," he admitted. "If I am caught and these people are left behind, they will surely be persecuted in my absence. I am willing to risk everything for their freedom. And I know you are willing to risk for your people too."

The men shared a solemn nod, understanding the gravity of their mission. "We will need provisions for a week-long voyage at least," Jean stated matter-of-factly.

A wide smile spread across Jeremiah's face, revealing a full set of white teeth and a gleam of excitement in his eyes. "Consider it done," he said confidently. "I have a plan."

The murky July night in Savannah was thick with an eerie fog that seemed to cloak the city in a foreboding stillness. The air was hot, humid, and heavy, suffocating in its silence. Jean and Andre, two men on a dangerous mission, stood tense and alert as they waited for Jeremiah's arrival.

"Seems like our Ayisyen Voodoo Gods have followed us here," Andre muttered, his voice barely audible over the oppressive atmosphere.

"If I had any doubts about their power before, they're gone now," Jean replied grimly, his eyes scanning their surroundings. "This weather is perfect."

As the minutes ticked by, Jean could feel the tension building in his chest. The ocean lay quiet behind them, giving no solace or reprieve from the stifling heat. Suddenly, the church bells began to toll, signaling the agreed-upon time for their rendezvous. Jean's gaze flicked towards the dock where their ships, Laura and Le Matin, sat guarded by four sentries.

"The guards are leaving their posts," he whispered urgently to Andre. "Joseph must have come through."

But as Jean watched the four figures walk away into the darkness, panic set in. Where was Jeremiah?

"Can you see him?" Jean asked frantically.

Andre's heart raced as he scanned the shadows, desperately searching for their new ally. With each passing second, the reality of failure loomed closer with the four guards disappearing into the night, destined to return within thirty minutes. But there was still no sign of Jeremiah.

Sweat dripped down Andre's forehead as five more tense minutes ticked by. Just when he thought all hope was lost, Captain Marbot approached. "What is taking so long?" he barked.

"Jeremiah assured us he would be here in plenty of time," Jean replied, his voice strained with worry. "Something must have happened."

"How much longer do we wait?" Andre asked, his frustration and fear mounting.

"As long as it takes." Jean's tone brooked no argument. "Be ready to subdue the guards."

"We promised Joseph there would be no violence, nor harm to them," Andre whispered urgently.

But before they could come up with a plan or explanation for their failure to retrieve the prisoners, a voice cut through the tense atmosphere. "I am here," came Jeremiah's hushed voice. "We had some interruptions on the road, but I will explain another time."

Behind him stood a crowd of over seventy people - fifty from his group and twenty-one members of the crew. Relief washed over Jean as he recognized Pierre, the first mate on the Laura, among them.

"Thank God you have come for us, boss," Pierre said with tears in his eyes.

Jean wasted no time giving orders. "Are you all in good health? Any injured?"

"We were just in despair and the work was grueling, but we are all good," Pierre replied.

"Jeremiah, get your people on those ships. Split them up into two groups," Jean commanded. "Marbot, let's get this party going now."

As the people scrambled to carry out their orders, they heard Jeremiah pleading with two young boys and a woman. "You must leave now, my sons," Jeremiah said with tears in his eyes. "Your father cannot go with you."

Runaway slaves dash towards the Bayard ships, Le Matin and The Laura, as Jean and Andre Bayard, with Captain Marbot, witness Jeremiah bidding his wife Karen and two sons a tearful farewell.

"What do you mean you're not coming?" Jean asked, his heart sinking at the thought of leaving his new friend behind.

"I cannot abandon the rest of my people. There is a group of us here who will begin the fight, as you have done in Ayiti," Jeremiah explained. "Now that my family will be safe, I will join them to free our people. They have asked me to be their commander."

Jeremiah's wife begged him to come with them, but it was clear that his decision had already been made. With heavy hearts, they said their goodbyes as the ships slowly began to move away from the dock.

But there was no time for lingering emotions. A sailor came running down the plank, panic etched on his face. "The ships are ready to pick up speed! We must board now!"

"Go," Jeremiah ordered to his young family. "The time is now. We will be together soon one day!" He then turned to his wife, Karen, and said, "Trust me woman, I promise you that we will see each other again."

Karen jumped in his arms for a final embrace as the sailors leaped off the gangplank and took her by the hand. She took one final look towards Jeremiah, tears rushing from her eyes, as she turned to leave, scurrying the boys up the gangplank behind the sailors as the ship slowly left from the dock.

In a frantic rush, Andre and Jean reached Le Matin, which was already four feet from the dock. They had to jump and hold onto ropes as the ship was rowed away into the night and sailors grasped their arms to haul them aboard.

As the crew began to hoist their sails, the men from the tenders began to board the ships, hoisting three tenders each to the ship deck and leaving the remaining ones to float in the water back to shore. As they sailed away from danger, Jean couldn't help but feel a sense of dread as he heard the guards yelling in the distance as gunfire rang out towards them, a rehearsed act he was sure to provide an alibi so as not to be accused of duplicity. He prayed that Jeremiah would make it safely to his destination.

The powerful currents helped carry the ships and their passengers towards their uncertain future in the new land called Ayiti as the ships groaned and creaked with the effort of breaking free from their long months at the Savannah docks. The wood, weathered and worn, seemed to protest as the sails were hoisted and they set off on their journey south towards the inviting waters of the Caribbean.

"Au revoir, my friend," Jean whispered under his breath, hoping that one day they would meet again, the next time Jeremiah being a free man.

And as for Jeremiah's parting words - "Take care of my people" - Jean vowed to honor his request with every fiber of his being; he would ensure that these now free citizens of Ayiti would be settled and safe.

Jeremiah had been tirelessly preparing for this voyage, sending over sacks filled with provisions that were carefully hidden away on board. Cornmeal, rice, sugar, and dried vegetables filled enough space to sustain all of the passengers during the week-long journey ahead.

As they set sail, a sense of relief seemed to wash over the ship, lifting the weight of despair that had weighed down their spirits during their lifetime. And as they settled in for their first night on board, the passengers slept soundly, grateful for the hope of a new beginning.

The following morning, Jean noticed Jeremiah's wife, Karen, leading a group of passengers, young and old alike, in an impromptu lesson. With patience and grace, she taught them words and how to properly pronounce them.

Curiosity getting the better of him, Jean joined in on the class until Karen dismissed them for lunch.

"Are you a school teacher, Karen?" he asked.

Karen's eyes twinkled with pride as she replied, "Our masters never allowed us such luxuries. We do this in secret, passing down knowledge to each generation in hopes that one day we will be free."

"I am deeply sorry that Jeremiah could not join us on this journey," Jean expressed with a tinge of regret in his voice.

"My husband's true name is Cheikh Anta, a man of great importance to his people. I am named Ngozi," she continued. "But the masters gave him the Christian name of Jeremiah, and me, Karen. We were forced to use these names in front of the whites."

Jean listened intently as Ngozi shared more about her family and heritage. "My sons are named Abdu and Kwasi," she said proudly.

"I believe the name Ngozi means *'blessing'* in Igbo, does it not?" Jean remarked, much to Ngozi's surprise. Her eyes lit up like two candles just lit, thrilled to know that Jean was familiar with African names, and maybe African culture. "Who taught you these things?" she asked.

"An old friend named Toussaint, unfortunately, was taken from this earth by the French.

"Do you speak of the great Toussaint Louverture?" Ngozi asked eagerly.

"The one and only," responded Jean with a sense of reverence. "A hero for all of us in Ayiti."

Ngozi's admiration for Jean grew as they bonded over their shared knowledge of Toussaint. "My husband also holds him in high regard, along with Jean-Jacques Dessalines. He aspires to be like them."

"Please, tell me more about Cheikh Anta. I only had the pleasure of meeting him briefly, but I was immediately struck by his intelligence and strength," Jean requested.

Ngozi's voice quivered with emotion as she spoke of her husband. "He comes from a line of royalty - his great-great-great grandfather was Ezeoha, the powerful leader of the Nama people. But his legacy was nearly erased by the white masters who sought to strip us of our names, languages, culture, and history."

Jean listened intently, captivated by their story of resilience and determination despite being forcefully taken from their home during wars a hundred years ago. "And how did Ezeoha end up here?" he questioned.

"Like so many others, he was captured by a rival tribe during the African wars who sold him to the white slave traders. He never saw his family again as they were separated and sent to different parts of this land. But my husband's ultimate goal is to end this atrocity in America and reunite our family," Ngozi declared with fierce determination.

Jean couldn't bear to shatter her hopes with the reality that ending slavery in such a strong nation would be nearly impossible. Instead, he asked her to tell him more about her husband, the man named Cheikh Anta.

"My husband follows in the footsteps of Virginia slave rebel Gabriel, who cried out *'Death or Liberty'* before being hanged with 25 others several years ago. Gabriel was also inspired by the Ayisyen slave uprising in 1791, even though he ultimately failed."

Jean nodded, having heard of these events before.

"But there is another man named Charles Deslondes, a mulatto slave on a plantation in Louisiana, who is quietly recruiting followers for the cause. He too was moved by your revolution in Ayiti," Ngozi revealed.

"Do you know him personally?" Jean asked.

"No, only through stories. I've heard he is light-skinned but kind to black slaves, much like yourself," Ngozi said confidently, meeting Jean's gaze without fear.

Jean was struck by her strength and pride, qualities that white slave masters tried to eradicate from slaves through the generations. "I see no difference in a person's character based on their skin color or background," he declared.

Ngozi shifted the conversation, her voice tinged with curiosity. "Is this your first time in America, Mr. Jean?"

Jean's eyes sparkled as he shook his head. "No, I was here about 25 years ago, in 1779. In the very city of Savannah, or rather, on its outskirts."

Ngozi's eyebrows furrowed in confusion. "What brought you to Savannah?"

A proud smile graced Jean's lips as he replied, "I was fighting for your freedom during the American Revolution."

Ngozi's eyes widened in surprise. "You fought for our freedom? Well, not our freedom, Mr. Jean. The founding fathers may have said 'All men are created equal', but they had no intent to apply it to us who are treated no better than livestock. But you're...French, not American."

Jean chuckled at her reaction. "Yes, I was French. Now I am Ayisyen. At that time, I fought for the French army against the British. We were trying to liberate Savannah from them. I served under a great man, Charles Henri Hector, the Compte d'Estaing."

"That is quite the name," Ngozi remarked.

"He was also quite the man," Jean said with admiration. "He was honorable and just."

Ngozi couldn't help but ask, "Did he also own slaves?"

"In France, slavery was not permitted. Only in the colonies. And being an Admiral of ships, he did not own any. However, there was a brief period when he rescued a young slave boy named Henry from a British island and entrusted him to me for his upbringing."

Ngozi's eyes widened in surprise once more. "And where is this boy now?"

A fond smile appeared on Jean's face as he replied proudly, "He is now a general in the great army of Ayiti. General Henry Christophe, Supreme Commander of the Northern forces."

Ngozi couldn't contain her excitement at the thought of her sons potentially achieving such greatness. "I cannot believe that my sons could one day be these things. And what happened to your great Admiral?"

Jean's expression turned solemn as he revealed, "That is a different story altogether. During the revolution in France to overthrow the monarchy, he was asked to renounce his friend, Queen Marie Antoinette. He refused and they took his life by guillotine - chopped his head off," Jean recounted using a gesture with his finger to slice his neck.

Ngozi gasped, her hand flying to cover her mouth in shock. "My gosh!"

Jean couldn't help but let out a laugh at her reaction. "But before his execution, he famously declared 'When my head falls off, offer it to the British as they will pay a dear price for it!'"

Both Ngozi and Jean laughed together at the irony of his words, despite the tragic end that befell the great Admiral.

Jean and Ngozi engaged in daily sessions of conversation, a delightful exchange in which Jean imparted knowledge about the island of Ayiti. He spoke of its rich history, vibrant language, colorful culture, mystical voodoo practices, mouthwatering food, intricate government system, and powerful military force. Ngozi eagerly soaked up every word and incorporated them into her daily instructions to her fellow passengers.

Each day followed a similar routine - filled with brilliant sunshine and gentle breezes that cooled their skin as they sailed across the open waters. The sailors skillfully cast out fish lines, providing an abundance of fresh catches to satisfy everyone's appetites.

On the morning of the seventh day, there was a noticeable change in the air. As they approached the horizon, the scent of salt water took on a sharp and distinct aroma. Ngozi found Jean standing at the bow, gazing ahead toward their destination - the island of Hispaniola and the new country of Ayiti.

The passengers on deck could feel the excitement rippling through their fellow travelers as they made their way, eagerly awaiting their first glimpse of their new homeland. As the ships neared their destination, flocks of seagulls descended from the sky, eagerly anticipating their regular feeding from the crew.

With a sudden shift, the ships began their starboard tack, rounding the sharp Fort Picolet point and setting sail towards the bustling dock of Cap Français.

The passengers burst into joyful folkloric songs as Jean watched on, marveling at the sailors' expert maneuvers after nearly a year away from the sea as if it were yesterday's routine.

Finally, they reached their destination where crowds of curious townspeople had gathered to see the historic arrival, adding to the already electric atmosphere.

A young dock boy had frantically raced to the Bayard offices, shouting at the top of his lungs that the ships had finally arrived. Without a moment's hesitation, Marie sprinted to the docks, her heart pounding in anticipation as she caught a glimpse of Jean descending from the gangplank of the Laura. Behind him was a group of followers, along with Andre from the Le Matin, equally surrounded by a crowd.

Marie lunged towards Jean, her arms outstretched for the long-awaited embrace. It was like a scene from a romantic novel, but there was an underlying urgency and tension in the air. Meanwhile, Ngozi stood back patiently, waiting for her introduction and taking in the exchange between husband and wife.

Jean looked upon Marie and remembered the first sight of her, her skin glowing in the sunlight, her dark hair cascading down her back. Now, wrinkles etched the corners of her eyes and a few strands of gray hair adorned her temples, but to Jean, she was still the most beautiful woman he had ever laid eyes on. And, at 54, there was a wisdom in her gaze, a depth that only added to her allure, making her more distinguished and captivating than ever before.

As Jean and Marie finally parted, he turned to Ngozi and made sure she was still present before turning back to Marie. "Marie, may I introduce you to Ngozi, wife of the great Cheikh Anta - the man responsible for freeing our crew."

"It is an honor to meet you," Marie said in her basic English. "Welcome to Ayiti! And accept my gratitude for the rescue of our crews."

"The pleasure, and equal gratitude, is all mine," Ngozi replied with a respectful bow of her head.

"Ngozi, please make sure your people do not wander off. I need Marie's counsel for a moment," Jean instructed.

"Yes, Mr. Jean," Ngozi obeyed before turning to address her people with open arms, embracing those she had been away from during their week aboard Le Matin.

Andre arrived next to Jean with a triumphant grin on his face. "See Marie! We told you we would bring them all back!"

"You have done well, Andre. You are a man of your word indeed," Marie praised him with a beaming smile.

"But the woman...Ngozi. I promised her husband who rescued our crew- I mean the enslaved ones that..." Jean trailed off, struggling to find the right words.

"Enslaved?!" Marie exclaimed in shock. "What do you mean by enslaved?"

"It's a long story, but to put it simply, all of our black and mulatto crew were sold into slavery. Ngozi's husband freed them in exchange for us setting up our new Ayisyen citizens - his family and friends - here in Ayiti, their new country," Jean explained with a heavy heart and furrowed brow.

Without hesitation, Marie turned to her young dock boy assistant, no older than twelve, "Ale chache Rambart nan depo prensipal la" - *Go fetch Rambart from the main warehouse*, Marie ordered as the young boy sprinted off towards one of the buildings.

"How many are there?" Marie asked.

"Fifty in all," replied Andre, not wanting to be left out of the conversation.

Robart and the dock boy returned. When they did, Marie ordered the dock boy again, "Al chache Yolande lakay" - *Go fetch Yolande from home*. The boy quickly sprinted away.

Marie turned to Robart and instructed him, "Prepare the empty warehouse for these individuals to stay in. Make sure it is cleaned thoroughly so they can be comfortable. Also, send Grando to the hardware store to purchase 50 field cots, and Acefie to the general store for 50 sets of bed linens."

Robart quickly responded, "Yes, Madame," before hurrying off to carry out her instructions.

"Jean, Ngozi will stay with us at the main house," Marie commanded.

"She has two sons with her," Jean replied quickly.

"What are their names?" Marie inquired, her demeanor still authoritative.

"Abdu and Kwasi. Good boys. One is eight and the other is ten," Jean rattled off, proud of his memory for details.

"We have plenty of room at the house. It will be nice to have some spirited boys running around and making noise," Marie quipped with a smile, picturing the energy and chaos that would soon fill their home, as it was when their son Junior was Abdu and Kwasi's age.

Yolande arrived, her apron dusted with flour from the kitchen. She spotted Jean and exclaimed excitedly, "Monsieur Jean! You are back!"

"Yes, I am, Yolande. Happy to be so," Jean replied with a warm smile.

"Oui Madame?" Yolande turned to Marie, awaiting her orders.

"Prepare 50 meals immediately. Hot and ready by dinner, please. We have hungry people to feed. Get some extra hands to help cook for the next few days until they are settled in," Marie instructed efficiently.

"Oui Madame," Yolande nodded before scurrying off to begin preparations.

Ngozi returned with Abdu and Kwasi by her side, their eyes wide with wonder at the grand city before them. "My sons, meet Madame Marie. Madame Marie, this is Abdu and this is Kwasi," Ngozi introduced proudly.

Marie kneeled to meet the boys at eye level and smiled warmly as she hugged them both tightly. "Welcome to your new home Abdu and Kwasi."

They both looked up at her with big grins on their faces. "Ngozi, we have made provisions and food for your people. Jean and I invite you to be our guest in our home," Marie extended the invitation gracefully.

"I am so thankful Madame Marie. Thank you so very much. However, it is my place to stay with my people. Would you allow me to do so?" Ngozi asked humbly, her gratitude shining in her eyes.

"Of course, whatever you prefer. But do know that the invitation is available at any time," Marie reassured her warmly.

Ngozi's voice trembled with gratitude as she turned to Marie, her eyes brimming with tears of thanks. Her people, who had endured unimaginable suffering and cruelty, now kneeled in reverence, kissing the ground where they stood. Ngozi's gaze shifted back to Marie, her words dripping with emotion. "We will do anything to repay your kindness, Madame Marie. Anything."

"And you are no longer slaves," Jean declared to them all, his words echoing through the air like a battle cry. "You are now the free citizens of Ayiti by law."

With these words, a wave of relief and hope washed over Ngozi and her people as they let out a cheer, many crying with tears of joy and others once again kneeling in thanks. For so long they had yearned for freedom, and now it was finally within their grasp.

They would never forget the generosity and bravery of Monsieur Jean and Andre for bringing them to this land of promise and of Madame Marie for her kindness on arrival.

From that day on, Ayiti became known as a sanctuary for those seeking asylum and freedom from the shackles of slavery. The patriating of countless slaves from the United States had begun, forever changing the course of history.

The new arrivals were greeted with open arms by dock workers and common folk, welcoming them to their new country.

Ngozi, a woman with determination etched on her face, approached Marie and quietly said, "You know, this is only a temporary home for my children and me."

Marie's brow furrowed in confusion. "What do you mean, Ngozi?"

"My husband has stayed back in the United States to fight for what was promised in our constitution: *'All men are created equal.'* Unfortunately, that right is not yet afforded to us slaves."

Marie nodded solemnly, understanding Ngozi's words all too well. This may be a temporary sanctuary for Ngozi and her family, but their true home was back in the United States. "Of course. Your home here is for as long as you want it to be. But from here forward, your friendship will be forever, no matter where you are."

This would be the beginning of a lifelong bond between Ngozi and Marie. Ngozi smiled towards Marie, though it pained her to be away from her husband, Cheikh Anta.

She and Marie will watch her sons, Abdu and Kwasi, grow into fine young men, find employment with the Bayard companies, and know a friendship that would never waiver.

However, the sons would never see their father Cheikh Anta again. He had stayed behind and joined Charles Deslondes in Louisiana, about 40 miles North of New Orleans. The rebellion that followed became known as the German Coast Uprising of 1811, originating from the Andry plantation there.

In the end, one hundred rebels were executed, their heads severed and placed along the road to New Orleans as a warning to others. One southern planter remarked that *'they looked like crows sitting on long poles'.*

Cheikh Anta's name forever joined the ranks of other brave Africans who fought and died for the freedom of slaves in the United States, including the Stono Rebellion of 1739, The New York City Conspiracy of 1741, Gabriel's Conspiracy of 1800, Denmark Vesey's 1822 rebellion in Charleston South Carolina, and Nat Turner's Rebellion of 1831. They all lost their lives, but their sacrifices will never be forgotten.

Eight

HAIL TO THE EMPEROR

La Croix
September 1806

The whip slashed across the man's exposed flesh, sending jolts of agonizing pain throughout his entire body. A gathering of workers formed around the spectacle, their faces twisted into a mix of morbid curiosity and fear.

The crack of the whip echoed once again through the air, causing shivers to run down the spines of those watching. The punisher, well-versed in administering this brutal discipline, wielded the tool with expert precision as he had done dozens of times before.

General Jean-Jacques Dessalines sat astride his horse Galipot, overseeing the punishment with an aloof expression. It was just another day at Plantation Splendide in the town of La Croix southeast of Gonaïves, where any minor transgression was met with harsh retribution. This laborer's crime? Attempting to leave without permission to meet his fiancé in the nearby town of L'Estère.

With each lash, the man's cries pierced through the air, muffled only by the large branch shoved between his teeth to prevent him from biting off his tongue. Each strike elicited a visceral reaction from the onlookers, who couldn't help but imagine themselves in his position.

As the whip cracked against his back for the 24th time, the punished man let out a guttural cry. The punisher, a tall black muscular figure with a menacing glare, folded his whip and coolly walked away.

The overseer of the plantation, a captain in Dessalines' army, stepped forward and addressed the crowd with authority. "I have warned him and all of you of the consequences for breaking the law. It is on full display here," he bellowed. He then pointed to two men in the crowd and commanded, "Cut down this punished man and tend to his wounds. I expect him back to work by morning," he added sternly.

Dessalines congratulated Captain Estimé on his handling of the situation. "Well done, Captain. This will make your workers think twice before breaking our laws."

"Yes, mon general," replied the Captain dutifully. "However, despite our harsh punishments, some workers continue to defy these laws."

"Rules and laws are meant to be followed," Dessalines barked in response. "There is no room for flexibility when it comes to maintaining order."

As they untied the punished worker from his position on a tree limb, he collapsed to the ground, too weak and injured to stand. His heavily whipped back was bleeding and welts were forming on his skin. He rolled over onto his back, wincing in pain as dirt from the ground entered his wounds.

The two men who were tasked with caring for him gently lifted him and carried him away to wash his skin, while Dessalines watched with an unwavering gaze.

Captain Estimé hesitantly approached General Dessalines, his eyes darting nervously as he prepared to speak. "May I speak frankly, General?" he asked.

"Speak your mind, Captain," replied Dessalines in a deep, commanding voice.

"The workers, General. They are growing restless and do not believe in your labor requirements," the Captain blurted out as if he had been holding onto this concern for some time.

Dessalines raised an eyebrow in interest. "Is that so? Please, continue."

"The workers are claiming that these conditions are no different than slavery. They are forced to work on the very lands they were once enslaved on and have no say in where they live or work. They question if there is a difference between this and slavery, between us and their former masters."

The General let out a deep sigh. "We have an economy that must produce. How else are we to pay for the repairs of our ports, roads, and equipment for our army? Without revenues, how are we to survive?"

"The workers simply want to lead peaceful lives with their families on their plots of land. They long to farm their own food instead of being forced to work on these plantations," explained Estimé.

"I do not care what their desires may be. The law requires them to work and that is all that matters," said Dessalines with an edge of anger.

The General's voice boomed through the plantation, silencing all protests. His eyes bore into the Captain, daring him to challenge his authority. "I do not need to remind you," Dessalines exclaimed, "that maintaining order and discipline is in your best interest, as well as that of all of my chosen officers overseeing seized plantations."

The Captain's shoulders slumped in defeat as he stated, Qui Mon General," and promised to be more diligent knowing his livelihood depended on it.

"Good," he declared coldly. "I will see you at your next inspection."

As the sound of Galipo's hooves faded into the distance, the Captain knew he had narrowly escaped being replaced. But the weight of the General's expectations hung heavy on his shoulders, a constant reminder of the consequences if he failed to meet them.

This was the reign of Dessalines after the hard-won fight for freedom, a time of tumultuous change and shifting power. The land, once claimed by wealthy and cruel owners, now lay confiscated at the feet of the new leader. He dismissed or executed the former masters and placed his loyal military officers in charge, forcing ex-slaves to work the very fields they were once bound to with chains.

Dessalines ruled with an iron fist, punishing any who dared to defy his orders or oppose his policies. His obstinate leadership left both fear and admiration in its wake.

As he departed the plantation on Galipot, his mood was dark and brooding. But as he traveled towards Saint-Marc for a much-awaited rendezvous with his wife, Marie-Claire, his spirits lifted. The battalion arrived in Saint-Marc the following day, setting up camp just outside the bustling city.

Dessalines rode ahead with six of his guards to a quaint hotel within the city. There, he was reunited with his beloved wife and they savored a wonderful dinner together on their first night.

The next day, Marie-Claire and Dessalines lounged in the hotel courtyard that had been cleared of guests for them and heavily guarded with soldiers encircling the building.

She filled him in on the events of the time they spent apart, including updates on his seven children from seven different mothers. Marie-Claire had taken on the role of mother to all of them, living in their spacious home with nearly all of their mothers' blessings.

As they enjoyed a leisurely afternoon lunch, Marie-Claire eagerly shared her activities in providing healthcare and food to those in need. She spoke with pride about her kindness and compassion towards those who were struggling. Dessalines listened intently, finding solace in her acts of charity amid the strict discipline he had to enforce as the Governor General.

Eventually, Marie-Claire steered the conversation towards a more difficult topic - the growing displeasure among the people about his labor practices, which were being compared to slavery. The use of corporal punishment and whippings was also a hot topic on everyone's lips.

"It is a complex matter, my love," Dessalines sighed, as servants cleared his now empty plate. "The people are desperate for a way to rebuild and start anew after years of suffering under the slavery regime. But they must understand that we cannot simply gift them land and resources without a solid foundation. We need to establish a strong economy and infrastructure before we can truly claim our independence."

Marie-Claire bit her lip, her eyes filled with concern. "But they only know slavery, and now, they are forced into labor once again. And, making matters worse, on the same plantations with the same scarred memories of where they were once enslaved. This is causing many to lose hope and even join the rebellious factions against us."

Dessalines nodded in agreement. "We cannot ignore these complaints, nor can we let the rebellions continue to grow in strength. I have been considering, Marie-Claire, the idea of instituting reforms. We could offer land to those who complete a set term of labor, and we could incorporate taxation that is fair and beneficial for all. This way, the people would have something to work towards and an incentive to stay loyal to our cause."

"But how would you justify this new system to the people who have experienced such hardship?" Marie-Claire inquired, her concern for the well-being of the people palpable.

Dessalines knew this was a delicate matter, and he took a moment to gather his thoughts. "The people have been through so much, my love, and their trust in us may be faltering. But I believe that with time, and by demonstrating our commitment to their welfare, we can rebuild that trust while rebuilding our economy.

"We must also address the issue of corporal punishment. While I understand the need for discipline, we cannot continue to inflict such violence on these people by the whip. We must find a more humane way to enforce our laws and maintain order." Marie-Claire stated.

Dessalines shifted uncomfortably, trying to steer the conversation away from the tense topic. "It is not as simple as that," he said, avoiding Marie-Claire's intense gaze. "Our efforts are not solely focused on the plantations; we are making progress in other industries as well."

Marie-Claire pressed on, her voice filled with frustration. "But why can't our farm laborers find jobs in these other industries? Why can't they relocate to different regions?"

Dessalines bristled at her questioning and was quick to cast blame elsewhere. "It's a delicate situation, Marie-Claire. The United States is limiting trade and enticing our merchants to do business with our former colonizers, France, England, and Spain as opposed to our new country. President Jefferson hasn't even had the courtesy to respond to my letter of introduction and cooperation, forcing me to now court the British to once again form a working alliance."

His anger flared, his normally composed demeanor turning dark. "But we will show him," Dessalines declared, his tone defiant. "If the United States doesn't want to trade with Ayiti, we have thriving partnerships with other colonies - Cuba, Jamaica, and others in the Antilles, and the Eastern side of our island - who have been left behind by their European oppressors."

"But you must address the rampant cruelty of your soldiers towards the laborers on the plantations, Jean-Jacques."

His face hardened at her words. "Enough," he growled. "You will come with me tomorrow and witness for yourself that not all planters are disgruntled. I am making a routine inspection of the Tourneau plantation on the outskirts of Saint-Marc. You will accompany me." His voice brooked no argument.

Marie-Claire knew better than to push the issue further. She had learned when to hold her tongue to avoid further conflict with her husband. Now, she decided, was one of those times. The air between them was thick with tension as she nodded silently in response to his command.

The day was starting beautifully, and the couple decided to take a horseback ride instead of traveling in a carriage. After enjoying a delicious breakfast, their horses were brought to the entrance of the hotel.

Dessalines' prized warhorse, Galipot, looked magnificent with his well-groomed coat and eager stance. In all his years of battle, Dessalines had never been injured, which he credited to the intelligence and agility of Galipot.

It took them two hours to reach the Tourneau plantation, but the scenic countryside and cool mountain breeze made for a pleasant journey. Accompanying them were a demi-brigade of well-equipped soldiers, 125 of them, handpicked from the army.

As they arrived at the plantation, workers emerged from the fields to cheer on their military hero and leader. Little did Marie-Claire or even Dessalines know that these cheers were forced under threat of punishment by the Captain in charge. "You will not embarrass me in front of the General!" he had warned, knowing all too well the harsh penalties for disobedience.

Marie-Claire couldn't help but be in awe of the efficient and orderly management of the plantation. The captain, a charming and hospitable host, had his staff expertly butcher and roast a goat to perfection for a lavish early afternoon meal for Marie-Claire and the officers of Dessalines' brigade before their departure.

As they set off towards Saint Marc, the sun began its descent towards the horizon, casting a warm glow over the surrounding fields. The group knew they had to reach the city before nightfall, so they made haste along the winding roads, passing by quaint villages and colorful markets along the way.

The air was filled with the sounds of chirping birds and distant laughter, making it feel like a peaceful journey despite their destination being surrounded by a tumultuous population.

Diédoné Lespwa's eyes bore into Ricardo Desbardes with a seething mix of suspicion and hatred. What was it about this Frenchman that set him on edge? Was it his deceptive nature, typical of a spy, or was it something else? The answer eluded Diédoné, but he knew one thing for sure - he would never trust this man.

"They should reach this point by late afternoon," Desbardes stated, tracing a makeshift map in the dirt with a sharp stick. "This is where you should attack."

"And how do you know this?" Diédoné demanded, his voice laced with incredulity. "Where do you get your information?"

"The where and the how are none of your concern, my friend," Desbardes quipped casually. "You just worry about taking down Dessalines."

"I am not your friend," Diédoné spat venomously. "And I never will be. The only reason we are here together is because we both share a common enemy - Dessalines. Apart from that, I would sooner slit your throat than work alongside you."

Desbardes shrugged off Diédoné's hostility with indifference. "I couldn't care less about your opinion of me. You have a job to do - to avenge your leader Lamour Desrances. And I represent France, so you must now be loyal to me."

"I, and my fellow Maroons, have no loyalty to France," Diédoné growled menacingly. "We would gladly slit the throats of all Frenchmen. But you are right - my hatred for Dessalines outweighs any other feelings right now. He brutally murdered Lamour Desrances, and for that, he will pay with his life." With grim determination in his voice, Diédoné vowed to exact revenge for his fallen leader at any cost.

As Dessalines' demi-brigade rode through the countryside, a trail of dust followed in their wake. They slowed down to a walk for a few miles, giving their horses a chance to cool off.

The afternoon was pleasant, with a refreshing breeze from the nearby ocean as they neared Saint-Marc. "So, what did you think of your visit, my dear?" Dessalines asked his wife.

"I must confess, I was taken aback," Marie-Claire replied. "Everything seemed to be in perfect order, almost too good to be true compared to what I've been hearing."

"Well, you have to admit, you were led astray by those who take pleasure in discrediting our government, and my leadership of it," Dessalines responded with a knowing look.

"Alright, perhaps I overreacted yesterday. People made it seem like discontent was widespread. But now it seems that not all plantations are run in such a manner."

Marie-Claire's blood ran cold as the whistling of arrows pierced the air and struck down soldiers all around her. She watched in horror as Dessalines barked orders, his voice drowned out by the sounds of war.

With a steely determination, she followed his command and took refuge with a group of guards, surrounded on three sides for protection.

Dessalines surveyed the chaos unfolding before him. He quickly dispatched his troops to pursue the enemy, but they were soon met with a barrage of gunfire from both sides of the road. The small contingent stood their ground, valiantly fighting against overwhelming odds.

The battle was intense as Galipot fell to the ground after being shot in the leg. Without hesitation, Dessalines unsheathed his sword and fought alongside his men, knowing that he was the main target of this savage attack.

As more enemies charged towards them, Marie-Claire appeared on horseback with an extra steed and urged Dessalines to flee with her. However, he refused to abandon his men.

"You are no longer just a soldier, but a leader of this country. You must survive and guide your people," she reasoned.

Dessalines realized the truth in her words and mounted the spare horse, riding to safety as other soldiers chased down the retreating enemy. The attack was over within minutes, with maroons lying dead or running away.

But the damage had been done. Dessalines and Marie-Claire returned to find many of their soldiers dead, and the remainder killing wounded attackers who lay on the ground. There was no need for interrogation; Dessalines already knew these were maroon soldiers under the command of Diédoné Lespwa, following their dead leader Desrances.

"You narrowly escaped assassination here, Jean-Jacques," Marie-Claire said with concern.

"Yes, I see that now. It was wise of you to come back for me."

Dessalines made his way to Galipot's side, lying on the ground in pain. The horse tried to rise when it saw its master approaching but could not, pathetically trying again and again in confusion and pain.

Dessalines knelt next to the horse and coaxed it down gently as Galipot obeyed his commands. He stroked the animal's mane as moisture developed in his eyes, wiping it away to avoid Marie-Claire getting a glimpse of his vulnerability.

Marie-Claire had never seen her husband emotional before. He was kneeling at the horse's side and she put her arm around his massive head and brought it to her waist as they both looked down at the animal.

"Since you are a nurse, what should we do?" Dessalines asked.

"Say goodbye, my love, and walk away. I will take care of him."

Dessalines looked into her eyes and knew what needed to be done. He got up and they embraced before he knelt one last time to bid farewell to Galipot.

As he walked away to speak with his officers, Marie-Claire wasted no time in pulling out her musket from her saddlebag and putting an end to the loyal beast's suffering with a single shot that echoed through the countryside. Dessalines closed his eyes as he continued to walk away.

General Henry Christophe gracefully dismounted from his horse and handed the reins to an awaiting lieutenant, whose eyes widened in respect as he took them. The General's gaze rose to the towering cross on the building of the Our Lady of the Assumption Cathedral, its presence felt even from a distance in the heart of Cap Français.

He paused to take in the magnificent structure, still standing proud since the 17th century. It had weathered countless storms - hurricanes, earthquakes, and war - even surviving the fires that he had ordered when he torched the city two years ago.

As he stood in front of the cathedral, memories flooded back to him. This square was where the proclamation of liberation for slaves had been made in August of 1793. And it was here in this same church that he and Marie-Louise had exchanged their wedding vows before God.

A lump formed in his throat as he looked at his captains flanking him on either side, their finest parade uniforms adding to their imposing presence. They all knelt and made the sign of the cross, as Toussaint would have required, before rising and climbing the steps.

Toussaint, Henry thought bitterly. The mere mention of his name was now forbidden in Ayiti by order of Governor General Jean-Jacques Dessalines. But that was about to change. Not the ban on speaking about Toussaint, but rather something equally monumental.

The title of Governor General was about to be changed to that of Emperor. Dessalines had twisted the arms of every last General for them to declare him ruler over Ayiti as an Imperial Lord. The thought made Henry scoff inwardly - how could such a man be fit for such a regal title?

But despite his grievance with Dessalines and his actions, there was nothing Henry could do to change it. He felt a twinge of guilt for not being able to prevent this turn of events - a man like Toussaint Louverture, who had sacrificed so much for the nation, was now wiped from history by one man's power-hungry ambition.

And yet, amidst all of this turmoil, something else weighed heavily on Henry's heart. The recent killing of Bayon de Libertad - a kind and fair man who had treated his slaves with respect and was the first to free them at the Breda plantation, before the official decree, at Toussaint's behest. He had also played a crucial role in ensuring the safety of returning planters, only to pay with his own life in the end.

These thoughts consumed Henry as he made his way into the cathedral with a heavy heart. Despite his disagreements with Dessalines and his growing paranoia, he couldn't deny that the Governor General was a haunted man - haunted by the innocent lives he had taken in the name of power.

Their footsteps echoed loudly as they walked into the grand cathedral, the high ceilings making their presence even more pronounced. Waiting for them at the front of the church was the Archbishop, flanked by his two senior priests from the Catholic diocese.

Led by Henry, the group made their way down the long aisle toward the ornate altar adorned with symbols of wealth. As they approached the priests, they all stopped and kneeled in reverence.

The Archbishop of Ayiti, Jean-Baptiste-Joseph Brelle, extended his hand to show off his prominent ring that symbolized his rank within the Catholic religion. He was a white French priest who had spent many years in the colony and had witnessed its many changes. As the chosen representative of the Roman Catholic Church in Ayiti, Brelle held great power over a large congregation but still followed directives from the Vatican.

After kissing the Archbishop's ring, Henry and his captains rose to their feet. The Archbishop greeted them with a stern smile and invited them to sit at a long mahogany table surrounded by twenty chairs in a nearby room.

Without hesitation, Brelle took his place at the head of the table and gestured for Henry to sit on his right side. The two priests quickly took their seats on Brelle's left, while Henry motioned for his captains to join him at the table as well.

Henry began, "It is the wish of our Governor General, Jean-Jacques Dessalines, that you preside over his grand coronation as Emperor of Ayiti," Henry's words rang out with an air of formality and authority.

"All except for General Christophe are to leave this room immediately," the Archbishop declared with a tone that brooked no argument. The captains hesitated, but an affirmative nod from Henry confirmed the order and they all filed out of the room.

The Archbishop turned his piercing gaze to Henry, "Has the Governor gone mad? How can he claim to be a monarch without any royal blood running through his veins?"

"His ascension has been sanctioned by the Generals of our Revolutionary Army, your grace," Henry replied calmly.

"Nonsense. I do not doubt that they were coerced by the Governor into making such a proclamation," the Archbishop retorted dismissively.

"Nevertheless, he will become Emperor and it is his request, or rather, his command, that you perform the coronation ceremony," Henry stated firmly.

"I do not take commands from government leaders and refuse to be a part of this farce!" The Archbishop's voice rose with indignation.

"In that case, one of your regional Bishops will perform the ceremony on your behalf. But make no mistake, your grace, if you choose to defy our Emperor's wishes, you and any other Bishops who refuse will be immediately deported back to France," Henry spoke with unwavering determination.

The Archbishop's face paled with anger. "How dare he!"

"Our new sovereign's word is now law. May I remind you that life in Ayiti has been quite comfortable for you thus far? Is returning to the cold, harsh weather of France worth opposing our Emperor?" Henry's calm demeanor never wavered as he delivered his ultimatum.

"When does this atrocity take place?" The Archbishop's voice shook with suppressed rage.

"The Emperor has set the date for Saturday, September 22nd. Can we count on your cooperation, your grace?" Henry asked in a perfectly polite tone.

"It shall be done," the Archbishop conceded defeat with a deep sigh.

Without waiting for any further words from the Archbishop, Henry rose from his seat and made his exit. "Thank you for your cooperation, most reverend," he declared as he left the room. The tension in the air was palpable, and both men knew that this was only the beginning of what would surely be a tumultuous reign for Ayiti's new Emperor.

As the carriage carrying the Governor General, Jean-Jacques Dessalines approached the cathedral, a dozen fanfare trumpets began to blare. Fifty horsemen rode in front of and behind the carriage, creating a grand entrance.

The streets were packed with citizens eagerly awaiting the historic event. Street vendors sold delicious foods like fried plantains and yucca, meats of goat, pork, and fish. They also offered souvenirs including little carved statues of the new Emperor and Empress that would soon be crowned.

At the final block, soldiers in their finest dress uniforms lined the streets, holding their swords high as the carriage passed by and stopped at the steps of the magnificently decorated Our Lady of Assumption Cathedral.

General Henry Christophe opened the door for Dessalines, who stepped out regally in a never-before-seen uniform adorned with gilded epaulets, medals, and fine cloth that shone in the light. His wife, Marie-Claire followed, dressed in a designer gown made by Dessalines' niece and seamstress to the first flag of Ayiti, Catherine Flon.

Amidst the VIP guests filling up every seat in the cathedral, two bishops stood at the front doors to begin the procession down the

Jean-Jacques Dessalines arrives with Marie-Claire Heureuse Félicité Bonheur in regal style to the Our Lady of Assumption Cathedral in Cap Français as Henry Christophe awaits to receive them. He will arrive as Governor General and will depart the church as Emperor.

main center aisle. The sweet smell of incense filled the church as they swung their thuribles suspended by chains while the choir sang hymns. Following them, many generals from the Revolutionary Army took their seats in the first two rows.

Despite any reservations he may have had, Archbishop Joseph Brelle presided over a magnificent ceremony that made history with the first monarchs of the Atlantic community.

As the ceremony unfolded, the cathedral was filled with a mix of emotions. Some in the congregation were proud and hopeful, seeing the coronation as a triumph of Ayiti's independence and a symbol of the nation's resilience. Others were filled with a sense of unease and even despair, worrying about the repercussions that the rise of a monarch would bring.

As the coronation ceremony reached its climax, Archbishop Brelle placed the crown upon Dessalines' head. The sight of the newly crowned monarch triggered a wave of conflicting emotions among the congregation. Some cheered with joy, others whispered in hushed tones, while still more remained stoic.

In the seat next to Dessalines, Marie-Claire held her breath, her gaze fixed on her husband's face. She had advised against this move but could see the weight of his decisions etched into every line of his features. She knew that this moment was not just about him as an individual but about the future of their nation and the people who looked to him for leadership.

As the ceremony drew to a close, the sound of applause reverberated throughout the cathedral. Despite the mixed feelings in the room, there was no denying that this was a monumental moment in Ayiti's history.

After the ceremony, the newly crowned Emperor addressed the crowd outside the cathedral. He spoke of his dreams for a united Ayiti, free from the shackles of colonialism and oppression as he recounted the hardships and sacrifices that had paved the way for this moment.

"We have fought long and hard for this freedom, and we must not let it slip through our fingers," he declared. "We are a nation of many cultures and backgrounds, but today we stand united as one people, bound by a shared vision of a better future."

His words resonated with the crowd, who listened intently as he outlined his plans for the new Ayiti. He spoke of a society built on the principles of equality, justice, and prosperity, where every citizen would have the opportunity to thrive, even though it was quite contrary to the current day's realities.

As he finished his speech, there was a chorus of cheers from the crowd. Many embraced each other, tears streaming down their faces. Some even fell to their knees, overcome with gratitude and hope for what the future might hold, while others remained terrified.

The sound of horse hooves echoed as Emperor Jean-Jacques Dessalines' Demi Brigade made their way into Plantation D'esprit, located east of Jacmel. Dessalines was familiar with this plantation; it was one of the places he suspected Alexandre Pétion had sought refuge nearly five years ago in the aftermath of his escape from Jacmel during the War of Knives.

The previous owners had been executed by Dessalines himself and now the plantation was occupied by a mulatto family who claimed to be managing the property on behalf of the owners, the Belgiers family, who resided in France. As the horses thundered down the plantation road, a cloud of dust rose, causing fear and panic among the inhabitants and workers.

Emperor Dessalines had begun to seize plantations in the name of land reforms mostly directed towards the Southern region. Any owner who could not substantially confirm ownership of the land would be subject to immediate removal and the plantation would revert to military administration.

Dessalines had stalled his plans in respect for the Southern regional mulatto General, Nicolas Geffrard, but when he had suspiciously died on the last day of May, he decided that the timing was now at hand to begin the enforcement.

These plantations were almost all run by mulattos of the south, whom he had detested since they had tried to become an autonomous colony under General Andre Rigaud during his failed and brutal Civil War of Knives.

As the horses barreled down the plantation drive, workers scrambled out of the way as the contingent approached. The troops stormed towards the grand plantation home, their horses trampling over any signs of life in their path. The flag of the Emperor's Demi Brigade flapped fiercely in the wind, a symbol of their power, arrogance, and authority. As the Emperor stepped off his horse, his gaze fell upon a man who appeared to be in charge, approaching from the stables to greet them.

"Bon après-midi," the mulatto man stated to Dessalines, his voice trembling with fear. "It is an honor to have a visit from the great Emperor of Ayiti," he said as he awkwardly bowed, sweat trickling down his forehead.

"Are you in charge here?" Dessalines barked, his eyes blazing with fury.

"I am. My name is Louis LaPorte. I am the manager. I reside here with my family," he replied, trembling under Dessalines' intense scrutiny.

A beautiful young woman with smooth skin of café au lait and a small child at her side, no more than five years old and barefoot, emerged from the doorway. She held an infant in her arms, her face drained of color and filled with fear.

"Under whose authority?" Dessalines roared, causing LaPorte to stumble backward in fear.

"By the request and approval of the Belgiers of France, Your Excellency," LaPorte stammered.

"Do you have a document proving this?"

"Yes...yes. I have a contract in my office, of course notarized. May I retrieve it?"

"That will not be necessary. You stated that the owners reside in France and I assume they are French citizens. They have no ownership rights in Ayiti to be able to contract as to this property's disposition. It is hereby confiscated," Dessalines declared, his voice booming with finality.

"But your excellency. This is also my family's home. My livelihood. How we feed ourselves. The workers depend on my management for their livelihood as well. You cannot just have us abandon that!" LaPorte pleaded, desperation creeping into his voice.

"This plantation is hereby confiscated as the property of the government of Ayiti. I will grace you with 3 days to leave the premises," Dessalines declared, unmoved by LaPorte's pleas. "Captain Bouchard will be the new manager, so you need not worry for your workers."

"This is an outrage!" LaPorte yelled, his voice rising in anger and defiance as soldiers menacingly drew their swords.

"Mind your tongue. The decision is made and you have my order to leave," Dessalines said coldly, mounting his horse and leading his men down the plantation road, leaving behind a contingent of 20 soldiers with Captain Bouchard to ensure obedience, and a cloud of dust in their wake.

The property confiscations continued through September of 1805 until Dessalines was satisfied that the task was complete. He had personally remained in the South through July and returned in October for a final review with his Demi-Brigade. They arrived at the Southern Military Headquarters in Jacmel, where Dessalines entered to meet with the new Commander, General Bouchard.

"Emperor Dessalines," General Bouchard greeted him at the entrance. "We were informed of your arrival. Welcome to Jacmel."

"I hope all lands in the Southern region have been properly surveyed and evaluated for ownership," Dessalines asked sternly.

"Yes, your majesty," replied Bouchard. "We have seized 332 properties and put them under government control with new management. The other 647 properties appear to have legitimate Ayisien owners with proper documentation. I must warn you, Your

Majesty, there are already talks of rebellions arising. This will not sit well with the mulattos."

"Good. If the people of the South do not revolt after what I have done, they are cowards and not true men. I did not target mulattos specifically. I targeted those who had no legal right to properties and others who continue to oppose my rule in the south," Dessalines responded with anger.

"Of which, almost all of them happen to be mulattos," Bouchard added cautiously.

NINE

THE END OF DESSALINES

Morne Baptiste
September 1806

The crisp mountain air enveloped the three mulatto men as they climbed the path to the camp of Diédoné Lespwa, high in the mountains overlooking Saint-Marc. The mountain chain of Matheux, dominated by the maroon communities, was located between the Artibonite Plain and the Cul-de-Sac Plain. The highest point is the summit of Morne Baptiste which rises to 1,575 meters (5,200 ft.)

The Morne Baptiste peak towered over them, with its summit disappearing into the clouds above. The men knew that Diédoné opposed Dessalines and they sought to align with him and the maroons to plan his demise. It was the fall of 1806.

The men made their way through the winding paths of the camp, escorted by four of Diédoné's fierce-looking men. Finally, they arrived at what appeared to be a village square, surrounded by small structures made of rock and mud. Thatch roofs provided shelter from the elements.

From one of the huts emerged a wirey and imposing figure, dressed only in rough short trousers despite the chilly October weather. "We are not accustomed to seeing mulattos venture this high up in the mountains," Diédoné spoke to the men. "I understand from your messages that you seek an accord to rid this land of Dessalines."

"Yes," answered the leader of the mulattos. "He has brought nothing but turmoil and misery to the south. Our leader, Andre Rigaud, once fought against him alongside your leader Lamour Desrances. Dessalines murdered him. We seek to align with you."

"Sit," Diédoné commanded, gesturing towards a straw mat on the ground near a fire that was boiling coffee. "Drink," he offered as women approached with metal goblets filled with coffee and rum, their smiles warm and welcoming.

Diédonés's eyes narrowed as he gestured to one of his men, who immediately brought forward a bound and gagged Frenchman. The man was Ricardo Desbardes, the notorious spy working for the French. The men forced him to kneel before Diédonés.

"This man," Diédonés began, his voice dripping with disgust, "made many promises and assurances to us. None of which have come true." He listed off the broken promises with a cold and calculating tone. Then, with a quick motion of his hand, Diédonés's man removed the gag from Desbardes's mouth.

"What do you have to say for yourself, my French spy?" Diédonés asked, his voice heavy with menace.

"It has been more difficult than I had imagined," Desbardes replied, his words strained.

"Difficult? The last time we trusted you, sixteen of my men lost their lives in an ambush thanks to your faulty information," Diédonés spat. "And let's not forget the white massacre that followed your enticement to the planters and the remaining soldiers of France to join you."

"I gave you and them the best information I had at the time," Desbardes pleaded.

"But it wasn't good enough," Diédonés growled. Without hesitation, he rose from his seat and grabbed a machete from the ground beside him. With years of experience as a cane cutter, he swung the blade down in one swift motion, severing Desbardes's head from his body.

As blood splattered across the square, Diédonés gave a cold order to his men: "Feed the traitor's remains to the wild boars."

They dragged away Desbardes's lifeless body while Diédonés stood expressionless. He then turned to the three mulattos and declared, "This is how I handle those who break their promises."

The mulattos exchanged glances before addressing Diédonés, "We will not disappoint as we will work alongside you, not from the shadows."

With a finality in his tone, Diédonés responded, "Then let us plan the downfall of our common enemy."

By October of 1806, the two generals, Henry Christophe and Alexandre Pétion, were exhausted from the constant turmoil caused by the Emperor. Every week brought news of more discontent, strife, and injustices, as well as rumors of insurrection. The air was heavy with tension and uncertainty.

Despite their clear differences in ideology, Henry and Pétion knew they needed to address the pressing matters that had engulfed their new country. Henry once again turned to his adopted brother, Jean-Baptiste Bayard Junior, for help in arranging a meeting with Pétion and himself, and later to meet with Dessalines in attendance. After negotiations, the date was set for October 17th at Pont Rouge in Larnage on the northern end of Port Républicain.

For Dessalines, this location was an easy journey as he would be traveling north from Jacmel on the way to Leogane before heading east to Port Républicain. It was also convenient for Pétion who lived on Rue l'Enterrement in the city. Junior would be traveling from Jérémie and Henry from Cap Français.

As Dessalines rode towards Larnage on a cool Friday afternoon, he couldn't help but feel a sense of unease. While he was eager to return to Marie-Claire and their home at Marchand in L'Artibonite, the meeting ahead filled him with apprehension. He had sent his Demi Brigade ahead towards Marchand to assure the road was safe for passage while he attended the meeting, but he couldn't shake off the nagging feeling that something was not right.

Pétion arrived with minimal security, while Henry came with a noticeable presence. Dessalines, on the other hand, only brought a small security detail headed by his trusted mulatto colonel, Charlotin Marcadieu. Despite the tense atmosphere, Dessalines didn't waste any time getting to the point.

"I want this meeting to be brief," he stated firmly, "I need to be back on the road by four to meet my brigade in Sibert by nightfall."

Henry nodded in understanding, "Yes, Your Excellency," while Pétion remained silent, refusing to acknowledge Dessalines as a monarch, this being the first awkward meeting since his coronation.

"First things first," Dessalines began, addressing Henry directly. "My Generals appear to be dying of suspicious circumstances, I believe being poisoned. General François Capois La Mort was assassinated near Limonade last week, however, ambushed with no poisoning involved. And many are saying you were responsible."

Henry's face contorted in anger. "Why would I do such a thing?" he retorted.

Dessalines' tone hardened. "I'm not sure," he replied, his suspicion growing. "But your denial sounds like an admission."

Faced with the accusation and unable to provide a convincing denial, Henry fell silent. In reality, he had ordered Capois' death out of jealousy and insecurity but had no part in any of the other general's demise. But now, confronted by Dessalines, he was forced to confront the truth and bear the weight of his actions.

Pétion's voice cut through the tense atmosphere like a knife, his words sharp and confident, and saving Christophe from further prosecution. "You and Christophe can handle this interrogation at another time. You wanted this meeting to be brief, and so it shall."

Dessalines' glare shifted from Christophe to Pétion, then encompassed the entire room of those present. "Before we begin, clear the room. We will speak in private as leaders should."

Without hesitation, everyone obeyed his order. Junior anxiously looked to Pétion for guidance, receiving an affirmative nod before being dismissed, confused by the accusations leveled at Henry concerning the assassination of a fellow General.

"Pétion, Christophe," Dessalines addressed them sharply. "You called for this meeting. What is on your mind?"

It was clear that Henry was rattled by the accusations, a fact not lost on Pétion. He couldn't say if there was any truth to them, but in the treacherous game of political power, anything was possible and no one could be trusted. "General Christophe and I have grave concerns."

"Speak your mind, Pétion," Dessalines commanded.

"The state of our country is chaotic," Pétion began, his voice rising with passion. "You have marched against our mulatto brothers in the south, causing further division among our people. Your black Maroon brethren view you with suspicion and disdain. Your bloody massacre of the whites has led us to be seen as barbarians by other nations, causing our trade to suffer, and your generals are being assassinated one by one."

Dessalines took a deep breath before responding, his eyes darkening with anger.

Jean-Baptiste Bayard stepped into the Grand Hotel in downtown Port Républicain. He had just finished a meeting at the docks with two of his ship captains and was eagerly anticipating a relaxing evening with his wife, Marie.

A warm bath, a delicious dinner, wine, indulgent desserts, and perhaps some intimate time together. As he made his way up the stairs, Louis, the front desk manager, called out to him. "Monsieur Bayard, there is a note from Madame Bayard here for you."

Jean-Baptiste turned and went back down a few steps to retrieve the note. He opened it and read the message.

Jean,

Something terrible is about to happen. I have received word that there will be an assassination attempt on the Emperor this afternoon at Pont Rouge at Larnage. He is attending a meeting with Alexandre and Henry that our son Junior organized. I fear for their safety and am riding to warn them. Please meet me there – #16, Rue 87.

With all my love,
Marie

"When did she leave this damn note?" he demanded, his voice dripping with urgency.

"A mere half hour ago, Monsieur Bayard," the innkeeper replied, fear etched on his face.

Jean wasted no time and bolted towards the livery stable, his heart racing with worry for Marie's safety. He rented the fastest horse available, knowing that every minute counted in finding her.

He whipped the beast into a gallop, disregarding any rules about riding speed within city limits. The streets of Port-Republicain blurred as he flew past, his mind racing with thoughts of what danger could happen to Marie. With each passing second, his anxiety grew until it was nearly suffocating him. Only twenty minutes to Larnage at this speed. Twenty minutes to find her before it was too late.

Dessalines' voice shook with anger as he spoke. "What do you mean that I am not ruling in the best interests of my country and its citizens?"

Henry's calm demeanor contrasted sharply with Dessalines' fury. "The land reforms are causing a divide between the government and the people we are meant to serve. Let us not forget that the majority of our population was once enslaved, nearly half a million. The rest -

Gens de Couleur, Afranchi, and white Europeans who were not slaves - make up less than 100,000 citizens."

Dessalines scoffed at Henry's words. "So what? These former slaves need direction, guidance, and strong leadership. And I am their emperor!"

"But at what cost?" Henry countered. "You force them to work on plantations where they were once subjugated. They are still subjected to brutal discipline through whippings. What real difference have you made for them?"

"Our empire needs exports," Dessalines retorted fiercely. "We must defend ourselves from foreign aggression!"

"You speak of defending against aggression, yet it was you who invaded the Spanish side of our island without provocation," Henry pointed out. "You attacked first, not them."

"This island must be unified as one for the benefit of all!" Dessalines shouted.

"The French still hold possession of that side of the island," Henry clarified. "We have no claims there. But more importantly, you attempted to seize it before consolidating our strengths here. Your actions were so rash that you couldn't even finish the march and had to retreat, fearing rebellion within your own empire."

Dessalines' face turned red with rage, and Henry knew that their relationship had reached a point of no return. Would this despot kill him after this meeting or throw him into prison?

Pétion's voice trembled with barely contained anger as he interrupted Dessalines. "You forced your army to commit unspeakable atrocities during the retreat," he accused.

Dessalines turned to face him, his eyes blazing with fury. "Do not dare to challenge my authority," he growled.

"It is not a challenge, Dessalines, but counsel," Pétion shot back calmly.

"I am the Emperor and you will address me as such," Dessalines snarled.

"This is part of the problem. Many do not recognize you as their Emperor," retorted Pétion, his voice rising in defiance.

"The Generals of the revolution have voted that I am to be monarch of this land, Pétion. Do not forget that," Dessalines reminded him coldly.

"These generals fear you. They acquiesce to your every wish. But here stand two generals who fought by your side, Christophe and I, who have come to give you real counsel. Things you need to hear, not what you want to hear," Pétion reasoned with frustration.

"We have accomplished great things in a short period, Pétion. We have built fortresses, expanded trade, and revitalized the plantation system," Dessalines countered confidently.

"Yes, but at what cost? You have left destruction in your wake in the southern peninsula, where tensions run high against our government. You slaughtered innocent whites and sparked outrage from other nations towards our country. And now you crown yourself as royalty!" Pétion exclaimed, his voice trembling with emotion.

"Do you not see what I am trying to accomplish?" asked Dessalines, his defenses starting to crumble under Pétion's accusations.

"You have taken on the title of Emperor, imitating our enemy Napoleon Bonaparte. And you seek to unify the island just as Toussaint Louverture had done before he was betrayed and killed. Why do you follow in the footsteps of men you claim to despise?" Pétion challenged, his voice ringing with righteous indignation.

Dessalines' face twisted in anger as he struggled to contain his temper.

Marie arrived at the meeting point on Rue 87, her horse galloping furiously as she approached Jean Junior and a group of men. Without hesitation, Junior helped her dismount, but she was out of breath and wasted no time in delivering her urgent message.

"Junior, I've received word that there is an imminent attempt on the Emperor's life!" The other men gathered around them grew visibly alarmed, unable to hear their conversation.

Charlotin Marcadieu, commander of Dessalines' guards, approached them with concern etched on his face. "What's going on?" he demanded.

"I have reliable information that assassins are on their way to kill the Emperor," Marie blurted out urgently.

Charlotin quickly scanned their surroundings, but everything seemed normal. He turned back to the group of armed men, all highly trained and capable. As Marie and Junior headed inside the building, they could hear Dessalines engaged in a heated argument with Pétion and Henry.

"What is this intrusion?" barked Dessalines angrily. "I explicitly ordered this meeting to be private! Why are you here?"

"We're here because assassins are coming for you!" Marie exclaimed without hesitation.

"How do you know this, Madame?" Dessalines thundered as both Pétion and Henry closed in on Marie.

Suddenly, gunfire erupted outside, bullets whizzing past them in rapid succession. Pétion and Henry quickly drew their weapons as Dessalines rushed to the window, taking in the chaos outside where four men lay dead on the ground.

"Do you see the attackers, Charlotin?" Dessalines yelled through the window, already aiming at their enemies.

"Not yet, but we're under attack from multiple directions. Our reinforcements should arrive soon. Be ready to move," Charlotin replied urgently.

A dozen horsemen soon arrived to secure the Emperor's safety, braving a barrage of bullets as they rode towards him. Dessalines quickly mounted a horse and they galloped down the street. However, halfway down the block, they were met with a blockade of at least two dozen armed assailants who hailed on them a barrage of gunfire, dropping several soldiers, and forcing them to retreat where they had come.

A chaotic scene where the soldiers guarding Emperor Jean-Jacques Dessalines are overpowered by maroons and mulatto insurgents as many lay dead or injured in the street outside of the building they were meeting at.

Pétion and Henry returned fire from inside the building, providing cover for Dessalines and his soldiers as another group of attackers closed in from the opposite side of the street. "Take cover, Emperor!" Charlotin shouted above the chaos, as another round of bullets rained down on them.

As Dessalines urgently dismounted from his horse, Charlotin's sharp eyes caught a group of Maroons charging towards them. One of the men raised his rifle towards the Emperor and Charlotin immediately sprang into action, using his own body as a shield to protect Dessalines.

However, both Charlotin and Dessalines were both struck by a barrage of bullets intended for the Emperor and fell to their knees, blood gushing from both. Still determined to defend his leader, Charlotin managed to draw his two side pistols, taking down two assailants before falling to the ground next to Dessalines, gasping for air to fill his failing lungs.

The scene descended into chaos as the rest of Dessalines' guard was mercilessly slaughtered. Shocked and confused, Dessalines watched as his loyal colonel lay dead beside him, a mulatto who had sacrificed everything, including now his very own life for him. The irony did not escape the Emperor - he had spent years resenting and mistreating the mulattos, yet here was one who had given his life for him.

As the Emperor's lifeblood spilled onto the ground, he couldn't help but think about all that he had endured during his rise to power - surviving slavery, a bloody revolution for thirteen years without ever being injured, surviving two previous assassination attempts unscathed. And now, on this fateful day, he lay on the ground helpless and vulnerable.

His thoughts turned to his faithful generals - Nicolas Gefrard, another mulatto who had remained fiercely loyal to him despite his prejudices against their race; Clerveaux, Bonnet, Bazelais, Vernet, Romain, Guérin - all mulattos who had fought alongside him in the name of freedom. He couldn't help but question himself - why had he been so against them all these years?

As the sounds around him faded and his vision began to blur, Dessalines found himself surrounded by a mob of angry black citizens. The very people he had fought for, now turning against him and seeking his blood. It was a cruel irony that he couldn't bear to face.

He closed his eyes and searched for Marie-Claire, knowing that he would never see her again in this lifetime. He could now feel the mob dragging his near-lifeless body to the government square as he lost consciousness and succumbed to his wounds.

There they proceeded to mutilate, defile, and tear his body apart for over an hour in celebration of their victory over the once brutal Emperor, then leaving the square to the children to pelt his cadaver with stones.

Amidst the chaos, an old woman named Dédée Bazile, known as Défilée-La-Folle – *the crazy* – appeared. She was unafraid of the violent mob of children, teens, and some adults surrounding her who remained. She was once a peddler working in the wake of the warring troops of the indigenous army. She had seen her three brothers and two of her three sons massacred by Rochambeau's French army during the revolution. Strongly shaken by this shock, Dédée Bazile sank into madness, while continuing to follow the indigenous army who coined her nickname Défilée-La-Folle – *The Crazy.*

When she saw the mutilated remains of the Emperor, her once hero General Dessalines, her wild eyes suddenly became calm as she stared at the mob. The crowd grew terrified, never had they seen her in a state of composure, and ran away. She retrieved a sack and carried his body parts to a nearby cemetery where she gave him a proper burial with the help of others who also adored the Emperor.

As Jean Baptiste Bayard dismounted from his exhausted horse, he was met with a scene of absolute carnage. Bodies lay strewn across the streets, some hanging from windows in grotesque displays that sent chills down his spine. His heart pounded with fear and dread for Marie as he entered the building.

Inside, Pétion, Henry, and Junior kneeled before Marie's lifeless form. Blood gushed from her side where a bullet had pierced her skin, and Junior was desperately trying to stop the bleeding.

"Mare has been shot," Henry yelled as Jean burst into the room.

Rushing to his wife's side, Jean frantically checked for signs of life. The faint rise and fall of her chest and the weak beat of her heart filled him with both relief and terror.

"I'm going to get a surgeon right now," Pétion declared as he rushed out of the room to mount a horse.

"I'll make sure this place is secure," Henry bellowed as he headed outside in search of the remnants of his guard detail.

"Junior, bring water and a cloth," Jean commanded his son, trying to keep his voice steady despite the panic rising in his chest.

As if on cue, Marie moaned and opened her eyes. "Jean?"

"It's me, my love."

"How bad is it? Tell me the truth, Jean" she pleaded as she tried unsuccessfully to get up.

"You've been shot...but you're strong. We'll get help and you'll be alright," Jean reassured her through gritted teeth.

But Marie knew the truth. "I'm dying, Jean. I can feel it."

"No! You're not allowed to leave me!" Jean felt tears prick at the corners of his eyes.

"Have I been a good wife to you?" Marie asked weakly.

"Don't talk like that. Of course, you have," Jean replied fiercely, feeling anger bubble up inside of him at the thought of losing her.

"Will you remember me always, or just replace me?" Marie's voice was barely audible.

"You will never be replaced in my heart, Marie. Never," Jean vowed, his voice breaking with emotion.

"Kiss me, Jean."

Bending down, Jean pressed a kiss to her forehead.

"No, my love. Kiss me the way I want. On my lips," Marie demanded stubbornly. "Let me breathe my last breath into you."

Their lips met in a desperate and bittersweet embrace. Tears streamed down Jean's face as he felt Marie slip away from him, her last breath mingling with his own before her eyes closed as she lost consciousness.

Ten

THE BATTLE OF SIBERT

Port Républicain
October 1806

The city of Port Républicain was engulfed in chaos and bloodshed, torn apart by the aftermath of Emperor Jean-Jacques Dessalines' assassination. Each person took a side, whether it be celebrating his death as a victory for the country or mourning the loss of their leader and father of Ayiti.

As heated debates raged throughout the city, Pétion rushed back with a doctor to tend to Marie, her life hanging on by a thread as blood oozed from her gunshot wound. Her husband, Jean-Baptiste Bayard, frantically whisked her away with the surgeon towards the finest hospital in a carriage escorted by an honor guard provided by Pétion.

Meanwhile, soldiers tirelessly worked to clear the streets littered with bodies and transport the wounded to military facilities. A team of officers struggled to uncover the truth behind Dessalines' murder - was it the maroons seeking revenge for the death of Lamour Desrances? Were mulattos seeking retribution for lost lands? Or perhaps it was an enraged mob, fueled by years of oppression, who had taken matters into their own bloody hands.

Amidst the chaos and confusion, one thing was certain that Henry and Pétion agreed upon - vengeance was at play. Dessalines had made countless enemies during his short reign as Emperor. As

Pétion lit a cheroot and took a long drag, he couldn't help but feel a sense of foreboding about the far-reaching consequences this event would bring.

"As I am the senior officer in the army and General Commander of the North, it is my duty to take command and restore order," declared Henry with authority.

"But there are still unanswered questions, Christophe," replied Pétion coolly, taking another drag from his cheroot. "What about Dessalines accusing you of murdering General Francois Capois earlier today?"

"Nonsense and irrelevant," retorted Christophe quickly.

"I demand an answer. On your honor as an officer, did you have any involvement in the planning or execution of Capois' murder?"

"I do not answer to you Pétion. My responses to the Emperor should have made that clear," replied Henry, growing increasingly agitated.

"Your evasiveness towards Dessalines and now me speaks volumes about your guilt. I wonder, if they were able to examine the Emperor's body, would they find a bullet in his back?" Pétion's accusatory gaze bore into Henry.

"How dare you suggest that I would betray and murder our Emperor?"

The tension in the air was palpable as the two leaders stood across from each other, their words hanging heavy like the smoke from Pétion's cheroot. The streets had been cleaned of the last remnants of battle and the wounded had been transported to military facilities, but the stench of death lingered in the air.

Henry could feel his blood rushing as his anger boiled over at Pétion's insinuations. He took a deep breath to calm himself and replied with a cold fury in his voice, "I would never betray Dessalines or our country. My loyalty lies with Ayiti and its people. I will not let you drag me into your baseless accusations."

Pétion stared at Henry, the cheroot between his lips glowing faintly in the dim light. "You are a clever man, Christophe, but your words ring hollow. Your involvement in Capois' murder has marred your reputation and cast a shadow over your leadership. You are now a man with something to hide, and that will come at a cost."

The weight of Pétion's words bore down on Henry like a thousand-pound burden, crushing his spirit and jeopardizing his dreams as the future leader of Ayiti. The realization that his actions may have not only compromised his integrity but also put his future in jeopardy gnawed at him relentlessly.

"I must make haste to Gonaïves and the Northern cities," Henry declared, breaking the tense silence between them. Without even waiting for Pétion's endorsement, he stormed out with determination etched on his face.

Pétion stood motionless, his mind racing as he contemplated the dangerous power vacuum that now existed. He knew that Henry would undoubtedly make a move to seize control during this chaos, and he needed to act swiftly. But how? Any attempt to arrest the general on mere suspicion would only further destabilize the country.

As Pétion plotted his next move, he couldn't help but feel a sense of foreboding and fear for what lay ahead. The fate of Ayiti hung in a precarious balance, and only time would tell if they could weather this storm.

The journey north was fraught with unease for Henry and his men. As they rode towards L'Artibonite, he couldn't help but feel guilty for not being able to prevent the Emperor's death. Pétion had accused him of having a hand in it, despite his innocence.

They pushed their horses hard, desperate to reach the Empress before anyone else could deliver the news. Their arrival in Marchand was met with relief as the town seemed blissfully unaware of the tragedy that had occurred. But as they made their way to the main house, Henry's nerves were on edge, unsure of how The Empress, Marie-Claire Heureuse Félicité Dessalines would react to the news.

He found her sitting on the veranda, sipping coffee as if nothing had changed. But Henry knew her peaceful existence was about to shatter into pieces.

Marie-Claire's eyes met his somber gaze with a mix of curiosity and concern. She knew something was amiss, and the look on his face told her it was serious.

"What is it, General Christophe?" she asked gently, setting her cup down and rising to her feet. She could sense the tension in the air, and she hoped that whatever news he bore would not be too grave.

Henry closed the distance between them, bowing to her as the Empress. "I fear I must inform you of the Emperor's demise," he began, his voice low and strained.

Marie-Claire felt the blood drain from her face as she registered his words. The death of her husband was something she had feared, even expected, since the coronation. A combination of jealousy, fear, and revenge towards him mixed with the overreach of his authority had become a lethal mix.

"How?" she asked.

"An ambush during our meeting in Port Républicain. Many men perished alongside him."

"Who is responsible?"

"I am not certain. Maroons, Mulattos, a mob of disgruntled laborers, and maybe even…" Henry stated, casting a calculated doubt into the mix.

"And even what, Henry?" Marie Claire asked, using his first name to endear him.

"I dare not think it so," your Majesty.

"Speak your mind, General. That is a command, not a request," Marie-Claire stated with the authority of a seasoned Empress.

"I have my suspicions that Alexandre Pétion may have been involved or possibly the one who may have shot the Emperor himself."

Marie-Claire took both hands and for the first time showed emotion as she brought them to her mouth. "Do you know this for sure?" she asked.

"This is why I did not want to speak of it. I only divulged it by your command to do so."

"You must ensure that there is no rebellion during this difficult time. Go about your duty," Marie-Claire said, anxious to be left alone to grieve.

Henry bowed, "Your Majesty," and turned and walked away as he heard sobs of her grief as he exited the room.

The horsemen continued their journey, turning west towards the town of Saint Marc before heading north through Ester, La Croix, Gonaïves, Ennery, Plaisance, and Marmelade. Along the way, they also stopped at each major town in the Plaine du Nord, spreading false rumors of a plot conceived by Pétion and the mulattos of the South.

As they made their way towards Cap-Français, whispers of revenge for the late emperor spread like wildfire throughout the northern region. Past grudges and disagreements over his reign were quickly overshadowed by a common enemy - the Mulattos.

Finally, Henry arrived home after days of travel. Exhausted but relieved to be back with his family. He was greeted by his wife Marie-Louise and their three children: nine-year-old Françoise-Améthyste, seven-year-old Athénaïre, and two-year-old Jacques-Victor Henry. The absence of their beloved oldest son François Ferdinand hung heavy in the air; he had tragically succumbed to malaria the previous year at the age of eleven.

Marie-Louise clung to her husband, her nails digging into his skin as he shared the unsettling news. They both stood in silence, contemplating the uncertain future that lay ahead.

"We must take action," Henry's voice trembled with anger. "The traitorous people of the south will pay for this betrayal."

"Are you sure, my love?" Marie-Louise's voice quivered with fear. She knows how passionate and impulsive Henry can be, especially since the death of their eldest son. His once gentle heart has turned cold and callous.

"The Emperor showed them no mercy. He confiscated their lands. "I am certain it was Pétion who orchestrated this treachery."

"But can you truly be sure?" Marie-Louise pleaded. "Remember the rumors about you and Capois? People were starting to believe you had him killed."

Henry grabbed a flask of rum and poured himself a glass, downing it in one gulp before pouring another. Marie-Louise sensed the turmoil within him, a storm brewing beneath his calm exterior.

"You know I had no choice," Henry finally admitted, unable to lie to his wife any longer. "Capois was a hindrance to our plans."

Marie-Louise's eyes filled with tears as she gazed upon her husband, a man driven by ambition and ruthlessness to fill the void left by the loss of their son François. She now fears what he may become in his pursuit of power, but cannot stand against him because of the love she still holds for him.

It had been less than two months since the murder of the Emperor and hero of the country, yet it was as if the assassination of Jean-Jacques Dessalines was merely a footnote in the annals of Ayiti's history. Without hesitation the representatives had met, all senior generals of the army, and each represented a region under their control with the western and southern delegates in the majority.

The representatives quickly drafted a constitution, organized a senate, and went about the task of appointing a new President. As per the protocol of the time, the most senior of the army's generals, without any consideration of forming a civilian government, nominated Henry Christophe to lead the country as its President. He was not the eldest, but the general with the most tenure, having joined Toussaint Louverture long ago.

However, the leadership mandate would come with a stipulation to avoid the type of excesses and power grab of Dessalines. The new president would be directed by the newly formed senate, consisting of these same generals, who would ratify and approve nearly every decision he would make.

During November and early December, Henry solidified his grip on the north, amassing an army of 22,000 soldiers ready for battle. Regiments of cavalry, artillery, infantry, reconnaissance, and a new group known as saboteurs are now all at his disposal.

He plans to arrive at Port Républicain and accept the nomination, however demanding he be placed with powers above the Senate. And if that fails, they will take control by force. With his army fully mobilized, the future waits to be shaped by Henry's iron fist.

Hushed whispers of President Christophe's discontent, of his disdain for being reduced to a mere figurehead—a puppet president—rippled through the masses. It was this very constitution, which he viewed as a shackle upon his authority, that spurred him onward, the 22,000 men at his back a testament to his resolve.

As the year waned, word of Henry's march towards Port Républicain, the seat of the government, caused fury. Soon the Senate's proclamation rang out, branding Henry an enemy of the Republic should he dare approach with his legions. Yet, there was no turning back, for the die had been cast, setting the course for confrontation.

The New Year dawned with a sky cloaked in somber hues, the darkened clouds releasing their burdens in a torrential downpour onto the already tense city. Pétion, clad in determination and the weight of leadership, mustered his modest force of 3,000 and departed at the appointed hour, ten o'clock in the morning, to meet the army of Christophe, however underestimating its strength.

As Henry marched with the entirety of the combined army of the North, less a couple of thousand left back for security, Pétion had only his brigade of the west. The South and West armies were scattered amongst the land, performing their duties in the hamlets they protected and served.

Regardless, as Pétion departed from Port Republican, his departure was not one of retreat, but rather a strategic advance toward Sibert, where he would meet Christophe and allow destiny to unfold.

Sibert lay quiet, the Batardeau River murmuring between its banks, ignorant of the history about to be inscribed along its shores. Here, Pétion and his Republican force positioned themselves with hope as their rampart, facing the ominous silence from the north.

Then, without warning, Henry and his army emerged, his presence on the horizon casting a long shadow over the scattered Republican line. He and his army appeared not as a specter but as a solid force of nature, his eyes reflecting the steel of his will and the depth of his love for Ayiti — a love that compelled him to build, to discipline, to envision a future forged by his hands without the interference of others.

The rain intensified, droplets like the tears of the heavens, mourning the division of brothers below. The northerly wind carried the scent of damp earth and the faintest trace of gunpowder—a harbinger of what was to come. The river, once a benign barrier, now marked the threshold between unity and fracture, its waters swelling with the unspoken fears of brothers soon to face brothers.

On the left bank, the Republicans shuffled uneasily, their muskets slick with moisture. They were soldiers, yes, but they were also sons and daughters of Ayiti, torn between the oaths they had sworn and the uncertain path that lay ahead. On the right, the Northerners stood resolute, their silent vigil a stark contrast to the chaos that reigned across the water. Of the twenty-two thousand soldiers, over two thousand were battle-tested women, respected for their fierce warrior skills by all.

At this moment, Henry saw not just a battlefield but the canvas of his nation's future, one he envisioned painted with broad strokes of discipline and order. Each drop of rain that fell upon his skin was a reminder of the trials he had endured, the resilience of his people,

The soldiers of Pétion's Southern army in the foreground are shocked by the enormity of Henry Christophe's Northern army across the Batardeau River.

and the freedom that had been so dearly won, squandered by the decisions of the slain Emperor.

The stage was now set, the actors in place, and all that remained was the unfolding of the drama that would tip the scales of power within the young Republic. Soon the first drops of blood will mingle with the rainwater of the Sibert, and the reflection of a nation's soul would be left trembling upon its surface.

Henry Christophe's eyes surveyed the scene before him with the discerning gaze of an eagle as the army advanced south towards the river and the capital beyond. The edge of the Sibert was a line drawn in the silt, a boundary between defiance and conquest. His vanguard, the heralds of his will, had halted at the water's churned banks, the river's tumult an echo of the storm brewing within men's hearts.

Pétion was positioning his men from a distance as the silence at the banks of the river was broken by Colonel Metellus of the 11th Regiment of Port Républicain as he called out to Christophe's army; "Where are you going? Is it to Port Républicain, to punish the misdeeds of what you deem as traitors?" his voice laced with a mocking undertone that danced above the sound of the river. His laughter was a fleeting affront to the northerners concerning the gravity of the moment.

Christophe's Generals, Guerrier, and Longueville, men of stature hardened by conflict, stood firm as if cast from the very earth they sought to claim. They awaited their leader's order before uttering a response.

Without hearing one, Metellus again shouted; "What can so many troops come to do in full peace?" challenging them, questioning the very fabric of their intent. "Does the Constitution allow the President of Ayiti to transport himself in arms to the city where the Senate holds its sittings? The inquiry hung in the air, a specter of legalism amidst the clamor of impending strife.

But already the words had pierced the veil of uncertainty in Christophe's soldiers, carrying across the divide like embers on the wind. They looked towards their generals to untangle their confusion.

Longueville was the first to assure them and cast doubt to his opponents on the other side of the river; "Comrades, what! Are we going to fight for an absurd constitution, for the ambition of Pétion, who is an enemy of the Fatherland, brothers against brothers, Negroes of the North against Negroes of the South? Long live General Christophe, the legitimate head of the state!"

These cries, fervent and impassioned, struck at the resolve of the Southern Republican soldiers. A tremor ran through their ranks, a palpable hesitation as if their very souls were caught in the balance, weighing loyalty against fraternity, servitude against sovereignty.

Amidst this maelstrom of doubt, Pétion, could not let the minds of his men be swayed as he shouted across the river; "President Christophe and the Generals of the North. Your march on the capital is unlawful and I warn you to turn back your legions except for the lawful quantity of troops to accompany the President if he desires business with the Senate. You have one-quarter hour to comply."

As the deadline approached, Pétion could see they were not making any attempt to turn back and allowed several minutes to prevail after the deadline, then shouted. "This is your last opportunity to turn back in peace. We have an honor guard ready to escort President Christophe to the halls of the Senate if he so wisely chooses."

More time elapsed without an answer from the Northern army. Pétion was stalwart in his convictions and called his army to open fire, unleashing a commanding thunder that shattered the tenuous calm. A tempest of lead and smoke unfurled over the waters, and the heartbeats of men thrummed with the cadence of battle drums and cannons.

Henry, ever the architect of his destiny, stood firm near a small bridge that arched modestly over a stream. The Moleart plantation lay quiet behind him, a silent witness to the crossroad of destiny. He wasted not a breath nor a heartbeat; his command was swift, his intent unyielding.

"Forward!" he bellowed, his voice the clarion call that unleashed the fury of his soldiers. The fight was upon them all, a conflagration of wills set ablaze under the darkened sky of the land.

The clash resonated with the sounds of grappling iron and the cries of the determined and the doomed alike. Each drop of rain mingled with the blood of patriots and loyalists, painting the earth with the hues of sacrifice and the essence of the struggle for domination and self-rule.

In each stroke of combat, Henry saw more than the fray; he saw the enduring resilience of his army, the hope that cleaved to the promise of a brighter tomorrow. The Republic's heartbeat was syncopated with the rhythm of revolt, each pulse a testament to the unwavering quest for order that had birthed a nation from the ashes of oppression.

As the din of battle echoed in the distance, the reflections in the turbid waters of the Sibert whispered of the dreams and despairs of a people who had known chains and now sought to forge their destiny, unshackled and sovereign, whichever their chosen destiny.

The tumultuous symphony of war crescendoed as Henry Christophe's Northern forces descended upon the Republican lines with a fury that brooked no opposition. The once orderly ranks of Pétion's men, incredibly outnumbered seven-to-one, and surprised by the sheer breadth of Christophe's army, shattered under the weight of the relentless onslaught, their formation dissolving like sugar in the tropical rains that now lashed the battlefield.

Steel clashed against steel, the metallic ring punctuated by the grunts and cries of men locked in the dance of death. The earth beneath their feet churned into a treacherous mire, grasping at the boots of the living and the fallen alike, indifferent to their allegiance, their rank, or their cause.

In the thick of the chaos, Pétion stood out like a beacon, his parade hat braided with gold glinting dully in the dim light—a target for every eye, friend, and foe. His visage was a mask of grim determination, the weight of leadership pressing upon him as heavily as the sodden fabric of his uniform. He had underestimated the resolve and the power of Christophe who had organized a massive war machine in record time. This would surely turn into a disaster.

"Disperse and retreat!" he roared over the din, his voice carrying the authority of command yet tinged with an undercurrent of desperation. "To the woods to regroup!"

But his words were swept away by the clamor of battle, heard by few, heeded by fewer. The dragoons of the Artibonite, loyal protectors of the Republic's fleeting dream, gathered close, their mounts snorting and skittish amidst the bedlam, already charging to their certain death.

Henry, astride his charger at a vantage point, surveyed the field with the critical eye of a master tactician. He saw the disarray among his adversaries, the fear that gnawed at their resolve. With a terse nod, he signaled his troops forward, his lips set in a firm line.

"Victory is ours!" he declared, his voice resonating with conviction. "Press on to Port Républicain!"

His soldiers, emboldened by their leader's confidence, surged ahead like a dark wave ready to break upon the city's gates. They pursued the fleeing Republicans with a zeal born not merely of duty but of belief in the righteousness of their cause.

The thrum of fear pulsed through the cobbled streets of Port-Républicain, a city held captive not by chains but by the shadow of an impending siege. Henry Christophe, with the weight of betrayal and unfulfilled ambition heavy in his heart, led his formidable army southward. The manifesto he had dispatched as a prior warning of his discontent had now materialized. He had heralded that their march was as much a promise as it was a threat, the words etched into the minds of the city's inhabitants, who now scrambled in confusion to escape the wrath they believed inevitable, the usually vibrant marketplaces now barren, save for the hurried footsteps of families seeking refuge elsewhere.

As Pétion navigated the pandemonium of the battlefield, the Barthelemy squadron of the North's chief, Mirault, caught sight of the gleaming hat and raised his arm high, his finger pointing accusingly at Pétion. "Fire upon that man!" Mirault commanded, the venom of betrayal lacing his order. "He shall not escape justice this day!"

Bullets whistled through the air, seeking flesh and blood. Pétion wove his charger between the specters of death, each step defiance of fate, his heart pounding a staccato rhythm of survival and hope.

The beleaguered Republicans scattered, some paralyzed by dread, others propelled by calculated resentment. Henry's victory was complete, not in the conquest of territory, but in the disintegration of opposing wills.

The clamor of battle had receded into a dreadful silence as a republican soldier, Coutilien Coutard, his mind unclouded by the fear that gripped so many others, seized the moment to act with a courage that bordered on the divine. He reached for the hat of Pétion — the symbol of leadership that was now a beacon for death and plucked it from Pétion's head with a swift, selfless gesture. The world seemed to pause, acknowledging the gravity of his sacrifice as he hoisted the bright hat above his head.

Coutard mounted his horse with an air of grim resolve and became an instant target by the enemy during his ruse. Blades unsheathed with the cold intent of executioners advancing on him. With every second, the breath of freedom he sought for his leader grew thinner, until the inevitable fall came at the Blanchard Bridge. His horse, overwhelmed by the force of the attack, collapsed beneath him, and before the dust settled, sabers descended, carving a tragic end for the young hero.

The brutal tableau did not escape the northern general Mirault's attention. In the aftermath, he strode forward through the mire, his boots squelching against the sodden earth, to retrieve the gilded hat. Holding it aloft like a macabre trophy, he approached Christophe, the builder of nations, whose eyes betrayed neither joy nor sorrow.

"General-in-Chief," Mirault intoned, his voice a mere echo of the chaos that had preceded, "Here is the New Year's gift that I offer you." The words hung heavy in the damp air, a somber reflection on the cost of ambition and power, but unbeknownst that the soldier slain who wore this prized hat was not Pétion at all.

Meanwhile, the forest became Pétion's sanctuary, its labyrinthine greenery swallowing him whole as he stumbled away from the carnage seeking safety in his retreat. His progress was labored, each step an assertion of will against the odds stacked high as mountains. Thorns snagged at his clothing, roots threatened to unbalance him, but onward he pressed with his few comrades towards the distant promise of the sea to escape to fight another day.

At the Truitier settlement, salvation appeared as a simple fishing boat near the shore, its sails billowing like the wings of some great bird taking flight as the enemy continued their chase. Yet, as Pétion motioned frantically for it to return, it seemed fate would deal yet another cruel hand—the vessel continued its retreat. Desperation clawed at his throat, manifesting in a shout lost on the wind as he shook his head in defeat towards his comrades.

But hope, ever resilient, found form in the recognition of a woman aboard the boat. Her eyes, sharp and discerning, cut through the masquerade of circumstance. With the persistence born of countless struggles endured by women just like her, she invoked shared dreams of liberty and unity, until the boatman, swayed by the woman's conviction, turned the vessel back towards shore.

Pétion, along with his officers Bedouet, David, Troy, Covin, Meyronne, and Bouzy, who had remained steadfast at his side, were pulled aboard. They huddled together, a mosaic of weary souls united by purpose, as the boat cleaved through the waves, carrying them away from the blood-soaked land toward an uncertain horizon.

The following day, palls of smoke rose in ominous plumes, blackening the sky above the Cul-de-Sac plain northeast of Port Républicain in the path of Christophe's advancing army as the clamor of panicked voices and the clatter of arms filled the air. Republican forces General Magloire Ambroise, his brow furrowed with a gravitas born of countless campaigns, watched from atop his steed as the disarray unfolded before him. Soldiers were running from the enemy towards him as the news of Pétion's defeat and narrow escape hung heavily in the air, mingling with the scent of charred earth and the lingering anguish of betrayal.

"General!" cried an aide-de-camp, breathless from sprinting. "The enemy advances upon us! The army of the north is mighty and huge in numbers."

General Ambroise nodded curtly. His keen eyes swept over the remnants of shattered ranks—the weary, the wounded, the crestfallen. With urgency propelling his every move, he spurred his horse forward, rallying the scattered troops with a voice that cut through the chaos like a saber's edge.

"Brothers! To arms! Our nation's heart beats within these walls, and we shall not let it falter! Ready all defenses and be ready for a siege," he yelled from inside Fort Portail Saint Joseph.

Soldiers took position behind him, a resolute barrier against the tide of conquest. Along the pits, Ambroise's call to battle echoed, finding kindred spirits in the soldiers with names of Yayou, Lys, Canneau, and Lamarre—men who bore the scars of liberty's arduous journey and knew all too well the price of freedom.

"Stand firm," Lys bellowed, gripping his musket with hands calloused by both toil and war, as the men took up positions along the fortifications.

"Fort Portail Saint Joseph will hold," Lamarre declared, his gaze unwavering as he surveyed the preparations for defense.

As the sun reached its zenith, word arrived like a fleeting gust of wind: Pétion had landed at Truitier de Naucresson. A collective sigh, a ripple of hope, surged through the beleaguered defenders as they steeled themselves for the inevitable onslaught in honor of their leader.

Pétion, narrowly escaping death at Sibert, returned with a burning vengeance. He dispatched horsemen to the farthest corners of the South and West, summoning armies to defend the capital from Christophe's siege of the city. With careful precision, he positioned his artillery in the treacherous mountains of Boutillier, readying them to rain down a barrage of punishing cannon fire on any enemy foolish enough to march towards them.

Days later, as dawn broke on January 6, Pétion's ears were assaulted by the ominous roll of drums and the distant thunder of cannons. The ground shook beneath his feet as Christophe's forces threw themselves against the outskirts of the city with a ferocity born of desperation. The air was thick with gunpowder and blood, screams and cries mingling with the sounds of battle.

But Pétion stood firm, a master of artillery whose skills began to decimate Christophe's regiments sending them crawling from the city like wounded animals. However, despite heavy losses, they continued to push forward with determination despite the punishing of Pétion's cannons.

Yet Fort Portail Saint Joseph remained unyielding, a symbol of resilience that struck fear into Henry's heart. Fort Nationale also held strong against wave after wave of invaders, the loyalists within the city fighting back with unwavering determination, united in their vision of what Ayiti could be as Pétion's constant explosions rained down on the enemy from the distant hills.

Amidst the chaos and destruction, Republican forces from the distant provinces arrived, with wave after wave thrown into the battle to defend their capital. Ambroise could not help but contemplate the fickle nature of fate. How many times had they faced this threat before? And yet, they always persevered. They resisted. They hoped. For deep within each person's soul there burned an ember of hope, refusing to be extinguished even in the darkest moments. Fearing that this war would spur rebellion within his dominions in his absence, Christophe retreated on January 8th after many days of relentless battle. In a fit of rage, he ordered 200 Republican prisoners to be burned alive as a grim reminder of his anger and his power.

Christophe's forces retreated and took the road to Arcahaie, leaving behind a trail of smoldering ruins in the Cul-de-Sac, Port Républicain, and surrounding hamlets. The people emerged from hiding, their spirits unbroken by the destruction around them, for though their homes may lay in ruins, the light of hope burned bright within their hearts, guiding them towards a brighter future beyond the ashes of a war between brothers.

Despite his best efforts, Henry found himself fruitlessly pleading with the Senate representatives from his camp in Arcahaie, desperately trying to convince them that he held full executive power as designated by his office. However, after witnessing the death, destruction, devastation, and chaos he had caused in the capital, their ears were deaf to his arguments and instead met him with fierce resistance.

Meanwhile, Christophe's armies remained stationed in Arcahaie, carrying out a campaign of terror through acts of intimidation, brutal killings, and destructive burnings. The Reconnaissance Regiment proved invaluable in gathering intelligence on pockets of resistance and utilizing a network of spies within the city to monitor the political climate and sentiments of its citizens.

As for the Saboteur Regiment, they lived up to their name, executing calculated attacks on critical infrastructure such as bridges and roads, effectively crippling the economy and demoralizing the populace.

In early March, multiple sessions were convened by the senate to debate and hear arguments regarding Christophe's demands. After much deliberation, they issued a decree denouncing his actions and declaring him an outlaw. A warrant for his arrest was issued along with a reward for his capture. Furthermore, an official proclamation was made against his army for their crimes against the government and its people. This proclamation was unanimously passed, calling for the dissolution of Christophe's army.

Marie-Madeleine 'Joute' Lachenais sat in the opulent sitting room of Alexandre Pétion's home on Rue l'Enterrement in Port Républicain. The walls were adorned with elegant tapestries and the furniture was made of rich mahogany wood. She had moved in with Pétion at his request, along with her aging parents, seeking solace and protection from Christophe's threatening army stationed near their home in Arcahaie.

As Pétion's mistress, she knew she was at risk of being arrested or detained by Christophe, She couldn't help but feel a sense of comfort and security in Pétion's presence, as he exuded confidence and authority with every step.

"Cherie," Joute greeted him as he entered the room. "I have a cup of this exquisite coffee waiting for you." She gestured towards a small table where a steaming cup stood, its aroma filling the air.

Pétion smiled warmly at her before removing his sidearm and saber and placing them carefully on a nearby table. He washed his hands in a basin from a pitcher filled with water and lime, dried them on a towel, and wiped his face with the damp cloth, a refreshing customary ritual after returning from the senate where he had been every day for the past five days.

He walked over to Joute and kissed her tenderly on each cheek before sinking into the plush sofa beside her. "How are Mama et Papa?" he asked, his voice filled with regard for her parents.

"They, as am I, are worried about you, Cherie," she replied, using the endearing term that Pétion often called her by.

"What has you worried, my dear?" Pétion questioned, taking a sip of the coffee that Joute had prepared for him just how he liked it - strong with a lot of sugar. He gulped the rest of the cup, savoring its taste.

"You haven't been sleeping well, only three or four hours per night," she explained, her worry evident in her voice.

"There is much to be done," Pétion sighed, "the senate finally declared Christophe an outlaw today, as they should have from the beginning of his onslaught. I don't know what took them this long."

"What has gotten into him? He couldn't possibly think that the senate would give in to his demands," Joute said shaking her head in disbelief as she poured Pétion another cup of coffee.

Pétion closed his eyes and breathed in the rich, comforting scent. "Ah, the simple pleasures in life. Why do we men always make things so complicated?"

"But what could have caused this change in him?" Joute pressed on.

"I do not know or recognize Henry Christophe anymore," Pétion replied with a heavy heart. "First, he had Capois killed, then I suspect him of shooting Dessalines, and finally mobilizing this massive army to try and take control of the government. I spoke with Jean-Baptiste Junior today about it."

"And what does he make of this madness?" asked Joute.

"He is just as bewildered as I. He will visit with his father for guidance and counsel. However, he believes that the recent death of his son, François Ferdinand, may have had a profound impact on Christophe. The poor boy was only eleven years old and was Christophe's favorite, as well as the eldest. They say he died from Yellow Fever."

"Do you think that could have caused him to act so irrationally?"

"I asked the same question, but no one can say for sure. All I know is that Henry Christophe has become consumed by power and I fear for what he might do next."

"And what will you do next, Alexandre?"

"My duty, as always."

"But is it not truly your duty to become president of the Republic? To lead a country and its people?" Joute's words were laced with an air of authority, almost like an order.

"I am not fit for such a formal role. I am not a politician," Pétion replied with uncertainty.

"But the people look up to you. They listen to you, even adore you. You have already replaced André Rigaud as the leader of the West and South. General Geffrard is gone and they need someone to guide them. You called upon the armies and they marched to Port Républicain without hesitation," Joute argued persuasively.

Despite his doubts, on March 7, 1807, Alexandre Pétion was appointed as President by the senate. But unlike the confident acceptance predicted by Joute, Pétion couldn't help but feel conflicted about taking on such a powerful position. Would he truly be able to fulfill the expectations of the people? He couldn't help but wonder if he had made the right decision but understood that Joute would play a collaborative and pivotal role in their future and that of the new republic, of which he was certain.

"How dare them!" Henry's voice boomed like thunder as he stood flanked by his top two generals, Guerrier and Longueville. His fists clenched in rage as he paced back and forth, the weight of an outlaw and a warrant for his arrest heavy on his shoulders.

"Not only that, Mr. President," Guerrier spoke up, "but they have also demanded that you disband our army."

"When did you receive this news?" Henry growled.

"Moments ago from a spy within the city. It will be made public tomorrow, along with another decree," Guerrier replied cautiously.

"What other decree could there possibly be?" Henry's eyes blazed with fury.

"General Pétion will succeed you as the new president of the Republic," Guerrier revealed.

"Pétion? The same man who betrayed us during the Civil War and then returned with Napoleon's forces to take back our lands? That traitorous Pétion? Have they all lost their minds?" Henry seethed.

"It seems so, Mr. President," Longueville added. "They have reason to be angry at you."

"I am not their president if my position is not legitimate. I prefer to be called General in Chief anyway," Christophe sneered. "But make no mistake; if they disband our army, we will either lose our heads or be forced into exile."

"We are fully aware of the consequences," Longueville stated. "What is your decision regarding this matter?"

Without answering, Christophe stormed out of the room followed closely by his two generals. They stood on a hilltop overlooking their military encampment which stretched out below them.

"Do you see that?" Christophe asked, gesturing towards their vast camp.

"The line of tents as far as the eye can see?" Guerrier asked.

"Yes. From east to west, that line will become the southern border of a new country. Our country. Pétion and the others have succeeded in their secession of the South. I declare that they are the outlaws now, not us," Christophe shouted.

"Their so-called republic is a renegade state, just as Rigaud wanted," Longueville added.

"The mulattos have achieved their malicious plan to claim our land for themselves. Let them have it, I don't want to see any of them in my presence!" Christophe's face was twisted with hate.

"Are you suggesting that we form a new republic?" Longueville asked cautiously.

"Yes, that is exactly what I am saying. From this line northward will be the State of Ayiti. The true and legitimate country of Ayiti, not some puppet government controlled by hidden manipulators hiding behind the senate's curtain. And I will be President for life, with the power to choose my successor to ensure stability for generations to come. We will go down in history as the founders of the one and only rightful State of Ayiti!"

Guerrier and Longueville's eyes gleamed with excitement as they locked onto Henry Christophe, eagerly awaiting his command. "Oui, Monsieur President!" they exclaimed in unison, their voices filled with fervent zeal. "What is your first order?"

Without hesitation, Christophe's voice boomed with authority. "Have the regiment of Sabateurs slaughter every single mulatto they come across on their journey from here to Cap-Français during their march north. We will send a clear message for them to leave their lands and flee south."

Longueville's hand shook as he spoke up, a hint of fear audible in his voice. "Mr. President? Are you sure this is necessary?"

Christophe fixed him with a steely gaze. "You heard me. I want every last mulatto north of that line dead or fleeing for their new country in the south."

Guerrier and Longueville exchanged a nervous glance before quickly saluting their leader once again. "Oui, Monsieur President," they choked out, their hearts heavy with the weight of this ruthless command.

Jean-Baptiste knelt tenderly at the edge of the bed, careful not to disturb his wife's fragile form. With a small spoon, he carefully ladled hot soup into her mouth, a hearty bouyon filled with chunks of succulent chicken and an array of vibrant vegetables - potatoes, carrots, sweet potatoes, plantains, yuca, malanga, with added dumplings, her favorite non-vegetable ingredient. Each bite was rich with nutrients and vitamins, nourishing Marie's weakened body.

Her lips curved into a grateful smile towards her husband, a silent thank you to God for his unwavering vigil by her side. It was Jean who had saved her life when she lay unconscious for three long days after the surgeon successfully removed two bullets from her body. One in her arm, the other perilously close to piercing a vital organ. It was this second bullet, laced with filth and infection that became her greatest threat.

For months they had been confined to the Grand Hotel in Port Républicain since the fatal shooting of Emperor Dessalines, Marie, and countless others in an attack whose true perpetrators remained unknown. The early days were filled with uncertainty and fear as she battled high fevers, chills, and an inability to eat or drink. But through it all, Jean never left her side - tending to her physical needs while holding on to hope for her survival.

After three harrowing weeks of ups and downs, Marie finally began to show signs of recovery. Though weak, it was clear she would survive this ordeal - at least for now. Slowly but surely, she made progress in regaining her strength over the following weeks until finally, her usual laughter and humor returned - bringing joy not only to herself but also to Jean who had never given up on her.

A gentle knock on the door broke the silence of their quiet lunch. "It is I, Papa… Maman?" The familiar voice belonged to Jean-Baptiste Junior, and his presence instantly brought a smile to Jean's face as he stood to greet his son. With open arms, they embraced in a warm hug before Junior made his way over to his mother's bed to kiss her. Marie had grown used to these visits from her son and cherished those more and more as she recovered from her injuries.

"So you haven't forgotten your maman yet, my son?" Marie said with a touch of sarcasm. "I hope the day never comes when you do."

"Maman!" exclaimed Junior. "Stop that talk. You know I will always be here for you."

"Please, sit down, my son," Marie said, gesturing towards a chair. "How are things?"

"Everything is good, Maman," Junior replied.

"And what about your beautiful wife, Marie Victoire?"

"She is also doing well, Maman," Junior answered. His mother was unaware of their struggles to conceive another child after losing their first during birth.

"Now, tell us everything," Marie urged. "It's been almost a week since your last visit. There must be plenty to catch up on."

Junior glanced at his father and then at Marie, silently asking if it was appropriate to speak freely in front of her while she was still recovering.

"Just say what's on your mind, Junior," Marie said with determination in her voice.

Junior turned to his father for confirmation. "You better do so before your mother gets out of bed and backslaps you," Jean Baptiste joked with a smile.

Marie began to sit up straighter, wincing slightly from the pain as Jean quickly came to her side to help. He placed an extra pillow behind her back and asked if she was comfortable. "I think this pain in my back is from being in bed for too long," she complained. "We need to walk more than twice a day, Jean."

"Go ahead, Junior. I'm ready now," Marie stated.

"First, regarding our business. Our ships are all sailing smoothly. The Marcelle has been diverted to assist the Solange with trade in the lesser Antilles as business is picking up there. The Jacqueline is currently operating in Guadeloupe, Martinique, and Saint Barthelemy. The Laura and Le Matin are sailing exclusively to Cuba and Puerto Rico, while the Michaele is trading in Jamaica and the Marcelle is making stops along the South American coast. The remaining two ships are used for inter-coastal trade. So far, we haven't encountered any issues and profits are well above projections."

Marie nodded in approval. "That sounds promising. Have you heard from Bunel or André about resuming trade with Philadelphia and Boston?"

"They advise against it," Junior replied. "There's talk of an embargo on Ayiti and, as you may recall, we did take back our ships from Savannah. Needless to say, they are not pleased with us."

"We had no choice, my son," Marie interjected, taking Jean's hand in hers. "Those ships belonged to us and we were simply reclaiming our rightful property."

"And I was following your orders to retrieve them," Jean added with a mischievous grin as he leaned down to steal a quick kiss from his wife.

"Excuse me for interrupting your romantic exchanges," Junior chimed in teasingly. "But I am still your child, you know."

Marie's eyes flickered with determination as she addressed her son. "Alright, Junior, back to you," she said, her voice commanding the attention of the room. "You have our full attention now. What's next?"

"It's about Henry," Junior stated, his usually confident tone faltering slightly. "He has been labeled an outlaw by the Senate and a warrant has been issued for his arrest."

Marie's eyebrows furrowed in concern as she turned to her husband. "When?" she asked, worry evident in her voice.

"Today," replied Junior, his expression grave. "It will be published in tomorrow's Nouveliste newspaper, Alexandre has informed me."

"I was afraid of that," sighed Jean. "Is he still in Arcahaie?"

"Yes," confirmed Junior. "And he has been demanding that he be the president without any interference from the senate or any other governmental body. But the senate will have nothing to do with him after the destruction he wreaked on Port Républicain. They will name Alexandre as president to succeed him."

"How bad is it?" Marie asked, her hand reaching out to grasp Jean's comfortingly.

"Henry's army got deep into the city and destroyed many buildings before they were repelled," reported Junior. "Pétion's cannon created much damage to roads and bridges to slow him down and what was not destroyed, Henry's military completed." His face twisted in disgust as he added, "Henry even has this new regiment named the Saboteurs, no need to explain their mission."

"Henry was always the efficient administrator," Marie said with a slight smile revealing her pride, though there was no humor behind it.

"Expect delays in all supplies moving forward from inland roads," warned Junior. "We will need to maybe charter a vessel or two to bring in supplies from other regions to supply the city."

"Good thinking son," praised Jean. "Get on that right away before there are none left to charter. Make long-term commitments based on today's prices. You will need more than two ships. Charter for four."

"Yes sir," replied Junior, his voice tinged with concern. "However, this behavior is not like Henry's. I don't know what has gotten into him. The last time I spoke with him he was not himself, that is for sure. It's like he believes it is his destiny to not only take over from Dessalines but secure his legacy through military might and political power."

"What does Marie-Louise think of all this?" Jean asked Junior.

"She is worried for him," Junior replied with a heavy sigh. "She believes that much of this is a result of their son François Ferdinand's death. He's never been the same since the funeral."

"When is your next ship departing for Cap Francais?" Marie inquired, her mind already working out a plan.

"Two days hence," answered Junior.

"It's time to go home, Jean," determination clear in her voice.

"But my love, you are not ready yet," protested Jean.

"I've been ready for two weeks," smirked Marie with a mischievous twinkle in her eye. "I've simply been enjoying your undivided attention, Jean." She leaned back on her pillow, relishing in the pampering she had received during her convalescence. "Wonderful massages with Madame Karine's oils of my hands, feet, and neck. Pampered by the finest foods, even at times spoon-fed by my handsome husband." She let out a contented sigh as she added with a broad smile, "I was hoping it would never end!"

Jean couldn't help but laugh at his wife's playful antics. "Why you little conniver!" he exclaimed fondly.

"And as for our son here," continued Marie, her expression turning serious once again. "What better training could he have received? Being in charge while you were away, he had to swim on his own and he has done remarkably well. Look how smoothly things have been running with him at the helm."

"I can't believe you, Maman!" exclaimed Junior, standing up and putting his fists on his waist. "You have been playing us all this time?"

"Now, make sure that the ship's best stateroom is cleaned and ready for Jean and I," ordered Marie, changing the subject. "I want to get back to Cap before Henry arrives. We need to plan an intervention of sorts with Marie-Louise. Henry needs us to talk some sense into him."

208

Eleven

PÉTION'S REPUBLIC
& CHRISTOPHE'S STATE

Port Républicain
May 1807

The Grand Hôtel was abuzz with excitement on a clear, starry evening in late May of 1807. Guests gathered to celebrate the inauguration of the newly appointed Président of the Republic of Ayiti, Alexandre Sabès Pétion. By his side stood Marie-Madeleine Lachenais, known affectionately and reverently as Joute, as well as Jean-Pierre Boyer and Jean-Baptiste Bayard Junior.

Pétion's tailored military uniform caught the candlelight, every fold and seam crisp and precise. The gold embroidery along the edges glinted, adorned with gleaming epaulets, and polished buttons. His accomplishments and rank were proudly displayed through colorful patches and decorations.

The crowd consisted of Port Républicain's elite; high-ranking military officers, government officials, men of commerce, and distinguished citizens, dressed elegantly for the occasion. An orchestra played while couples danced in the grand ballroom.

As the final notes of a waltz echoed through the room, an officer whispered to the conductor who then motioned for a brief intermission. Boyer stepped forward, holding a glass of champagne, and addressed the guests: "Ladies and gentlemen, it is my great honor to introduce to you the new Président of the Republic of Ayiti, His Excellency, Alexandre Sabès Pétion!"

The crowd cheered with a roar. Pétion straightened his posture, his gaze sweeping over the assembled guests with a mix of gratitude and determination. His voice resonated through the grand ballroom, filled with unwavering conviction as he began to address the gathering.

"My fellow Ayisyen," Pétion's voice carried the weight of his words, each syllable carefully enunciated. "Tonight, as we stand on the cusp of a new era, I am humbled by your trust and honored to lead our great nation forward."

Joute, stood beside him, her poise elegant and unwavering. Her eyes sparkled with a mixture of pride for her partner and an acute awareness of the challenges that lay ahead. She exuded a silent strength that complemented Pétion's charismatic presence.

The audience listened intently, captivated by Pétion's words, which resonated with promises of progress and unity. "Under my leadership," Pétion continued, his voice unwavering, "we shall forge a path to prosperity for all Ayisyen. We have battled against oppression and tyranny, and now, it is time to build a nation that stands as a beacon of hope and resilience." His words echoed in the hall, stirring something deep within the hearts of those present.

Joute watched him with a mixture of admiration and concern. She knew the weight of the responsibilities that now rested on Pétion's shoulders would also be hers to bear. The road ahead was fraught with challenges, both internal and external. But she also knew his unwavering determination and resilience.

As Pétion spoke of land reforms to empower the peasantry, and of abolishing slavery abroad, wherever their influence could reach, murmurs of approval and some concern rippled through the crowd. His vision was grand, his dreams lofty, but there was a fire in his eyes that left no room for doubt.

The grand ballroom fell into a hushed reverence as Pétion's words lingered in the air, like a promise of a new dawn. Joute's gaze never wavered from him, her admiration for the man she stood beside mingling with a deep-rooted affection that transcended mere partnership. Their journey together had been one of shared ambitions, whispered fears, and unspoken sacrifices. She would become his présidential partner, vowing to shape the country in their mutual vision.

The crowd cheered their new leader and toasts were both short and lengthy from distinguished guests present. When all was said, the orchestra began again, and the celebration continued.

Junior raised his glass and pointed out, "You certainly have their attention, Monsieur Président."

"The country is young and full of potential," Pétion began, then glanced at his mistress before turning back to Junior and Boyer. "Joute and I will rely on your support."

"You have it," Boyer acknowledged, nodding in agreement with Junior. Three more of Pétion's loyal allies joined the group - Générals Borgella from Port Républicain, Bonnet from Léogâne, and Bazelais from Saint Marc. They all lifted their glasses as well, following the lead of Junior and Boyer.

"I am grateful for your unwavering loyalty to our President," Joute declared, surprising the group. Aside from Junior and Boyer who knew her well, these Générals were not accustomed to a woman speaking with such authority and influence.

"We and our armies are prepared to defend your presidency," Général Borgella affirmed, showing no acknowledgment towards Joute. "You can count on us." As was common during this time, each Général held enormous power over their territory, and their armies were always ready to follow their orders.

"I am certain of that, Général," Pétion replied before asking about the state of the regions under their control.

"Most regions are stable and remain loyal to you. We will handle any rebellions," Bonnet offered and continued with an encouraging report of a somewhat stable country.

Between 1807 and 1809, Pétion rewarded his most loyal soldiers with government-owned land as a token of appreciation and compensation for their services. This was also an attempt to increase tax revenue by encouraging these lands to become productive farms or light industrial businesses.

However, the results were lackluster, disappointing, and not as successful as Pétion had envisioned. Many soldiers struggled with farming on small plots of land and lacked the necessary expertise in the discipline of farming. In a meeting with his cabinet members, Pétion expressed his concerns and sought new ideas.

"We have exhausted our supply of fertile government-owned land that can be used for agriculture," stated one of the members present, Paul Auguste, who was a mulatto. "And even if we did have more available, our soldiers are not capable of successfully farming."

"The soldiers have already received enough land and others are not willing to sign up for it. They prefer money instead," Pétion added firmly. "But I believe we can reclaim unlawfully rented lands from the land barons and redistribute them to the peasant farmers for agricultural purposes."

"Mr. Président, many of those lands belong to the elite class in the South. How can we confiscate them?" questioned Charles Haspel, the minister of finance.

"I disagree with Mr. Haspel," chimed in Pierre Dejean, the minister of agriculture. "These so-called property owners have taken control of unowned land near their habitations and claim ownership without legal rights."

"But they have been cultivating these lands for years, even generations," argued Haspel. "Confiscating them now would only cause chaos and resentment towards the government."

"Those landlords have no right to rent out land that they do not legally own! Their actions resemble feudalism rather than landlords," countered Dejean.

Joute had been silently observing the discussion until she finally stood up to speak. The other cabinet members were surprised but

Pétion seemed open to hearing her opinion, though being his mistress.

"Gentlemen, remember that the peasantry is our power. We represent them, not these deceitful landowners who exploit their labor for personal gain," Joute passionately expressed. "It is time to right this wrong and relieve the peasants of their burdensome rent. Let us identify these lands and take action."

"Madame Lachenais, you cannot be serious..." started Haspel.

"Dejean and Haspel, I believe you both have valid points. You will work together on this project - Dejean will identify properties eligible for confiscation and Haspel will present arguments for or against it. If there are any disagreements, I will have the final say on each property," Pétion declared.

Both men nodded in agreement as the other cabinet members marveled at Joute's influence over Pétion's decisions. She would certainly be a powerful force to reckon with in the future. "Now, let us move on to the next item on the agenda," said Pétion.

The late afternoon sun cast a golden hue over the parlor of Marie-Louise Coidavid Christophe in Cap Français where she sat entwined in hushed conversation with her confidante, Marie Bayard. The air was thick with the scent of blooming jasmine from the garden, but its sweetness did nothing to alleviate the acrid taste of concern that lingered on their tongues.

"Marie," whispered Marie-Louise, her voice barely rising above the rustle of silk skirts, "the man who stands before me now, garbed in the regalia of power and authority, bears little semblance to the Henry I once knew."

Marie Bayard's keen eyes, which had seen much of life's vicissitudes, met those of her friend. She noted the subtle tremble in

Marie-Louise Coidavid Christophe and Marie Bayard enjoy each other's companionship and concern relative to the uncharacteristic behavior of Henry Christophe.

Marie-Louise's hands, an outward testament to an inner turmoil. "The tales that reach my ears are fraught with sorrow. To think that children were not spared death at Moca and Santiago on their march back from the Spanish campaign... It is unconscionable," Marie stated, referring to Dessalines' aborted attempt to conquer the Spanish East and their bloody retreat in 1806.

"Under Dessalines' banner, he acted," Marie-Louise continued in her husband's defense, her words punctuated by despair.

"But it was Henry's hand that steered their fate," Marie countered, "turning towns like Monte Plata into charred relics of what once was. And the people... treated as chattel on the very soil they toiled upon. His grief, Marie-Louise, it has eclipsed his humanity," Marie offered gently, though her own heart was heavy with the gravity of the misdeeds recounted.

"His heart turned fallow the day our eldest was claimed by the heavens," Marie-Louise confided, her gaze falling to the floor where the shadows grew longer with the waning day. "Where once there was a wellspring of compassion, now lies a barren wasteland. He has built a fortress around his sorrow, and within its walls, empathy cannot breach."

"Yet, I have seen the flicker of torment behind his eyes, the silent scream for the son he lost." Marie-Louise's voice cracked as she beseeched her friend. "We must find a way to navigate him through this maelstrom of pain. If left unchecked, I fear the whole nation will be consumed by the fires of his rage."

"The Senate's denial of absolute power only fueled his indignation, propelling him toward rebellion." Marie's countenance hardened at the memory of the ensuing strife. "His quest for dominion bathed our land in the blood of countless souls, even those who surrendered in captivity found no mercy, burned alive and immolated in a grotesque spectacle."

"However, hope yet endures for him, I know it, Marie-Louise," Marie insisted, her words imbued with the resilience that had carried her through tumultuous years.

"Help me, Marie. Help me guide him back to the path of righteousness," pleaded Marie-Louise, her eyes beseeching. "He listens to you. I cannot bear to watch the legacy of our revolution, and that of my husband, birthed from the hunger for freedom, be sullied by the hands of one of its most valiant champions."

Their exchange was a quiet symphony of shared resolve and unspoken fears, each note weighed down by the knowledge that the road ahead was fraught with uncertainty. In the stillness of that room, amidst the opulence that concealed the scars of a nation, two women stood as silent sentinels of hope, vowing to salvage the soul of a leader, and through him, the spirit of Ayiti itself.

Marie Bayard's somber gaze drifted to the portrait that adorned the mahogany-paneled wall of Général Christophe's mansion. The youthful visage of a twelve-year-old boy, captured in oils, looked back at her with eyes full of promise while he stood next to her husband, both in military attire. A soft sigh escaped her lips as she recalled the day when Henry, then but a child in the aftermath of war, had first crossed the threshold of her life. She had commissioned an artist who painted the work of art, entitled 'Jean et Henri', from her memory of the first days Henry had arrived in then Saint Domingue with the painting's name spelled with an 'I' for the French spelling of Henri, instead of the 'Y' like the British form 'Henry' that he had changed when he became emancipated.

"Chérie," she murmured, the endearment meant for the past and its long-lost innocence. Her husband Jean had returned from the Battle of Savannah during the American Revolution, his expression shadowed by the toll of conflict yet alight with compassion for the young slave who accompanied him. They took Henry in, fed him, clothed him, schooled him in manners and letters, and witnessed the blossoming of his intellect and spirit.

It was within the walls of Hôtel de la Couronne that Henry's true talents unfurled like sails against the Caribbean breeze. As the Hôtel manager, he navigated affairs with an adeptness that belied his youth, his acumen breathing prosperity into the establishment. He became more than an employee; he was kin, an older brother to young Jean-Baptiste Junior, and a confidant to Jean himself.

"Look how well he has assimilated," her husband used to say, pride lifting the corners of his mouth as they watched Henry skillfully mediate a dispute between two patrons or charm the local gentry into another night's stay.

Marie closed her eyes, allowing herself a moment's escape into the sepia-toned corridors of memory before the pressing darkness of the present pulled her back. Outside, beyond the opulent isolation of the estate, the land bled under the march of Général Christophe's army.

With grim resolve, the troops had retraced their steps from the scorched earth policies enacted in the southern region. But even as they neared Cap Français, their departure heralded no peace. Instead, a clandestine unit, veiled by the shadows of twilight, dispatched violence upon those whose skin bore the lighter hue of mixed heritage.

Whispers of terror wound their way through marketplaces and into the homes of families. Tales of mulatto men and women, children clutching at their skirts, cut down where they stood or fled. Silent screams echoed in the stillness of the night, and the air was thick with mourning—a testament to the unchecked wrath of a leader whose heart had hardened against his people.

"Mon Dieu," Marie breathed, her hands clenching into fists. How could the same hands that once expertly arranged a floral centerpiece for a diplomat's banquet now be stained with the blood of the innocent?

The stark juxtaposition haunted her, gnawing at the edges of her stoic demeanor. Hope, the persistent ember that had endured the hurricane of revolution, flickered beneath the onslaught of such merciless reprisal. Yet still, it persisted, fueled by the steadfast resilience etched deep within the soul of every Ayisyen who dreamt of liberty.

In the quietude of reflection, Marie stood—a pillar of strength against the tide of despair, her heart heavy with the burden of history, but her spirit unyielding in the pursuit of a brighter dawn.

The sun heated the earth of Cap Français, its heat mirroring the burning fury in Général Henry Christophe's heart. His elite brigade, a legion of a thousand men, marched with solemn precision, their boots pounding the cobblestone streets like the relentless beat of a death drum. The air was thick with tension, cut only by the sharp jangle of bridles and the heavy breathing of horses.

Henry rode at the forefront, his posture rigid, eyes scanning the horizon with a predatory gaze. His once vibrant spirit, which had shone brightly in the salons of Hôtel de la Couronne, had been dimmed by the shadows of war and defeat. His officers flanked him, their voices low and measured as they ventured words of solace and strategy, but he swatted them away like pesky flies, his mind awhirl with thoughts of retribution and the establishment of a new dominion in this land of the north.

For three weeks after his arrival, he had distanced himself from home, from Marie-Louise and his children. The fear of an assassin's blade kept him ensconced within the grim perimeter of his military encampment, where the echo of revolt whispered through the ranks. Yet now, as he approached the grandeur of his residence, a fortress against the chaos that swelled outside its walls, unease tugged at his steely resolve. Fifty soldiers, handpicked for their unwavering loyalty, remained close, a living shield against the invisible menace of betrayal.

Upon entering the serene sanctuary of his home, the clamor of the city fell away, replaced by the soft cooing of doves and the murmur of fountains. Marie-Louise awaited him, her elegance undiminished by the sorrow that weighed upon her delicate features.

"Mon amour," she greeted, her voice a tender whisper, yet it carried the weight of mountains. It broke the spell of warfare that clung to Henry's skin, leaving behind a man vulnerable to the echoes of his past deeds.

In the presence of his children, Henry's mask of severity softened. He embraced them with arms that had commanded battalions, now gentle instruments of paternal affection. Their laughter, unburdened by the complexities of their father's world, offered a reprieve from the reality that loomed over him like an ominous cloud.

But Marie-Louise could not ignore the signs—the distant look in his eyes, the subtle clench of his jaw. She confronted him later, in the quiet of their chamber, where the truths they shared were stripped of ceremony.

"Your anger, it has become a tempest within you," she said, her gaze steady though her heart raced. "It frightens me, Henry."

"Anger? Meanness?" he countered, his denial swift as a rapier's thrust. "No, I am driven by necessity, by the will to forge a future for you, our children, and our people."

"Is it necessity or is it grief?" Marie-Louise pressed, undeterred. "Our son—" Her voice cracked, the name too painful to utter.

"Silence!" The word exploded from him, shattering the fragile peace. He turned away, embarrassed by his inability to control his emotions and his temper, taking it out on her as his broad shoulders heaved, a bulwark against the onslaught of memories best left buried.

"Hope can still be salvaged from despair," Marie-Louise whispered, more to herself than to him. Her words that floated in the room imbued her resilience that had endured, much yet still dared to dream.

Outside, the night settled over Cap Français, a blanket of stars watching over a land caught between the throes of revolution and the yearning for tranquility. In the hearts of its people, the flame of freedom flickered defiantly, a testament to the enduring human spirit that no tyranny could ever extinguish.

The hushed stillness of the room lay in stark contrast to the storm that brewed within Marie Bayard's chest as she awaited Henry Christophe's arrival. The air was thick with the scent of tropical flowers, which had been arranged meticulously around the parlor, an attempt at normalcy amid chaos. The rustle of silk announced her husband's approach before his somber figure appeared, lending a silent strength to her side.

"Marie," Jean Baptiste whispered, his hand finding hers, both cool and grounding. "Are you certain you wish to confront him? Let me do this alone to spare you from that anguish"

"Silence is complicity," Marie responded with quiet resolve, her voice laced with the weight of impending confrontation.

The tension coiled tighter as footsteps heralded the entrance of the great Général Henry Christophe, but to them, just Henry. His silhouette filled the doorway, the lines of his uniform sharp, his countenance betraying nothing of the turmoil reported in hushed whispers throughout Cap Français.

"Henry," Marie greeted, her tone informal, as she rose to meet his gaze, noticing he was not approaching her quickly as he always did. She went to him and extended her cheeks for their customary pecks.

"Madame Bayard," he replied, a frosty veneer over his words. "You requested my presence."

"And when did you become so formal with me? You have always called me Marie. How you have changed so," Marie began, her composed exterior belying the fervor of her spirit.

"Forgive me, Marie. Jean, it is good to see you both once more," Henry said, attempting to be kind as Jean approached him, taking his hand for a brisk shake. "You asked to see me as soon as possible. I am here."

"Your campaign has left deep scars upon our land, Henry. The devastation that cuts into the very heart of Ayiti," Marie accused as she lunged into the subject matter at hand.

Jean Baptiste stepped forward for support, not expecting Marie to be so abrupt, his voice a steady baritone. "We have stood by you, fought beside you, but this path you carve now concerns us deeply."

Henry's eyes, dark pools reflecting an unspoken history, remained impassive. "My actions are for the good of our nation. To protect it from enemies, both foreign and domestic."

"By killing mulattos?" Marie's question hung heavy between them. "Jean and I, we share their blood. Do we also stand amongst those you deem as traitors? Are we also in danger from your death squads?"

"Your loyalty has never been in question," Henry retorted, his voice low. "But understand, my war is not against a color, but against division, against those who would see Ayiti crumble."

"Yet division is what you sow," Jean Baptiste countered, imploring sense to a man he could once reason with.

As the silence stretched, Henry's stance shifted imperceptibly, a façade of control over a tempest of conviction. "I will unify this country," he declared, "under one flag, one rule. The State of Ayiti shall rise in the North, and I shall lead it towards greatness."

"Through force, fear, intimidation… murder?" Marie challenged, her resilience hardening in the face of such unbending determination.

"Through necessity," Henry insisted. "And through order. I have seen too much chaos and too much weakness. It ends now."

Marie watched the man who once stood as a brother to her husband, now cloaked in the mantle of power, his vision for Ayiti crossing the boundaries of tyranny. Yet beneath the ironclad exterior, she glimpsed the shards of a soul burdened by loss, twisted by grief into something unrecognizable.

"Order must be underpinned by justice, Henry," Marie implored softly, hoping to reach the vestiges of the man they once knew. "Without it, freedom is but an illusion."

"Freedom," Henry echoed, a hint of the old fire flickering in his eyes. "It has always been about freedom. And I will secure it for our people, ensure their prosperity, even if it requires them to bend to the yoke of discipline."

"Discipline to what extent and with what penalties?" asked Jean.

"Discipline that shapes a nation," Henry affirmed. "One where each man, woman, and child knows their place, their duty. My reforms will bring about a new era of civility, progress, and prosperity."

In the waning light, the shadows played across Henry's face as he spoke of his dreams, a tableau of a leader torn between the nobility of intent and the despotism of method. Marie felt the pang of sorrow for what could have been, for the harmony that seemed to slip further away with each passing sentence.

"Hope, Henry," she whispered, the word a benediction for the haunted look that passed fleetingly across his face. "Let it not be lost in your quest for order."

"Hope," he repeated, softer now, and for an instant, the mask lifted, revealing the vulnerability of a torn man. "Hope will indeed reign in Ayiti, Marie. You have my word."

With that, Henry, Général Christophe, and the self-proclaimed President of the new State of the Grand Nord of Ayiti turned on his heel, his departure leaving a wake of unanswered questions and a fragile thread of hope that clung desperately to the idea of a future where freedom and peace might yet flourish in this battered land.

Twelve

THE STARK DIFFERENCE OF ADMINISTRATIVE GOVERNENCE

Southern Penninsula
May 1809

Two more years had passed, and Pétion stood before the vast expanse of green that stretched out from the grand habitation, his eyes reflecting a vision far beyond the horizon. The weight of his name—an homage to Jérôme Pétion de Villeneuve, a staunch abolitionist and prior mayor of Paris during Pétion's studies there, whose ideals he carried like a sacred flame—pressed upon his shoulders as heavily as the humid air of Ayiti itself. He gazed at the opulent home, a symbol of colonial grandeur and oppression, its walls blending into the verdant landscape, a relic of an era that Pétion had vowed to dismantle with fervor.

His fingers traced the rough bark of a nearby mahogany tree, grounding himself in the reality of his mission. The air was thick with the scent of tropical flowers, the constant hum of insects, and the chirping of exotic birds.

"Général Pétion," a familiar voice called softly from behind, breaking the reflective silence. Jean-Pierre Boyer approached, his presence as a reminder of their interconnected struggles for freedom and their shared mission.

"Jean-Pierre," Pétion acknowledged without turning, his gaze still locked on the fields. "You see before you the remnants of chains we have broken. What remains are not plantations but opportunities—lands waiting to be nurtured by those once bound to them."

"Indeed," Boyer replied, stepping beside him. "Your actions echo loudly in the hearts of men who yearn for liberty, not just freedom. But tell me, how will you ensure these lands do not fall into the tyranny of neglect?"

Pétion turned, finally facing his most loyal ally and one he dared to call friend, his expression solemn. "We redistribute. We entrust these acres to hands that have tilled without reward and who have been extorted by the inhabitants of that house, and many more like them. We will distribute the land to the families who have never reaped the fruits of their labor. They will claim ownership, not merely through papers but through the sweat that merges with the soil."

"An ambitious undertaking," Boyer mused, his brow furrowed with both admiration and concern. "But the wealthy, the previous proprietors—how will they take to this new order?"

"Monsieur Baglet sitting fat in that habitation over there has no rights to the lands that surround him which he claims as his own and then rents for profit from the unknowing peasantry. Soon that will be corrected. They will resist," Pétion admitted, a shadow crossing his visage. "They still cling to the old ways and the illusion of superiority and entitlement. But it is an inevitable resistance that we must overcome. For what is a nation if not the sum of its people's well-being?"

"Revolutionary," Boyer said softly, the word carrying weight. "To build from the ashes and to sow seeds where there was once despair."

"Revolutionary indeed," Pétion echoed, his voice a steady thrum of determination. "It is a path fraught with difficulty, but one we must tread. These lands shall be divided among those who have been denied their due by those like the residents in that grand habitation, extorted of their hard-earned sweat, forced to pay homage to these barons through their crops. They shall now cultivate hope from the very earth that has witnessed their sorrow and reap more of their labor's fruits instead of appropriating them to those who take advantage of their privilege and stature, as does Mr. Baglet, eating their fruits in there without giving them proper compensation."

As the two men contemplated the future, the sun dipped lower, casting a golden hue over the land—a silent promise of the harvests to come. Pétion knew the road ahead would be tumultuous, marked by the discontent of those who saw their power waning. Yet within him burned the unquenchable desire for fairness, a legacy he intended to embed in the fertile ground of Ayiti. The warm breeze carried the sounds of distant drums and laughter from nearby villages, reminding Pétion of the resilience and spirit of his people. As the fiery sun descended beneath the horizon, he couldn't help but feel a sense of hope for a future where all Ayisyen could thrive on their land, free from oppression and injustice.

A year later, the sun's descent brought a cooler air over the verdant fields, where men and women worked with diligence that spoke of newfound purpose. Président Alexandre Pétion stood at the edge of one such plot, his gaze surveying the rows of crops that swayed gently in the evening breeze. These were the lands reclaimed, the tendrils of independence taking root in the very soil that had been the bedrock of colonial exploitation.

'Papa Bon-Coeur'- *Father Good Heart*, the new name branded the new Président, whispered an elderly man as he straightened his back, pausing in his labor. His hands, though gnarled with age and work, cradled a yam like a precious gem. A respectful nod was exchanged between the two; no grand gestures were needed to convey the depth of gratitude that flowed from the heart of the farmer as he handed the fruits of his labor to the Président as a gesture of thanks.

"Work well, my friend," Pétion encouraged, his voice warm yet tinged with the gravity of their shared endeavor. "This land is now yours to nurture," as Pétion took the fruit, brought it to his nose, and took in the ripe scent.

"Oui, Président Pétion," the man replied, his words carrying the weight of years spent in bondage now broken. "We will make this soil sing with our sweat and toil."

As Pétion turned away from the man, continuing his inspection, he could feel the pulse of the land underfoot—a steady rhythm that beat in time with the hearts of its cultivators. They were forging a new Ayiti, one furrow at a time.

A subtle scent of ripening sugar cane drifted on the wind, leading Pétion's attention to where the fruits of the farmers' labors were being gathered. Young and old alike bundled the produce, preparing it for transport to the markets and docks. The system, while not without its critics, provided sustenance and a modicum of stability in these tumultuous times.

As Pétion lost himself in a daydream of progress and prosperity for his beloved country, a familiar voice jolted him back to reality. It was Jean-Baptiste Bayard Junior, his face etched with worry and the weight of responsibility as he climbed down from his carriage. "Monsieur Président," he began, "export shipments of coffee and sugar are dwindling. Our once prosperous farms are no longer producing these goods in abundance."

Pétion's heart sank at this news, but he forced a reassuring smile onto his face. He could not show weakness in front of his young senator. "It will recover, my friend," he said with optimism. "Just wait until these farmers experience progress and the luxuries their hard-earned money can buy."

But there was more bad news to come. Junior continued, "And that is not all. With the embargo imposed by Jefferson, we now have a surplus of indigo, cotton, and cacao. We were once the leading exporter in the world of these products, but cannot sell them to our largest markets in the United States."

Pétion's heart dropped even further at this revelation. He asked, "What is this costing us?"

"Trade in 1805 with the states amounted to nearly seven million dollars. Last year it shrunk to less than two million," Junior replied with clear worry etched on his face. "It's a huge problem and an enormous loss of tax revenue, Mr. President."

"What is Christophe doing about it in the north?" Pétion asked.

"They are not dependent on the United States. It is their smallest market. They sell mostly to the British, whereas we have now lost trade with the U.S. and France.

"This too shall pass, my young senator," Pétion reassured him with a smile. "Let us go and ease your worries over a scrumptious lunch."

But despite Pétion's confident words, things did not improve as he had predicted. The landowner farmers, newly freed from paying rent to wealthy landowners, began to work less and spend more time enjoying life with their families. The United States refused to lift the embargo until well into 1810, leading to a prolonged struggle for Pétion's country.

Month after month, there were fewer and fewer produce available for local markets as the farmers consumed more of their crops for sustenance. The money supply began to dry up due to the United States embargo, causing inflation to soar and a recession to take hold of the country. Despite Pétion's best efforts, the economy began to unravel alarmingly.

The silhouette of Président Pétion cut a stark outline against the burgeoning dawn sky as he strode through the cobblestone streets of Port Républicain. The rising sun cast long shadows over the quiet early morning, painting a serene picture that belied the tumultuous undercurrents of the nation he led. As he approached a sturdy building, its façade unadorned yet dignified, Pétion was struck by a sense of pride and purpose. This was the Lycée Pétion, the embodiment of his belief in education as a transformative force.

The school's student body encapsulated the children of working-class artisans, professionals, government employees, and shopkeepers. There was also a mixture of the children of well-to-do farmers who had carved out some relative wealth and impressed the government as future leaders in the new country. The children of the elite, mostly comprised of mulattos and European whites who had remained, were not part of this school as they had the benefit of personal tutors or were educated in salons with others of their privileged class. The peasantry enjoyed no education at all, something Pétion hoped to change one day.

"Good morning, Président Pétion," greeted a young man sweeping the entrance, his voice tinged with reverence.

"A la yon bèl jounen – *What a beautiful morning*," Pétion replied with a warm smile, offering a nod of acknowledgment. His eyes lingered on the youth, recognizing not just a caretaker of brick and mortar, but a custodian of a future forged by knowledge.

Inside, the halls were alive with activity. The sound of fervent discourse filled the air as young minds engaged in lively debates and discussions. Their eyes shone with curiosity and determination. The aroma of ink and parchment mingled with the subtle musk of new mahogany furniture. Pétion stood at the back of a classroom, observing as an instructor expounded upon the principles and responsiblities of freedom—concepts dear to Pétion's heart.

"Liberty is more than just a word," declared the teacher passionately. "It is a continuous pursuit that must be nurtured within the walls of institutions such as this," as he stole a glance towards Pétion.

"Indeed," Pétion whispered to himself, his words barely audible among the chorus of learning, moving from class to class of mathematics, history, reading, and the like.

He thought back to his decision to dismantle the plantation system, which had brought economic hardship, but also emotional prosperity to the country. Yet even amidst doubts and criticism, he remained steadfast in his conviction that true prosperity could only be achieved through embracing these ideals.

A few days later, the sun shone brightly in Port Républicain, over the bustling streets and a cool winter breeze brought a welcome respite to the heat of the day. As his carriage made its way through the busy city, the Président could feel the excitement building within him for his plans to spend the afternoon with Joute and his secret plans for a picnic.

Across from him, his staff had prepared a mobile feast with Joute's favorite culinary delights. The succulent duck was cooked to perfection, accompanied by boiled potatoes and carrots smothered in a creamy butter sauce, and an assortment of breads and fruits. And to top it off, there was a beautifully decorated cake specially baked for the occasion.

As they arrived at their destination, L'Orphelinat de Port Républicain Pour Filles - The Orphanage of Port Républicain For Girls, the Président couldn't help but marvel at the grandeur of the structure before him. It stood tall and proud, a testament to Joute's unwavering dedication to providing a home for orphans. Across the street stood an identical building, with only one word changed in its name: *Garçons* instead of *Filles*, indicating that it was exclusively for orphan boys.

As Pétion gazed upon the impressive building, he noticed two young girls darting into the entrance, most likely scouts planted by Joute to report his arrival. She always had a flair for pomp and circumstance, and he eagerly anticipated whatever program she had planned for his visit.

Stepping into the grand hallway Pétion would not be disappointed as he was greeted by at least one hundred boisterous boys and girls who cheered "Bonjour Monsieur le Président!" He smiled warmly as two older girls, complete with white ribbons in their hair, rushed to his side and escorted him to a large chair adorned with flowers and fabric in his honor. They gestured for him to take a seat.

President Alexandre Pétion enjoys the boys and girls choir at L'Orphelinat de Port Républicain as Joute, and the orphanage directors; Madame Fombrun, and Monsieur Boncy look on.

Amidst cheers and applause, the children began singing a beautiful melody in chorus. Pétion watched with pride as Joute stood in the background, beaming with joy. The concert lasted for four songs with each executed flawlessly. Afterward, everyone took to the courtyard at the rear of the building to enjoy a refreshing tropical fruit punch and delicious meat patés.

Joute approached him with a man and a woman by her side, formally addressing him as "Monsieur le Président." She was radiating with pride. Pétion took her hand and tenderly kissed it, saying, "It is my honor to be here, Madame Lachenais."

Joute then introduced him to Madame Fombrun, the mistress director for the girls, and Monsieur Boncy, the director for the boys. Both gave a slight bow of their heads as Pétion shook their hands and praised them for their work with the children of the country. "The country thanks you for your commitment to our youth and your devotion to their success. By what I have just witnessed, their future is in good hands."

"Merci, Monsieur le Président," they both replied in unison.

Pétion, with Joute and the two directors, stood at the head of a line as children waited to meet and shake the Président's hand. Once the procession was completed, Joute and Pétion walked to the carriage. It was a heartwarming and memorable visit that left Pétion feeling grateful for all those who dedicated their lives to helping the future generations of Ayiti thrive.

The carriage ascended the winding roads of the hills, taking nearly an hour to reach their destination. Pétion's anticipation for the divine meal he had prepared was almost palpable.

"We are almost there, my love. Just a few moments longer," he reassured Joute, his anxious companion.

As they reached the crest of a mountain and a grassy area nestled halfway up the steep slopes, the sprawling capital city came into view several miles below. Pétion helped Joute out of the carriage and directed two servants from the trailing wagon to set up a lavish outdoor dining area with tablecloths, silverware, and all the necessary accouterments under a large mahogany tree. The servants then left, along with the six soldiers on horseback who were stationed as guards nearby.

"It is in moments like these that you always have something delightful up your sleeve," Joute exclaimed with a smile as they settled in to enjoy their afternoon together.

After nearly three hours of tasty foods, desserts, wine, and lively conversation filled with refreshing laughter in the perfect weather and magnificent view of the Ayisyen mountainside, Pétion's gaze shifted towards a distant cliff.

"What are you looking at?" Joute asked curiously, sensing his attention had wandered away from their joyous picnic.

"Do you see anything over there?" Pétion replied, directing her attention towards the high peak of Boutilier overlooking Port Républicain.

Joute peered closely but saw nothing out of the ordinary. "No," she said confused. "What should I be looking for?"

Pétion continued to stare before finally revealing his discovery. "If you look closely enough, now and then you can catch a glint of sunlight off of a shiny piece of metal. Those are cannons placed strategically on the cliff to protect our city."

Joute's eyes widened as Pétion got up and retrieved a spyglass from his ornate hunting bag. She eagerly took it from him and scanned the horizon, successfully spotting each cannon he pointed out.

"Can these cannons shoot that far, Alexandre?" Joute asked in amazement.

"From here, yes. We are at a high elevation," Pétion explained with pride. "It's one of my favorite tactics. With the right angle precisely calculated, and a measured increase of gunpowder, those cannons can hit any ship entering our harbor or an advancing army many miles away."

Joute couldn't help but be drawn to Pétion's passion for artillery and the way he excitedly spoke about it. "You are very sensuous when you speak of artillery, Alexandre." She became more motivated to show him extra affection tonight. "You make me want you even more when you share our bed this evening."

Pétion smiled as they gathered their belongings and called for the staff, it was clear that their time in the mountains had come to an end. But Joute couldn't help feeling grateful for this brief moment of peace and beauty amid constant threats and turmoil in their country.

The afternoon sun poured into the chamber where Pétion sat, surrounded by his Générals. Tension crackled in the air, thick with the weight of military men confined within bureaucratic walls.

The Générals, decorated with medals and bearing scars of battle, sat stiffly in their chairs, their discomfort evident in the tightness of their jaws and the rigidity of their posture.

"Brothers," Pétion began with a solemn tone, "Ayiti stands at a crossroads, a new era where the pen must wield as much power as the sword."

Murmurs rippled through the room, skepticism etched on the faces of men accustomed to the clarity of battlefields rather than the abstractions of governance.

"Many of you may struggle with letters and laws," he continued empathetically, "but we must remember that strength lies not only in our arms but also in our wisdom as leaders."

"Président Pétion," one grizzled Général spoke up, his calloused hands betraying years of campaigns, "we are soldiers. Our expertise lies in strategy and combat."

"Indeed," Pétion acknowledged, "but now that we have achieved independence, our focus must shift towards stabilizing and growing our nation. We must adapt and embrace new skills if we are to guide Ayiti towards lasting sovereignty."

Silence descended upon the room like a heavy cloak as they absorbed his words. These men who once looked down musket barrels now faced a daunting realm of parchment and laws, their gazes shifting nervously between each other.

Joute rose from her seat and addressed them with authority. "My fellow Généraux, speak freely and honestly. As I have observed these discussions, it is clear that your hearts are still on the battlefield rather than in these halls of government, am I correct?"

The Généraux turned to Pétion for permission to speak; unaccustomed to a woman speaking so openly.

"What say you, Général Borgella?" Pétion asked one of his staunchest allies.

"With all due respect, Monsieur Président," the Général replied, "I would be much more effective and prefer to lead my men in the fields rather than being confined to an assembly hall, as Madame Lachenais has correctly observed."

"As would I," added Général Bonnet.

"And I as well," confirmed Général Bazelais.

"Then it is settled," Pétion urged, "let us come together for the sake of our people who look to us as architects of their destiny. We will seek out those in our communities who desire their voices to be heard in these halls."

As the Généraux filed out of the room, some with reluctant nods and others with furrowed brows, Pétion remained with Joute and Boyer.

"Well, that could not have gone any better," Joute remarked after the last Général had left.

"Agreed," Jean-Pierre Boyer added. "I thought we would face far more resistance to them sharing power with non-military citizenry."

"They understand that they are out of their element. Most cannot compose a sentence on parchment and the others can barely read one. They are good men but not suited for this role. Unlike you and me, Jean-Pierre, who were educated at the finest universities in Paris," offered Pétion.

"Now begins the process of organizing elections for replacements in the outlying districts," Joute interjected. "We will tell the people that we want them to elect their representatives, and more importantly, have a voice in their future. But we must steer these elections towards those who will support you best."

"Very wise, Madame Joute," Boyer said, using her informal nickname as a sign of friendly familiarity. "But we cannot be seen as manipulating the elections. Perhaps someone else should spearhead this political move."

"May I suggest Jean-Baptiste Bayard, Junior?" Joute immediately responded without hesitation. "He is intelligent, highly educated, articulate, and extremely loyal to our Président, possesses strong administrative capabilities, and can be extremely persuasive when in debate. Let him be the one to organize your supporters."

As the sun slowly disappeared behind the horizon, a warm, golden light enveloped Jean-Baptiste Bayard Junior's sprawling estate. Amidst the growing shadows, a group of distinguished black and mulatto men and women gathered in the grand salon, their faces exuding an air of contemplative authority.

"Education is the very soul of a republic," murmured Pétion, his gaze sweeping across the room filled with individuals from various professions. Businessmen, farmers, lawyers, physicians, educators, intellectuals, and others mingled together, exchanging ideas and strategies over glasses of rum cocktails, champagne, and wine.

"Jean-Baptiste," Pétion addressed Junior as he made his way towards him, his voice resonating with a weight that seemed to draw the walls closer. "Your counsel has been our guiding compass through these tumultuous times. Your work and connections throughout the regions are very much needed and appreciated."

Junior, a symbol of discretion and insight, nodded solemnly, the lamplight glinting off his piercing eyes. "Président Pétion, it is our collective duty to ensure that Ayiti's legislature is composed of not only loyal but also competent individuals capable of advancing our cause with wisdom and foresight."

A sense of gravity hung heavy in the air as Junior outlined his strategy to strengthen their ranks with erudite senators. Without their knowledge, the candidates in this very room were being quietly studied, evaluated, and rated for these abilities. Meticulously, Junior detailed to Pétion the profiles of potential candidates - each one a pillar in their respective communities possessing intellect and integrity - while gesturing to indicate those whom he would choose for the task. Each person a crucial piece of the puzzle in Pétion's grand vision for the nation's success.

"And so, we must entrust our future to those who can wield knowledge as deftly as a Général wields his sword," Pétion said, keenly aware that there were no military men present.

As the conversation shifted towards strategic planning, Joute appeared in the salon. Her entrance was unannounced, yet her influence could be felt by all, like a silent tide lifting all ships. She moved with grace and poise, belying her sharp intellect. Her eyes sparkled with unspoken thoughts as she commanded the attention of everyone in the room. Both men and women admired her.

"Joute," Pétion greeted with a respectful nod, acknowledging her not only as his confidante but also as the hidden force guiding the nation's affairs.

"Président," she replied, her voice conveying both power and persuasion. "The work we do here will be remembered for generations to come. To ensure its purity, we must remain vigilant against corruption and weakening resolve."

Joute seamlessly wove her insights into the ongoing discussion, her observations sharp and her suggestions incisive. For those familiar with Ayisyen politics, her role was undeniable; she was the key to redefining the identity of a nation.

"Your perspective is invaluable as always," Pétion acknowledged, his admiration for her wisdom evident in the softening of his features. "Together, we are laying the foundations of a new nation brick by brick, rooted in unity and enlightenment," he acknowledged, as he toasted Junior and Joute before continuing their conversation.

Outside, the stars began to twinkle silently, bearing witness to the unfolding drama of a country striving for an ideal - a beacon of hope amidst human struggles. This evening was just one step in finding the best individuals to lead in building this nation. Jean-Baptiste Junior would continue these gatherings throughout the southern part of the country as elections were organized to choose representatives selected from this very room.

As Junior excused himself to join other candidates in their search for the best leaders, Pétion and Joute shared a moment of mutual understanding. In this intimate setting, their partnership was more than just two individuals - it represented resilience and the promise of a better future, free from the shackles of the past.

"Papa Bon-Coeur," they affectionately called him, and in moments like this, Pétion felt the weight of that endearment. For in the eyes of common people and history alike, his legacy would not be measured by battles won, but by lives uplifted and a society transformed through the pursuit of freedom. These men and women gathered tonight, who are educated, wealthy, and prominent, were essential in achieving this goal for those who have not what they possess.

Cap Français

The British government had kept good relations with the new country, first with Dessalines' government and later with Henry's in the North. The governor of Jamaica had initially coaxed Dessalines to become a king, but he had opted for the title of Emperor, in part to best his French rival, Napoleon Bonaparte who proclaimed himself an emperor several months after.

Upon the death of Dessalines, the British seized on the opportunity to enjoy good diplomatic relations with Henry, preferring the northern president over Alexandre Pétion in the south. After all, Henry was born on St. Kitts in the British West Indies and spoke perfect English. Within a short period, Ayiti became a major supplier to the British navy and her other colonial islands as British gold began to fill the coffers of Henry's government. The British lobbied him continuously to crown himself king of the new nation so they could continue to enjoy good, strong relations and an exclusive partnership. This was very appealing to Henry's zest for more power.

Four years later, in 1811, Henry declared the northern state of Ayiti a kingdom and had himself crowned by Jean-Baptiste-Joseph Brelle, the archbishop of Cap Français. An edict on April 1st, 1811 proclaimed his full title as King of Ayiti, Sovereign of Tortuga, Gonâve, and other adjacent islands, Destroyer of tyranny, Regenerator and Benefactor of the Ayisyen nation, Creator of her moral, political, and martial institutions, First crowned monarch of the New World, Defender of the faith, and Founder of the Royal Military Order of Saint Henry.

Henry named his son Jacques-Victor Henry heir apparent, giving him the title of Prince Royal of Ayiti, and his wife regent if he died before the prince was of age, as he was only seven at the time. He was also named a future Colonel in the army.

In July 1811, Henry instituted a commission to elaborate laws that would be submitted to the Privy Council of the Grand Council of State for consideration. He would arrive early, take an active and dominant part in the discussions, present his arguments, and shed light on the debates. The conferences lasted about six months; and, at the end of January of 1812, nine new laws were passed and compiled together under the title of the Code Henry, using the first name of its creator.

The laws on agriculture were divided into eight parts. The first three dealt with the reciprocal obligations of the landowner and the farmer who cultivated the land. The landowner was to treat the workers as well as possible; otherwise, the latter could complain to the King's lieutenant.

The owner was obligated to construct the essential buildings and provide the mill and the tools needed to make sugar. He had the responsibility of keeping the mill in good condition, making sure that the sugar cane was planted, taking care of the fields, and cutting the cane in time to make sugar of impeccable quality. Coffee plantations had to have a good location, drying sheds, and a crushing and winnowing mill. The old coffee trees had to be pruned and cut back.

Part four governed the distribution of a quarter of the revenues that went to the cultivators. All rural habitations that owned a workshop following the law had to first sell their crop and then distribute a quarter share to the eligible parties. The last part of this law regards offenses and penalties. Infractions were punished with fines, imprisonment, and coercion of labor.

Due to the Ayisyen Army's system of structure, just as it was in the south, it was consistent in the north. Générals of the army that would oversee different regions were granted enormous power and virtual autonomy. Their armed forces were loyal to them first and to the kingdom second. This concerned Henry a great deal, making him more paranoid about insurrection than he already was.

In conversations with the British admirals, he learned that there were African warriors in Dahomey who desired to relocate. The appeal of a free nation governed by blacks enticed many to want to relocate across the Atlantic. As Great Britain was very active on the African coast, the British arranged for some of the Dahomey leaders to visit Ayiti on British warships to consult with King Henry.

Soon, a deal was struck for the importation of African warriors which Henry utilized for palace security and to balance the power in case wayward Générals would want to overthrow him. Between the years of 1808 and 1809, nearly two thousand of these mighty Dahomian warriors had migrated to Ayiti to form a security force separate from the army. They were already trained in guerilla warfare, and upon arrival, Henry supplemented their skills by personally training them on conventional warfare. He told his Générals that they would be strictly used for policing the population to relieve the army of that burden. However, the Générals were very weary of them.

Henry set about acclimating them to the ways and customs of Ayiti without the loss of their focus and African warrior attributes. To enhance their stature, he had special uniforms designed that were regal; white uniforms made of Egyptian cotton highlighted by tassels of gold. Instead of boots, they kept their open-toed sandals that they much better preferred and more effective wearing.

The imported soldiers, now named The Royal Dahomets, became the police force in the countryside, assuring strict adherence to Code Henry. Everything was scrutinized, from work ethic, cleanliness of property, obeying the laws, truancy, and even dress codes. Every plantation was inspected at three o'clock in the morning by an agent of the Royal Dahomets who was in charge of surveillance. The cultivator was obligated to work the land and could not leave as he wished, wander from one habitation to the other, or live wherever he wanted. It was required that all citizens have a job and have to be able to prove their employment.

On this day, in the burgeoning light of dawn, Cap Henry unfurled itself like a grand tapestry beneath the watchful gaze of King Henry Christophe. His silhouette cut against the morning sky as he surveyed the northern expanse from his balcony. The vibrant Cap Français had been christened with a new name by a new king, and with it bore the weight of his ambitions. The city was now named Cap Henry.

The air was thick with the scent of moist earth and sugarcane, a testament to the fertile lands that stretched across his dominion. Beneath him, the plantation system thrived under the rigidity of fermage—the system he had refined with an administrative acumen reminiscent of his days managing the Hôtel de la Couronne. The laborers moved rhythmically in konbit – *teamwork* – through the fields, their bodies bending and swaying in a dance dictated by survival rather than the spirit. Each stroke of their tools echoed the surrender of personal freedoms, forced to work where the government dictated, and the reality of restricted movement across the realm, for the promise of a quarter share in the harvest.

Henry's eyes narrowed as he considered the wealth accumulated through the bilateral trade with Britain, the British pounds that filled his treasury reaffirming the potency of his rule. Yet, despite the affluence that lined the coffers of the north, a restlessness stirred within him. He knew all too well that the glitter of gold could not mask the growing discontent among those who toiled on the plantations—better off, perhaps, but trapped in gilded misery.

Within the palace grounds, the newly crowned Queen Marie-Louise commenced her day with a quiet dignity befitting her station. Her chambers were adorned with the simplicity of elegance; the soft rustle of silk and the whispered consultations with her ladies-in-waiting underscored her new role. She carried her title as queen with a solemn grace, understanding that the honor bestowed upon her by the nation carried with it the weight of silent expectation. Her tasks were ceremonial, yet she approached each with the earnestness of one who understood the symbolic power of her presence.

As regent in waiting, should her son ascend to the throne prematurely, the gravity of potential governance rested uneasily on her shoulders. She did not meddle in the affairs of the state, but her influence was felt in the subtleties of court life and the compassionate glances she offered to those who suffered under the king's rigid edicts.

Henry descended from his vantage point, his footsteps echoing along the corridors, the sound mingling with the distant clinking of chains and murmurs of labor outside the palace walls. He paused before the grand tapestry that depicted the phoenix rising from ashes—the emblem of his rebirth and resilience. The truth of it resonated within him; out of destruction, he had forged a new kingdom, but at what cost?

"Je renais de mes cendres - *I am reborn from my ashes*" he murmured, a metaphor from his burning of Cap Ayitien back in 1802 by order of Toussaint Louverture when the French had invaded, the words more a question than a declaration. Could the ashes of his past truly birth a future of hope? Or would they only smother the flames of revolution that had once burned so fiercely in his heart?

As he turned away from the woven scene, the sun crested higher which would shortly blaze hot over the land. And somewhere between the harsh lines of discipline and the soft curves of hope, King Henry I contemplated the legacy he would leave upon the Kingdom of Ayiti—a realm caught in the throes of its turbulent birth.

The morning sun pierced the horizon, casting its first light upon the disciplined rows of Royal Dahomets who stood motionless within the encampment just outside the borders of Cap Henry. Their shadows stretched long and lean across the dew-soaked earth, a silent testament to the order King Henry had brought to these lands.

King Henry sat atop the huge charger, steadying the horse as he observed his warriors through the telescope that had become an extension of his reach. Citizens observing him in constant possession of his spyglass were convinced that he saw all in the kingdom.

The Royal Dahomets, his chosen enforcers from the distant shores of Dahomey, were a sight to behold—stoic, unyielding, and fearsome in their loyalty. They inspected the populace with almost surgical precision; no detail was too small, and no infraction too minor. The king's edicts on cleanliness and honesty were not mere suggestions but mandates etched into the bedrock of his kingdom.

"Your Majesty," an aide approached, bowing deeply. "The people grow ever more diligent under the gaze of your Dahomets."

"Vigilance breeds order," Henry replied without taking his eyes off the glass. "And order is the foundation of a strong nation."

Below, in the bustling markets of Cap Henry, one of the Dahomets discreetly placed a leather wallet bulging with coins near a fruit stall to test the honesty of the citizens as the King focused his instrument on it. The Dahomet then retreated to the shadows, his gaze unwavering as he watched the throng of early risers. The morning pedestrians passing would notice the wallet, but would not dare think to touch it. However, a young boy, his hands stained with the juice of mangoes, eyed the wallet before snatching it up and darting away.

Within moments, the Dahomet emerged, seizing the boy before he could disappear into the labyrinth of streets. The message was clear: even the smallest act of dishonesty would not escape the king's justice by any citizen – young or old. The boy would be administered his corporal punishment equal to his crime. The King was pleased.

Whispers fluttered through the crowds like startled birds—King Henry saw all, they said. He punished all. A shiver ran down the spines of the common folk, for in his quest for righteousness, the king had become omnipotent, omnipresent, serving as judge, prosecutor, executioner, and heavily feared.

Thirteen

CHALLENGING ECONOMIES, UPRISINGS, AND FOREIGNERS

Port Républicain
September 1811

The sun descended below the horizon, setting the sky ablaze with fiery reds and ominous purples as Alexandre Pétion stood motionless on the balcony of the senate building in September of 1811. The colors evoked a nation in turmoil - a nation he had sworn to guide towards its destiny four years ago when he became Président in 1807. From the harbor of Port Républicain came echoes of shouts and tolling bells, a haunting reminder of the fragile balance between progress and stability.

"Président Pétion," Général Jérôme Maximilien Borgella's voice pierced through the peaceful evening air, thick with salt and earth as his boots thundered with the announcement of his arrival. "We must discuss urgent matters."

Pétion turned, his gaze steady upon the Général's furrowed brow. "Speak, Général. What shadows now loom over our path?" his words hinted at those who opposed his presidency - like Général Yayou, who had attempted to assassinate him in June of 1807 and was later killed. And Magloire Amboise from Jacmel who had disobeyed orders and met a mysterious death, suspecting his loyal officers responsible, similar to Borgella, for their demise.

"Général Gérin has raised the banner of defiance in the south," Borgella reported, his tone sharp like the sound of marching soldiers. "He openly mocks you, calling you 'Mademoiselle Pétion' in contempt for Madeleine Lachenais' counsel!"

A flicker of annoyance passed over Pétion's face before he composed himself with a smile and light laughter. Joute - Marie-Madeleine Lachenais - was not just his mistress, but a trusted partner whose wisdom and strength were vital to his rule. Her presence at meetings was not simply tolerated but welcomed, a radical step that traditionalists like Gérin could never understand or accept. He wondered if deep down, Général Borgella and his other trusted Générals felt the same.

These Générals, even those most loyal to him, were like warlords. Their armies pledged allegiance to them first, wherever they resided in the south and west, and to the country second. They only united behind Pétion when faced with a common threat of invasion, except for his most loyal; Boyer, Bonnet, Bazelais, and the Général before him, Borgella. Should he also take this rebellion seriously?

These men were the protectors of his presidency. They could sniff out descent and insurrection and snuff it out before taking root. These were his mop-up men who could clean out trouble as efficiently as a housekeeper can clean a house.

"Let them mock," Pétion declared after a moment, his voice heavy as stone. "For while they jest, we build. And when history looks back, it will not remember their ridicule, but the progress of our hard work."

"Nevertheless," Borgella persisted, "we must address Gérin's uprising. It festers and poisons the unity we have fought so hard to establish."

"Then address it we shall," Pétion replied, his resolve unshakable. "With caution and no mercy for those who would see our republic crumble."

Borgella nodded in understanding, feeling the weight of command in Pétion's unwavering gaze. Those eyes had witnessed the horrors of war and the glimmer of hope in the hearts of a people finally freed from oppression.

Borgella and other loyal Générals marched their armies towards Gérin's rebellion, ultimately defeating him. But when they went to arrest Gérin, they found his lifeless body punctured with a self-inflicted gunshot wound ending his futile fight against Pétion's rule.

As the ship moaned and groaned against the turbulent waves, Andre Rigaud stepped off onto Ayisyen soil for the third time in the island's history. The air was thick with anticipation and whispers of unrest, and the scent of sea salt mingled with the uneasy shifting of his supporters who stood by his side. His body, once a fierce warrior of numerous battles, now seemed fragile, but his eyes burned with an unquenchable fire of sovereignty and defiance.

"Liberté!" he rasped to the gathering crowd of landowners and military loyalists, his voice weakened by years in French prisons and self-inflicted liver poisoning from excessive drinking. But it still held the power of a man who once commanded legions. "Our cause is not yet lost."

Rigaud quickly established himself as a leader among his followers who had urged his return, despite his physical frailty. He declared Les Cayes as the capital of his reclaimed State of the South ceded from Pétion's republic, drawing in desperate mulatto elites who saw him as their ticket back to wealth and status with a border north to Jérémie.

Meanwhile, far to the east in Port Républicain, Pétion felt the weight of leadership press upon him as he received news of Rigaud's return, a man he had once respected and served, following him into a failed rebellion and civil war in 1799 against Toussaint Louverture, Dessalines, and Christophe. That alliance still caused him much strife with Christophe even today.

In his garden filled with fragrant jasmine and damp earth, he pondered the unfolding power play before him. This move by

Rigaud was unexpected, and it came at a critical time when unity was crucial for their nation.

He entered back into his study, surrounded by the books he cherished most, describing great warriors and leaders; Alexander the Great, various Roman Caesars, Genghis Khan, and Ahmed Alba, the leader of the Songhai Empire of Africa, amongst others.
Pétion looked at maps of his fractured country and considered Rigaud's fate.

"Alexandre," Joute appeared like a ghost at his side, her voice a soothing balm and her presence a reminder of the complexities of power. "The South will return to us with time, not through brute force. You must exercise patience, Alexandre."

"Patience," Pétion repeated her words, feeling the meaning of them settle within him. He knew that force alone would not extinguish the dying ember of mulatto opposition in the South; it required a delicate touch and calculated reprisal. "But, Joute, patience comes at a cost, and it is often paid in human suffering. We must build a future where such costs are no longer necessary."

Joute nodded in understanding. "Then let us lay the foundation with care, for upon them we will build a nation that embodies liberté, égalité, fraternité - as you once sought and cherished."

Months passed, and Rigaud's grip on power weakened under the relentless march of his diseases. His death, a short six months after his return, left a void that could never be filled by those who had pinned their hopes on him. The south, aimless and fragmented, slowly reverted to Pétion's vision of unity and freedom under the bright blue sky above them.

It was the end of 1811, four years after taking office, and the economy had still not improved. Although it wasn't getting any worse, the scarcity of exports made it difficult to stimulate foreign exchange for trade. The once thriving port city now seemed desolate and quiet, with only a few ships docked in the harbor.

During this time, a wave of immigrants from the Middle East began to arrive on Ayiti's shores, seeking refuge from the violence in their home countries. Among them were Syrians, Moroccans, Palestinians, Jordanians, and others from the Ottoman Empire. These new arrivals brought much needed goods to the struggling country, as inflation and lack of imports had made many necessities scarce.

To simplify things, the Ayisyen referred to all these immigrants as Syrians, since they were unfamiliar with the entire Middle East. It didn't matter if you were from Palestine, Jordan, or elsewhere in the Middle East, in Ayiti, you were Syrian. Despite some initial skepticism from the locals, these frugal and shrewd merchants quickly integrated into society and became valued members of their communities.

Using wagons as their mode of transportation, they traveled from town to town selling their wares. Eventually, many of them settled down and opened shops, selling hardware, linens, and other Général store items. While they did interact with the local population, they tended to stick together and maintain their cultural customs, though over time eventually intermarrying amongst the Ayisyen population.

The arrival of the Middle Easterners provided a much-needed boost to an otherwise depressed country. Despite facing challenges like scarcity of food and the dwindling purchasing power from wealthy landowners who had lost their land due to confiscation by the government, the general mood in Ayiti was one of "happy depression," characterized by relative calm and low crime rates but also a sense of hopelessness due to economic apathy.

The peasants, once downtrodden and oppressed, now reveled in their newfound freedom as landowners. They toiled fewer days and hours in the grueling sun and were able to roam freely throughout the country, unlike the haunting tales of the north's Kingdom of Ayiti, where Général Christophe, now King Henry, ruled with a merciless iron fist and his forced labor policy of fermage.

It was a cruel irony that Alexandre Pétion's mulatto government of the Grand Sud could provide more happiness to their black population than King Henry's black government could provide for the benefit of their black population of the north.

And so, with grateful hearts, the black peasantry of the south counted their blessings, never forgetting the atrocities of their past and the fragility of their present peace, patient that Président Papa Bon-Cœur would lead them to eventual prosperity and total happiness.

It was the night of the opening celebration of his new Présidential palace - Volant-Le-Thor, as Alexandre Sabès Pétion gazed out at the horizon. The sky was a canvas of fiery colors, painting promises of renewal and hope for a better future. He stood tall, a symbol of resilience and determination, surrounded by the people who had gathered to celebrate the inauguration of their new Présidential palace.

The festivities were filled with laughter, dancing, and an abundance of delicious food and drink. The crowds outside joined in the celebration, people from all walks of life united in their belief that their Président Papa Bon-Cœur would lead them toward a brighter future someday.

But amidst the revelry, a somber note hung in the air. News had just arrived of the tragic end of Général Delva, a man who was respected by many and hated by others, and who had plotted to overthrow Pétion's government. He had been imprisoned for his actions and scheduled for release the next morning. He was found dead with his throat slit by an unknown assailant.

Whispers of conspiracy quickly spread throughout the palace like restless spirits, casting a shadow over the joyous occasion. Many believed that Pétion himself had played a hand in Delva's demise, but no evidence could be found to support such accusations.

As news reached him, Pétion maintained a stoic facade, knowing that every death was a stain on the fabric of freedom he fought to uphold.

Amid his contemplations, Joute approached him. Her silhouette glowed ethereally against the lanterns behind her as she spoke softly. "Papa Bon Coeur," she said, using his affectionate nickname. "Even fathers must discipline their children when they stray from the right path. But I know you did not harm Delva."

He turned to her with a questioning gaze, "And how do you know this?"

"Because you would have sought my counsel first," she explained confidently.

Pétion nodded in understanding. "Discipline is one thing," he murmured. "But I did not hold the knife that ended Delva's life. His blood is not on my hands, though some may try to paint me as the villain."

"History will absolve you," Joute assured him, placing a comforting hand on his arm. "For it will be written by those who know your heart and your actions."

He gave her a small smile, finding solace in her words. But as they stood together, united in purpose and resolve, Pétion couldn't help but feel the weight of uncertainty for the future ahead. As guests began to leave the palace, the promise of tomorrow whispered through the rustling leaves of the courtyard below, a reminder that their journey toward progress would not be an easy one.

Throughout the year 1812, each decision, each action, bore consequences that ripped through the lives of those he sought to uplift. The weight of his Présidential role pressed down on him like a crushing boulder as he faced the relentless challenges of nation-building and constant defense against power-hungry military men and dissenters who opposed even the slightest disagreement.

The looming threat from his rival, Henry Christophe, and his new Kingdom, relentlessly plagued Alexandre Pétion's every thought since 1807. He had waged war against Christophe to protect the capital and now his continuing treacherous attempts to invade his republic truly tormented him. Twice, in 1810 and again in 1812, Christophe's forces had tried to overthrow his rule, driven by their tyrannical leader's thirst for power and vengeance, especially after Pétion was once again nominated for a second term as president.

But Pétion was not one to back down. He demonstrated his unparalleled military prowess as cannons thundered from the mountains, decimating three brigades of enemy soldiers in a matter of days. With the help of his loyal Générals, Boyer, Borgella, Bonnet, and Bazelais, Pétion's combined army emerged victorious, each time forcing Christophe's humiliation and retreat once again.

As Pétion stood at the window, looking out over the city, Joute's gentle voice interrupted his troubled thoughts. "What troubles you, my love?" she asked, handing him a glass of rum.

"I can't help but think about all we've endured," Pétion replied wearily. "Why did I agree to this presidency in the first place?"

Joute's touch brought him some peace. "You agreed because you love our country and you are its greatest leader," she reminded him.

"And now," Pétion continued with frustration lacing his words, "our new monarch to the North continues to attack us and has even appointed this man named Goman, a former maroon and an enemy combatant, as the Comte of Jérémie! Can you believe it?"

Joute poured another drink for her husband. "Let go of your worries about Christophe. We both know he has gone mad."

But Goman's appointment served as a constant reminder of the resistance and opposition that Pétion faced daily - not just from the old guard, but from those who had only known struggle and conflict under colonial rule. Despite their efforts, Goman's newest rebellion was like a relentless wave crashing against the rugged cliffs of Pétion's leadership - fierce, persistent, but ultimately futile.

The citizens despised Goman and his forces, who hid in the mountains and periodically and without reason would attack supply lines, army units, and innocent civilians.

But Pétion knew that over time, Goman's attempts to sow dissent would fail. The people were tired of war and yearned for peace and stability above all else. And though it weighed heavily on him,

Pétion stood firm in his belief that peace and progress were within reach for his beloved country.

The sultry air of the southern plains hung heavy with the scents of earth and sea, enveloping Général Borgella as he rode atop his chestnut steed. As he crested the ridge that overlooked Port Républicain, his sharp gaze swept over the sprawling city beneath him. The return of the South to Alexandre Pétion was more than just a military allegiance—it was an affirmation of their shared vision for Ayiti, a vision that had been disrupted by Rigaud's brief resurgence and Goman's stubborn rebellion.

Pétion stood on the balcony of his palace, Volant-Le-Tort, his piercing eyes scanning the distance as if he could sense the approach of his trusted Général. The sound of the hooves of the army's horses clattering against the cobbled streets officially announced Borgella's arrival.

Pétion descended the grand staircase with measured steps, his mind already weaving through the implications of Borgella's report. The air in the foyer was thick with electricity, tangible proof of momentous events unfolding.

"Président Pétion," greeted Borgella, dismounting from his steed with a grace that belied the urgency of his news. "The Southern Penninsula is once again yours."

"Your unwavering loyalty has been our compass through turbulent seas, Général." Pétion clasped Borgella's forearm in a firm grip. "What is the sentiment among our people down there?"

"Hope, sir," replied Borgella, his baritone voice carrying echoes of countless conversations with soldiers and civilians alike. "They yearn for stability and the freedom you espouse."

"Yet with stability comes the challenge of sustenance," interjected Pétion, furrowing his brow slightly. He understood all too well that their independence hinged not only on ideals but also on the very land that sustained them. "We must ensure that our lands are tended, and our people do not simply survive, but thrive."

"Yes, Monsieur Président. And with your reforms, they shall have the means to do so. But they must also be patient."

As they walked through the corridors, their footsteps were a soft counterpoint to the whispering of palm fronds against the windows. The setting sun cast long shadows, painting the walls in hues of determination and resilience.

"Général Borgella," Pétion began, "our path is fraught with peril, but it is also paved with potential. As we aid our brothers in the South, we must remain vigilant. We cannot allow the fires of discord to be kindled anew."

"Rigaud's time has passed. Goman's resistance will wane. The people look to you, Papa Bon Coeur," reassured Borgella, using the affectionate moniker bestowed upon Pétion by the common folk.

"Then let us not falter in our duty to lead them towards a future where freedom is more than just a word spoken, but a life lived." Pétion's gaze returned to the window, where the last light of day began to give way to the first star of the evening.

"Let us build a nation worthy of their hope," he added solemnly, his words a sacred vow to the spirits of those who had fought and died for this dream—a dream of Ayiti, unfettered and unbroken.

The year was 1814, and for the past two years, a sense of relative calm had settled over the country. The occasional raid from the notorious scoundrel Goman was the only disruption to the peace and stability that had been welcomed with open arms. Pétion was confident in the country's forces that they would soon capture Goman and put an end to his disruptive ways. But he knew it would require patience and strategic planning. The treacherous mountains where Goman often retreated made it futile to directly pursue him, so Pétion focused on shoring up security in the towns.

As Pétion gazed out at the harbor, he couldn't help but wonder when the great trading fleets that once filled it would return in abundance. But for now, there was only one ship approaching the docks to join the handful of merchant vessels already there, slowly making its way through the waters of Port Républicain. Retrieving his spyglass, Pétion focused in on the vessel's flag - unmistakably the tricolor of the French Republic. What brings old enemies to our shores, he wondered.

A few hours later, a knock on his office door interrupted Pétion's thoughts, his aide de camp informing him of a request from the captain of the French warship to dock and assuring them that they came in peace. Several hours later, a diplomatic pouch was handed to Pétion, announcing the arrival of three representatives from the French government - Lavaysse, Draverma, and Medina. They were seeking an audience with the Président of the Republic.

Pétion graciously invited them to dine at the Présidential palace as honored guests. As they arrived, they were escorted to a grand parlor and seated comfortably while they waited for their host. Pétion's staff informed him that the men were dressed in fine suits of silk and linen, exuding an air of snobbery.

With calculated delay, Pétion finally descended the grand staircase, accompanied by his loyal advisor, and mistress, Joute. His regal presence was enhanced by his finely tailored military dress uniform and the delicate arm of Mademoiselle Marie-Madeleine Lachenais resting on it. As they entered the room, Pétion's Aide de Camp announced their arrival with a flourish.

The three Frenchmen, accustomed to the pomp and ceremony of their empire, were surprised by the grandeur and formality displayed in this supposedly "backward small country". They exchanged uncomfortable glances as Pétion and Joute made their way towards them.

Pétion greeted them formally, his French accent and mannerisms refined and polished from his years spent in Paris. He invited them to the dinner table, where a sumptuous five-course meal would be served with impeccable precision.

As they began to partake in light conversation, the Frenchmen grew increasingly impatient and steered the discussion towards the main reason for their visit. Monsieur Lavaysse, clearly in charge of the group, addressed Pétion. "Monsieur le Président, I bring you greetings on behalf of King Louis the Eighteenth."

Pétion raised an eyebrow and replied with a hint of sarcasm, "Ah yes. I have heard that France has reverted to having monarchs rule over it. How is that working out for the country?"

Lavaysse maintained his composure and responded, "The country is pleased to have his majesty and the monarchy back in power, Monsieur Président."

Pétion smirked knowingly as he retorted, "Yes, I can imagine Napoleon's reign didn't work out too well for you over there. We had to remove his representatives from our island. Quite ironic that he is now exiled to another island."

Draverma and Medina exchanged concerned glances as they realized that they had underestimated Pétion. Despite their previous reports of turmoil and economic collapse, everything in Port Republicain seemed to be in harmony. The opulence of the new palace only added to their surprise and realization that they were dealing with a formidable leader and nation.

Lavaysse cleared his throat, a subtle signal for the conversation to return to more diplomatic grounds. "Monsieur le Président, we are here on behalf of the French government to discuss matters of mutual interest and cooperation between our nations. We seek to establish diplomatic exchanges and trade that would benefit both Ayiti and France."

Pétion listened attentively; his expression composed yet guarded. He knew all too well the delicate balance of power at play in such discussions. "Trade agreements can indeed be beneficial for both parties," he acknowledged, "but they must be fair and respect the sovereignty of our nation."

Draverma, sensing an opportunity to sway the conversation in their favor, added smoothly, "Of course, Monsieur le Président. France is willing to offer favorable terms that would ensure the prosperity of your people and ours. We understand the importance of maintaining good relations with Ayiti."

Pétion's gaze was steely as he replied, "Prosperity is indeed vital for our people, but it must be achieved on mutually beneficial terms. We will not bow to any attempts at manipulation or exploitation, whether overt or veiled under the guise of diplomacy."

The Frenchmen exchanged uncomfortable glances, realizing that their initial approach had been too presumptuous. Monsieur Lavaysse, regaining his composure, spoke up, "Monsieur le Président, we also come in good faith to petition on behalf of those who have been injured financially from the changes in this land.

"We understand that the transition has not been easy for everyone," Pétion responded with a hint of empathy in his voice. "But our reforms are aimed at creating a more equitable society for all, not just a privileged few. We are open to discussions that benefit both our nations, but they must be built on a foundation of respect and fairness."

Draverma's eyes narrowed as he caught on to Pétion's tone, knowing that the conversation was about to take a dangerous turn. He tried to steer it towards a compromise, but Pétion had already made up his mind. His reforms and progress in Ayiti were non-negotiable.

Joute, sensing the tension, stood ready to enter the conversation at Pétion's cue. With a small nod, Pétion granted her license to speak.

"To be frank, gentlemen," Joute began, her voice dripping with contempt. "What I believe you are attempting to do is have this government compensate those who have oppressed and stolen from the Ayisyen people for generations. Is that where this conversation is headed?"

Lavaysse shifted uncomfortably in his seat, not used to being challenged by a woman in such a bold manner. "May I ask, mademoiselle, what position do you hold in this government?" he sneered.

Unfazed by his condescending tone, Joute replied calmly, "I am a citizen of the Republic of Ayiti, Mr. Lavaysse. A free and sovereign country that has gained its independence from France after years of oppression. My position in this government is of no concern to you."

The tension in the room was thick as Joute's words hung heavy in the air. Lavaysse, visibly taken aback by her assertiveness, struggled to regain his composure.

Before Pétion could come to her defense, Joute continued, "The Ayisyen government will not compensate a single centime to those who have raped and plundered this land for generations. They are no longer property owners; their lands were confiscated for payments due to the enslaved population they exploited."

The staff broke the tension when they entered the room with trays of decadent desserts, freshly brewed coffee, and fine brandy, much to the delight of the Frenchmen who had been eating meager rations aboard their ship for weeks. Pétion whispered to the head waiter before he left the room, signaling an end to the conversation.

"Gentlemen," Pétion said with finality. "My patience for this discussion has ended. I intend to enjoy the rest of this beautiful evening with Mademoiselle Lachenais. I bid you farewell and Godspeed on your journey. I expect you to have your captain weigh anchor and leave our shores at first light."

As if on cue, the captain of the guards entered with four soldiers, their weapons ready. The Frenchmen looked at each other. Reluctantly, they left without another word, leaving behind the uneaten delicacies on their plates, much to their chagrin.

The room fell silent once again as Pétion and Joute settled in to enjoy their evening together, surrounded by the remnants of a tense and heated conversation. They then both looked at each other, raised their glasses in a toast and laughed, easing the tension that had existed.

The warm sun of March in 1814 welcomed a grand French ship as it sailed into the harbor of Cap Henry. On board were three men -

Lavaysse, Draverma, and Medina – the very same French government officials who had attempted to negotiate with President Pétion for financial compensation for the confiscated lands of the wealthy Grands Blancs. Unsuccessful in the south, they sought a more receptive audience with the king in the north.

An officer was sent ashore to request an audience with King Henry. Two days later, they found themselves standing at the steps of Sans Souci Palace, ready to meet the ruler. The opulence of the palace took their breath away even more than the presidential palace of Pétion in the south.

As they were given a tour of the magnificent royal grounds, designed by Christophe's military engineer Henri Barre, they marveled at its blend of European and Afro-Caribbean architecture. Ornate columns, arches, and carvings adorned every corner, reflecting the luxurious lifestyle of its inhabitants. Lush gardens and intricate waterworks added to its splendor. They gazed up at a baroque staircase and classical terraces, inspired by Versailles' Grand Canal, leading up to a grand façade.

Stretching across the grounds were administrative buildings, stables, barracks, a prison, an arsenal, a workshop, a hospital, the prince's residence, and even a chapel. However, there were whispers among the staff that certain secrets were being withheld from their tour - like the underground tunnel large enough for galloping horses that connected Sans Souci to the nearby military mountain fortress of the Citadelle for emergency escapes.

They also learned that the palace shared its name with another Ayisyen revolutionary leader - Jean-Baptiste Sans Souci - who had met his end ten years before construction of the palace had begun. It was rumored that King Henry had him killed, and then built this extravagant home over the very spot where Sans Souci, the man, had fallen. The French officials exchanged uneasy glances, wondering what kind of man this powerful ruler truly was.

As Lavaysse, Draverma, and Medina were led to the grand hall where King Henry held his court, they couldn't help but feel

French government officials Lavaysse, Draverma, and Medina arrived at Sans Souci palace for a meeting with King Henry

overwhelmed by the opulence and grandeur of the space. The hall was filled with over two dozen people, including his son the prince, a duke, four counts, five barons, and two knights or chevaliers. The king himself sat upon a magnificent throne carved from dark mahogany, with gold painted accents, with Queen Marie-Louise regally seated at his side.

The air was thick with tension as the king completed the deliberation on a land dispute when the men entered. They were escorted to the throne as the king dispensed his final ruling, finding for the plaintiff. The Sergeant at Arms bowed low and announced their arrival: "King Henry, I present Monsieur Lavaysse, Monsieur Draverma, and Monsieur Medina, official envoys of King Louis XVIII of France."

Reluctantly, the men stepped forward and bowed before the monarch, feeling awkwardly small and insignificant under his gaze. Surrounding the king and queen were four imposing Dahomet guards dressed in striking all-white uniforms adorned with gold braids - a clear display of power and authority.

But what truly caught their attention were the two massive dogs flanking the king's throne. They would later find out that the dogs were a breaded mix of Cuban attack dogs, those brought over by French Général Rochambeau to hunt runaway slaves, infused with the size and strength of Mastiffs, gifted to Prince Jacques-Victor Henri on his birth several years ago by a British Admiral. They sat calmly at their master's feet, their mighty jaws muzzled and tightly secured to protect any innocent bystanders from their sometimes unpredictable behavior, a characteristic of their Cuban ancestry. However, their intimidating size and fierce genetics were enough to frighten any person of intelligence.

With bated breaths and hearts pounding in unison, the men repeated in chorus: "Your majesty."

"Now, what do we have here? Frenchmen, with their noses held high with arrogance, dare to set foot on the land they once enslaved and the people they treated like mere beasts?" He then addressed the crowd in Creole, "Yo gen grenn nan bounda yo! - *They have big balls in their asses,*"

The laughter of the court echoed through the hall with conversations of amusement flowing in Creole from the crowd, mocking the unsuspecting Frenchmen who had no understanding of the language. Henry spoke refined French, tinted with a slight English accent, and addressed them, his tone seething with contempt. "What is it that you desire with my kingdom?"

Lavaysse, the most outspoken of the trio, replied with a smug smile. "We have noticed your harbor overflowing with British ships and your docks bursting at the seams with trade. Your city is wealthy beyond measure."

Henry's eyes narrowed as he immediately saw through their facade. "So, you suddenly realize that black men from Africa can become successful and rule their lands?" he spat.

Lavaysse backtracked quickly. "No, Your Majesty, that is not what we meant precisely. We were in the southern country and-"

Before he could finish, Henry stood up abruptly, his anger evident in his posture. "You dare visit that outlaw Pétion before paying homage to me, the King? How dare you!"

But Henry was already well aware of their visit to Pétion's republic. His spies had reported everything - even overhearing conversations between the three Frenchmen as they dined with Pétion. Henry knew they sought reimbursement for wealthy property owners whose lands had been rightfully confiscated by Pétion's government.

"No, your majesty," Lavaysse lied smoothly. "Our ship was forced to dock there for repairs before heading to your shores, which we had all good intentions to visit first."

As Draverma and Medina nodded in agreement, Henry's grimace deepened. "And what did you find in the southern republic?"

"A government in denial, Your Majesty," Draverma spoke up. "Their harbor is nearly empty, their docks bare, and very few stores in the principal city filled with goods."

Henry's eyes gleamed with pride and he exclaimed loudly, "Aha! The Kingdom of Ayiti prospers while the Republic languishes. Proof that my administration is superior and my rule just."

The Frenchmen could only nod in agreement, their true intentions hidden behind false flattery. Henry was onto them, and they knew it.

"Step forward and bow before the Duke of Marmalade, Supreme Commander, and the Comte de Limonade, Secretary of State," Henry commanded.

Medina suddenly broke out into laughter, but as the Frenchman did so, the serious faces of his counterparts turned to looks of warning. Henry, clearly agitated, demanded an explanation.

"What is it that amuses you, Monsieur Medina?" he asked sharply.

Ignoring the subtle signals from Lavaysse and Draverma, Medina continued to laugh uncontrollably. "Duke of Marmalade and Comte de Limonade? Oranges? Lemons, Fruit juice? This cannot be real!"

The Duke and Comte stepped forward, their eyes narrowing in suspicion at Medina's disrespectful behavior.

"I find your crude humor both odd and disrespectful, Monsieur Medina. These regions were named by your countrymen and these men represent their people," Henry scolded, as Marie-Louise placed a calming hand on his arm.

"And would you also mock the Prince of L'Orange of France, and call him a piece of fruit?" Henry's voice rose with anger. The queen knew all too well how volatile her husband could be when provoked as she squeezed his hand for attention.

Medina suddenly realized his blunder as Henry continued to berate him. "And by the smug look on your face, I can tell you do not know of what I speak."

Lavaysse intervened, trying to defuse the situation. But Henry was not finished yet. He raised his voice even louder as he schooled Medina on geography.

"The title you so ignorantly mock comes from Orange in southern France, a property of various noble houses before passing to the House of Orange-Nassau. Clearly, there are many things you are not educated about," he spat out.

Thoroughly embarrassed and humiliated by his ignorance, Medina stumbled over his words in apology. "I-I was not aware," he stammered.

"You will address me as 'your majesty' from now on, Monsieur Medina. And you are dismissed for the evening. We will continue this discussion tomorrow at precisely eight in the morning."

With a bow of his head, Medina scurried out of the room, his face red with shame. Lavaysse and Draverma began to apologize as Henry raised his hand, an obvious gesture to be silent, and flickered his hand in a gesture to push them away to leave.

This interview had not gone as planned. Lavausse thought.

The sun had just risen over the horizon when a carriage pulled up to the palace with the three French government officials, Lavaysse, Draverma, and Medina precisely at 8 am.

As King Henry descended the steps of the grand building, they bowed their heads in deference. "Your Majesty," they greeted him. A line of horses awaited each with a Royal Dahomet seated upon its back.

"Good morning, my Frenchmen," Henry exclaimed cheerfully. "Allow me to introduce you once again to my Secretary of State, the Comte de Limonade." The Compte's expression was stern and cold as he acknowledged the Frenchmen's presence. "He will guide you upon your arrival. In the meantime, you are in good hands with my royal guards."

With a swift kick to his charger's side, Henry galloped off towards their destination, followed by two dozen Royal Dahomets. The remaining guards began to walk down the road, leaving the

Frenchmen behind. "Are we not riding horses there?" asked Medina incredulously.

The captain stepped forward and replied, "No, the king believes it would be wise for us to walk so that you may better understand the countryside. We will meet him there."

With that, he set off at a brisk pace, his men following close behind. The three Frenchmen looked at each other in disbelief before quickly following suit. "Can you believe this?" Medina grumbled. "Who does he think he is?"

Lavaysse gave him a stern look and reminded him, "He is the king, you fool. This is the price we must now pay for your idiotic behavior yesterday!" Their conversation was cut short as they continued their journey on foot.

By the time they reached the town of Limonade, it was nearly two o'clock in the afternoon. They found King Henry and his entourage dining on an afternoon lunch in a stunning courtyard garden. "Ah, my Frenchmen!" boomed the king upon their arrival. "Welcome to Limonade!"

The three men, sunburned, dehydrated, lathered in sweat, and exhausted from their long walk, collapsed onto the nearest chairs. "A quick lunch, my Frenchmen," announced Henry. "We have much to see and do before we must hurry back to Cap Henry before nightfall."

A bowl of fresh fruit was placed in front of them, along with a pitcher of cool water and three glasses. As they savored the juicy mangoes, sweet bananas, and tart oranges, the Compte finally spoke up. "Pierre will give you a brief tour of the town, then you will return to Cap Henry." With that, he walked away and was not seen again.

Pierre led the trio on a quick tour of Limonade, pointing out its notable landmarks and features with boredom. As they reached the edge of town, they were met by the royal guards who would escort them back to Milot on foot.

When they arrived at the Sans Souci Palace in Milot, exhausted and famished from their long walk, they requested an audience with the king but were denied. Their carriage awaited them at the front of the palace, with orders to take them straight to the dock where their ship awaited them and ordered to depart at first light.

The Frenchmen left without saying a word of reparation to the king, relieved to be leaving behind the chaotic island and its two unpredictable leaders with their limbs and lives intact.

In the grand hall of his palace, the seriousness of international politics weighed heavily upon Christophe. French ambition, it seemed, had not been quenched by the loss of Napoleon. Letters seized from captured agents revealed a plot to reclaim Saint-Domingue, now Ayiti, for King Louis XVIII. The Treaty of Paris restored Santo Domingo to Spain and permitted the monstrous slave trade of human lives to continue unfettered. Outrage at the reversal of anti-slave laws spread like wildfire throughout the kingdom, igniting a fervor for defense and sovereignty among his people.

"Ministers," Henry addressed the men gathered around the heavy oak table, "We must be vigilant. Our freedom is once again threatened by the chains of our former oppressors."

"Your Majesty," one minister rose, holding out a freshly printed pamphlet. "Our campaign has begun. The Atlantic world will hear the truth of our plight."

Henry nodded, his expression solemn, as he took the document containing the printed words of its author, Pompée Valentin Vastey. Vastey, a mulatto with a French white father and black Ayisyen mother, served as a secretary to King Henry and a tutor to Prince Victor Henri and was one of the king's staunches supporters.

The book entitled Le Système Colonial Dévoilé (*'The Colonial System Unveiled'*) became a rallying cry for those who dared to dream of a world free from colonial shackles. The literary work defended the Ayisyen monarchy in writing against the dreaded return of the French, a description of abuses committed by the former colonists during their reign, and a list of the names of the torturers most guilty. The book became one of his major works.

"Send word to William Wilberforce," Henry commanded, his voice carrying the weight of hope and resilience as he spoke of the British politician and philanthropist who was most prominent in the movement to abolish slavery. "Tell our friend that Ayiti stands firm, that we seek allies in our struggle against tyranny."

"Of course, Your Majesty," the minister bowed, retreating to carry out the royal decree.

As the king returned to his solitude, he gazed out upon the burgeoning expanse of his kingdom, where the sweat of laborers watered the fields and the laughter of children intertwined with the songs of freedom. His heart swelled with pride, yet a whisper of doubt lingered in the corners of his mind.

"Will our resilience be enough?" he pondered. "Can hope alone fortify the walls against the tides of greed and conquest?"

Daniel J.D. Bayard

Fourteen

CITADELLE LA FERRIÈRE

Bonnet à l'Evêque mountaintop, Milot

The sun dipped low behind the towering silhouette of La Citadelle Laferrière, casting long shadows over the newly laid stones that formed the fortress's formidable walls. Henry Christophe stood at the precipice of the grand fort, his eyes tracing the horizon where sea and sky merged into an indistinguishable blue. The sounds of work tools filled the air, a testament to the day's tireless efforts to expedite the fortress's completion.

"Your Majesty," a voice called from behind, breaking the contemplative silence. It was one of the British architects, holding a leather satchel filled with the duplicated plans of the Citadelle. "The final inspection is complete."

Henry turned, his gaze as impenetrable as the bastion he had erected. The Citadelle was commissioned back in 1805 by Henry Christophe under the orders of Emperor Dessalines and had taken well over a decade to construct thus far, but still not completed to Henry's satisfaction. The fortress was built as part of a system of fortifications, with other forts and batteries, designed to thwart potential foreign incursions; notably the French, and to prevent any attempt at seizing the country again.

The Citadelle was built by the forced labor of more than 20,000 citizens and cost over 5,000 lives due to accidents, heat exhaustion, and hard labor, several kilometers inland atop the 3,000-foot Bonnet à l'Eveque mountain, as a means of providing the optimal military vantage point.

The colossal physical dimensions include its walls that rise 130 feet from the mountaintop covering an area of 110,000 square feet, at times twenty feet in thickness. Workers laid the large foundation stones of the fortress directly into the stone of the mountaintop, using a mortar mixture that included quicklime, molasses, and the blood of cows and goats— as well as cows' hooves that they cooked to a glue and added to the mix to give the mortar added strength and bonding capabilities.

Large water cisterns and storehouses in the fortress's interior were designed to store enough food and water for 5,000 defenders for up to one year. The fortress included palace quarters for the king and his family, in the event that they needed to take refuge within its walls from a secret tunnel leading from the King's palace to the mountaintop fortress. Other facilities encompassed dungeons, bathing quarters, barracks, bakery ovens, gunpowder rooms, and all else to remain self-sufficient.

The location enabled Ayisyen forces to strategically keep watch over a vast distance, from the nearby valleys to the coastline, where Cap Henry and the adjoining Atlantic Ocean are visible from the roof of the fortress. It is the largest fortress in Ayiti and arguably the largest in the New World.

In the event of a massive invasion like that of 1802, Henry planned to have his military burn the valuable crops and food stocks along the coast, then retreat to the fortress, setting ambushes along the sole mountain path leading to the Citadelle.

"Very well," he responded, accepting the satchel with a nod. That evening, the great halls of the Citadelle resonated with the clinking of silverware and the murmur of voices as a celebration dinner unfolded. The king had invited his most senior military officers from different regions of the kingdom to celebrate with him. Toasts were made to the ingenuity of design by the British architects and the persistence of will that saw the massive structure rise from the earth.

Yet, even as laughter warmed the stone chambers, a cold resolve settled in Henry's chest. He knew that the secrets of his fortress—the intricate tunnels and hidden chambers—were too vital to risk exposure. And so, as the British architects departed several days later with smiles, pouches of gold and handshakes, sailing off into the harbor of Cap Henry, a saboteur stow-away drilled a hole into the hull of the ship and its lifeboats before lighting the kegs of gunpowder in the storage hold.

Flames engulfed the departing ship after the deadly explosion, ensuring the silence of the ocean floor would be the sole keeper of the Citadelle's mysteries with no one the wiser of the clandestine operation. Days later, young teen Dayiva's, divers with lungs enlarged from years of deep fishing. were commissioned to recover the gold payments from the clutched hands of the architects at the bottom of the ocean for a percentage of the treasure returned under the watchful eyes of the palace's Dahomet guards.

Amidst the verdant hills of Milot, the regal splendor of Sans-Souci Palace stood in stark contrast to the austere might of the Citadelle. Here, Henry had built an oasis of opulence, a palace named for the carefree spirit it embodied but underscored by the shadow of its namesake's tragic end. The palace's gardens sprawled like a canvas painted with every shade of green, punctuated by bursts of color from exotic flowers. The water danced through artificial springs, the sound mingling with the laughter of courtiers who wandered the paths.

Within these walls, the king and queen hosted feasts that were the envy of all and royal galas that set the rhythm of hope for a nation reborn. Yet, beneath the revelry lurked whispers of the countless laborers whose sweat had watered the gardens and whose hands had chiseled the stones. Their sacrifices, though uncounted, were etched into every corner of the palace—a silent testament to the cost of the king's greatness.

In the stillness that followed the merriment, Henry would often walk the empty halls of Sans-Souci, his footsteps echoing against marble floors and high ceilings. The waterworks continued their endless cycle, a symbol of life's constancy amidst the flux of power and ambition. In the quiet reflection of the pools, Henry sought solace, pondering whether the resilience of his people could truly fortify the walls of freedom they had fought so fiercely to erect.

"Freedom," he whispered into the night, "is a fortress of the soul, impregnable yet ever under siege." The flame of a single torch flickered in the dark, a beacon of hope that burned as relentlessly as the spirit of Ayiti itself—a flame that would never be extinguished as long as men such as he, Henry Christophe, drew breath and dared to dream of liberty's enduring light, he convinced himself.

The sun dipped low on the horizon, casting a golden shade over the lush gardens of Sans-Souci Palace. Queen Marie-Louise, adorned in the finery befitting her regal status, greeted the ten British officers with the grace and poise that had become the hallmark of her regal role as hostess. The air was perfumed with the scent of blooming jasmine, mingling with the subtle aroma of the feast being prepared within the palace's grand dining hall in their honor.

"Welcome to Sans-Souci," she said, her voice imbued with warmth yet underscored by a firmness born of her duty to her nation. "May your stay here reflect the strength and beauty of our land."

King Henry, towering and resolute beside her, nodded cordially at their guests, his eyes betraying none of the tumultuous thoughts that roiled beneath his stoic exterior. His lands were extensive, his wealth monumental, and yet this display was not merely for pomp—it was a statement of Ayiti's resilience, a testament to freedom hard-won and dearly held.

As night fell, laughter and music filled the air, echoing through the corridors where the British officers marveled at the opulence surrounding them, their words laced with thinly veiled surprise at the sophistication they encountered in what they had presumed to be a young and unrefined nation.

"Your Majesty, your palace rivals the grandeur of Europe's finest," one officer remarked, his gaze sweeping over the frescoed ceilings and intricate tapestries.

"Sans-Souci stands as a beacon of hope for our people, a reminder that from the ashes of oppression, we have risen to craft our destiny," King Henry replied, his tone measured,

The evening waned, and the revelry subsided into a somber dawn. As the first light of day broke over the Citadelle, Henry led the contingent by horseback up the steep incline to the fortress that crowned the mountain's peak. On arrival, the soldiers stood in formation, an unyielding line of determination and might, their uniforms a sea of blue against the backdrop of stone and sky at the parade flats of the mighty fortress's upper level.

"This fortress is very impressive," stated Major Jones of the British Navy. Tell me of the defenses you have here."

Henry turned to the captain by his side and nodded his approval to speak.

"The fort is outfitted with 365 cannons of varying size. They were assembled from the abandoned munitions left behind by the European forces that formerly occupied the island; the French, the Spanish, and you, the British as well," remarked the Captain with a grin. "We have enormous stockpiles of cannonballs, over 12,000 in all, stacked in pyramidal shapes at the base of the fortress walls and in storage, with gunpowder held dry in special rooms".

"Thank you, Captain," Henry interrupted, not wanting him to provide all of the secrets of his mighty fortress.

"A fortress is only as good as the discipline of its occupants," British Captain Clarke added. "Are your men up to the task of manning this fort and do they have the discipline to do so? Aren't most of your army just former slaves?"

"It is one thing to marvel at our splendor," Henry said, addressing the British officers. "It is another to witness the discipline of our troops. So, to better satisfy your wishes, follow me for a demonstration."

Le Citadelle La ferrière, considered one of the 8th wonders of the world, located atop the Bonnet à l'Evêque mountain in Milot was built by the forced labor of more than 20,000 citizens and cost over 5,000 lives

To prove the loyalty and bravery of his army, King Henry ordered the squad of soldiers to march to their deaths until halted to impress his British counterparts.

A murmur of condescension rippled through the ranks of the ten visitors, the skepticism in their eyes a challenge to the king's pride.

Without a word, Henry turned to the Captain of the Guard, his command slicing through the crisp morning air. "Captain, have your men march until I give you the order to halt."

"Sòlda yo nan sitadèl la, avanse mach - *Soldiers of the Citadelle, forward march!*" commanded the captain without a fragment of hesitation.

The soldiers moved as one, boots thudding in unison upon the hard surface of the fortress, their faces set with a resolve that knew no fear. Onward they marched, toward the edge of the parade grounds, where the earth met the sky in a precipitous drop.

"Discipline," Henry boomed to the British officers, watching as the first row of five soldiers stepped off the edge, plummeting to their deaths into the abyss below. "Under fire or the weight of sacrifice, it is the cornerstone of our freedom."

The British officers stood in stunned silence, their earlier arrogance washed away by the stark demonstration before them as the second row of five troops dropped out of site. In that moment, they understood the depth of Ayiti's resolve, and the lengths to which its ruler would go to protect the sovereignty they had so fiercely claimed.

As the third row approached the edge without a sign of fear, Captain Clarke yelled, "Stop! Please Your Majesty!" as he felt guilty as the one who had instigated these useless deaths.

Henry slowly turned to the Captain of the Guard and casually spoke, "Halt the march, captain."

The captain yelled "Halt!" as the third row stopped mere inches of the ledge where they would have also plunged to their deaths. As the captain looked on at the British officers, he was unsure if it was more the heat or fear that had their uniforms and faces bathed in a lather of sweat. Probably the heat, he supposed, piercing their fragile white skin.

As the echoes of the fallen faded, and the officers were escorted from the grounds, Henry stood alone atop the Citadelle, his gaze lingering on the horizon where the sea met sky. Freedom, he knew, came at great cost—these British officers would repeat this display of resistance over and over until all foreigners understood that every Ayisyen would die over being enslaved once again, Henry reasoned. These ten brave men have given the ultimate sacrifice without ever firing a single shot to save tens of thousands from invasion, he was convinced.

"Resilience," he whispered to the wind. "Our legacy shall be woven with threads of undying fortitude." And with that, he descended back to Sans-Souci, to the queen who shared his burden and the children who embodied their nation's future—a future forged in the crucible of revolution and sustained by the unwavering dream of liberty.

Fifteen

BOLÍVAR AND PÉTION

Aux Cayes
December 1815

As he approached the Caribbean shores of the new country of Ayiti that he had heard so much about, he thought of his own journey. Simón Bolívar remembered a day, before the sun rose, standing solitary on the mountain that overlooked the valley cradling Caracas. His figure was outlined against the sky, breathing in the cool air that carried whispers of rebellion and unrest. The land itself seemed to pulse under the weight of colonial rule, mirroring the hearts of men who longed for freedom.

Born into a wealthy Creole family in Caracas, the Captaincy Général of Venezuela, Bolívar lost both parents at a young age and was raised and educated abroad in Spain. During his time in Madrid from the age of seventeen through twenty, from 1800 to 1802, he was exposed to Enlightenment philosophy and married María Teresa Rodríguez del Toro y Alaysa.

Tragically, she succumbed to yellow fever during their return to Venezuela in 1803. A devastated Bolívar then embarked on a Grand Tour through Europe as he grieved his wife's death, ending up in Rome where he made a solemn vow to free his home from Spanish control, in part in honor of his lost wife. Upon his return to Venezuela in 1807, he began advocating for independence among other wealthy Creoles.

Bolívar's gaze swept across the valley, each inhale heavy with the responsibility of shaping an unwritten future. His return from abroad had not only brought him Enlightenment ideals; it had also ignited a fiery passion for revolution, sparked by the tales and struggles of fellow revolutionary, Sebastián Francisco de Miranda.

As he stood on the hillside, Bolívar could almost hear Miranda's voice once again: "We must break these chains, Simón. It is not enough to survive; we must thrive as free men." These words had taken root in Bolívar's heart and now grew uncontrollably, driving him to awaken his fellow Spanish Creoles from their complacency.

As the sun began to rise, casting its warm light over the city, Bolívar descended from the hills with purpose, feeling the earth beneath his boots as a reminder of the land longing to be liberated. He arrived at an assembly of wealthy Creoles like himself who held power but lacked the vision to use it for a greater purpose.

"Señores," he began, his voice filled with conviction, "the time has come to break free from the chains that bind us to a distant crown. Do you not feel the winds of change? Will you sit idly by while our countrymen suffer under Spanish oppression?"

His plea was met with apathy, resistance, and murmurs of practicality and fear. They spoke of trade and stability, warning of the personal risks involved in rebellion. But Bolívar saw through their hesitations to the heart of their discontent—the same yearning for autonomy that echoed throughout every corner of the Venezuelan colony.

"Open your eyes," he urged them, gesturing towards the window where sunshine illuminated the city below. "Our land is brimming with potential, our people resilient. We are masters of our destiny, and if we do not seize this opportunity, history will remember us as cowards." But after his passionate pleas throughout the colony, very few would join his cause.

Beginning in 1808, when the far-off Iberian Peninsular War with France's Napoleon Bonaparte sapped Spain of its strength, Bolívar seized the opportunity. With a fervor that belied his years, he donned the mantle of a soldier and plunged into the crucible of war.

Bolívar began his military career at age 27 in 1810 as a militia officer in the Venezuelan War of Independence, fighting Royalist forces for the first Venezuelan republic and the United Provinces of New Granada. His transition from the salons of discourse to the chaos of battlefields was as swift as it was resolute.

The clash of steel and the thunder of cannons became the harrowing symphony to which Bolívar set his life's work. He led his militia with a zeal that inspired both admiration and awe, driving back Royalist forces in skirmish after skirmish. Each victory, whether large or small, was a testament to the enduring spirit of those who fought beside him—the indomitable will of a people who had tasted the possibility of freedom and found it sweet.

The year was 1812 and the Confederation was on the brink of collapse. The once-hailed leader, Miranda, had been forced to relinquish command of his army to the fierce Spanish marine frigate captain, Domingo Monteverde. With a small but determined force, Monteverde began his march toward Valencia, quickly amassing a powerful army as he went.

Meanwhile, Miranda's grasp on central Venezuela weakened with each passing day. A devastating earthquake on Maundy Thursday, the day during Holy Week that commemorates the Washing of the Feet and Last Supper of Jesus, struck the superstitious citizens of Republican-controlled areas as a sign from Providence that the government was not to be trusted. This event only added to the mounting pressure against the young Republic.

As whole provinces began to defect against the new Republican side in favor of the royalist side, Miranda was left with only a small territory under his control. Even their supposed allies refused to send reinforcements, leaving them vulnerable and isolated.

In July of 1812, Miranda surrendered to the Cortes of Cádiz in the final battles between Miranda and Monteverde. The remainder of the Republic's forces crumbled as Monteverde's victorious army marched into Caracas on August 1, 1812.

The weight of defeat pressed heavily upon Bolívar's heart, a burden he bore with the stoicism that had marked his character since Miranda's fall from grace. Bolívar had watched from the sidelines as Miranda, draped in the mantle of power, had succumbed to the inexorable tide of Spanish royalist forces.

The subsequent armistice was a wound that festered in the souls of all who yearned for liberty—a surrender that Bolívar could neither forgive nor forget. And when the proud Miranda was led away in shackles to meet his grim fate in a distant Spanish prison cell, a part of Bolívar's resolve hardened into something unbreakable.

And so, amidst the turmoil of war, Bolívar resumed the fight as his legend began to take root. The Liberator, they called him, champion of the oppressed, bearer of hope. In the smoke-filled aftermath of each encounter, he would stand, his uniform marred by the grit and grime of battle, his eyes alight with the promise of a nation's birth.

"Liberty is a right, not a gift," he would remind his weary soldiers, his voice ringing out over fields strewn with bodies of followers and enemies alike, the cost of their struggle. "We fight not for glory or gain, but for the birthright of every man, woman, and child to live unfettered by tyranny."

Even as the horizon stretched endless before him, fraught with obstacles yet to be overcome, Bolívar's resolve never wavered. For within him burned the unquenchable flame of freedom—a flame that, once kindled, would illuminate the path toward a new dawn for all of Venezuela.

Bolívar continued his struggle with as many victories as defeats. In January 1814, he was made the dictator of the second coming of the republic of Venezuela in the devastated Western section. However, his government retained the weaknesses of the first republic, allowing him to only govern western Venezuela which was economically devastated, could not support the republic's armies, and the people of color remained disenfranchised and thus unsupportive of his new republican government. The republic was assailed from all sides by slave revolts and Royalist forces, especially the Legion of Hell, an army of llaneros – the horsemen of the Llanos, to the south.

The horsemen were led by José Tomás Boves who was the head of these irregular forces and ruled the politically distinct territory in Llano. Boves was a staunch royalist supporter who was brutal in committing atrocities, considered the Rochambeau of Venezuela, against any who supported Venezuelan independence.

In Bolivars' army encampment, the canvas flap of his tent rustled softly, and a slight figure slipped through, bringing with it the sweet aroma of fresh corn. Simón Bolívar's eyes remained intently fixed upon the crisscrossing lines and shaded regions of the Venezuelan Republic that sprawled across the map before him. His mind wove strategies and counterstrategies, a silent war raging on paper in the subdued glow of the lantern light.

"Señor Bolívar," came the tentative voice of young Juan, his words slicing through the hush of concentration. The boy's small hands balanced a plate of Cachapas, the rustic corn pancakes, an homage to a time before conquest and subjugation.

Twelve summers had scarcely brushed Juan's skin, yet the rifle he carefully placed aside spoke of the heavy burdens he bore far too soon as a boy soldier. "This one is for you, Señor Bolívar. I bring it for you," Juan said, his voice barely rising above a whisper, yet imbued with a gravity far beyond his years.

"You are wonderful, Juan. Thank you," he replied, a smile softening the hard lines of his face as he accepted the offering. "Mmmm, that smells good," Bolívar murmured, the rich scent breaking his reverie and drawing his gaze away from territorial disputes toward a more comforting battlefront. He regarded Juan not just as a soldier—a child among men—but as a living testament to the resilience of a people long trodden under the heel of a colonial empire. A descendant of the Arawak, Juan carried within him the bloodline of those who first tilled this land, the first to have shed their blood for freedom, their legacy interwoven with the soil itself.

In the dimness of the tent, Bolívar watched as Juan's eyes brimmed with a mixture of pride and sorrow. These Cachapas were not merely sustenance; they were relics of a culture that thrived in harmony with the earth, cultivating yuca, sweet potatoes, maize, and beans—crops that had once nourished a flourishing society. Juan's ancestors had greeted the Spanish with open arms, sharing their bounty and their knowledge, only to be repaid with treachery by the theft of their lands and farms, forced labor, Christian indoctrination, and the road toward extinction.

Juan watched, pride lighting his features as Bolívar took a bite, savoring the taste of resistance and resilience baked into the humble fare. Each chew was an acknowledgment of the blood and toil that had soaked into the land, of the countless hands that had labored to birth a dish that now nourished the very soul and Juan's reasons to join the revolution.

"Your people were great farmers, Juan," Bolívar said, his voice a low rumble of reflective respect. "They nurtured this land, and their spirit endures in these simple pancakes, even after all the pain inflicted upon them."

Juan nodded solemnly, his youthful face hardened by the realities of a world where freedom was paid for in blood and loss. "The Spaniards took everything... our crops, our gold, our freedom," he whispered, the weight of centuries resting uneasily on his shoulders. "They even forced us to have Christian names, like my name Juan, instead of our Arawak names. I have always wondered what my proud Arawak name could have been if my parents were allowed to name me as they chose. So many could haves, Señor Bolívar".

"Si, mi niño," Bolívar agreed, the title of endearment slipping out naturally. He felt the sting of injustice, the echo of chains and cries that haunted the landscape of his beloved country as he glimpsed a tear ready to escape Juan's eye. "But we are here to reclaim it all—every grain of corn, every inch of land. Your heritage will not be forgotten; it fuels our fight."

"Say your name again, please Señor Bolívar?" the boy asked, breaking the meditative stillness that had settled between them. His young voice carried the eagerness of one who found strength in the repetition of hallowed words.

"Simón José Antonio de la Santísima Trinidad Bolívar Palacios Ponte y Blanco is my name, Juan." His intonation rose and fell with the cadence of a well-loved song, each syllable a testament to the legacy he was determined to forge. Bolívar looked up, the corners of his mouth curling into a gentle smile as he indulged the boy's request. "I have told you this many, many times before!"

Juan's grin was infectious, an unspoken acknowledgment of the bond they shared—not just as commander and soldier, but as kindred spirits united by a vision of freedom. He settled down beside Bolívar, his youthful frame dwarfed by the gravity of their cause.

"Every time you say it, it sings like a battle cry," Juan said, eyes alight with admiration. "Like it carries the hope of every person fighting alongside you. With a name like this, you must have the strength of many great warriors!"

"Perhaps it does," Bolívar mused, his gaze returning to the map as he contemplated the roads to victory that lay ahead. "And perhaps in that name, there is a promise—a vow to those who came before us and to those who will come after."

"Will our children speak it with pride?" Juan whispered, half to himself, the weight of history pressing upon his slender shoulders.

"More than pride, Juan," Bolívar assured him, his voice the emblem of unwavering conviction. "Our descendants will inherit not just a name, but a land unshackled, a people sovereign. We are crafting a story that will be told through the ages."

In the quietude of the tent, surrounded by the ephemeral dance of shadows, they found solace in the shared reverie of a future forged by their resilience. It was a moment suspended in time, where the echoes of battles fought and yet to come converged with the enduring spirit of hope. And in that space, Simón Bolívar and Juan, the Général and the boy soldier became more than mere architects of revolution—they became the guardians of a dream, etched into the soul of a nation waiting to be molded.

He slowly returned to the present-day from his dream of the past. The Caribbean sun hung low in the sky, casting long shadows across the deck of the timeworn vessel as it cut through the cerulean waters. Physically and mentally devastated, Simón Bolívar stood at the prow, his gaze fixed on the horizon, where the silhouette of Ayiti began to take form like a promise whispered by the wind. Around him, the creaking of wood and the slap of waves against the hull were the only sounds that pierced the silence.

"El Libertador," they had called him, but now, exiled from the land he vowed to free, Bolívar questioned the title. The murmurs of his followers huddled together below deck—men and women bound by a shared vision of freedom, and the reality of defeat—were a constant reminder of the responsibility that lay upon his shoulders. They were the survivors of battles with scars as witnesses to their trials. The sacrifice of so many more, like the death of his little comrade Juan, the boy soldier, could not be in vain; the dream of independence must be rekindled, even from the ashes of despair.

As night fell and the stars emerged to cast their indifferent light upon the world, Bolívar felt the solitude of command more acutely than ever. The heavens, strewn with constellations that told tales of old, seemed to mock the frailty of human endeavors. Yet, amidst the vast tapestry of the cosmos, there remained a single, unwavering point: the Pole Star of freedom, guiding him onward.

He had been exiled to Jamaica since May of 1815 and it had been a refuge, albeit a precarious one. The specter of extradition loomed over the exiles like a menacing storm cloud, and Bolívar knew they could linger no longer. With whispers of plots and Spanish spies weaving through Kingston's alleys, the urgency of departure had driven him to the black market in search of ocean passage, where secrecy was the currency of survival.

Now, as Ayiti grew larger before his eyes, Bolívar considered the irony of seeking solace in the arms of a nation born from the very institution he wrestled with internally. Slavery was an abomination, a blight upon humanity, yet its eradication was a complex entanglement that threatened to fray the fragile tapestry of alliances he sought to weave in his home country.

But for now, the pressing matter was survival and regrouping. Ayiti represented a flicker of hope—a hope that Alexandre Pétion, the leader who had helped turn this land into a beacon of emancipation, might extend a hand to a fellow revolutionary. Ayiti had shed colonialism and in Pétion's success, Bolívar saw a reflection of what could be achieved: a people risen from subjugation, forging their destiny with fire and blood. He had chosen Pétion's Grand Sud of Ayiti, as opposed to the Kingdom of Ayiti ruled by a monarch to the north, the very system of government he fought so desperately to shed.

The ship finally anchored off the coast of Aux Cayes on Ayiti's Southern Peninsula, in December of 1815. As Bolívar stepped onto Ayisyen soil for the first time, he could feel the earth beneath his feet resonating with the echoes of revolution. Here, in this land of defiance, he would find the strength to continue the fight. The struggle was not merely Venezuela's—it was a struggle for all of humanity against the chains of oppression and colonialism. He had been told that other exiles from Venezuela had sought refuge in this country and he sought to find them. He would convince them to be his followers and reengage in the fight for the freedom of their homes.

"Libertad o muerte," he whispered to the waves, the words a solemn vow to himself and to the legions who looked to him for guidance. "Freedom or death."

And as the darkness enveloped him, Simón Bolívar knew that the road ahead would be fraught with hardship and sacrifice. Yet within him, the flames of resilience and hope burned ever brighter, illuminating the path toward a future where the yoke of tyranny would be cast off, once and for all.

Several weeks later, Simón Bolívar, with the weight of a continent's freedom resting upon his shoulders, followed the gilded path leading into the opulent plantation headquarters of Alexandre Pétion in Aux Cayes. The habitation before him, an edifice of grandeur and power, stood in stark contrast to the rugged battlefield tents he had grown accustomed to, its walls were bathed in the golden hues of the Caribbean afternoon sun.

Bolívar's leather boots echoed on marble floors, polished to mirror-like perfection, reflecting the high ceilings adorned with intricate frescoes that depicted the bygone era of dominance by the French colonial Grands Blancs who had dominated the land and abused its people. These buildings were now confiscated by the government and repurposed for their needs.

His associates—men of war now dwarfed by the splendor surrounding them—exchanged muted expressions of awe. Such luxury was foreign to their cause, yet here on Ayiti's Southern Peninsula, wealth was no stranger. The Liberators were ushered into Pétion's office within the stately home, a chamber where elegance met governance. Heavy drapes framed windows that revealed the lush gardens beyond, the scent of blooming jasmine subtly permeating the air. Pétion rose from behind a mahogany desk, his charismatic presence filling the room. He extended a hand, not as a ruler to a supplicant, but as one revolutionary to another.

"Welcome, Señor Bolívar, El Libertador," Pétion warmly greeted, his voice carrying both authority and warmth. "Your reputation precedes you."

"President Pétion, your support is our salvation," Bolívar replied, the clasp of their hands marking the union of two destinies intertwined by the same relentless pursuit of freedom from colonialism.

Pétion next shook hands with Bolívar's two associates and signaled for them to sit. Together, Bolívar and Pétion sat across from each other, the weight of their respective struggles hanging heavy in the air. The incoming sun, occasionally shaded by the fronds of palm, danced upon the mahogany furniture, casting elongated shadows that seemed to mirror the complexity of their mission.

"As you well know, President Pétion," Bolívar began, his voice steady yet filled with a quiet urgency, "the fight for liberty in Venezuela is at a critical juncture. The Spanish forces tighten their grip on our land, and we find ourselves in need of allies who understand the true cost of freedom."

Pétion's gaze held a mixture of empathy and resolve as he listened intently. His fingers drummed thoughtfully against the polished surface of the desk before he spoke, his words measured yet carrying a fierce determination. "I have heard tales of your valor, Señor Bolívar," Pétion began, his tone resonating with respect. "Your quest for liberation echoes the very essence of our struggle here in Ayiti. It is a battle not just for land or power, but for the very soul of humanity."

A gentle knock on the door announced the arrival of a server, who entered with a silver tray laden with treats. The enticing aroma of rum, fruit juices, coffee, and meat-filled pastries of beef and fish, known as Paté's to the Ayisyens, filled the air. The servers were followed by Joute, and she was introduced by Pétion to Simón Bolívar and his entourage as Mademoiselle Marie-Madeleine Lachenais.

"Eat, my fellow revolutionaries. You must be famished after the ordeal you have had to endure these past few months," Joute said.

The Venezuelans' eyes had lit up at the sight of the spread, their mouths watering in anticipation. As they reached for their desired Paté, the room was filled with sounds of appreciation and contentment.

"Señor Bolívar, it is a pleasure to finally meet you," Joute's voice was soft yet carried a hint of unwavering determination as her gaze held a depth of knowledge and experience, a silent acknowledgment of the sacrifices made in the name of freedom.

Simón Bolívar, captivated by the radiance of this Ayisyen beauty before him, returned her greeting with a courtly bow. "The pleasure is truly mine, Mademoiselle Lachenais," he replied, his tone carrying a hint of admiration.

"Please call me Joute, all my friends do," she warmly offered as she exchanged pleasantries with the Venezuelan entourage, Bolívar leaned back in his chair, his gaze wandering to the garden outside that unfurled its splendor before their eyes, a tapestry of vibrant colors and intoxicating scents that seemed to embrace the very essence of life itself. Bolívar found himself utterly captivated by the beauty that surrounded them, his gaze drifting over the riotous blooms on trees of flamboyant, red hibiscus and beautiful Bougainvillea, amongst other verdant foliage, manicured to perfection.

"President Pétion, Mademoiselle Joute," Bolívar began, his voice filled with genuine awe, "your home here is a testament to the magnificence of Ayiti and the resilience of its people. The garden is like a paradise on earth, a sanctuary amidst the tumult of our world."

Pétion smiled at Bolívar's words, a glint of pride shimmering in his eyes. "Thank you, Señor Bolívar. Our garden has weathered storms and witnessed victories, much like our nation. It is a reflection of our unwavering spirit. We love coming to Aux Cayes and taking advantage of this splendor when we are in town. However, business at the capital always prevents our full enjoyment."

"And tell us about your homeland of Venezuela," Joute inquired, ever gracious and composed.

Bolívar's eyes lit up as he expounded upon his homeland with pride, a spark of passion igniting within him as he spoke, "Imagine vast plains stretching as far as the eye could see, bathed in the golden hues of the setting sun encased by the majestic Andes mountains, their snow-capped peaks piercing the azure sky like ancient sentinels guarding the land below".

The air in the room seemed to come alive with the sounds and scents of Venezuela as Bolívar painted a vivid picture with his words. He spoke of the rich tapestry of cultures that called his homeland home, from the indigenous tribes that still held fast to their traditions to the vibrant mestizo communities born from a blend of Spanish and African heritage.

As he wove tales of Venezuelan history and resilience, Joute found herself captivated by the vision Bolívar presented. She could almost taste the flavors of traditional dishes he described, and hear the strains of music that echoed through bustling streets.

Pétion brought the room back to the business at hand, informing Joute, "Señor Bolívar has asked us to be an ally in his quest for Venezuelan independence." The mention of such a weighty alliance hung in the air, momentarily dimming the lively atmosphere that had surrounded them.

Joute, ever perceptive, noted the subtle shift and glanced at Bolívar, recognizing the gravity of his mission. His eyes shone with determination, reflecting the fire burning within him, a passion for freedom that mirrored the flames of revolution. She saw in him a kindred spirit, someone willing to fight against oppression and tyranny at any cost.

A knock on the door signaled the arrival of Jean-Baptiste Bayard Junior, now a senator and forever the staunch ally of Pétion. He entered the room with a confident flair just having turned forty.

Joute wished him a belated happy birthday. Junior, with a striking resemblance to his father, flashed a charming smile in response, his eyes gleaming with a mixture of determination and passion. The weight of his responsibilities as a senator and his unwavering allegiance to Pétion rested comfortably on his broad shoulders, exuding an air of authority that demanded respect.

A chair was brought forward by a servant, and he took a seat amongst the entourage after formal introductions. Joute poured the strong and rich Ayisyen coffee of the Southern Penninsula into delicate porcelain cups, its aroma filling the air with notes of chocolate and spice. The steam rose in swirling tendrils, carrying with it the weight of unspoken words.

Pétion reconvened the conversation. "I have asked my good friend, Senator Bayard, to join us as I had tasked him to visit several upstanding citizens of the south and solicit assistance for your cause, Señor Bolívar."

"Your support, kindness, and hospitality, will forever be remembered Monsieur President," Bolívar replied, then looked at Junior. "Thank you for all efforts extended on our behalf."

"I have been successful in raising several thousand British pounds, a cache of gold, a commitment to sew 300 uniforms from a clothier, and several hundred guns, and rifles. My father will provide the use of a frigate to transport you and your comrades back to your nation to continue the fight, should you so choose."

Bolívar's face and that of his comrades lit up at the news as Bolívar stood and approached Junior, who rose as well. Bolívar then wrapped his arms around Junior giving him a warm hug as emotions within him towards the generosity provided so quickly ran deep.

Standing beside Pétion, Joute regarded the Venezuelan delegation with an assessing gaze. There was a solidity to them, a foundation unshaken by the tremors of upheaval. "Señor Bolívar," Joute interjected, "your quest for independence is noble, yet incomplete if it does not extend its grace to all souls shackled by chains."

Bolívar hesitated with the air thickening from the gravity of Joute's condition. "To promise the abolition of slavery is to venture into uncharted moral territory," Bolívar began. "Our battle thus far has been only for sovereignty, not societal reform. Many supporters in Venezuela still utilize slaves for cultivation and mining. They will certainly oppose this move and not support us," Bolívar said as he turned to Pétion to deliver the message.

"Joute is accurate in her request," Pétion said. "Ayiti is a country where slavery is illegal. To support a revolution that continues to allow slavery would be against our ideals, our laws, and probably our constitution."

Simón Bolívar, at left, strategizes with Alexandre Pétion and Jean-Baptiste Bayard Junior at right as his associates and Joute look on.

Bolívar was now cornered and looked at his entourage for guidance.

Yet, in the silent exchange between these men of the revolution, Bolívar understood the inextricable link between liberation and emancipation. He needed to be bolder this time around. In slaves dreaming of freedom, he would certainly find new freedom fighters by his side.

"Slavery," Bolívar began, his voice a solemn echo of resolve emerging within him, "Slavery will find no refuge in the lands we reclaim from tyranny. I vow it."

Pétion nodded and looked at Joute, exposing a smile and a spark of approval in his eyes. The pact was sealed, not with ink, but with honor—a covenant that would ripple through the ages.

As they conversed throughout the afternoon, ideas and strategies weaving together like threads in a tapestry of insurgency, Bolívar felt the bond of friendship fasten between himself and Pétion. Their dialogue transcended politics, touching upon the shared dreams of their peoples, and the resilience that coursed like lifeblood through their veins. Here, in this chamber of promises and pacts, hope was not merely an abstract yearning; it was a palpable force, ready to be molded into reality by their conjoined wills.

When the meeting adjourned, Bolívar stepped back into the sunlight. In Pétion's assurance, he found not just an ally but a kindred spirit, a comrade-in-arms against the specter of oppression. As they parted ways, the liberator's mind turned once more to the road ahead, arduous and fraught with peril.

Yet, amid the trials that awaited, Bolívar carried with him the luminous vision of a world reborn—the dream of a continent unchained, its destiny reclaimed by the indomitable spirit of those who dare to defy empires, such as his new Ayisyen friends had done, and continue to do.

The equatorial sun bore down with a relentless fury as Simón Bolívar surveyed the coastline of Caraballeda, from the deck of the creaking vessel. The dense Venezuelan jungle teemed with unseen life, its thick canopy unfurling like an emerald tapestry to the water's edge. The air was thick with the scent of earth and salt, carrying the distant calls of exotic birds that danced on the heated breeze.

"Peyi devan! – *Country Ahead!*" echoed the cry, a signal that stirred the weary hearts of his companions. They had returned home.

Bolívar's gaze remained fixed on the shore, his mind grappling with the immense task that lay before them. Alexandre Pétion had given them sanctuary, sustenance, and support; now it was upon their shoulders to carry forward the torch of liberation. With a nod to his men, a silent command was issued—they were to make landfall under the veil of the early morning twighlight, cloaked by the shadows of the towering palms.

As darkness enveloped the world, Bolívar's feet touched the Venezuelan soil—his homeland now foreign, yet achingly familiar. They moved stealthily; the soft thud of their boots muffled by the underbrush as they threaded their way into the heart of the jungle. Each step was laden with purpose, each breath a testament to the resilience that thrummed through their veins.

Hours turned to days as the band of revolutionaries labored through the dense foliage, the humidity clinging to their skin like a second garment. The mountains of Pico Naiguata loomed ahead, sentinels guarding the path to freedom. Bolívar could feel the weight of the guns, shots, and powder provided by Pétion, a tangible reminder of the Ayisyen leader's belief in their cause—a belief that fueled their march ever upward.

But word of Bolívar's arrival spread faster than the wildfires that sometimes ravaged the dry plains. Whispers of "El Libertador" ignited the passions of those who hungered for liberty and sovereignty, drawing both ally and adversary closer to their flame.

The Royalist militias were swift to respond, their attacks as severe as the jagged terrain they traversed. Bolívar's men, though stalwart, found themselves outnumbered, outmaneuvered by foes who knew every hidden trail and secret pass. The clash of gunshots and the steel of the swords rang through the air, a discordant symphony that echoed the chaos of battles.

In one such skirmish, just as he was rallying his forces to push back against the encroaching tide, Bolívar felt the cold grip of capture. His sword slipped from his grasp, clattering against stone, its sound a hollow echo of defeat just four months after his return.

Bound and surrounded by hostile faces, Bolívar's thoughts drifted—to Pétion's palatial halls, to the lofty ideals they had toasted under chandeliers that shimmered like stars. Yet even in this bleak moment, the fires of hope were not extinguished within him. His eyes, dark and unyielding, held the reflection of a dream undimmed—the vision of a continent unshackled, its people sovereign and free.

As Bolívar was led away, his resolve did not waver. Each step toward captivity was, paradoxically, a step closer to the ultimate goal. In the stillness of his heart, the liberator understood that the journey to freedom was often forged in chains. And so, amidst the cacophony of war and whispers of despair, the silent anthem of resilience played on—an unending melody that promised dawn would rise upon a new republic, born from the indomitable will of those who dared to dream.

The horizon bled with the first light of dawn as the crestfallen figure of Simón Bolívar stood on the Ayisyen shore once again in September of 1816, his gaze lost in the undulating embrace of the sea. The salty breeze tugged at his worn coat, a cruel mimicry of the freedom he so desperately sought but felt slipping from his grasp like grains of sand.

He and his followers, a scant few that had managed the harrowing escape in August with him, watched in somber silence. Each man bore the weight of defeat, their shadows stretching long and thin upon the sand as if reaching for something just beyond their tired reach.

Bolívar's mind was a tumult of despair and anger, each thought a sharp lash against the rawness of his soul. He had envisioned victory, a liberated land echoing with the cheers of its people, not this bitter retreat to the shores that had once heralded hope. Many of those who had shared his vision now faced the ultimate price for their audacity—the crack of the rifles of a royalist firing squad breaking the morning silence, a final punctuation to lives spent in pursuit of liberty. How many had been put to death because of him? His mind journeyed back to Juan, the boy of twelve, who had also met his death in following his lead.

"Général," a voice broke through his reverie, rich with the warmth of the Caribbean French-Creole accent that had become both comfort and catalyst in recent times. Alexandre Pétion approached, his stride confident yet imbued with an empathy that seemed to acknowledge the gravity of Bolívar's sorrow.

"Presidente Pétion," Bolívar replied, his voice a mere whisper carried away by the wind. "I fear I have led my men to doom, only to return with empty hands and a heart filled with grief."

"Simón," Pétion said, placing a firm hand upon Bolívar's shoulder, his touch grounding. "You have returned with more than you realize—the resilience to face adversity, the courage to continue despite overwhelming odds. These are the seeds from which new beginnings will sprout."

Pétion's words were a balm, though the scars they meant to heal ran deep and jagged within Bolívar. With a solemn nod, he allowed himself to be steered away from the water's edge, towards the promise of renewal amidst the verdant hills that cradled Pétion's estate in Ayiti.

Over the weeks that followed, the rolling hills of Ayiti bore witness to a unique melding of purpose and skill. A small cadre of men—two dozen in total, complimented by a fusion of Ayisyen soldiers and officers with Bolívar's top lieutenants—gathered under the tutelage of Pétion's army. They trained with a fervor born of shared conviction, their movements synchronized in the dance of guerilla warfare that would be essential in the battles yet to come.

The clashing of machetes during practice combat echoed with the clash of ideals outside these green enclaves. Sweat dripped onto the fertile soil as men learned to move as one entity, bound by the singular objective of shaping a future where the chains of oppression lay broken and discarded.

"Watch the terrain, use it to your advantage," instructed an Ayisyen sergeant, his eyes scanning the landscape with strategic acumen. "Surprise is our ally; strike swiftly, then vanish like the mist that clings to these mountains."

Bolívar watched intently, the spark of determination reigniting within his chest as he observed his men and the Ayisyen volunteers adapting, growing stronger and more cunning with each passing day. The camaraderie forged in the crucible of shared struggle sowed the seeds of hope in the furrows of his doubt.

As dusk settled over the encampment, painting the sky in hues of fire and shadow, Bolívar felt the resurgence of purpose within him. Here, in the company of those who refused to yield to tyranny, he found the strength to cast aside the mantle of defeat. In the silent communion of kindred spirits, the resolve to fight on was rekindled—a flame nurtured by the whispered promise of freedom, resilience, and the unyielding dream of a continent waiting to be reborn.

The residence in Aux Cayes of Alexandre Pétion radiated warmth against the crisp December evening air, its opulent walls echoing with the laughter and spirited conversation of the men and women assembled within. Crystal glasses shimmered under the chandelier's glow as they were raised in toasts, their contents a rich amber that caught the light like liquid sun.

"Por la libertad!" declared Simón Bolívar, his voice commanding attention despite the undercurrent of weariness that shadowed his eyes. The clinking of glass against glass was a symphony of solidarity, each note infused with the unspoken promise of camaraderie in the face of uncertainty.

Around the long mahogany table, the faces of friends and allies reflected the candlelight, revealing a tapestry of determination woven with threads of hope. Joute exchanged a knowing glance with Bolívar, his eyes alight with fervor, while the three Ayisyen officers who had volunteered to go on this mission nodded in solemn agreement, their features carved from the same stone of resolve. The Spanish Creole officers, weathered by struggle yet unbowed, mirrored the sentiment, their presence an embodiment of the shared conviction that tied them all to this noble cause.

The air was thick with the scent of spiced meats and tropical fruits, the sumptuous feast laid out before them a testament to the generosity of their host, who understood that the battle ahead was not only fought with swords but with spirits fortified by unity. Present at the dinner with Pétion and Joute were Jean-Baptiste Bayard Junior and Jean-Pierre Boyer.

Pétion, the Ayisyen President, charismatic as ever, rose and swept his hand across the assembly, his eyes reflecting the fire of ambition and a depth that hinted at the complex machinations of his mind. "Tonight, we dine as brothers," he proclaimed, his voice a velvet rumble that resonated through the chamber. "Tomorrow, you depart as soldiers united under one banner—the banner of liberty. May our actions ripple through the ages, and may history remember us as the architects of a new dawn in the land of Venezuela."

The meal passed in a blur of flavors and fellowship, each bite savored as if it might be the last in this land that had become an unexpected sanctuary. Laughter mingled with earnest discussions of strategy and tactics, the gravity of their mission never far from thought, yet tempered by the bonds forged between them.

Jean-Baptiste Bayard Junior was now the senate president and had led the drive to successfully amend the Ayisyen Constitution, this past June, to elevate the powers of the executive branch over that of the senate. He, Pétion, Joute, and Boyer felt that there had been too much ambiguity in governance which had posed a challenge to Pétion's effective leadership. Also, the amendment placed the president, Pétion, as President for Life with the ability to select his successor upon leaving office, granting him vast powers.

As a result, Pétion did not need to have the Senate ratify the assistance he was providing Bolívar. In the pre-dawn silence on the 22nd of December 1816, Bolívar stood on the deck of one of the four small ships bobbing gently in the harbor. Each vessel brimmed with supplies—1500 rifles, thousands of shots, powder, 12 small cannons, and a printing press, a silent harbinger of the revolution's voice yet to resonate with the people.

Pétion's instructions on the use of the press echoed in Bolívar's thoughts, a strategic weapon as critical as any sword or musket. "Words inspire hearts, Simón," Pétion had said to his protégé, thirteen years his junior, now at 33. His hand rested on the machine that would sow seeds of insurrection across the Venezuelan landscape. "Let them be your heralds."

Pétion had loaded the ships, provided by the Bayard family, with 350 experienced soldiers to augment Bolívar's men, some of which were Spanish Creoles from the other side of the island who had migrated to the Southern Peninsula seeking lands and wealth. Many decided to join the cause with promises by Bolívar of wealth, grandeur, and stature in a new government in their familiar tongue of Spanish and had rigorously trained for this opportunity with the Ayisian military. A force numbering 600 in all.

As the sails unfurled and the ships cut through the water, departing Ayiti with the first light of day, a sense of destiny settled upon Bolívar's shoulders like a mantle. The shores of Chichiriviche, Maiquetía, Caraballeda, and Naiguatá awaited them, each landing point a beacon in the darkness, signaling the resurgence of their campaign.

Upon reaching the South American northern coast in January of 1817, Bolívar watched the horizon where the sea met the sky as the empty Ayisyen ships began their return journey to Ayiti, there would be no turning back now, his mind heavy with the weight of expectations. Yet, amidst the rolling waves and the call of the wind, there was a steadfast certainty that this time, the tides of fate would turn in their favor.

The associates dispersed; each group was tasked with igniting the flame of rebellion in the hearts of potential supporters. They carried with them the whispers of change, spreading like wildfire through the towns and villages, calling the oppressed to gather at the foot of Pico Naiguatá Mountain. Their weapons were the printed words of a call to duty from El Libertador, Simón Bolívar, minted by Pétion's printing press which would be scattered across the land.

The sun had barely kissed the horizon, painting the sky in hues of orange and pink when Simón Bolívar set his eyes upon the Andean peaks. The chill in the air was sharp, a stark contrast to the warmth that throbbed in his veins as he envisioned the liberation that lay beyond those formidable mountains. His heart echoed with the rhythm of freedom, resilience, and hope, thrumming like a drumbeat against the canvas of silence that draped over the slumbering encampment.

"El Libertador," as he was known by his growing legion of supporters, moved quietly among the rows of tents where his Ayisyen counterparts and dissenters-turned-soldiers lay in the repose of the weary. They were a motley band, an amalgamation of fierce determination and unyielding spirit, bound by the shared dream of a continent unfettered by the yoke of oppression.

As the first light of dawn crept across the landscape, it cast long shadows over the figures of men and women who stirred from their rest, summoned by the urgency of the cause they had all sworn to uphold. Bolívar could see the fire of resolve in their eyes, a reflection of the flames that had burned in the hearts of those who had gathered at Pico Naiguatá, answering the call to rise against the tyranny that had long suffocated their hopes.

"Today, we cross into the annals of history," Bolívar proclaimed, his voice resonating with the gravity of the moment. "With each step we take across these mountains, we tread the path toward a future shaped by our own hands—a future where the Republic of Gran Colombia will stand as a testament to our unwavering conviction."

A murmur of agreement rippled through the ranks, each nod and clasp of hands reinforcing the camaraderie that had been forged in the crucible of struggle. They had come from disparate corners of the land, yet here they stood, united in purpose, their diversity a source of strength rather than division.

As they began their ascent, the terrain proved as unforgiving as the enemy they sought to vanquish. Steep inclines and treacherous passes tested both body and spirit, but the promise of freedom for some, and emancipation for others, spurred them onward, an invisible thread weaving their fates together in the intricate tapestry of revolution.

Months turned into years, and the relentless march of time saw Bolívar and his allies face the might of the Spanish in New Granada. With strategy and valor, they shattered the chains of subjugation, the reverberations of their victory resounding through conquered territory—each triumph a clarion call heralding the birth of future nations.

In the wake of conquest, the Republic of Gran Colombia emerged as an embodiment of grand aspirations, uniting territories of Venezuela, Panama, Ecuador, Peru, and Bolivia under a single banner. Bolívar, once a man propelled by personal grief and enlightened philosophy, ascended to the presidency, his name forever etched into the foundation of a dream realized.

Yet even as he navigated the labyrinthine corridors of power, Bolívar remained steadfastly attuned to the pulse of the people he served. He recognized that the true measure of independence lay not in declarations or titles, but in the lived experiences of those who had fought and sacrificed alongside him.

Years later, the fervor of revolution gave way to the solemnity of governance, but the echoes of revolution continued to resonate within the walls of Gran Colombia, shaping its destiny with every decision made, and every policy enacted. Simón Bolívar, the visionary whose longing for liberty had set an entire continent ablaze, now bore the weight of its future—a future born from the ashes of war and the unyielding belief in the indomitable human spirit.

A decade hence, the incessant rain whispered against the walls of the Casa de San Pedro, a somber serenade to the solitary figure within. Simón Bolívar, draped in a mantle of contemplation, stood before the towering windows, his gaze lost in the tumultuous skies that hung heavy over Bogotá. The coarse fabric of his uniform, which once seemed to merge with the very essence of revolution, now felt like an alien weight upon his shoulders.

"Libertador," they called him, yet as the tempest raged outside, he pondered the shackles invisible to the eye—those wrought by ideology and expectation. The dreams of unity that had once blazed like wildfire across the continent were smoldering embers, choked by the very hands that had borne torches in their name.

A cough rattled through his chest—a cruel herald of the ailment that ravaged his body. His breaths, once deep and commanding as he addressed his troops, now came in shallow gasps, a stark mirror to the faltering pulse of Gran Colombia. It was an irony not lost on Bolívar: the man who had breathed life into nations now struggled for every breath of his own.

The door to his chamber creaked open, and the faint scent of wet earth invaded the room as an aide entered, carrying dispatches from the provinces. Bolívar turned, his eyes narrowing with the strain of disillusionment that had etched itself into his features. As he took the documents, his fingers brushed against the crisp paper, each stroke a reminder of the fragility of the republics he had so ardently forged.

"Shall I light the lamp, mi Général?" the aide asked, a tremor of deference in his voice.

Bolívar nodded, his lips curving into a ghost of a smile—a wistful acknowledgment of the dimming light both within and without. The aide struck flint to steel, sparks leaping forth like fleeting hopes in the gathering gloom.

"Leave me," Bolívar murmured, his words scarcely more than a whisper amidst the patter of raindrops. Alone once more, he unfolded the dispatches, his eyes skimming over reports of unrest, of factions clashing, of a people divided not by borders but by beliefs.

Centralism—an anchor that he had once believed would stabilize the fledgling states, now seemed a chain that bound them to strife. With each passing day, his vision of a united South America ebbed further away, eroded by the tides of regionalism and personal ambition.

His tenure as president, marked by the fervent pursuit of cohesion, had become a crucible in which his spirit was tried and found wanting. Territory after territory fell from his grasp like autumn leaves, each departure a quiet surrender to the immutable forces of change.

Achingly, he rose from his chair, his body protesting the movement as if in solidarity with his weary heart. He approached the window once more, pressing a palm against the cool glass. Beyond the mists that clung to the pane lay the lands he had liberated, each victory now a bittersweet memory woven into the tapestry of his legacy.

"Freedom," he spoke the word to the storm, a solemn prayer to the ideals that had defined his existence. "Resilience. Hope." The tenets of his revolution echoed hollowly in the chamber, resonating with the ache of truths hard-won and easily lost.

As Bolívar's thoughts drifted to the distant shores of Ayiti, where he had once found friends, refuge, and renewed purpose, a sense of kinship with its people stirred within him. They too had risen from the ashes of oppression, their resilience a beacon that had illuminated his darkest hour. Yet, even as he admired their indomitable spirit, he knew that the path of freedom was fraught with perils unseen.

The candle flickered, casting elongated shadows that danced upon the walls like specters of the past. In their silent ballet, Bolívar saw the faces of those who had shared his journey—friends and foes, heroes and martyrs—each leaving their mark upon the canvas of history.

As the night deepened, the Liberator allowed himself a moment of reprieve from the harsh judgment of retrospect. In the solitude of his quarters, he crafted a final resolve, a testament to the undying flame of hope that had always guided him. With measured strokes of his quill, he penned his resignation, sealing the fate of his presidency with ink and parchment.

Simón Bolívar, whose name would come to echo through the annals of time, closed his eyes and drew a labored breath. He surrendered not to defeat, but to the inexorable march of time, trusting that the seeds of liberty he had sown would one day flourish in the hearts of generations yet to come.

And when death came to claim him in 1830, it found a man at peace with his mortality, his spirit unbound by the confines of earthly accolades or titles. For though his body would succumb to the ravages of disease, his legacy would endure—as enduring as the mountains he had crossed, and as vast as the skies he had once held in his revolutionary grasp.

Sixteen

THE DEATH OF THE PRESIDENT

Port Républicain
April 1817

The air held a balmy caress as the Presidential palace, steeped in grandeur and the echoes of a nation's tumultuous journey toward freedom, opened its arms to welcome the esteemed gathering. Lush velvet drapes whispered against marble pillars, and candlelight danced across silverware, setting the scene for President Alexandre Pétion's forty-seventh birthday celebration. The tables were laid out with opulence befitting the leader of the first republic to have shed the yoke of colonialism, an array of exotic dishes, and crystal goblets reflecting the light of numerous chandeliers.

Among the guests, a coterie of generals stood, their uniforms crisp, medals gleaming—a testament to their valor and the resilience that had birthed their nascent republic. General Bonnet, his posture rigid yet noble, conversed with a group of senators, whose eyes held the shrewdness of many battles. General Lys, a man whose presence was as commanding as his reputation, shared a quiet word with Boyer—the youngest among them, but no less respected.

The women, resplendent in silks and satins, added a vivacious color to the palette of the evening. None, however, outshone Mademoiselle Marie-Madeleine Lachenais, known affectionately as Joute. Her laughter rang like a chime, clear and melodious, drawing the admiration of all who basked in her radiance. With each graceful nod and clever repartee, she wove her charm through the hearts of men and women alike, encapsulating the hope and spirit of Ayiti.

In attendance at the grand event were the most prestigious members of the city of Port Républicain: distinguished Senators, influential business people, and wealthy landowners. They all swayed to the music and raised their glasses in honor of Alexandre Pétion's presidency and life.

The ballroom was filled with a sea of elegant gowns and tailored suits, as well as the intoxicating scents of expensive perfumes and colognes. Laughter and conversation filled the air, creating a lively atmosphere that seemed to embrace every guest in its warm embrace. It was a celebration fit for royalty, honoring a man who had risen to become a true icon of the nation. Papa Bon Coeur, he had been named by the people, the protector of the downtrodden, an educator to the young, a revolutionary who exported his ideals, instrumental in the creation of Gran Colombia and elsewhere, and a president who welcomed escaped slaves to his country.

As the evening unfolded, the air thrummed with the subtle strains of violins—each note a soft pulse in the rhythm of the night. Aromatic scents wafted from the feast, tantalizing the senses, while the clinking of glasses punctuated the hum of conversation. Here was a microcosm of the new Ayiti, a tableau of progress where leaders and visionaries mingled, their aspirations as heady as the wine they sipped.

Yet beneath the surface of revelry, there lay a reflective undertone. This was a celebration not just of a man, but of a hard-won freedom, a dream crystallized into reality after years of struggle. Pétion, a beacon of such dreams, moved with ease among his guests, his smile warm, and his gaze piercing. He understood the weight of leadership, the delicate balance of diplomacy and power. His thoughts, carefully guarded, were a tapestry of past revolutions and future ambitions—a narrative of a people unbound, a tribute to the resilience of the human spirit.

In this chamber of festivity, the narratives of lives interwoven by the threads of history played out. Each guest, a bearer of stories etched by the revolution's fire, found solace in the shared vision of hope that filled the palatial space. And as the night deepened, the reflection of a nation reborn shimmered in the glow of celebration, its promise written in the stars above.

The quartet's strings whispered a melody of elegance and grace, a tender caress to the ears of those who swayed in time with its rhythm. Couples danced in the grand ballroom of the Presidential palace, their movements' fluid as if the very air around them was infused with the spirit of the celebration. The soft shuffle of feet on marble, the rustle of silken gowns, and the murmur of admiring glances composed an orchestra of sociability that harmonized with the music.

Joute, resplendent in a specially designed gown for the occasion that captured the light with every turn, moved with an air of practiced poise. Her laughter, bright and clear, rose above the ensemble, drawing eyes like moths to a flame. With a glass of champagne held aloft, she toasted the man of the hour. "To President Pétion," she declared, her voice steady and sure, "whose virtues illuminate our beloved Ayiti like the sun itself. Happy birthday, Mr. President!"

A chorus of cheers followed, glasses raised in tribute to the leader whose vision had helped craft a nation from the ashes of oppression. Alexandre Pétion, his countenance both genial and inscrutable, nodded in acknowledgment, the corners of his mouth curving into a restrained smile. His eyes, those sharp windows to an astute mind, briefly met Joute's before sweeping across the room. He played his part flawlessly, the consummate host, yet behind the façade, he bore the weight of secrets untold.

Among the revelers, General Jean-Pierre Boyer stood with a posture of relaxed authority, his uniform impeccable, his expression schooled to neutrality. He offered a toast in kind, his respect for Pétion apparent. Yet when his gaze found Joute, a spark of something more than loyalty flickered there—a hidden fire that spoke of clandestine meetings and whispered promises.

Joute returned his look with a subtlety that belied the intensity of their shared history. Their secret, a precarious dance more intricate than any performed this evening, was veiled by the shadow of discretion. Around them, the celebration continued, the string quartet playing a tune that now seemed laced with the subtlest notes of intrigue.

Pétion, the architect of many a careful strategy, allowed himself a moment's contemplation as he observed the interactions of his guests. He knew of the discreet glances shared between Joute and Boyer; nothing in his domain escaped his notice. But as a master of international diplomacy and political maneuvering, he chose silence over scandal, understanding that the fragile fabric of unity must not be torn by personal grievances.

Thus, the night unfurled like a flag of resilience, each laugh and gesture weaving together the threads of hope and freedom that defined the new Ayiti. Pétion, ever the reflective leader, considered the past struggles that had brought them here and the future triumphs that beckoned. In the quiet corners of his heart, he embraced the paradoxes of power: the ability to harbor knowledge without action, to inspire loyalty amidst betrayal, and to celebrate the dawn of an era even as the specter of the past lingered close.

And so the birthday celebration of April 1817 continued, a testament to the human capacity for joy and endurance, an ode to a nation reborn from the crucible of revolution, dancing onward towards the promise of a hopeful tomorrow.

Senator Jean-Baptiste Bayard Junior strode gracefully towards Pétion, his wife Marie-Victoire gliding by his side. The room was alive with chatter and music, the soft glow of candles casting a warm light on the faces of guests. "This is quite the soirée, Alexandre," Junior remarked.

"I am blessed to have so many dear friends here to celebrate with me," Pétion replied, a genuine smile spreading across his face. "Madame Bayard, you are truly a sight to behold. Your elegance and poise fill this room."

Marie-Victoire blushed from Pétion's admiring words, and her husband's intense loving gaze upon her only added fuel to the fire. She was indeed as Pétion had described - stunningly beautiful - and Junior felt grateful to have her affection.

"I also wanted to commend you both on your two daughters, Janine and Henriette I believe, whom I had the pleasure of observing in their classes at the Lycee Pétion just the other day," Pétion continued, "The headmaster informs me that they excel in their studies."

"Yes, that is them. I hope they were on their best behavior, Mr. President?" Marie-Victoire asked with a playful smile.

"Of course," Pétion reassured her with a laugh before turning to Junior. "Jean, your amendments to the constitution a couple of years ago were brilliant and have greatly aided me in moving this country forward. I cannot thank you enough for that."

"As Senate President, it is my duty to enact laws that benefit our country," Junior replied humbly. "Your success and stability as president are proof of that."

A hint of a smile played on Pétion's lips. "Indeed, Jean. And I am aware that your support extends beyond the Senate. Your assistance in smoothening out diplomatic relations with the United States has not gone unnoticed." He raised his glass in a silent toast to Junior and Marie-Victoire, conveying his appreciation.

"I was very much aided by my Uncle Andre as he is now in Philadelphia," informed Junior. "He was very instrumental in persuading the administration to lift the embargo back in 1810.

"Forward him my thanks as well," Pétion added.

As the sweet notes of laughter and music wafted through the air, a thought settled over them like a quiet murmuring wind. They were all connected by an invisible tether, their fates bound together by the shadows of their past and the light of their future; they were the guardians of Ayiti's destiny, embroiled in a dance of diplomacy and power.

As the evening progressed, Pétion's guests mingled and danced, their laughter and chatter filling the room. Joute sashayed over to where Pétion, Junior, and Marie-Victoire were standing, a glass of champagne in hand, for yet another toast.

"To our dear President Alexandre Pétion," she toasted enthusiastically, loudly enough so that anyone within the vicinity could hear, clinking her glass against theirs. "May you continue to lead Ayiti with wisdom and grace."

"Thank you, Joute," Pétion smiled warmly at her. "Your continued support means everything to me."

Joute beamed at him before turning to Marie-Victoire. "Madame Bayard, your daughters are simply gorgeous! I couldn't help but notice them during our last visit to the Lycee Pétion with our president."

Marie-Victoire blushed again at the compliment. "Thank you, Joute. They are my pride and joy. I understand that your daughters Cecile and Hersilie are as gifted as they are pretty."

"They take after their mother," Pétion exclaimed.

During the conversation, Junior caught a glimpse of Joute's eyes as they scanned the room and landed on Jean-Pierre Boyer across the room. It wasn't a look of business; it was something else altogether. His gut instinct told him that something just wasn't right, but his friend Pétion seemed oblivious to it.

On the following Thursday, as the sun was just beginning to rise, casting a vibrant orange and pink glow over the cobblestone streets of Port Républicain, Président Pétion sat in his carriage, a striking figure in his new dress uniform, his profile cutting a stark outline against the burgeoning dawn sky. Beside him sat Joute, her usually warm and sensual demeanor replaced by a cold and calculating one since they entered the carriage.

As they made their way through the quiet early morning streets, Pétion couldn't help but wonder what was occupying Joute's thoughts. She had been distant lately, not in public where she always maintained her role as an able diplomat and political advisor, but behind closed doors.

The clattering hooves of their horses brought them to a stop in front of a sturdy building with an unadorned yet dignified façade. Pétion felt a swell of pride and purpose as he gazed upon the sign of the Lycée Pétion. This school embodied his belief that education was a transformative force.

Inside, the halls were alive with activity. The sound of fervent discourse filled the air as young minds engaged in lively debates and discussions. The students' eyes shone with curiosity and determination as they delved into subjects such as mathematics, history, reading, languages, religion, and more.

Pétion and Joute stood at the back of a classroom, observing as an instructor passionately expounded upon the principles of government - concepts dear to Pétion's heart. The aroma of ink and parchment mingled with the subtle musk of new mahogany furniture.

"Government exists to serve the people," declared the teacher emphatically, stealing a glance towards Pétion. "And the people must find productive ways to serve the nation."

Pétion nodded in agreement, thinking back to his decision to dismantle the plantation system that had brought wealth to a privileged few while causing heartache for the majority. Despite facing criticism and doubts, he remained resolute in his belief that true prosperity could only be achieved by embracing these principles.

The students were divided into groups based on age and ability, with classes starting at age five and progressing every two years; 5-6 years old, 7-9, 10-12, and so on until the 17-18 year old graduating class.

As Pétion and Joute walked from classroom to classroom, they were greeted with cheers and eager faces, some familiar and others unknown. When they entered the 10-12 class, they spotted their daughters Cecile (12) and Hersilie (10). The girls' teacher nodded and the two ran over to their parents as the other children watched in awe of the President and the mother of their classmate.

Pétion took time to speak with each student, encouraging them to pursue knowledge and use it for the betterment of their country. Joute listened to stories from the girls and reassured them that women were just as capable as men. The visit left him filled with hope and determination for the future of their nation.

Pétion had planned a drive up the mountains afterward as they were accustomed to doing. But Joute feigned a headache and wanted to go back home to the presidential palace. Pétion thought it a good time to bring up the delicate subject on the ride home.

"Joute, you have been distant lately. What is troubling you?" he asked, his tone tense with suspicion.

"What are you implying, Alexandre?" Joute responded coolly.

"Don't play games with me. Something has changed between us and I know it's not me," Pétion said sharply.

"I thought you knew what pleases and upsets me," Joute coolly remarked with a hint of anger in her voice.

"Then tell me, what is upsetting you now?" Pétion demands.

"Do I have to spell it out for you? We just visited a school where children are taught about love and commitment, yet I am still your mistress concubine instead of your wife," Joute retorts bitterly.

"We've discussed this before. As a military man, it is expected that I do not have a wife," Pétion argues.

"You are not just a military man, you are the president of a country. How can I be respected when I am only known as your mistress?" Joute challenges.

"I have given you a voice and power within our administration. Is that not enough?" Pétion asks, growing frustrated with the argument.

"No, Alexandre. It is not enough," Joute responds firmly, her dark eyes flashing. "I want to be seen as your equal partner, to share your name and have the world know that I am more than just another woman in your life."

Pétion feels a pang of guilt, looking into her fiery eyes. He can no longer avoid the truth; she deserves more than what he has given her. Silence descends upon them as they continue their journey, with only the rhythmic clopping of the horse's hooves breaking the quiet.

The carriage pulls up to the grand entrance of the presidential palace and as they alight, Pétion reaches out and takes Joute's hand.

He gazes at her for a moment before speaking, "Give me some time, Joute. I will make things right."

Joute pulls her hand away, her face hardened by his empty promises. "I've heard it all before, Alexandre." She turns and reaches for the carriage door, her fingers brushing against the polished brass handle, ready to walk away from Pétion's false assurances and into the marble-clad palace that had borne silent witness to their tumultuous relationship.

But just as she is about to step out, Pétion's hand shoots out across her and slams the door shut again, much to the surprise of the coachman. "Wait, Joute," he pleads, his voice echoing in the confines of the carriage. He looks at her, his dark eyes filled with desperation and, for the first time in a long while, vulnerability. The sight of this proud man, who led their nation with such unwavering conviction yet couldn't find a way to make their relationship right, tugged at her heart.

Joute sighs, a soft, pained sound that seems to echo the conflicting emotions swirling within her. "What is it, Alexandre?" she murmurs, her voice a mere whisper against the profound silence that engulfs them.

Pétion closes his eyes for a moment, gathering his thoughts before speaking. When he finally opens them again, there's a determination in his gaze she's never seen before. "My heart is yours, as it has always been. But I have been blind to your pain and your desires," he begins softly, his voice full of regret.

Overwhelmed by his admission, Joute turns her gaze towards the window, trying to hide the tears welling up in her eyes. She watches as the palace grounds stretch out beneath the crimson-gold light of the sun, manicured gardens and ornate fountains sparkling like jewels against the sprawling landscape. Her heart swells with bitter affection for this place... their home... and the man who she loves but knows she must share with an entire country.

"What is Jean-Pierre Boyer to you," Pétion asked as he glared into her eyes.

The question threw her completely off guard. The conversation was veering towards the direction she had intended, then suddenly, this. "What in heavens do you mean, Alexandre?"

Joute did not know at this point how much Pétion knew of their clandestine affair as she searched for the right words, the right direction. "Jean-Pierre is trying to help me. He's the only one who seems to understand me these days," she admits, her gaze locked with Pétion's. There was a heavy silence in the carriage, broken only by their shallow breaths.

Pétion's grip tightens on the brass handle, his skin pallid against the ornate metalwork. "Is there something between you and Jean-Pierre?" he asks, his voice barely above a whisper.

Joute's eyes flash defiantly, "It is not what you think, Alexandre. It's about connection, something you've never given me."

Pétion removes his hand from the door, sliding it back to his side. "I see. I didn't realize how far I have pushed you away by my actions, or lack thereof." His voice is steady but there is a tremor in his gaze.

Pétion closes his eyes for a moment, gathering his thoughts before speaking. When he finally opens them again, there's a determination in his gaze she's never seen before. "Again, I repeat to you; my heart is yours, as it has always been. But I have been blind to your pain and your desires," he begins softly, his voice full of regret. "How far has this relationship with Jean-Pierre gone?" asked Pétion.

"It is not like that. He listens to me. He understands me."

"I listen to you. I always listen to your advice, your counsel, your strategies," answered Pétion.

"That is not what I mean. All you need me for is politics. He needs, I mean wants. No, that is not what I mean. He speaks differently like all of that does not matter," Joute says in confusion as she reaches for the right words to say. She then rushes from the carriage, her heart pounding with guilt and shame as the truth of their crumbling relationship hits her like a ton of bricks, causing her to make her escape before the need to confess her transgressions to Alexandre.

The next several months were a challenge for both Joute and Pétion. There was an awkward air in their relationship as the months dragged out until it was the Christmas holidays.

Their days were full of frosty mornings, with bracing winds that seemed to carry the tension between them. The palace was a flurry of activity as they prepared for the holiday festivities, desperate to have an appearance of family normalcy in front of their daughters, but the joyous atmosphere felt hollow to both. They moved in parallel lines, never intersecting, their conversations reduced to cordial necessities.

Jean-Pierre Boyer, however, became an increasingly frequent presence in Joute's life. He often invited her for walks around the estate when Pétion traveled from the city, and his letters became a constant source of comfort when Pétion was home and Jean-Pierre was unable to visit. His words were like the soft glow of a hearth in the chill winter nights—warm and comforting—providing an escape from her strained relationship with Pétion.

However, Joute found it hard to keep up appearances when out in public with Pétion during the holiday galas and parties, where they were expected to perform as a unified front.

One such event was the annual Christmas Eve ball, a grand affair hosted by the mayor. The opulent ballroom was adorned with shimmering chandeliers and crimson poinsettias. The well-to-do citizens, nobles, and diplomats alike walked about in their finest attire, their laughter and conversation barely heard over the orchestra's festive serenade.

Joute watched as Pétion mingled with the guests, his charm and charisma on full display. He was a master at these social events, at ease among the politicians and aristocracy. It was during moments like this that she felt the most distant from him. He was a statesman first, a partner and lover second.

Amid her solitude, Joute's heart leaped at the sight of a familiar figure — Jean-Pierre. His concerned gaze pierced through her, a stark contrast to Pétion's cold and distant scrutiny. With a gentle gesture, he extended his hand for a dance, offering her an escape from her loneliness. As they glided across the dancefloor, Joute surrendered herself to the pulsing rhythm of the music. Each step brought her closer to Jean-Pierre and further away from her troubles, enveloped in the warmth and comfort of his touch.

"Have you spoken with Alexandre yet of his successor to the presidency?" Boyer asked.

"I have brought up the subject, but he shuts me down each time. He suspects us, though I have told him that our relationship is a friendship, and nothing more."

"Then it is time, Joute," Boyer murmured gently, his hands tightening around hers as he maneuvered them around the ballroom. "You cannot go on living like this, constantly torn between two worlds."

"But Jean-Pierre, it is not so simple..." Joute faltered, her gaze dropping to their entwined hands. "There is so much at stake; my family, my position, my daughters, the good of the country."

"I understand it won't be easy," he assured her, his voice barely audible over the rich melodies of the orchestra. "But Joute, you deserve a life filled with joy and warmth. You deserve to be heard and understood."

Joute's heart fluttered at his words, an unfamiliar sense of hope blooming within her. She looked into his eyes and saw sincerity there, a stark contrast to Pétion's dismissive glances.

The ball drew to a close with a final waltz. The couple moved in fluid synchrony across the floor as he gently stopped their dance, drawing them both to the side of the room, out of site by most. He held both her hands in his now, his eyes pleading. "I love you, Joute. More than just a friend," he confessed, his voice barely above a whisper but clear in the buzzing of the ballroom.

Jean-Pierre Boyer and Joute could not resist an up-close waltz during the Christmas ball, even though their clandestine relationship could be easily uncovered.

Joute's heart pounded in her chest, her breath hitched as she looked into Jean-Pierre's eyes, eyes that held so much sincerity and affection. An affection she longed for, one that had the power to break down all her insecurities. She was silent for a while, measuring the weight of his confession. "Jean-Pierre..." she began, her voice full of emotion. "I..."

Suddenly, they were interrupted by a loud applause as the orchestra finished their final piece. The room buzzed with laughter and joyous conversation as couples left the dance floor heading to the grand dining hall where a feast awaited them.

Jean-Pierre pulled away slightly, still holding Joute's hands within his own. He nodded toward the crowd with a resigned smile. "Perhaps this is not the right time," he said, carefully disentangling their hands.

Joute watched as he disappeared back into the sea of people, leaving her with an overwhelming sense of longing and the understanding that she must rejoin the president and head into the banquet to perform her duties yet another time.

Christmas and the lead-up to the New Year were festive but tense for both Pétion and Joute. What made matters worse was that Pétion had become ill with a lingering stomach virus that was stubborn to leave, and symptoms that lasted and progressively got worse over the next couple of months.

In mid-February, with the president bedridden, the palace was quieter and more somber than usual. Joute found herself having to step in and perform more of the public duties usually carried out by the president. She made appearances at events, dealt with inquiries from aristocrats, and even attended meetings with the Senate at his behest. The stress of handling their public image alone weighed on her heavily, but she did what she could to maintain a sense of normalcy for their daughters.

Jean-Pierre, ever the reliable friend and a discreet lover, was by her side through it all. He assisted her with military insights that were beyond her understanding, as her expertise was more of a political and diplomatic nature. His steady presence was a lifeline through the chaotic days of Pétion's illness.

In the heart of one such hectic day in February, Pétion called Joute into his room. There was a stark change in him-- his eyes had lost their luster, his skin was pale, and he appeared frail under the blankets. Seeing him like this shook Joute to her core. It was a stark reminder of the fragility of life and the fleeting nature of power and prestige.

"Joute," Pétion rasped, attempting to sit up in bed. He winced at the pain, hand gripping his abdomen. "Help me, please."

She rushed to his side, her heart heavy with empathy as she gently aided him into a sitting position. They were silent for some moments with only the soft crackling of the fire and the strained breaths of Pétion filling the room.

Finally, Pétion broke the silence. "I need to talk to you about...about my successor," he began, each word strained with effort.

Joute's heart pounded in her chest. She could hardly believe what she was hearing. Was Pétion truly revealing his greatest secret?

"Jean-Baptiste Bayard Junior," he announced, meeting Joute's gaze with a steely determination that belied his weakened state.

Startled by this revelation, Joute took a step back, her eyes wide in disbelief. "But why him? Why Bayard?" she asked, her voice barely above a whisper.

Pétion sighed, his hands trembling slightly as he reached for a glass of water on the nightstand. After a long drink, he set the glass down and looked up at Joute, his gaze steady despite his illness.

"Bayard is strong," Pétion admitted, his voice weak but clear. "He's a capable politician, and he has the respect of the Senate. No more should this country be ruled by the military. A civilian government and a civilian must be at the helm as its leader. He's also," Pétion began to cough continuously until he recovered, "...he's also loyal."

At that word, Joute couldn't help but feel a pang in her heart. She thought of Jean-Pierre and his unwavering loyalty to her and Alexandre.

Pétion continued, "He may not be my first choice, Joute. But given the current circumstances...Bayard is the best option we have."

Joute stood there silently, digesting Pétion's words. She was overwhelmed with a whirlpool of emotions, her mind racing to make sense of it all. Pétion's admittance of his mortality, his choice for a successor other than Jean-Pierre, and the underlying tensions... everything was changing too quickly.

"Does Bayard know?" she asked eventually, her voice barely audible.

"Not yet. All I have told him is a civilian government must now lead our nation, not the military," Pétion admitted, sinking back against the pillows. He looked drained, his eyes closing as he breathed heavily. "I plan on telling him soon... when I gather enough strength."

"And Jean-Pierre?" Joute couldn't help but ask, her heart stinging at the thought of his reaction.

"Boyer will understand," Pétion responded weakly, his voice barely a whisper now. "He knows the politics of our world better than anyone. He won't take it personally."

Joute nodded slowly, lost in thought. She had an uncanny suspicion that Jean-Pierre might not react as calmly as Pétion assumed.

"I need your support on this, Joute," Pétion continued, a hint of desperation creeping into his voice. "I need you to stand by me, to assure the people that this is the right decision."

Joute raised her head and met Pétion's gaze. "I have always stood by you, Alexandre," she said quietly. "And I will continue to do so."

Pétion nodded, relief washing over his features. He released a heavy breath he seemed to have been holding and sank deeper into the pillows. Joute could see the exhaustion etched on his face and knew that his confession had taken much from him.

She straightened up, determination welling up within her. "Rest now," she told him softly. "We'll talk more about this when you're feeling better."

But even as she said it, she knew that rest would not be easy for her. The revelation of Bayard as Pétion's successor would significantly alter the dynamics, as well as her plans, among them all. As she left Pétion's room, she was resolved with what she must do, even talking herself into it being her duty to do so.

Days passed, and Pétion continued to digress, Joute would arrive at the appropriate hour with papers to sign so that the government could continue to operate. Mostly routine and mundane, Pétion would sign them as she would read them out loud since his eyesight had diminished.

But on this day, the bottommost document was different. It was the official declaration of Pétion's successor, carefully detailed and worded by lawyers and advisors to assure its legitimacy.

Joute's heart pounded in her chest as she held the paper in her hands. She glanced over at Pétion. He looked feeble and worn, his hand trembling slightly as it rested on the edge of his bedcovers. Surely he wasn't ready to step down yet.

She cleared her throat. "This last document," she said slowly, "is a declaration naming your successor."

Pétion's gaze shifted toward her, a glint of surprise flickering in his eyes. "Already?" he rasped.

Joute nodded. "The Senate believes they must know your wishes, especially considering your.... condition."

Pétion grimaced but remained silent, his gaze dropping down to his hands as he considered this.

"I can read it aloud if you wish." Joute offered, watching him closely for any sign of resistance. The stark fear in his eyes hit her hard, making her feel suddenly hollow inside.

She braced herself before continuing. "It states that should you be unable to fulfill your duties as President for any reason, Senator Jean-Baptiste Bayard Junior will assume the position in your stead."

There was a long pause as Pétion processed this, his features set in a grim line. He took a deep breath before finally extending his hand towards her. "Give it here," he said softly.

Joute handed him the document without a word. As she watched him scan it, knowing the words were a blur, she pointed to the signature line. With shaky hands, he scribbled his signature, as her heart felt like it was being squeezed in a vice. "Would you apply the official seal for me please, Joute?" he sheepishly whispered.

It was real now. The future of their nation hinged on this single piece of paper, and there was no turning back.

As Pétion handed the paper back to her, he looked frailer than ever. His eyes showed a resignation that frightened Joute more than anything else she had ever seen before. It was as if he'd already resigned himself to his fate, and this act of signing off his power was a final acceptance of his mortality.

Despite the heaviness in her own heart, Joute forced herself to smile at him. "You should get some rest now, my love," she said gently, taking the document from him and slipping it into the leather pouch. "You've done more than enough today."

Pétion nodded, clearly drained from the weight of his decision. "Thank you, Joute," he replied in a barely audible whisper before sinking back against the pillows, his eyes fluttering closed.

Joute remained a while longer, watching over Pétion as he drifted into a restless sleep. Her thoughts were a whirlwind, embroiled with worry for Pétion's suffering and the future of their nation. But beneath it all was a glimmer of resolve. She would do what she must to ensure the new president's smooth transition into power and maintain stability in their country.

She got up and began to leave the room, pulling out the document from its pouch. She glanced at the signature of her lover, her president, as a whirlwind of memories came to haunt her. The bold strokes of his signature were now faint and shaky, a poignant reminder of the once vigorous man he had been. Her gaze lingered on the last two curved lines of his signature, a smile tugged at the corners of her mouth recalling all those times he'd signed off letters with his flamboyant 'Alexandre.' It was painful to absorb this sight and mystifyingly surreal. All she needed to do now was to apply the official seal and the proclamation would be official.

As she made her way out, she steeled herself before stepping into the hallway. She took one last look at the document proclaiming Jean-Pierre Boyer as successor to the presidency before she slipped it back into the folder and held it close to her chest, a protective shield against potential impending chaos. The gravity of what they had set in motion weighed heavily upon her, yet she couldn't show signs of weakness to anyone who would cross her path; the servants shuffling about their duties, the guards standing sentinel, the generals of their great army, or the senate minding the government's affairs. They would all still look to her for steadiness in these troubling times as her thoughts went to Jean-Pierre Boyer. He would shoulder his new responsibilities with her by his side. But, if it was indeed Bayard on that document, she would become irrelevant and drift into the lost sands of history.

Exactly seven days later, on the morning of March 29th of 1818, Pétion took his final breath in his sleep. The physician summoned by Joute is coaxed to declare Pétion's demise as a result of yellow fever, but the doctor's gut tells him otherwise. He has seen these symptoms before, but not in cases of the infamous la fievre jaune - this is something much darker, deadlier, and sinister.

Jean-Baptiste Bayard, Junior's opulent home was buzzing with excitement as his parents had arrived from Cap-Henry, marking a grand celebration. The air was filled with laughter and the tinkling of glasses as Junior watched lovingly while his mother played with his two young daughters. But the festive atmosphere suddenly turned grave as two soldiers appeared at the door, requesting to speak with

Junior - the powerful senate president. As the guests looked on in confusion, the soldiers left the room and Junior turned to them to deliver the devastating news.

"My family and friends, it is with great sorrow that I must inform you of our leader's untimely death." With a heavy heart, Marie stood by her son's side as he addressed the somber gathering. "Alexandre Pétion," Junior began solemnly, his voice steady despite the tremor of grief in his eyes. "My mentor, my guide, my friend... and our president, has passed away."

Shocked gasps echoed through the garden as Marie-Victoire swiftly ushered her daughters inside and gathered them close. An eerie silence fell over the group, their minds racing with questions and fears for their country's future. A few of the ladies gathered around began to sob quietly while others murmured a prayer under their breaths.

But as Bayard Junior held Marie-Victoire's gaze, she saw the unspoken words in his eyes - the knowledge that he was now in line to assume leadership as Pétion had not yet nominated a successor. The realization was, at once, overwhelming and humbling.

"There remains a task ahead of us – a task that necessitates courage and unity," he continued with newfound resolve. "Having been elected by the Senate as its president, I am constitutionally tasked with continuing in his footsteps until a new president is chosen."

His words hung heavy in the air for a moment before he added, "I seek your support and prayers to lead our beloved nation through these testing times until the clarity of future leadership is achieved."

Bayard Junior's words came as a shock to many present. Whispers began to pass through the crowd, some of surprise, others of approval. Marie felt a knot tighten in her chest as she watched her son stand tall under the weight of responsibility. As nervous as she was for him, she was also filled with an immense sense of pride.

Jean-Baptiste Bayard Junior locked his gaze with his mother, drawing strength from the silent encouragement in her eyes. He held himself together and continued, "I do not take this appointment lightly. I am ready to dedicate myself to our nation's needs and steer us through the storm that is brewing."

He took a slow, steadying breath. "The next few weeks will be difficult for all of us. We will mourn our lost leader and prepare for a future without him. But we must remember, my friends," he continued, his voice growing stronger, "That our nation was built on unity and resilience in the face of adversity. With that said, I must now take my leave to the presidential palace for meetings."

Junior's heart pounded with adrenaline and fear as he said goodbye to his guests, tightly embracing Jean and Marie, and passionately kissing his wife. He sprinted inside and quickly bid farewell to his young daughters, knowing the danger that awaited him on this mission.

Jean watched as Junior embraced his daughters from the front door and waited until he came to exit. "Listen to me, son. These will be dangerous times. Be careful of who you trust and leary of who you do not. Keep your wits about you."

Junior looked at his father. "Qui Papa," he said, needing no further communication as they both knew what the stakes would be moving forward. They embraced before Junior went out the front door.

The two stoic soldiers stood outside, their eyes betraying a mixture of respect and disdain for Junior being that he was not a man of the military. Without a word, they ushered him into a waiting carriage that would take him to the palace, where an uncertain future awaited. As he climbed onto the seat, a sense of awe mingled with overwhelming sorrow washed over him, knowing that this could be his last ride in this world if the generals had intentions of securing the country through military force.

As the carriage trundled through the empty Sunday streets of Port Républicain, Junior leaned against the plush backrest and watched as a ripple of shock and grief passed through the people milling about. News traveled quickly in this city - it would not be long before every home, every heart, was touched by the news of Pétion's passing. Occasionally, someone would recognize him in his carriage and either touch their breast in acknowledgment or look away in fear or suspicion.

When they finally reached the grand entrance of the Presidential Palace, a sense of dread gripped him. This was it - the next few hours would determine the path of a country and his path as well.

As he entered the palace, familiar faces had already arrived to hold a vigil after hearing the news. The staff served coffee, tea, and light bites. The butler, Charles, arrived at Junior's side. "Madame Lachenais has asked that you be brought to the president's chambers immediately upon your arrival.

As he was led up the stairs to the living quarters, the normally welcoming ambiance of the palace felt cold and foreboding. Each step echoed ominously in the grand staircase, reverberating against the marble walls.

Arriving at the chamber door, Junior found it slightly ajar, a single candlelight flickering from within. Taking a deep breath, he pushed open the door and stepped inside. The outer chamber of the bedroom had an air of somber tranquility.

Joute sat near the window, her body silhouetted against the pale sun streaming in from behind. Her face was partially obscured, her expression unreadable as she looked towards him. "Jean-Baptiste," she began in a whisper that somehow filled the room with a palpable heaviness. "You're here."

"Yes, Joute," Junior managed to reply in a low voice as he moved towards her, stopping at a respectful distance. "Please accept the condolences of myself and my entire family."

"Come here, Jean-Baptiste Junior," she said warmly as she extended her open arms to him. Junior went to her and at once she began to sob in his arms for several seconds before disengaging and stepping back. She studied him for an agonizing moment before addressing him again. "I have been expecting you," she said softly, offering him a grave smile that didn't quite reach her eyes.

Junior swallowed hard against the lump in his throat, "I am sorry for your loss, our collective loss, Joute."

Joute blinked slowly, her gaze still fixed on him. "And I for yours," she responded, her voice containing a hint of something he couldn't place. Was it sympathy? Sorrow? Or perhaps even relief? It was as if she had been expecting this moment too, somehow knowing that death would come to claim Pétion in his sleep.

"Thank you, Joute," he said, bowing his head slightly. He wasn't quite sure how to navigate this conversation, the weight of their new reality heavy in the air between them.

"There is much to discuss," Joute finally said, breaking the silence once more. She gestured to an antique chair nearby, indicating for him to sit. "But first, we must send a message to the country. The people must be reassured that their leader's passing will not lead to chaos."

Junior gave a nod in agreement, even though he had been dreading this moment. But he knew it was inevitable and couldn't avoid it any longer. "I understand," he said calmly, although his nerves were on edge. "I'll draft a message to be sent out at dawn."

Joute interrupted, signaling to Charles to call the generals back into the room. They quickly entered and Junior greeted General Borgella and Boyer with a slight bow before they all professionally shook hands.

Junior spoke up, "It pains me to switch so rapidly to governmental matters, but we must send a message to our citizens about the continuity of their government. As per our laws, it is my constitutional obligation as Senate President to take over as leader until a permanent successor is chosen since our president presented no decree before his death.

Joute stood, went to a desk in the room, and presented a document for them all to see, "This is one of the last official documents signed by our late president.

As they huddled around to read it, General Borgella appeared visibly shocked while Boyer seemed already familiar with its contents. After reading it, Borgella looked incredulous and Junior couldn't believe what he was reading either: Jean-Pierre Boyer was named successor and President for Life. Both Borgella and Junior examined the signature which appeared to be genuine, as did the wax seal.

Borgella's annoyance was apparent - he was senior to Boyer, had been a loyal ally to Pétion, and by all accounts should have been the chosen successor. Junior's mind, on the other hand, went to the recent memory of a conversation with Pétion where he was adamant that the military would no longer head the government upon his death, and that the civilians would lead the country forward.

Riding the tide of his shock, Junior tried to keep his composure. "This is unexpected," he said slowly, his gaze moving from Joute, who seemed to carry a quiet sadness and disappointment in her eyes, to Boyer who remained stoic and unreadable.

The room was filled with an awkward silence until Borgella broke it, his voice laced with frustration. "How is this possible? I've been at Pétion's side for years. And Boyer?" he turned to face the new president with a mix of disbelief and hostility.

Boyer met Borgella's gaze without flinching, his poise unchanging. "It seems Pétion saw fit to entrust the country to me. He must have had his reasons."

Borgella turned and marched out of the room.

Junior felt a surge of resentment towards Boyer. The declaration was completely against Pétion's express wishes, which had been communicated privately to him. As he snapped his head up, he caught Joute and Boyer exchanging a sly look, filled with unspoken secrets and shameless betrayal. The air crackled with unspoken tension, the weight heavy on Junior's chest as he felt his heart pound with rage and hurt.

"I want to see Alexandre," Junior asserted.

Joute hesitates with a flicker of fear in her eyes. "His body is in the adjacent bedroom," she finally replies.

Ignoring Joute's hesitation, Junior strode towards the door and cautiously opened it. As he enters the room, he senses an oppressive warmth that makes his skin prickle. The physician, seated on a chair inside, stands up abruptly at their entrance, followed by Joute and Boyer.

"Doctor, how could our powerful president succumb to this illness?" Junior demands, his voice cold and steely.

The physician avoids Junior's gaze and looks towards Joute for guidance. She gives him a subtle nod, urging him to speak.

"I cannot say for certain," the physician begins cautiously.

Junior takes a step forward, his jaw clenching with determination. "I am the senate president and I must officially record the passing of our great leader. It is your duty to tell us, what caused his death?"

"I cannot be certain," repeats the physician evasively.

Junior's patience runs thin. "Then what is your best guess, Doctor?" he presses.

Joute interjects anxiously. "Do we need to do this now?"

"Yes, we do," Junior replies firmly. He turns back to the physician, his eyes piercing. "What is your most calculated guess?"

The physician shifts uncomfortably before answering. "The symptoms resemble those of yellow fever, but there are some differences. Yellow fever typically lasts no more than two weeks before either recovery or death. Our president suffered for nearly four months before passing away."

Boyer cuts in impatiently. "Why are you not certain then?"

"Because…" the physician hesitates before dropping a bombshell. "Because it resembles symptoms of poisoning."

A stunned silence follows as Joute covers her mouth in shock and Boyer's glare turns icy. Junior's face hardens into a mask of fury as he orders the physician to leave.

Once they are alone, Junior turns to Boyer and Joute with fire in his eyes. "Explain this to me. What is going on?"

Joute's voice quivers as she speaks, "Forever...what do you mean?"

Junior's face is stone cold as he responds, "Our president made it clear that a military man would no longer lead as president. He was adamant that he wanted a clear separation of power between the government and the military. Yet here we are, with this document that goes against his final wishes and a physician who is asserting that foul play may be present."

Boyer's eyes narrow in suspicion as he steps forward, "Are you accusing Joute and I of being involved in his death?"

Junior's gaze turns cold and accusatory as he replies, "That is exactly what I am implying." Tension fills the room as Boyer moves closer to Junior, ready to confront him.

But Joute forcefully steps between them, her words laced with urgency and desperation. "This is not the time for petty divisions! Borgella's growing power threatens us all, and without a united front from the Senate and the executive branch, he will certainly launch a military coup. We must stand together and bring stability to our country. Borgella commands the support of his powerful allies, Generals Bonnet from Léogâne, and Bazelais from Jacmel."

The weight of responsibility and danger presses down on their shoulders, and the realization of how fragile their position truly is hits them like a ton of bricks. Boyer steps forward to Junior with an outstretched hand, trying to salvage their alliance. "You were once loyal to our good friend and president, Jean-Baptiste. Join Joute and I as we continue the progress that he fought so hard for."

Jean looks at Boyer's hand, but his mind is consumed with doubt and fear. Joute watches them both intently, her gaze shifting back and forth like a predator eyeing its prey. After what feels like an eternity, Junior refuses to take Boyer's hand, instead meeting his eyes with a steely resolve.

"I will only offer this hand once, Jean-Baptiste," Boyer warns him with a hint of menace. "Take it now or consider our alliance to be done."

Junior's jaw tightens as he stares down at the open hand before him. He knows that accepting it means betraying everything he believed in and possibly standing against his former ally and mentor, Alexandre Pétion. But refusing means certain defeat and potentially even death.

"What have you both done?" Junior growls before turning on his heel and storming out of the room, leaving Boyer and Joute to face the gravity of his accusations alone. The room falls into tense silence as they realize the true cost of their choices.

Daniel J.D. Bayard

Seventeen

THE YOUNG PRINCE

Milot
June 1820

Queen Marie-Louise, of the Kingdom of Ayiti, closed her eyes and let her mind drift back to a sunny June Sunday in 1813 when Henry took her hand and led her on a tour of the magnificent Sans-Souci palace. After years of construction, it was finally completed and stood tall, three stories high with walls covered in vibrant yellow brick, topped with a roof of brilliant red tiles.

As they entered the grand hall, Marie-Louise's heart swelled with awe at the sight of the regal stairway flanked by stone sentry boxes at intervals. Her husband guided her through the spacious terrace, pointing out each lavish room - the audience chamber, the offices, the banquet hall, and upstairs to their private quarters as king and queen.

But it was not just the opulent rooms that impressed Marie-Louise. In the gardens and grounds, she marveled at every flower and fruit she had ever desired, now flourishing under her husband's care. They visited the chapel, the arsenal, and the barracks where the special African regiment of guards known as The Royal Dahomet Palace Guards were housed. And then back to their palace, where every detail was carefully curated; marble floors, polished wood paneling adorning the walls, mirrors reflecting tapestries and paintings, and a library lined with richly bound books.

Overwhelmed with emotion, Marie-Louise couldn't hold back tears as she gazed at her husband. "It's all so beautiful," she said with a brave smile. "But I fear all of this luxury will also bring us trouble in the future, Henry. Our true happiness was once found under my father's hotel's pepper tree or in our humble mountain hideaway when we were being chased by the French army. We do not need all of this opulence to be happy."

But Henry squeezed her arm reassuringly and replied, "Let go of your fears and enjoy the present moment. That is what you taught me under the pepper tree at your father's hotel."

Her mind drifted back to her childhood, a time when the Coidavid family lived in a grandiose two-story home across town from the hotel that her father had built. The luxurious abode was a stark contrast to the humble beginnings of her parents, Gabriel and Christiane, who had been born as slaves but eventually gained the coveted status of Afranchi, free ex-slaves in the French colonial caste system.

However, Marie-Louise was born free, a Gens de Couleur, and her parents were determined to provide her with the best education that money could buy. Sent to study in Paris at a young age, Marie-Louise excelled in both scholastic and artistic pursuits, particularly in music and oil painting. But despite her privileged upbringing, she remained grounded and approachable like her father, inheriting his easygoing disposition.

Growing up in a hotel presented Marie-Louise with a unique perspective on life. She interacted with children from the full gamete of the population - playing with the elite children on palm-shaded streets, mingling with middle-class Petits Blancs at Cap Français's picturesque main square, and befriending ragged-clothed black slave girls in the alleyways of the town. To her, one's social station and skin color held little importance.

This diverse environment shaped Marie-Louise into a well-rounded individual. Home from her studies abroad, she would eagerly listen to stories passed down by the hotel's slaves who performed tasks such as scrubbing floors and cleaning rooms. These tales spoke of ancestral heritage from West Africa - or Guinée as they called it - where they believed their souls would return upon death for eternal happiness. Stories of powerful kings, fierce warriors, exotic tribes, and wild creatures filled her imagination. She often wondered if her ancestors had similar stories, but they were never spoken of by her parents.

Among these tales were also scandalous ones told by Avril - a free colored woman who sold her vegetables and fruits to the head chefs of white-owned plantations in the Plaine du Nord. Avril brought gossip of theft, corruption, fraud, and deceit throughout the region to her father who always told his daughter to be cognizant of the pulse of the people around her.

As Marie-Louise's mind returned to her current surroundings, she found herself surrounded by a group of laundry women who were her informants and supplied an unfiltered gauge of the peasantry. Their voices were hushed as they whispered about the latest gossip being spread at the river regarding her husband, the King. Marie-Louise couldn't help but feel a sense of unease wash over her as she listened to their words.

They spoke of the Code Henry outlined in the 750-page legal law that contained a set of rules imposed on every adult man, and woman, which required them to work from sunrise until eight o'clock, with only an hour break for breakfast. In the summer months, the heat and humidity of the tropics made it impossible to work without taking breaks for siestas, so the King allowed two hours for this during the hottest part of the day. But even this wasn't enough for the women at the washing place who cried out "This is slavery!" in unison.

The King, it seemed, was determined to keep his subjects working without rest or respite, the women would grumble and complain, saying that even in their days as slaves they had been treated better, even though in reality, it was not so.

Marie-Louise knew that Ayiti, and before that the colony of Saint Domingue, had always been a powder keg, ready to explode at any moment. And with tensions already running high due to the King's actions, any small spark could set off a violent rebellion. She feared not just for her safety, but for that of her husband and children.

This was the reality and the worry that Marie-Louise dealt with daily. Her deep love and respect for her husband and the seeds of turmoil he was sewing in the people. She feared for him.

King Henry was a visionary ruler who saw the importance of education for his people. He wanted not only his three children to be properly educated, but also the general population. "The future of our kingdom lies in the hands of our youth," he would often proclaim. As a result, the king spared no expense when it came to education. He built schools across his entire kingdom and brought in teachers from England and the United States to lead them, with English as the primary language for all students.

King Henry made sure to prioritize the proper education of his children; His son Victor, the Prince Royal, and his two daughters Princesses Amethiste and Athenaire. The girls were both bright and curious and were initially taught by their mother, who had received a good education befitting her status in her hometown and in Paris. However, as the princesses grew older, she felt that her knowledge was insufficient for their needs of the present day.

That's when Pompée Valentin Vastey, the secretary and historian of the king's cabinet with the title of Baron, stepped in. Having lived in America himself before joining the royal court, he handpicked female teachers from abroad to instruct the princesses. This included two proper and reserved women for general studies, as well as two younger and livelier instructors for music, dance, and painting.

Although the king approved of all the teachers chosen by Baron Vastey, he found Mademoiselle Ducette, the music and dance teacher, to be particularly intriguing. She was talented on both the piano and with her voice, earning her praises from everyone at court.

It was another Thursday and King Henry's court had assembled, as usual every Thursday evening, to hear the enchanting music being played on the piano she had insisted be imported for her. "The music is splendid indeed," Henry complimented as he leaned towards Marie-Louise.

Marie-Louise smiled, appreciating the delicate harmonies. "She is a wonder, isn't she? A true virtuoso. I only hope our girls can learn even half of her musical talents."

The courtiers hummed in agreement, swaying gently to the rhythm of the music. The soft light of the chandeliers cast a warm glow on the polished wooden floors and the silk-clad audience. It was a scene straight from Versailles, but here in Ayiti, it held its own unique beauty and charm.

Yet even amidst this serenity, Marie-Louise could not shake off the undercurrents of unease that pervaded through the crowd. Whispers had gotten louder, discontent had become bolder. She knew that their world was balanced on a delicate precipice and it would take only a minor incident to tip it over.

When the tune completed, a polite applause came from the court as Henry stood up and continued to clap loudly and energetically, "Bravo, Bravo!" he declared, his eyes sparkling with genuine admiration.

Mademoiselle Ducette curtsied, a blush creeping up her cheeks at the king's praise. The courtiers followed suit, their applause louder and more heartfelt this time, echoing the king's actions throughout the grandeur of the palace.

At dinner that evening, the music still melodied in Marie-Louise's ears as she found herself seated next to Baron Vastey. She much enjoyed his company as conversations flowed around them; men discussed politics and women whispered about the latest fashions imported from Paris. Amidst it all, a cloud of unease hung heavy in the air.

Vastey had become her confidant of late. He possessed enormous political and government knowledge from his days in the Department of Finance under the Dessalines administration, was a secretary on the commission that developed the Code Henry, and was rewarded with the title of Baron by her husband. He has always been a staunch supporter and defender of the king by writing major papers and books on the evils of the French empire as well as his past negative writings towards Pétion's government to the south while the late president was still alive.

He had impressed the king so much so, that this past August of 1819 he was made a knight of the Royal and Military Order of Saint Henry and was appointed Field Marshal and Chancellor. His latest published literary work, '*Essay on the Causes of the Revolution and Civil Wars in Ayiti',* was critical of Pétion's Grand Sud, much to the approval of the king.

"Baron," Marie-Louise began, folding her hands neatly on her lap. "I'm concerned about... unrest."

Vastey's gaze softened, understanding dawning upon him. "You've heard the whispers too," he noted, more of a statement than a question.

"I have," she admitted, looking down at her untouched plate of food.

He sighed, running a hand through his greying hair. "It's a complex situation, Madame," he replied, his voice low so as not to be overheard by the courtiers nearby. "There's a growing tension between the different factions in our country, and between the Grand Sud and Grand Nord. It's creating a divide we can't ignore."

Marie-Louise nodded seriously, studying the intricate patterns of her china plate. "Can anything be done to alleviate this tension?" she asked cautiously.

Baron Vastey regarded her thoughtfully for a moment before responding. "The King is attempting to create a singular Ayisyen identity, however, he needs the Kingdom to succeed and prosper so he can export that success to the south" he explained. "But it will take time and patience."

"And courage," Marie-Louise added softly, turning her gaze back to the baron. She saw in his worn face a mirror of her fears and hopes for their beloved country.

"Yes," agreed Vastey, his voice firm with conviction. "So wish me luck as it is time for me to have some." as he stood to make a toast.

Vastey commanded the crowd with his baritone voice and their utter respect for his literary talents. "Ladies and Gentlemen. Please join be in a toast to our King of Ayiti, Sovereign of Tortuga, Gonâve, and other adjacent islands, Destroyer of tyranny, Regenerator and Benefactor of the Ayisyen nation, Creator of her moral, political, and martial institutions, First crowned monarch of the New World, Defender of the faith, Founder of the Royal Military Order of Saint Henry and husband to Queen Marie-Louise", as he lifted his glass towards the king.

All in attendance stood at attention and lifted their glass as well, waiting for the king to rise, which he did. The queen remained seated until he did so and began to speak,

"My good people," began King Henry, his voice resonating deeply through the ornate hall, reaching every ear with its commanding firmness. His eyes scanned the room, taking in every face - faces etched with hope, expectation, and a wary sense of anticipation.

"I stand before you today not as an invincible monarch, but as a man who shares your dreams for a united Ayiti. An Ayiti where our diversity is our strength, and our unity is our invincibility." He paused briefly, letting his words sink in.

"Let us not let petty squabbles divide us. Let us not allow the winds of colonial influence to drive a wedge between us. We are one nation." His gaze swept over the crowd once again - this time more intensely - challenging all present to dispute his proclamation.

"Baron Vastey speaks truth when he writes in his books that 'it will take courage'. It will take courage to forge a new path against the clashing currents of culture and influence. But courage, I see, is not lacking amidst us. Just as we fought for our independence, so too shall we fight for our unity and progress." His voice echoed through the hall as he raised his glass, toasting a brighter future for Ayiti. There was a distinct intensity to his gaze that held everyone's attention spellbound.

His words were met with a thunderous applause that resonated within the high-vaulted ceiling of the majestic hall. Glasses clinked against each other in agreement, faces smiling with newfound hope and determination. A spark had been ignited in the hearts of those present - a spark that promised to grow into a raging flame under the right guidance."

The evening continued until the king and queen departed the hall. No one was permitted to leave until they first did so.

The ground shook beneath the hooves of two dozen soldiers on horseback, their weapons glinting in the sunlight as they thundered down the main street of Cap Henry. The townspeople caught sight of them from their windows and doorways, awe and fear stirring in their hearts at the approaching cavalry of young men and boys led by Crown Prince Jacques-Victor Henry.

At the front of the procession rode the prince himself, awkwardly perched atop a massive black stallion named Éclair. Despite his obese figure, Victor held his head high with newfound authority, his fingers tight around the reins as he commanded his regiment to slow down.

The townsfolk watched with mixed emotions as the prince and his men stopped in front of a popular restaurant, the establishment bustling with activity. In a matter of minutes, the captain of the guard and a sergeant dismounted their horses and entered the establishment with an announcement for everyone to leave.

Hungry customers grumbled and cursed as they exited the restaurant, making way for Prince Victor and his entourage to enter. The air was thick with tension as he and his men enjoyed their meal, leaving without so much as a word of gratitude or a dime of payment for the twenty-plus meals consumed.

Prince Victor-Henry leads his young members of the cavalry on a charge down the main street of Cap Henry to have lunch downtown with total disregard for the citizens

Disgust twisted in the stomach of the manager and the servers, but none dared speak out against the prince's actions. After all, he was the son of the king - a formidable force to be reckoned with. But when the manager asked about payment for services, he was simply told to send the bill to the palace, knowing it would be months or never before payment would be received.

As they rode off into the distance, leaving chaos and unpaid bills in their wake, the townspeople could only watch with wary eyes and pray that they never crossed paths with the royals again.

In the library, Princess Françoise-Améthyste and Princess Anne-Athénaïre patiently waited for their daily class to begin. However, as usual, the 16-year-old crown prince was nowhere to be seen.

"Can we start without him?" twenty-two-year-old Princess Françoise asked the teacher.

"I have strict instructions from your father to never begin class without the crown prince," she replied firmly.

"It's not fair. Every day we waste time waiting for him to wake up, take forever to get ready, and then finally show up late!" complained Princess Anne.

"He's not even learning anything anyway," added Princess Françoise. "We all know that."

Right on cue, the crown prince strolled in and took a seat at the table. "What did I miss?" he asked casually.

"You are the most immature, irresponsible, arrogant, rude...," Princess Anne began before being interrupted.

"Enough, Anne. I am a prince and you are just a princess," he said snidely.

"Grow up," stated Princess Françoise. "How do you expect to one day rule this kingdom when you can't even manage yourself? You're sixteen going on ten!"

"That's it. I've learned enough for today. Have a lovely day, you two foolish girls."

With those caustic words, the crown prince sauntered out of the library, his figure receding into the lush palace garden.

His departure left an uneasy silence in its wake, the tension hanging palpable like the tropical humidity outside. Françoise-Améthyste and Anne-Athénaïre exchanged weary glances, their frustration mirrored in each other's eyes, as well as their teachers.

The Prince Royal proved to be an endless burden on his teachers, causing them countless sleepless nights and endless frustration. Unlike his diligent and hardworking father, King Henry, Victor was a carefree soul, more interested in play than the weighty responsibilities of learning to rule a kingdom one day.

His lack of interest and motivation also hindered the progress of the two princesses who were eager to learn and excelled in their studies. The four educators, exhausted and at their wits' end, decided to take their concerns to Baron Vastey, their employer and the man tasked with the royal children's development.

The Baron, whose main occupation did not involve the daily education of the royal children, was caught off guard by this meeting. As he leisurely strolled from his opulent apartment within the palace to the opposite wing that housed the offices of government, he was suddenly accosted by the four women educators outside his office.

The eldest and most severe-looking among them, Agatha Williams, a British spinster from London, spoke up first with an air of authority. "My Lord, we must bring to your attention a dire situation that has been unfolding about the education of the royal children."

But it was difficult for Vastey to focus on their words as his mind was still fixated on the conversation he had with the queen over dinner about growing unrest within the empire. He knew that this situation would require immediate attention and action from all those involved in ruling the kingdom.

"Indeed? A dire situation?" His reply held a veiled apprehension as he reflexively stroked the silver medallion hanging from his neck. It was a precious heirloom trusted to the Baron by King Henry himself, symbolic of his bond with the monarch.

Vastey led the educators to his office where Agatha Williams replied "Yes, my Lord.", her voice firm and steady as the other three teachers; Carol Davis of history and literature, Emily Miller of arts and crafts, and Mademoiselle Ducette of music, stared intently at his reaction.

"The Prince Royal is not taking his lessons seriously," blurted Carol Davis.

"He is always late, disrupts our lessons, and refuses to follow any form of instruction," added Emily Miller.

"And this, despite our repeated efforts to engage him," concluded Agatha Williams.

Baron Vastey paused for a moment, his gaze lost in the distance beyond the palace walls. The looming mountains were bathed in the warm hues of the morning; yet darkness seemed to emanate from them, a stark reminder of the nation Ayiti had risen from.

"I see," he finally muttered, torn between the urgency of a competing political crisis and the apparent educational crisis at hand. "And how does this impact Princesses Françoise-Améthyste and Anne-Athénaïs?"

The teachers exchanged glances before Mademoiselle Ducette responded, her French accent heavy. "Their Highnesses are diligent in their studies, especially the Princess Françoise-Améthyste. She excels in her music lessons, possessing an innate understanding of rhythm and melody. However," she hesitated, the corners of her mouth tightening, "their progress suffers due to the distractions caused by the Prince. He infuriates them."

Agatha Williams jumped back in. "We believe that perhaps a... more firm hand might need to be applied, or a change in his curriculum to better suit His Highness's... temperament."

A silent heaviness filled the room as the Baron contemplated their words. He knew they weren't wrong - he had noticed a defiant streak in the young prince himself. Put bluntly, the boy was a spoiled, entitled brat raised predominantly by a protective father who had lost his eldest son years ago and overcompensated his grief with Jacques-Victor Henry's lax discipline.

His gaze fell upon an antique map of Ayiti on his office wall, its thickly inked boundaries stark against the aged parchment. The north was marked with strong, decisive lines - a reflection of Henry's unwavering vision for his realm. In contrast, the south bore softer curves, its edges feathered as if still uncertain - much like Pétion's consensus-driven approach to governance. Two distinct ideologies shape one nation.

"Spare the rod, spoil the child," he murmured, barely above a whisper, his gaze tracing the sinuous spine of the Massif de la Selle, boasting the highest peak of Ayiti, at 9,000 feet, he had once visited. He knew a drastic change was needed to nurture responsibility and discipline in Victor Henry. The question was how this could be accomplished without subjecting the king to undue distress.

The Baron turned back towards his visitors. "Thank you for bringing this to my attention," he said, his voice resonating with firm resolve. "I will speak with His Majesty about this matter."

Later that evening, the Baron found himself in the company of King Henry, sharing a bottle of fine aged rum under the warm glow of lantern light and spirited conversation. The King was a formidable presence, his dark eyes reflecting the complexity of a man torn between his dreams for a prosperous Ayisyen kingdom and the tremulous reality of the task before him. Vastey truly liked the man, especially on nights like this where the king was in a good mood.

"The boy is merely expressive," the king offered, his deep voice resonating with the authority he wielded. "He is strong-willed, like me, his father."

The Baron regarded him quietly over the rim of his glass. "Strong-willed or a spoiled brat, time will be the judge of that. But Jacques-Victor Henry's tutors fear his behavior is growing disruptive. They suggest firm intervention."

No one could speak to the king this way and live to see another day. But Baron Vastey had acquired the license through loyalty and intellect to do so. He was indispensable to the king and his mission, and he knew it.

A flicker of annoyance flashed across Henry's face, his broad forehead creased with slight irritation. He picked up an ancient brass compass from his desk, its edges worn smooth from decades of use. "He is but a child. He has years to learn discipline."

"He does not have years, Your Highness," asserted the Baron, setting down his glass with a gentle thud. "Not if he is to assume the mantle of leadership someday. He is constantly being observed by your subjects every day who analyze his every action, and many of them, not so good."

King Henry leaned back, his ebony fingers gently tracing the weathered lines etched into the brass instrument. The sigh that escaped his lips carried the weight of battles won and most recently, battles lost, of numerous sacrifices, and was not born of exasperation but rather of deep-seated concern. "Discipline should not be borne out of fear," he said quietly, more to himself than to Baron Vastey.

"Indeed not," responded the Baron, softly meeting his gaze. "But respect should be borne from understanding one's position and responsibilities. Jacques-Victor Henry might benefit from learning some humility. It might serve him well in the future. Your subjects watch his behavior."

A silence fell over them, carrying with it the echo of Ayiti's turbulent past, the specter of its uncertain future. The night outside embraced their somber gathering, as if nature herself shared their concerns for a land that continued to fight for its freedom against all odds. He could not let his son interfere with the complications of ruling a kingdom. "Advise the prince to meet us here first thing in the morning. I will know what to do with him by then."

The sun rose in a golden blaze, casting its warm rays across the kingdom. The king, his heart full of joy and purpose, had decided his son's future. He would personally take on the task of educating him, bringing him along on official trips and patiently guiding him through the complexities of ruling a nation. Despite knowing his son's stubborn nature, the king was determined to mold him into a capable leader through firsthand experience.

As they waited for Victor's late arrival, the king and baron sat in a grand hall adorned with rich tapestries and gilded furnishings, their anticipation growing with each passing minute efficiently reminded by the tick-tock of the clock on the wall. Finally, after an hour of waiting, the heavy doors swung open and Victor stormed in, his face flushed with anger and defiance. "What is so important? I had plans to go to the oceanshore today! You have ruined everything!"

The king's resolve only strengthened as he prepared to embark on this journey of fatherly guidance and royal education. The room seemed to shrink under Victor's fiery gaze, his chest heaving with unsaid words caught in his throat as he stared at his father with contempt and stalked toward the ornate seat across from the king. Not a word was spoken as he lowered himself onto the cushion, the tension in the room thick enough to be cut with a blade.

"Victor," began Henry, his tone steady, though he could feel the sharp edges of his son's anger biting into him. "I have decided that your education is of utmost importance, and it should fall upon me to take this mantle."

The words hung heavily in the air, Victor's dark eyes wide with disbelief. He opened his mouth to retaliate, but Henry lifted a hand to silence him.

"I understand your frustration," Henry admitted, "but you must also understand that our country is at a crucial juncture. Ayiti needs more than just soldiers now; it needs leaders who can guide it towards stability and prosperity."

Victor's protest died on his lips, his anger giving way to confusion. He looked at his father searchingly, trying to discern any hint of jest in his stern gaze. But all he saw was an unwavering determination and a firm belief in his words. After a few seconds of tense silence, Victor sighed, slouching into the plush cushion of his chair. "When does this new… education… begin?"

"Immediately. Instruct your cavalry that they will be subordinate to my regiment and they will ride out with us at first light towards L'Artibonite. Pack for several days."

"Are you serious?" Victor protested. I have a life you know. I have made plans to…

"Enough!" shouted the king. For the first time, the king's cool composure cracked, a hint of raw frustration tingeing his words.

Victor recoiled at his father's fury but held his ground. "Fine," he spat, folding his arms stubbornly across his chest. "But don't expect me to be happy about it."

"I do not expect happiness, Victor," Henry said, a note of weary resignation creeping into his voice. "I only expect duty." He rose from his seat, towering over his son with the same imposing presence that had made him a revered leader on the battlefield. "Do not disappoint me."

Victor swallowed hard, his anger temporarily extinguished by the burden of expectation that was suddenly thrust upon him. He watched as his father and the baron exited the room, leaving him alone with his thoughts.

Later at the palace, Jean-Baptiste and Marie Bayard found themselves grappling with their own set of uncertainties. As owners of the shipping and luxury hotel businesses, they were acutely aware of the political tensions simmering beneath the surface of everyday life in Ayiti and requested a meeting with the king.

Jean was engaged in a discussion with Marie about the implications of King Henry's push for a total ban on French commerce. This was in retaliation for France's continuous meddling and refusal to recognize Ayiti and open full diplomatic channels. He worried about the potential pushback from the elite, fearing it could ripple through their customer base and disrupt the delicate balance they had worked so hard to establish.

"I understand your concerns, Jean," said Marie, her dark eyes reflecting the flickering candlelight. "But Henry is not unreasonable. He sees the value in having a strong commercial sector. He just also believes in a strict social order."

The couple had worked tirelessly over the years, navigating through tumultuous periods of political instability and economic uncertainty. Their success was a testament to their resilience. But now, more than ever, they felt the weight of their responsibility not only as business owners but as community leaders.

They were interrupted by a knock on the door, breaking them out of their somber conversation. The door opened to reveal a messenger, panting heavily. "The king wishes to see you," the man wheezed, his hand pressed against his chest.

Jean and Marie exchanged a glance of understanding before rising from their seats. The meeting they had requested was upon them, but whether it would bring reassurance or more disquiet, they couldn't predict.

As they followed the messenger through the ornate hallways of the palace, Marie braced herself for what was to come. Her mind replayed Jean's worries; he had not been wrong about the intricacies of their situation.

King Henry awaited them in his private study, a room that simultaneously spoke volumes about his military prowess and intellectual acumen. Maps highlighting strategic trade routes hung on one wall while others showcased an impressive collection of classic literature from around the globe.

"Thank you for making time," Jean began respectfully as they entered. They knew Henry long enough to dispense from the customary royal rituals and for all of their sakes, just get to the point. The time when they would banter niceties at each other was long gone with a relationship somewhat strained between them nowadays.

"We understand your desire to place a total ban on French commerce. Yet, our businesses, and those of countless others, heavily depend on those relationships. How do you suggest this country navigate this turbulence?"

King Henry, sitting behind his grand oak desk, looked at them with a contemplative gaze. His eyes, hardened from the countless battles fought, held a glimmer of understanding. He paused before addressing them, pouring over his thoughts carefully.

"This decision is not made lightly," the king said, his voice echoing in the vast room. "We are establishing our own identity – one independent of our past colonizers. This is about more than just commerce; it's about our dignity as a nation."

Marie interjected gently, "And we strive for the same dignity, Henry. But uprooting established trade relations overnight may lead to social unrest and economic instability…" Her voice wavered slightly at the enormity of what they were discussing. The future of their nation hung in balance along with their fortunes. "This will cause staggering inflation as commodities will run scarce as we all develop new supply chains. At that point, the people will not be able to afford life as they now know it."

The king leaned back, "Yes, you're right. New supply chains will need to be established for trade to occur," King Henry agreed, his steely gaze softening. "It will be a period of significant adjustment. For you, for me, and all the people of Ayiti."

He leaned over the maps strewn across his desk, tracing out new potential trade routes with his finger. "But we cannot continue to cower under the shadow of our colonizers, flourish under their terms," he continued, turning back towards Jean and Marie. He saw in their eyes a shared worry, "We must stand independently as a nation and show the world that we are not just survivors but victors."

Jean nodded slowly, seeing a sliver of hope in Henry's conviction. Perhaps this drastic step was necessary to cut Ayiti's ties with its painful past, allowing them to carve out a future crafted by their own hands. His business acumen recognized the potential profits that could be reaped from these new trade routes as many frustrated or lazy competitors would surely drop out of this new challenge, but also the risks they posed. The room fell into a contemplative silence as each pondered over the weight of the impending changes.

In the quiet, Marie found herself reflecting on the vast disparities within their homeland. The Grand Nord, heavily influenced by English culture, thrived on a strict social code and literacy whilst the Grand Sud, steeped in French refinement, clung tenaciously to a vibrant lifestyle full of leisure, music, and dance. The two halves of Ayiti seemed worlds apart, yet she traveled both and concluded them to be undeniably Ayisyen, wishing she could just throw them into a melting pot to combine the best of the two. She was reminded of how her own life mirrored that dichotomy - her resilient spirit shaped by brutal hardships yet yearning for an age of peace and prosperity.

"Perhaps," she began, breaking the silence. "There is a way we can gradually shift our economy's reliance away from French imports and still get much-needed products produced there. Yes, we can instead increase trade with the English colonies, as well as the Spanish ones, but that is not enough. We especially need the Danish West Indies as they trade heavily with France and we can trans-ship from there by using our current suppliers through St. Thomas and St. Croix as a port of entry to the Caribbean. That would respect your decree, non? It will be seen as an official rejection of French trade, while still importing French goods until new supply routes are solidified. But, understand that our Danish trading partners will want a profit, resulting in an inflation of probably ten percent or so," she said as her ingenious proposal hung in the air, a beacon of hope amidst the turbulent sea of uncertainty.

King Henry, with his ever-calculating mind, considered her suggestion. "It is a thought," he declared, running his finger along the carved arm of his chair. "The English are known for their naval prowess and are no strangers to trade on the high seas and the Danish are experts of importation to the Caribbean. It would further consolidate a valuable ally, while also challenging our people to adapt and grow. Then done, it is settled. I must depart now for another rendezvous. The Queen asked that you remain as she longs to see you both. I will send for her. Please excuse me." And at that, he stood and left the room.

Marie-Louise arrived shortly thereafter with Princesses Amethiste and Athenaire in tow, all happy to see one another again. It was nearly three that afternoon and as usual, it was tea time. As servants entered with a tray of tea, finger sandwiches, pâtés, and delicious cakes, the princesses scurried to Marie and Jean, offering kisses and hugs to whom they affectionately called Aunt and Uncle in their extended family.

Amid the clinking of porcelain, Marie allowed herself a pause to appreciate the simple pleasure of eating warm cake and drinking sweetened tea, while sharing lighthearted stories. The sight of the young princesses laughing with their mother was a stark contrast to the serious discussions that had taken place earlier with the king.

Across from her, Jean studied his wife's face, his eyes softening at Marie's smile. He also appreciated these moments of tranquility; they were rare in this world that constantly demanded their attention and decisions. His gaze shifted to Marie-Louise and her daughters, and he felt a warmth creep into his heart. These strong women were also part of Ayiti's future - their intelligence, resilience, and spirit were symbolic of what the nation could become.

As they continued in conversation the subject of the prince, Jacques-Victor Henry, came to the table. "He is incredulous," complained Princesses Amethiste. Any more of his nonsense in classes and we will lose our teachers, I know it."

"What do you forever mean?" asked Marie.

"They hate him. The way he talks down to them. He is arrogant, corrupted, and spoiled rotten," offered Princess Athenaire.

Marie-Louise sighed heavily, closing her eyes momentarily as if summoning the strength to handle the delicate subject. "Jacques-Victor Henry has...a strong will, no doubt," she finally said, her words carefully chosen. "He is being shaped still, much like our country. It's difficult to mold a future when the past haunts so persistently," referring to the loss of her firstborn son, François Ferdinand, at the young age of eleven.

Jean, who had kept silent until now, chimed in with his characteristic candor. "It is essential for him to understand the value of humility and respect. We are all part of this nation's tapestry," he commented, his gaze thoughtful.

Marie, seeing an opportunity to impart wisdom, leaned forward and addressed the young princesses. "Remember, my dears, that true leadership is not about wielding power over others but service to them. As women of this country, we must counsel our men, however young, and direct power through them, as you must do with your brother. He will need your guidance as the future king one day. Do you understand what I am saying? You must guide him without him being the wiser. That is your power as a woman."

Her words hung in the air momentarily before Amethiste nodded slowly, her young face furrowed in thought. "We must...show him the right path? Is that what you mean, Tante Marie?

"Yes," Marie affirmed gently, "and more than that. You must stand firm in your convictions and principles. It is through your example that he will learn best."

"Ladies," Marie-Louise stated. "Please leave us at this time. I have a matter to discuss with your Aunt and Uncle.

"Yes Maman," the girls said in practiced unison. They stood, hugged, and kissed Marie and Jean, and bid their farewell to the group.

When the girls left, Marie-Louise looked at the Bayards and asked, "What is the feeling downtown?"

"What do you mean by 'the feeling'?" asked Jean.

"The consensus as to the rule of Henry. Are they pleased with their king or do they despise him?

Jean glanced at Marie before turning his gaze back to Marie-Louise. "It's...complicated," he began, rubbing the stubble along his jawline thoughtfully. "Many respect him for his strong leadership and the steps he has taken towards rebuilding our nation. His regimented society has brought a semblance of order to Ayiti in these turbulent times."

"However..." Marie continued, her gaze distant as she stared at Marie-Louise, her eyes reflecting the flickering candlelight. "There are disquieting whispers too. Some say his strict code of conduct borders on tyranny. While they appreciate the peace and infrastructure he provides, they fear and despise his methods."

Marie-Louise nodded silently, her face schooled into neutrality. Despite the calm veneer, an undercurrent of concern etched lines into her delicate features. Jean studied her closely, sensing the gravity behind the queen's question.

"Marie-Louise," Jean spoke earnestly, leaning forward in his chair, "the truth is that the situation is as delicate as a house of cards. One wrong move and everything could come tumbling down. The citizens are restive, teetering between gratitude for the stability and resentment towards the strictness. Henry's vision is noble but implementing it has been...problematic."

Marie added, "People are not used to this level of discipline and control since the days of slavery. Even though life is better for them, their perception of it is that it is not. And that perception is your reality. They have tasted freedom, and now they feel as though they have traded one master for another."

The silence that followed was fraught with implications. Jean rose from his chair and moved to the window, gazing out into the afternoon's shade. His mind was a whirl of thoughts, a turmoil of strategies and calculations as he turned back towards her, "There is another delicate issue at hand as well. You must get control of Prince Jacques-Victor Henry's behavior. It is disturbing as he is next in line to the throne.

A shiver ran down Marie-Louise's spine at the mention of her wayward son. She gripped the armrests of her chair tightly, knuckles turning white under the strain. "I understand the gravity of the situation, Jean," she acknowledged with a sigh. "Henry and I will do what we can to control him. The stability of our country depends on it."

Marie extended her hand and held onto Marie-Louise's forearm as Jean nodded, relief evident in his eyes that she understood there was a definite problem and hadn't put up a defense about it, as he glanced at his wife.

Sixty horsemen rode into the town of Belle Rivière, the location of the new palace that Henry was having built for his trips to monitor the lush and productive Artibonite region. The area was adjacent to the Grand Sud of Ayiti, so the king was extremely protective of the area, especially watchful of the ambitions of the Grand Sud's new president, Jean-Pierre Boyer, anticipating that he could flex his power in an attempt to invade this fertile region.

The commander of the local militia came out to greet the king and the prince. His face was lined with years of hard living, but his eyes were bright and alert. He bowed low, showing his respect for the monarch and his successor.

"Your Majesty, Prince Jacques-Victor Henry," he greeted, straightening up and giving them a stern salute. "Welcome to Belle Rivière. We're honored by your visit."

Henry nodded, allowing himself a moment to survey his surroundings before addressing the commander. His sharp eyes took in the well-tended fields, the solid fortifications, and the nervous faces of the onlookers who had gathered to catch a glimpse of their king.

"Thank you, Commander," he said finally, his voice carrying across the silent courtyard. "We've come to see the progress of our new palace as well as the yield of the crop. On the surface, all appears to be in good order."

The commander seemed relieved at the king's words. He gestured towards several completed buildings not far from where they stood. "Yes, Your Majesty. It's this way. We worked day and night to ensure everything was according to your vision for completion. You will be pleased, I assure you."

"Has our meals been prepared, Commander?" asked the prince.

The commander looked puzzled at his question, his furrowed brow deepening. "Indeed, my Prince," he responded, his tone laced with a subtle confusion. "Our cooks have been preparing since dawn. I had assumed you'd prefer to tour the palace first, as it is early in the day, my Prince?"

"Actually," Jacques-Victor Henry interrupted, his voice smooth yet commanding, "A meal sounds splendid. Let us see to that first. The palace can wait."

Henry glanced at his son, a flicker of surprise and annoyance crossing his stoic face. He had not expected this diversion but gave a curt nod to the commander in agreement. There was wisdom, he considered, in breaking bread before discussing matters of politics and power, giving the prince the benefit of the doubt.

As they were led to the grand dining hall, Henry reflected on their surroundings. The air held an intoxicating mix of tropical blooms and the distant scent of burning firewood. In the distance, the rolling hills of fertile land bore testament to the intense labor poured into this region. Marie-Louise will like it here, he imagined.

Then, to his amazement, Jacques-Victor Henry insulted the commander right there in the dining hall in front of the entourage of officers and staff. "Commander, the table setting is all wrong," he scoffed, picking up a glass and squinting at it as if it were an offending object. "My mother has been schooled in France and has a taste for the refined. This... this is far from it."

The commander blinked, taken aback by the blunt critique. It was an affront to his preparations, yet he held his tongue, aware of Jacques-Victor Henry's royal blood. Henry watched them silently, his jaw tightening. The prince's audacity was becoming a thorn in his side but Henry could not embarrass the prince in public and expect him to be respected.

"Apologies, my Prince," the commander replied respectfully. "We did our best with what we have."

In 1816, English painter Richard Evans produced two of the most enduring images of post-revolutionary Haiti: portraits of the Caribbean's first king and prince. The portrait sets the prince outdoors, carrying glove and riding crop in his right hand as he leans confidently on a young horse, whose small dimensions make the then 12-year-old boy seem huge in comparison.

Jacques-Victor Henry waved off his apology dismissively. "Just remember next time," he said before turning to the king. "Father, when Mother arrives, I would like her treated with the dignity and respect befitting of her station, not subjected to these...primitive arrangements."

Henry held his sons gaze, a slow simmer of frustration brewing beneath his calm exterior. "Your mother," he said evenly, "will be treated with all the honor and respect due to the queen. However, this is Ayiti, not France. We have our traditions and ways of living here. Your mother fully understands that."

There was a tense silence that followed his words. The commander excused himself from the table, leaving father and son alone in the expansive dining hall. Jacques-Victor Henry opened his mouth to protest, but Henry held up his hand.

"Enough," he said quietly. "This isn't about table settings or finery. It's about understanding and respecting the people you will one day rule and follow you. Never forget that," Henry lectured now that they were alone.

The commander had a feast prepared with an array of familiar Creole dishes, each revealing the unique fusion of their complicated history - there were French influences in the hearty bouillabaisse that simmered with fresh seafood, African elements in the spicy griot made from juicy pork chunks, and Spanish touches in the piping hot empanadas that burst with flavor.

The conversation during the meal remained light and courteous, a careful dance around more pressing matters. After the lavish meal, the commander conducted a tour of the magnificent Palais de la Belle Rivière. It was perched atop a hill overlooking the Petite Rivière de l'Artibonite and situated one kilometer east of the Crête-à-Pierrot fortress, one that held great significance as it was the site of a major battle with the French during the Ayisyen Revolution in 1802.

Henry named it "The Palace of 365 Doors" due to his intention to have that many doors upon completion of the two-story building; one for each day of the year. During the tour, they were introduced to the architect and engineer, Louis Dupeyrac, who began the construction earlier this year and remained on schedule for completion.

The primary function of this impressive structure was to serve as a royal residence for King Henry to consolidate and ensure his power in the fertile Artibonite region, which shared a border with the Grand Sud once ruled by Pétion and now Boyer, through extended stays for him and his entourage,

The palace stretched out before them, its magnificent rectangular design covering an impressive 68 meters or 220 feet in length and 11 meters or 36 feet in width. This equated to a staggering 8,000 square feet on the first floor alone, with equal space planned for the second floor upon completion. As they approached the western facade, their eyes were immediately drawn to the sprawling rotunda that measured another 12 meters or 40 feet in diameter. The walls of the structure were expertly constructed with a combination of stone masonry and clay bricks, skillfully bonded together with lime mortar to create a formidable presence against its natural surroundings.

The king and the prince remained there for three days, surveying the land's fertile crops, but not without the prince's constant arrogance towards the people of the region – government, civilian, and staff of the palace, much to the king's chagrin.

During the day, they made their way through the fertile Artibonite region, which was named after the river that flowed like life's blood through its heart. Henry pointed out to his son the sprawling plantations that were beginning to burgeon with sugarcane and coffee, vital exports that he hoped would further bolster the nation's economy.

Each evening, as the tropical sun descended beneath the horizon, bathing Ayiti in hues of fiery orange and deep indigo, the king would discuss his vision for the Ayisyen kingdom as he attempted to mold, educate, and stimulate the prince toward a more responsible approach.

But the prince, a capricious character, showed little interest in his father's designs. He was more intrigued by the luxuries of the palace and the power his title bestowed upon him. King Henry, however, was not disheartened. He knew he had much work to do with the boy, blaming himself for his outlandish behavior.

Eighteen

DOWN WITH THE KING

Cap Henry
August 1820

The kingdom of King Henry flourished under a shroud of enforced labor, filling the king's coffers with a mix of European and American coins. Elaborate expenditures adorned the landscape - multiple palaces and grand châteaus that rivaled even Sans Souci, all connected by meticulously paved roads.

Yet, a lingering mystery hovered over the abundant wealth. Deep within the dungeons of the citadel lay vaults meant for the national treasury, safeguarding an astounding thirty million pounds, so it was reported. Whispers and rumors swirled about Henry's ambitions to acquire the Spanish portion of the island with a great portion of the crown's treasure set aside specifically for that purpose.

The people of Ayiti chuckled at these tales of vast riches. If King Henry could amass such wealth for the state, how much did he divert for personal gain? Speculation ran rampant that his private hoard equaled or even surpassed what he allocated to the kingdom.

Suspicions bred vigilance as eyes keenly scrutinized his every move in hopes of uncovering his secret cache. To them, any discovery would be just recompense since this fortune belonged to the state and its citizens - except for the annual forty thousand pounds lining the king's own pockets as his salary by law.

Despite amassing immense riches, King Henry held little attachment to money itself; his true concerns were dedicated to

Queen Marie-Louise and their daughters' security, well-being, and the future destiny of his heir apparent, the lazy Prince Royal.

Henry's chivalrous nature dictated ample provisions for the women in his household. His unwavering devotion to Marie-Louise was evident; she was not only beloved but instrumental in his rise to power. Knowing that enemies lurked nearby necessitated protecting and securing her future should he meet an untimely end.

The sun was setting over the bustling port city of Cap Henry as King Henry stepped off his ornate carriage escorted by a dozen royal guards and made his way to the entrance of the British consulate. He was dressed in a crisp, white military uniform with gold buttons and epaulets adorned with the royal crest.

The butler announced his arrival to Rear Admiral Sir Home Riggs Popham, who had served as Commander-in-Chief of the Jamaica Station for the past three years, and was visiting Ayiti to inspect the British presence there. As they embraced, Henry could see that the aging admiral had grown thin and frail.

"Your Majesty," Popham said with a bow. "I wish I had known you were coming. I would have arranged for a proper salute."

Henry waved off his concerns. "This is not a formal visit, my friend," he replied. "I have come to see an old comrade," Henry said with a warm smile.

Popham's eyes lit up with recognition as they settled into comfortable armchairs by the window overlooking the harbor. They reminisced about the past and discussed Popham's upcoming retirement. "I long to be back home in Cheltenham, Your Majesty," Popham admitted with a wistful sigh.

"Cheltenham?" Henry repeated. "I have heard wonderful things about that town – on the edge of the Cotswolds, correct? A region renowned for its natural beauty?"

Popham looked pleasantly surprised at Henry's knowledge of English geography. "Indeed, Your Majesty," he replied. "I highly recommend a visit if you ever have the opportunity. How do you know of this region?"

"I owe my knowledge to one of your countrywomen," Henry confessed with a sly smile. "Agatha Williams, one of my family's tutors. She teaches me personally on certain evenings to expand my knowledge, as do all my children's tutors."

The admiral chuckled heartily at this revelation before tea was served. As they enjoyed their refreshments, Popham looked at Henry and said, "A correspondence came the other day from my son. He was marveling at your portrait, the one painted by the artist Richard Evans. It now hangs in the Royal Academy in London, to much acclaim."

"I was surprised when the painter arrived," Henry stated. "He proclaimed that he was commissioned by King George himself who wanted to see my likeness. I am happy it did not end up in the royal trash heap," they both laughed heartedly.

But soon, they delved into serious matters, discussing British interests in the Caribbean to expand lucrative trade with the British colonies, leaving out any mention of the Danish plan proposed by Marie Bayard, and the pressing need for Henry to send some treasure back to England. Henry knew that one day his wife Marie-Louise and their children may need it, so it was vital to secure and protect their future.

"Sir Popham," Henry began, "as you may know, we've just started to carve out a space for ourselves here in Ayiti, but the future remains uncertain. As such, I find myself thinking about what may lie ahead for Marie-Louise and our children."

"It's often said that uncertainty is a sailor's only certainty," Popham said slowly as he listened intently and sipped his tea.

"I have decided to set aside part of our treasure," Henry continued, "to be sent to England. A sort of insurance, if you will, for the wellbeing of my family should anything happen to me. Can I trust you with this task?"

Understandably ruffled by the gravity of the request, Popham hesitated before replying. His eyes studied Henry's determined face, and he asked, "Are you certain of this decision, Your Majesty?

Christophe appears as a gallant, middle-aged man with graying hair in an interior space. He is dressed in a dark green coat carrying the star of the Order of Saint-Henry, light breeches, and leather boots. His right hand holds his cane and bicorne (two-cornered) hat, and his left rests in the pocket of his coat giving him an almost casual air. Portrait by British artist Richard Evans – 1816.

.Sending away such treasure is no small matter, and can be rather complicated."

Henry simply nodded, his gaze steady. "I am," he said. "I have been thinking about this for some time now. It is not merely for my family's security; it is also a symbol of my trust in your nation and in you my friend."

Popham's visage softened into one of understanding. "Very well," he finally murmured, his voice imbued with emotion and the responsibility of the request. The weight of this decision was palpable in the room as they both savored their tea pensively.

True to his word, the admiral wasted no time in depositing a hefty sum of money into the Bank of England. Papers were drawn up and sent to the king by a trusted messenger, confirming the deposits. However, just months later, the admiral met his end in September in Cheltenham at the age of 57, leaving behind a large grieving family. Despite his high status, he was buried with little fanfare in the churchyard of St Michael and All Angels at Sunninghill, Berkshire, close to his grand home. The loss of such a powerful and influential figure left a void in Henry that could never be filled.

Henry's next challenge lay in discreetly hiding some wealth locally without alerting prying eyes constantly monitoring him. Among pervasive distrust towards those surrounding him, one Baron Rouanez stood out as a solid confidant - a former comrade from Dessalines' army now stationed as the Citadelle's commandant.

One fateful night, after twilight had descended and the world slept, the king rapped at the baron's door. The unexpected visit at such an ungodly hour prompted an anxious response from both him and his startled wife, who stood by with quivering candlelight casting eerie shadows around them. Despite initial trepidation, reassurance from the king allayed their immediate fears of danger while hinting at impending significance or perilous tasks ahead.

Later, as dawn approached with roosters heralding its arrival, the baron had returned and whispers echoed within their home revealing a clandestine mission undertaken on behalf of Queen Marie-Louise – secretly burying a treasure within her garden unknown to her but safeguarded by the Baron's sworn secrecy under penalty of death if divulged prematurely.

In silent contemplation following this revelation, his wife, the baroness, acknowledged with quiet reverence, "Well, it is clear that the king holds deep affection for our queen."

As the warm August air filled the cathedral of Saint Joseph in Limonade, southeast of Cap Henry. King Henry took a deep breath and walked beside his wife, Queen Marie-Louise. They were dressed in their finest attire, ready to celebrate a formal mass. The rich harmony of the choir echoed through the grand hall as they made their regal entrance, greeted by the solemn faces of the congregation.

Behind walked the Royal Prince and the two Princesses, their faces a mirror of the solemnity that had overtaken the occasion. The Prince, a young man bearing the unmistakable likeness to his father, and the Princesses, both lovely and graceful as flowers yet to bloom fully, their innocence a stark contrast to the gravity of their surroundings.

As was customary, King Henry visited a cathedral in a different town once a month to attend a formal mass. The church was filled with the staunchest supporters of the king, all gathered for the grand celebration by the bishop and looking forward to the evenings planned state dinner for that evening. The air was tense with anticipation as the most trusted Generals; Rouanez, Prévost, Dupuy, Besse, Magny, Pourcely, Romain, Daut, and Brave sat at the front, resplendent in their finest uniforms.

However, a sense of unease hung over the room as some notable generals were absent - Alain, Nicolas Louis, Beauvoir, Jean-Claude, and other powerful men of the military from the North-West, and Saint Marc. Henry's suspicions were confirmed as his intelligence sources reported that a select number of them were suspected of participating in clandestine meetings with members of the Grand Sud's government.

As the service continued, Henry suddenly felt a sharp pain in his head. He grasped at Marie-Louise's arm for support as dizziness overwhelmed him and his vision blurred. Panic set in as he realized something was terribly wrong and reached for his painful head with his hands.

"Henry?" His wife's voice rang out, laced with worry. "What is happening to you?"

He tried to respond but his words came out slurred and unintelligible. Darkness crept into his vision, making it difficult to see or understand what was happening. Fear gripped him as confusion clouded his mind. What was going on? Where was he? Why couldn't he make sense of anything as he scanned the room for answers?

He vaguely registered the concerned faces around him, the hurried whispers filling the air, and the frantic rustle of his wife's gown as she pleaded for someone to fetch a doctor as the Bishop stopped the mass. His world spun faster and faster until finally, with a shuddering gasp, he succumbed to the darkness and slumped heavily against Marie-Louise, then collapsed in the pew.

The subsequent events were a flurry of confusion. The tension in the room skyrocketed as generals rushed forward, orders barked sharply amidst the horrified gasps of onlookers. Marie-Louise clung to her unconscious husband, her face white with fear, praying desperately for divine intervention.

His most trusted generals took the task of carrying Henry's limp form out of the church premises and into a waiting carriage, they sped towards the residence of the Duke of Limonade where medical assistance awaited them. His seemingly lifeless form lay heavily on his wife's lap, her trembling hands clutching his cold ones. The panic was almost tangible; it clung to them like a miasma, choking the life out of their hopes and dreams. The carriage ride felt like an eternity, every bump on the cobblestone road jolting her into renewed fear.

Meanwhile, back in the cathedral, the realization of the king's sudden illness had caused a ripple of apprehension as news of the king's collapse raged through the city of Limonade like an unstoppable wildfire. The bustling marketplace turned silent, the usually vibrant streets now filled with hushed whispers and worried faces. Men huddled together, discussing the implications of this unsettling development for their fledgling nation. Women clasped their children closer, their minds filled with thoughts of uncertainty and fear as others toasted the king's pending demise and a hopeful death.

The vigil lasted for days with Marie-Louise at Henry's side as he lay, drifting in and out of consciousness as a wave of paralysis consumed him. His speech was slurred and disjointed, a desperate attempt to form words with his weakened muscles. His left side was completely immobilized, rendered useless by the cruel grip of paralysis. Even the simplest tasks, like gripping or holding onto things, were now impossible feats for the once mighty king. And his once sharp mind now moved at a sluggish pace, struggling to communicate with the outside world.

After a week at the Duke's residence, where every possible necessity was tended to, Henry proclaimed to Marie-Louise, "I want to go back to the palace, I want to do so immediately.

Marie-Louise cast a doubtful glance at her husband. She knew, more than anyone else how stubborn and headstrong the once indomitable king could be. And yet, she also saw the determination etched onto his countenance, the steely glint in his eyes that spoke volumes of an iron will that refused to bow down.

"Very well," Marie-Louise relented, giving Henry's hand a gentle squeeze. "We shall arrange for your return."

Word of the king's decision to return to the palace spread across Limonade as swiftly as his illness had. The streets once shrouded in apprehension now buzzed with cautious optimism. Perhaps their king was not as near death's door as they'd feared. Citizens lined the streets to cheer their king as they observed him propped upright in the carriage and waving to them. What they did not see was that behind the king sat the queen he was leaning on and who was the one waving his arm to appear normal behind the carriage door.

The day Henry returned to the palace was one filled with mixed emotions. His generals and advisors surrounded him, their faces a mask hiding their concern and relief. However, the citizens of Milot, curious yet respectful, lined up along the streets, peering from behind their homes and shops, silently watching their king's return.

As the procession moved through the streets, the palace came into view - its grandeur standing undiminished despite the turmoil that had engulfed its inhabitants. Jean stood at the entrance, his face impassive. He had received word of his Henry's condition but seeing him being carried into the palace was a stark reminder of his own mortality. Henry was far younger at 53 than Jean's 70 years of age.

Inside, Marie had made preparations for Henry's arrival. Her face was a calm exterior masking the storm within. She had loved the boy, then the man, and now the king as she had watched him grow and rise to power. Now she could only watch helplessly as his health failed him.

Both Jean and Marie were well aware that their country now teetered on the brink of chaos. Jean had not long ago declared that the state of the kingdom was like a house of cards. Hope was now a once again fragile commodity in these times.

Henry gave the his generals more power to run the day-to-day aspects of the government. The Palace physicians, meanwhile, were at a loss as to how to treat the ailing king. Foreign as well as local doctors were brought in, but each remedy they proposed seemed to have no effect. His skin, once dark mahogany, now looked sickly pale in the dull candlelight; and his once vibrant eyes lost their spark. He was a shell of his former self. Marie-Louise, sat by his side day and night, holding onto his limp hand; her tears falling silently on the sheets of their marital bed. The children often came and peered into the room from the hallway, uncertain and scared. The Princesses didn't quite comprehend what was happening, but the prince understood their father was dying.

Marie and Jean Bayard would go home each night and arrive back at the palace each day before noon. They would be taken to the king's chambers where they would find a visibly exhausted Marie-

Louise holding vigil by her husband's side and relieve her to allow her time to bathe and rest somewhat.

Outside the palace, huge crowds of both supporters and detractors had begun to camp out in a sort of siege, with more arriving each day. The streets of Cap-Henry thrummed with the whispers that swept through the kingdom like a chilling undercurrent. Talk of revolt stirred in the heart of the masses who had been subjected to harsh treatment, many hungry to rid themselves of the tyrant, fueling their desperation. Yet, within the palace walls, life lingered in a state of suspended animation. Time seemed to stand still as they awaited news regarding the fate of their king.

After weeks of bed rest and constant care, the king's condition finally stabilized. He was now able to take on more meetings with his advisors and generals, slowly but surely regaining control over his kingdom. In one such meeting with Generals Romain and Daut, they informed him of troubling news regarding Colonel Poulin from Saint-Marc. As the three men sat around a large oak table, with maps and reports spread out in front of them, the tension in the room was palpable.

"What do you mean he's unwilling to follow orders?" asked the king, his brow furrowed in concern.

"Production in the surrounding areas of Saint-Marc has significantly decreased," General Romain explained, pointing to a graph that showed a sharp decline. "The sugar harvest was twelve metric tons less than the previous year – an over 15% decline."

Henry leaned forward, his eyes narrowing. "And why is that?"

General Romain hesitated before answering, exchanging a worried glance with General Daut. Finally, he spoke up. "It seems Colonel Poulin has been neglecting his duties and not enforcing production quotas as strictly as he should."

The king's jaw tightened. "And why wasn't I informed of this sooner?"

Romain cleared his throat. "We were waiting for confirmation before bringing it to your attention."

Henry nodded, understanding their reasoning but still perturbed by the news. "Go ahead, tell me everything." He braced himself for the worst as General Daut began to recount the details of Poulin's insubordination and its consequences on their economy and people.

Daut's fingers traced the rugged edges of the map as he elaborated on a rising disquiet among the workers. "It seems that under Poulin's rule, the lines between the Code and servitude have become blurred. His laxity has led many to believe they can abandon their duties without consequence."

King Henry rubbed his temple, the weight of his crown seemingly heavier with every new revelation. He had fought valiantly to build this nation from its war-torn ashes, and he wasn't about to lose it to indiscipline and insubordination.

Henry's booming voice echoed through the room, silencing all other sounds as he slammed his fist against the table. "Every plantation must be audited," he growled, his eyes blazing with unwavering determination. "No excuses. We need to know where our weaknesses lie and how we can strengthen them. And I will not tolerate any further disruptions in our production."

The generals shifted nervously, knowing the gravity of their task ahead. They rose from their seats, ready for the daunting mission. But just as they were about to leave, the king's expression turned even darker, a dangerous glint in his eye. "Arrest Poulin immediately and bring him before me," he ordered.

Romain hesitated, knowing that Poulin was a commander of a powerful demi-brigade. "Perhaps we should invite him for a meeting instead of causing a scene," he suggested cautiously.

But the king's patience had run thin. "I don't care how you do it, just get him here, forthwith," he barked, slamming his hand on the table once more. "We cannot afford to waste any more time."

Protesters outside the palace gates were forced to disperse as a cavalry of 25 horses galloped through the grounds. The commanders, Romain, Duat, and Poulin, rode their steeds towards the palace and were quickly escorted to the court where the king was presiding over a routine dispute.

As they entered, the sound of their swords clanging against their sides echoed throughout the grand room and caught the attention of the king. He was completing his current case before addressing them, commanding that a man be paid fifty gourdes for stolen chickens from his coop. If not, the guilty party would face thirty days of labor in the sugar fields. With four hours to comply, they were dismissed with the accompaniment of two Dahomet royal guards to ensure compliance.

The king then motioned for the two generals and Colonel Poulin to approach as courtiers observed with interest. The three men approached the king and queen and bowed. "Let us get straight down to business, shall we?" ordered the king as Marie-Louse put a hand on his arm. The King had two pillows propping him up on the wide chair they had built after his illness. His left side was still paralyzed and his speech was somewhat slurred, Poulin immediately noticed, and taken aback by the kings deteriorated condition.

"Poulin. Your plantation production is much lower than in previous years. Why?"

"We are attempting to adjust our labor codes in the area of Saint-Marc, Your Majesty," Poulin answered with confidence.

"What does that mean… adjust?" asked the king as Marie-Louise could feel the rise of her husband's tension from years of observation.

"We have shortened the work day hours in an attempt to boost the workers morale and production in the long run," Poulin responded.

"And who has given you the authority to change the Code Henry, the law of the land?" asked the king as Marie-Louise again squeezed his arm tighter as a signal to remain calm.

"We have taken it upon ourselves to do so. We feel that being so far from the capital, we should have more autonomy at self-rule, somewhat," Poulin responded, taking much more liberty to be frank with the king as a result of his apparent illness."

The King's eyes narrowed and his lips formed a thin line. "From where I sit," he said slowly, "I govern the Grand Nord. And in these territories, Code Henry is the law."

Poulin's gaze held steady, not wavering under the king's dark stare. "We're not negating your authority, Your Majesty. We simply implemented minor adjustments that we believe will be more agreeable to our workers and eventually beneficial to production at large."

As the King sat on his throne, Marie-Louise bit her lip nervously. She couldn't help but feel concerned as she watched the man in front of them boldly challenge the King's authority, obviously taking advantage of his frail health.

"Arrest this man immediately," the King commanded, his voice filled with undisputed authority. Four guards from the elite Dahomet forces stepped forward, ready to carry out their orders.

"You have no right," Poulin shouted, his defiance echoing through the grand hall. "I resist your authority, just like many others in this land, especially in the northwest and western territories!" His words caused gasps of shock and disbelief among those present at court.

But suddenly, there was even more astonishment as the King rose to his feet, slowly stumbling towards Poulin. His trusted generals, Romain and Daut, moved to support him on either side, helping him stay steady on his feet.

"Disarm this man," the King declared loudly. "He is hereby relieved of duty and is no longer a colonel in our kingdom's army."

One of the Royal Dahomet guards reached for Poulin's sword, but Poulin resisted fiercely, attempting to step back. However, he was quickly stopped and his hands were forcefully held behind his back by another guard. "These are not officers or even legitimate soldiers of Ayiti. I refuse to surrender my honorable sword of Ayiti to these mercenaries!" Poulin protested vehemently.

General Romain, heavy-hearted and understanding of Poulin's position, approached him and extended both hands toward him. With a sense of solemnity, Poulin unsheathed his sword and ceremoniously handed it over to Romain. "I surrender my sacred sword to you, General Romain," extending the sword towards him with two hands and bowing his head in respect.

Romain, as solemn as the occasion deserved, received the sword with a nod. He was a man of few words but his actions spoke volumes. He held no personal grudge against the fallen colonel, on the contrary, understanding his plight and struggle. But he was bound by duty, honor, and loyalty to his King and country.

The king strode towards Poulin with a fierce determination, his eyes blazing with anger and disappointment. The courtiers cowered in fear as the four Dahomet guards stood rigidly at attention, their hands gripping their weapons tightly. Despite the tension, Poulin held his ground and met the king's gaze with unflinching resolve.

The tension in the room was palpable as the two men stood face to face, their gazes locked in a fierce battle of wills. The audience held their breath, aware that they were witnessing a clash between two powerful figures. Suddenly, with a roar of pure fury, the King lunged forward and tore the medals from Poulin's chest, hurling them to the ground with a deafening crash.

"You have betrayed me!" bellowed the King, his voice echoing through the grand hall. His rage knew no bounds as he ripped off the golden officer's epaulet from Poulin's left shoulder and flung it aside like a worthless trinket. "Your actions have disgraced your position and besmirched your once esteemed career!" With a violent tug, he tore off the epaulet from Poulin's right shoulder and tossed it to the floor with disdain as Poulin struggled to contain his anger, hearing the prince chuckle from the sidelines.

"Take him away!" thundered the King, his face twisted into a mask of wrath as he turned to the prince with a searing scowl to stop the behavior.

As the Royal Dahomet guards dragged a defiant and humiliated Colonel Poulin towards the prison cells, Romain and Duat rushed to help the seething king back onto his throne. Marie-Louise clung to her husband's arm, her whole body trembling with fear and emotion. It was clear that Poulin's fate would be decided by the unforgiving ruler within a matter of days.

Whispering urgently to Henry, Marie-Louise warned, "This could spell trouble for us, my love. You must act quickly to secure your allies."

Henry looked into his wife's eyes and saw genuine concern reflected in them. He knew she spoke the truth - his hold on power was fragile and this public display of defiance by Poulin could easily lead to rebellion. He vowed to take swift action to protect himself and his kingdom from any potential threats.

The esteemed Generals Alain, Nicolas Louis, Beauvoir, and Jean-Claude of the North-West and Saint Marc battalions convened in the Saint Marc military headquarters at the start of September of 1820. The air was thick with tension as they gathered to discuss their plan; to overthrow King Henry and restructure the government.

Each man took his seat, shoulders squared and eyes sharp with determination. The room echoed with the weight of their whispered strategizing as if the very walls were listening in on their plot. The fate of the kingdom hung in the balance, and these men knew that their decisions could change the course of history forever or even cost them their lives.

A cask of aged rum was brought in, its deep amber liquid poured into each man's glass. It was a symbolic gesture. They were not just soldiers in an army, they were comrades navigating a turbulent sea of change, armed with a shared vision and undying patriotism.

The list of grievances was long and varied, each one a source of tension for the generals. The Code Henry, often seen as an extension of slavery, sparked anger among those who sought freedom. The presence of foreign Dahomet guards, deemed "mercenaries" by some, was seen as a slight to the military prowess of the country. The extravagant palaces and unnecessary military installations drained the treasury despite the country's wealth. And then there was the infamous stunt at the Citadelle - a desperate attempt to impress the British that ended in the tragic deaths of fifteen loyal soldiers. To top it off, the once powerful patriot Colonel Poulin, had been humiliated and arrested, adding insult to injury.

As tensions rose and alliances formed, it seemed that no one could agree on what needed to be done to solve these conflicts tearing at the fabric of their nation with a tyrant at the helm.

In the pale glow of candlelight, the generals discussed their plans late into the night. General Alain, his usually jovial demeanor replaced by a stoic one, proposed a swift and decisive strike at the palace. General Beauvoir, ever the pragmatist, argued for rallying support from the people first - a revolt without the heart of Ayiti behind it would surely fail. Nicolas Louis, hailing from an influential family in Saint-Marc, offered to use his connections to ensure they had enough resources.

As the sun slowly rose, casting a beautiful palette of pinks and oranges across the sky, Jean-Claude stood up from his chair and gazed out at the vast city below. After taking a moment to collect his thoughts, he found the courage to speak up: "Now is the time for our nation to come together. The divide between the North and South was created by old leaders like President Pétion and King Henry. But they are both relics of the past, with Pétion already gone and reports suggesting that the king will soon follow."

Jean-Claude continued, his voice rising with conviction, "We, the new generation, must strive for unity. The cultural divide that separates our people, the divide that has us warring against each other instead of standing together... this is what we must conquer."

His words hung in the air as the men took a moment to digest them. Unity was a concept that felt so distant, so abstract amid the complexities of their shared history. Yet as they contemplated Jean-Claude's impassioned plea, a shimmering image of a future Ayiti began to form in their minds.

"Jean-Claude speaks the truth," Alain affirmed solemnly, his gaze drifting to the horizon where daylight was gently erasing night's reign. "The power struggle between the French culture in the Grand Sud and the English culture in the Grand Nord has yielded nothing but discord and strife. We need to envision an Ayiti that celebrates both cultures and yet evolves beyond them with a mix of our African Creole heritage intact."

"The king has sold himself to the British, and our children are now taught in a foreign tongue! What is next?" added General Beauvoir.

"But it is already pre-ordained. When the king passes, his son, the royal prince will take his place," offered Alain.

"He must not rule!" Beauvoir passionately inserted. The king was a tyrant, but his son would be far worse; a Tyrant without knowledge, vision, empathy, or experience. He cannot rule! He will not rule!"

"For that to happen, we must join with Boyer as we are not strong enough to combat the combined armies of the king's staunches supporters; Generals Rouanez, Prévost, Dupuy, Besse, Magny, Pourcely, Romain, Daut, and Brave," reasoned Nicolas Louis.

"Additionally, I am told that Poulin's Demi-Brigade has already defected from the kingdom in protest and is marching towards Boyer's forces as we speak to join them," offered Jean-Claude.

"Then, we must do it all," argued Alain. "We must attack the palace, rally support from the people who are tired of being treated like indentured servants or worse, nearly slaves, and obtain the backing of the influential families of the country. "Each of us can play a role in this. One of us needs to approach Boyer."

Nicholas Louis seemed about to protest, but a steely look from Alain silenced him. It was clear that this was not a plan born of haste or desperation, but one carefully considered and reasoned over time. "I will speak with Boyer," Alain declared, meeting each man's gaze steadily. "I can negotiate terms that can ensure our mutual interests."

"And how do we stem the retaliation of the king's most ardent supporters and get them to stand down - The brigades of Generals Rouanez, Prévost, Dupuy, Besse, Magny, Pourcely, Romain, Daut, and Brave?"

"I will ride out and speak to each of them. They are loyal to the king, yes, but will not support his idiot son as a successor. Of that I am sure," stated Nicholas Louis. "We must convince them that Boyer will not confiscate their already gained riches and have them keep their military units. Once this is guaranteed, I know they will stand down once the king is gone."

A murmur of approval rippled through the group. Alain was a respected figure, known for his shrewd diplomacy and unwavering commitment to Ayiti's independence. Despite being in the throes of chaos, they trusted him to bridge the gap between their tumultuous present and their envisioned future through negotiation with Boyer.

"I am certain I can achieve Boyer's commitment towards the Generals. I will travel there, meet with Boyer, and send a dispatch once I have the assurance," Alain stated to Nicolas Louis.

The plan had been meticulously crafted, each detail carefully calculated. Now it lay in their hands, ready to be executed with swift and ruthless precision. The weight of the responsibility settled heavily on their shoulders as they prepared to set their dangerous plan in motion.

Weeks later, on Henry's birthday on October 6th, nearly two months since his collapse, all of the physicians were in agreement that he suffered from apoplexy, where blood to his brain had stopped or slowed in flow. They did not feel his chances for survival were good. Henry's condition deteriorated and he began to go in and out of consciousness as he dreamed of his nation that had flourished, yet beneath the gleaming monuments of his reign had nightmares of the seething undercurrent of resentment and discontent.

He had pushed himself, and his people even harder, striving for greatness and a legacy that would be etched into every stone, every road, and every mind. He dreamed of himself walking amidst a procession of adoring supporters chanting "Long live the King," then quickly turning into a nightmare with the echoes of dissent,

In moments of vulnerability, he confided in Marie-Louise about his unfulfilled dreams and constant doubts. "To be great is to stand alone. To be magnificent is to be despised," he lamented, bearing the weight of leadership with relentless labor and ceaseless worry gnawing at his spirit until his body began to fail him even more. He found himself at a crossroads where mortality met reality. He came to accept that his death would bring jubilation among the very people he had strived all these years to prosper and please.

Marie-Louise held her breath, her dark eyes welling up with tears. Fearful for the future and yet resolute in her love for her husband, she reached out and gently clasped his trembling hand. Her voice was a whisper against the chilling silence of the room as she replied, "And we understand your sacrifices, Henry. This kingdom owes you more than it can ever repay."

"Be strong, Marie-Louise," Henry urged with tears in his eyes. "Guide our children through this storm and ensure that Prince Jacques-Victor Henry reigns as king when I am no longer." With a mixture of fierce determination and overwhelming regret etched onto his face, the king's trembling hands handed her the documents of the British bank accounts - their only hope for survival in exile should the monarchy fall after his passing.

Now, take me to the Grand reception hall and summon my ministers and generals so I may give my final wishes."

An hour later, the king's ragged breaths filled the room as he commanded his ministers to swiftly install Prince Jacques-Victor Henry on the throne as his successor, and for his generals to protect his family from the turmoil brewing within their kingdom "I have been good to you all," he reminded them. "I have made you wealthy beyond your wildest dreams. Now, make me proud as I am laid to rest and watch upon you from the heavens."

Turning to Baron Rouanez, the king whispered secretly to reminded him of his promise to retrieve the hidden treasure should things go wrong after his death. "You know what to do, Rouanez," he ordered in private about the buried treasure in Marie-Louise's garden.

Whispers of the king's impending death echoed beyond the palace walls, stirring up a sea of unrest. Every day they brought more furious protests and demands for change. The Royal Dahomet guards stood strong, aided by the local militia, as the drums of rebellion grew louder and closer. Meanwhile, King Henry secluded himself in his chambers, unable to face the storm brewing outside.

The following day, Henry asked Marie-Louise to bring in the children. It was time he felt to wish them farewell. With a heavy heart, she complied. As they entered their father's chambers, the sight of the once robust king lying frail in his bed startled them. The hushed tone in the room only added to their confusion and apprehension.

Henry beckoned them closer with a feeble wave of his hand. "I am not a man who is given to tears, but seeing you all standing before me... I know what my departure means." He stared into their innocent faces and felt a profound sorrow that he would not be there to guide them through the tempestuous journey that lay ahead. His voice was hoarse from the ravages of disease as he spoke, "Jacques-Victor Henry, you are my heir to the throne, always remember that the strength of this nation lies in its people. The crown may set you apart but you must curb your desires to be arrogant and cruel."

Jacques-Victor Henry said nothing, his young face solemn. Instead, he nodded silently, his large eyes filled with a mixture of fear and determination.

The king turned to his daughters, Princess Françoise-Améthyste and Princess Anne-Athénaïre, their eyes tearful yet sparkling with fear. "You are the beating hearts of our family," he told them gently. "Preserve the love and unity that binds us together, even in the face of adversity. Life shall test you, but I believe in your strength. Support your brother. Take care of your mother. This, I ask of you."

He then turned to his wife, the only woman he had ever loved, the one he had made queen, and said, "Marie-Louise, my only solace is knowing that you will be here to support our children. You possess a strength beyond measure and an unyielding spirit, qualities that I have always admired." His voice cracked with emotion as he took her hand. "I love you. Promise me, you'll guide them through the trials that lie ahead."

Her eyes welled with tears as she squeezed his hand, whispering a vow that echoed in the silence of the room, "I promise, Henry. We will hold each other close and stay strong."

As the King slipped into a fitful sleep, Marie-Louise remained by his side, her heart shattering at the sight of her once vibrant husband reduced to a mere shadow of his former self.

The following day, on October 8th, 1820, after weeks of turmoil and uncertainty, Henry made his final decision. While Marie-Louise had left him to tend to some palace matters, he acted. With trembling hands, he retrieved a gilded silver sphere - a symbol of both power and inevitability - from its hidden cabinet. As he held the silver bullet tightly, he couldn't help but feel conflicted about what this act would bring.

But before he could think, or calculate his decision anymore, the deafening crack of a discharged pistol shattered the stillness within the palace grounds. In her office chambers, Marie-Louise closed her eyes at the sound and wept. She knew exactly what had transpired.

The once-adoring crowd was stunned into disbelief at their fallen monarch's abrupt demise. "Long live the King!" was now challenged by cries of "The King is dead!" - signaling the impending power shift that emboldened the crowd outside.

Reinforcements were brought in to subdue the crowd which was quickly turning into an angry mob. Some of the Royal Dahomet guards, reviled by the masses for their meanness towards them, began to secretly remove their uniforms and slip into the night, leaving the palace to its own devices.

On the third day after his death, rioters began to storm the palace. The Dahomet palace guards, defecting by the dozens, were replaced with soldiers from the militia who were confused and reluctant to fire upon their neighbors. They were soon overpowered by the mob who had now become rioters. They breached the entrance by the thousands onto the palace grounds to ransack the royal building. Finally, retribution was demanded for years of oppression.

The prince entered the palace grounds with several hundred galloping Calvary and pushed back the mob. The king's brigade, now under the command of the young Prince, administered deadly force by indiscriminately gunning down many assembled, even those peacefully doing so as well. They succeeded in repelling the attackers and the prince continued to show no patience and much less mercy for the mobs in waiting, ordering his soldiers to violently displace them off the palace grounds.

Amid this chaos emerged Queen Marie-Louise, her face transformed by a steely determination akin to her late husband's. She commanded her attendants to assist her while she, Baron Rouanez, and others veiled Henry's remains in linen shrouds and led them on the clandestine tunnel towards the citadel overlooking their besieged kingdom.

Marie-Louise now understood the importance and vision of her husband to have built it. The tunnel was large enough for a column of horses and led straight up the mountain to the citadel. She marveled at the structure, growing a newfound respect for the king departed. There were torches at the ready with kerosene being lighted by the guides who had gone in advance of the queen's party.

Upon their arrival, and with grim determination, she directed Henry's body into a vat of corrosive lime—a final act to protect his remains from the vengeful masses intent on erasing all remnants of royalty. Her husband would not suffer the fate of the Emperor Dessalines and be dismembered. Time pressed against them as they descended from their mountain refuge towards the safety of the British consulate in Cap Henry while unrest gripped Ayiti in its vengeful throes, leaving behind a once-great king and a shattered nation in its wake.

With the immediate danger supposedly over, Marie-Louise could still feel the tension and hatred lingering in the air. Ayiti was left shattered and struggling to regain its footing after the violent uprising. As she stared out of the window of the consulate, a 100-man regiment, installed by General Prévost protected the building. Marie-Louise knew that nothing would ever be the same for this ravaged country after the fall of its leader.

General Nicholas Louis had struck a deal with the former loyalists of King Henry, now cowering in fear at the thought of Prince Jacques-Victor Henry rising to power. They believed it was in their, and the country's, best interest to stand down, trusting General Nicholas Louis' promise that President Boyer did not seek war and would honor their military titles.

A mere three days later, the plan was executed with precision. Generals Alain, Nicolas Louis, Beauvoir, and Jean-Claude of Saint Marc led a relentless army of four thousand soldiers to the palace walls, outnumbering and overpowering the meager 200 guards protecting the palace. Without resistance, they breached the gates and flooded onto the palace grounds, capturing Prince Jacques-Victor Henry, Baron Vastey, and other members of the king's court who had foolishly stayed behind.

The triumphant cries of several members of Colonel Poulin's demi-brigade reverberated through every room as he was found alive and liberated from his captivity.

A military tribunal was convened and justice was swift and merciless. Baron Vastey, once a revered member of society, along

Baron Pompée Valentin Vastey, after a brilliant career and staunch supporter of King Henry met his fate in front of a firing squad where he courageously stated his case to the crowds who so loved him.

with high-ranking government officials and even the Prince-Royal himself were found guilty of unspeakable crimes against their people - treason being only one of many. The sentence - death.

On a crisp morning two days later, the deafening sound of rifle fire echoed throughout the land as each group of five traitors - four groups in total - was callously executed by the firing squad.

And at high noon, it was the turn of the esteemed Baron Vastey. As a sign of respect, the bodies of the others executed were removed and the ground scrubbed clean of blood, though the smell of death lingered in the air like a haunting reminder of their crimes.

As if granting him one final act of pride before his demise, Vastey was offered a chance to address the crowd that had gathered to witness his downfall. With passionate words dripping with patriotism and loyalty to a kingdom that no longer existed, he recounted the events that had led to this revolution and extolled the accomplishments of King Henry.

Surprisingly, perhaps out of admiration for his bravery, his past accomplishments, or simply out of spite for their now-deceased ruler, the crowd cheered for Pompée Valentin Vastey as the baron refused a blindfold. With the deafening sound of five rifles, the life of the once-great baron was extinguished, leaving behind a nation in turmoil and a legacy stained with blood.

The door to the cell burst open with a loud crash, and in marched four imposing prison guards. "I demand to be released immediately and brought to the British Consulate!" yelled the once-crowned prince.

"Your fate has been decided, Citizen Victor. Your sentence will be death," answered a prison guard.

"You cannot do this. I am a prince. My father was king! Release me at once!" cried the prince as tears began to stream from his eyes.

When he was dragged outside of the cell, a man familiar to him in a uniform arrived at his side. "Am I to face the firing squad? It is not fair. It was my father who did the things you allege that I have done. Release me, I am innocent!"

Colonel Poulin arrived at the group and looked at the once-titled prince. "Was it not you who laughed when the king removed my life-long earned medals and threw them to the ground?" he asked.

The prince looked upon Poulin with regret in his eyes, trembling at his past arrogance.

"And is it not you who mocked me during your visit to Artibonite and berated me for not preparing your place setting to your standards?" asked the commander he had once publicly insulted during a visit to L'Artibonite.

Victor now realized the error of his ways, but it was far too late as the commander was now slowly loading his pistol and Poulin already had his cocked.

"No, please, I beg of you. Don't take me to the firing squad. I beg of you, spare me," cried the prince as the child he was.

"Firing squad?" asked Poulin. "No, we do not plan to do that."

"Thank you, Colonel. Thank you for sparing me," cried Victor.

"He did not mean it like that, my boy," said the commander. "What the Colonel meant was that you will not be honored from death by firing squad. You will not have a crowd to cheer you. You will be killed in this very dungeon."

"What?" cried Victor as both the commander and Poulin brought their pistols to his skull and wasted no time in simultaneously pulling the trigger.

After learning of her son's fate, Marie Louise and her daughters, Princesses Françoise-Améthyste and Anne-Athénaïre, were quickly whisked away on a large ship anchored in the Cap Henry harbor. The salty sea air brushed against their faces as they sailed towards the safety of England under the protection of the British Admiralty with some treasure that was unearthed by Baron Rouanez to secure their future and get them settled, as the king had wisely planned.

From that point on, Marie Louise lived out the rest of her days without economic difficulties with assets that Henry had deposited in the banks of London.

In England, the family found refuge in Blackheath, a quiet and peaceful village where prominent abolitionists welcomed them with open arms. They eventually moved to 49 Weymouth St, London, which is now known as 5 Exmouth Place. It was a popular choice among wealthy and aristocratic Londoners who sought respite from the smog and bustle of central London. In 2022, blue plaques were erected to honor the Queen's time in England and celebrate her legacy.

However, living in London during the Industrial Revolution took a toll on Améthyste's health. The pollution and harsh climate proved detrimental, prompting them to decide to leave. In 1824, Marie-Louise and her daughters relocated to Pisa in the Grand Duchy of Tuscany (now Italy), where they would spend the rest of their lives. Tragically, Améthyste passed away shortly after their arrival at the age of 25 and Athénaïre followed in 1839 at age 39.

Before her untimely death, and with heavy heart, Marie-Louise wrote to Ayiti seeking permission to return home. Despite her wishes, she never did make it back and passed away in 1851 at the age of 73 in Italy having outlived her two sons and two daughters before her passing. Marie-Louise was laid to rest in the church of San Donnino, where a beautiful historical marker was installed on April 23, 2023, to honor her and her daughters.

Nineteen

REUNIFICATION

Cap Henry
October 1820

The sun cast a somber light over the citadel, its once impregnable walls now breached by the whispers of betrayal. The thunderous heart of King Henry Christophe, the architect of nations and harbinger of discipline, had ceased to beat. His loyal guardians, men who had marched through fire and blood at his command, stood statuesque in their grief, their faces etched with the agony of loss.

"Le Roi est mort," one whispered, the words slicing through the air like a blade. The prince, too, had been led to the slaughter, a young life extinguished before it could bloom into a legacy. And the queen, her sails disappearing into the horizon, carried with her the last vestiges of a crumbling dynasty.

A heaviness pressed upon the land as if the very soil mourned the passage of its king. The disciplined ranks that Henry had so meticulously forged were now adrift in a sea of uncertainty. Eyes that once glowed with purpose now searched the void for direction, their stoic resolve wavering in the face of an obscured future.

In the streets of Cap-Henry, confusion reigned. Men and women who had known the strict order of King Henry's rule found themselves lost amidst hushed conversations and furtive glances. "What now?" they asked one another, their voices barely rising above the rustle of leaves. Do we work? Who will enforce the codes now that the mean Royal Dahomet guards have scattered? Children clung to the skirts of their mothers, sensing the palpable shift in the air, their innocent questions piercing the heavy silence that hung like a shroud.

As conspirators slithered from shadowed corners, their eyes alight with the fire of ambition, it was clear that the power struggle had only just begun. They spoke in fervent tones, their hands gesturing wildly as they carved up the kingdom in hushed council. Yet even as they plotted, the doubt lingered; for the spirit of King Henry, though stilled, was not so easily quelled. It whispered on the wind, through the stone-laden streets, and in the hearts of those who had seen a nation rise from ashes.

His most loyal generals issued decrees of peaceful transitions, though not providing a roadmap of a transition to what. Soldiers were unleashed from their barracks to patrol the streets and the countryside to quash any outbreak of civil disobedience as they regrouped to understand the new order and way forward.

"Freedom," the people murmured, the word a talisman against the encroaching darkness. Resilience was the blood that coursed through their veins, hope the steady drumbeat that had long guided their steps. But as they looked toward a horizon muddied by intrigue, they could not shake the feeling that their battle for progress had been reset, that they must once again gird themselves for the toilsome journey ahead as they had for the past thirty-odd years - a generation in all.

And so, under the watchful gaze of the mountain fortress, Ayiti held its breath. For in the wake of a king's demise, the path forward was shrouded, and only time would unveil the destiny of this indomitable island and its unconquerable soul.

Under the cloak of a moonless night, General Alain dismounted his weary horse with the stealth of a seasoned warrior. The air was thick with the scent of wild jasmine and the distant murmurs of Port Républicain which lay sprawled beneath the starlit sky. His boots sunk softly into the earth as he approached the derelict sugar mill where his clandestine rendezvous was to unfold.

Inside, Joute waited, her silhouette barely discernible in the shadowed recesses. The lines of her face were etched with the weight of recent events, eyes reflecting a tumultuous mix of sorrow and resolve. The king's demise had left a void, and the death of Alexandre Pétion, her former lover, had severed the last tie to her past loyalties. Now, she stood on the precipice of a vision long held close to her heart—the unification of North and South. Pétion had coward at the task, reasoning patience. He did not live to see her vision, fueled by her mountainous ambitions, bear fruit.

"General," Joute's voice was a whisper, yet it carried the authority of one who had navigated the treacherous waters of politics and emerged with an unshakeable purpose.

"Madame," Alain responded, his form emerging from the darkness like a specter. He moved with deliberate steps, mindful of the gravity that cloaked their meeting.

"The king is gone," she began, her tone a blend of mournfulness and pragmatism, "and with him, the old order crumbles. We are at the crossroads of destiny. The people yearn for guidance amidst this chaos."

Alain nodded, his weathered face a testament to battles fought and scars accrued, both visible and veiled. "The soldiers look to us now. They seek a banner under which they can rally—a cause that will not betray their sacrifices. They are confused as to the way forward"

"Then let us weave together the threads of North and South," Joute proposed, her eyes alight with the fervor of her dream. "A united Ayiti is within our grasp. Without the king, without Pétion, we are free to forge a new path."

"Unity is a delicate tapestry," Alain remarked thoughtfully, his gaze fixed upon her determined countenance. "It will require patience, strength... and cunning."

"Patience we have cultivated, strength we have in abundance," Joute countered, moving closer so that her presence might impress upon him the urgency of her plea. "And as for cunning, we shall wield it as deftly as the sword and pen."

The general's voice was low and urgent as he leaned in close to Joute. "Have you laid out our plans with Boyer yet? It is time. You and I have been meeting in secret for over a year now, planning this moment," Alain replied, her eyes glinting with determination.

"President Boyer will soon know of this," Joute interjected, the rustle of leaves outside echoing the secrecy of their pact. "We must be the architects of this peace, as I make him believe it is his design."

Joute nodded in agreement, her jaw set in determination. "Tell me about your dealings with the Western and Northern generals."

"The demi-brigade led by Colonel Poulin is already marching towards us. They have defected as retaliation for his arrest. Generals Nicolas Louis, Beauvoir, and Jean-Claude are with us, though they believe I am only in contact with Boyer himself."

"And what about the commanders of the northern units?" Joute asked, strategically probing for more information.

"General Nicholas Louis is meeting with each one individually. They were all staunch supporters of the late king, but they agreed that the prince could not take his place on the throne. He has been executed, along with any loyal nobles who refused to change," Allain explained.

Joute's eyes narrowed at this news. "It seems our true power lies within these generals and their brigades. Will they stand down if our armies march north?"

"With certain assurances, yes. They have amassed great riches under the king's reign. That is how he bought their loyalty," Allain stated confidently. "If we guarantee them equal standing, non-confiscation of their wealth and property, and a role in the new government, Nicholas-Louis assures me they will stand down."

"Then I will give them that assurance," Joute declared without hesitation.

But Allain hesitated, his brows furrowing in concern. "Respectfully, you are not President Jean-Pierre Boyer. You cannot guarantee these things."

Joute's gaze turned steely as she leaned in closer to Alain. "Who do you think holds the true power here? I am the power broker. I am the one who placed Boyer in his position and kept the military in control. He will do what I ask, of that you can be assured."

"Then I must make haste and dispatch a rider to inform Nicholas-Louis of this. We need to move quickly before fear takes hold of the people. How soon can you convince Boyer to join our plan?" Allain pressed.

"Leave that to me," Joute replied with a confident smile. "I will handle Boyer while you handle the generals. When the dawn breaks, I will begin to shape his thoughts towards our ambition and will send a messenger when a meeting is planned for you to meet Boyer yourself."

"Then let us be swift," Alain concluded, sealing their alliance with a curt nod. "The heart of Ayiti beats with uncertainty. If we are to guide it towards hope, we must act before despair takes root. I trust you will send word within the next three days?"

"Or less, if I am able," replied Joute. "I will send word as soon as I can."

Their meeting was brief, a fleeting moment amid the untamed rhythms of the night. Yet within those hushed exchanges bloomed the seeds of a future bound by unity. As General Alain slipped away into the darkness, blending once more with the shadows, Joute remained alone with her thoughts, the silent guardian of a dream that promised to mend a fractured nation.

In the stillness that followed, the air seemed to thicken with anticipation, charged with the silent prayers of a people who had known too well the cost of freedom. It was a canvas upon which the colors of resilience and hope would be painted anew, stroke by painstaking stroke, under the watchful eyes of those who dared to envision Ayiti whole and sovereign once more.

The sun rose over Port Républicain, its first light piercing the horizon with a violent intensity. The city lay in a state of tense anticipation, still reeling from the news of the royal family's sudden demise in the Northern Kingdom.

At her side stood Jean-Pierre Boyer, President of the Grand Sud, but she was more than just his mistress and consort. He relied on her counsel and trusted her implicitly as his advisor and confidante, just as Pétion before him had as well. Together, they were the force that drove the country forward towards progress and unity.

Servants had just brought in their morning coffee, its rich aroma surrounding them with the familiar scent of the earth's crop. "Jean-Pierre," she began, her voice steady as she addressed him in the privacy of their chamber. "The North lies fractured, leaderless. Our people yearn for stability, for a sign that out of this chaos, unity will emerge."

Boyer met her gaze, a mix of admiration and fear shining in his eyes. He knew the weight of her power and influence, and he relied on it to guide their country towards a better future. "But to unify the North and South would be a monumental task," he argued.

Joute leaned in closer, holding his gaze steadily. "It is necessary for our country's healing," she said firmly.

Boyer regarded her, his eyes reflecting a mix of admiration and trepidation. He understood this woman and was keenly aware of her hold on the mantles of politics. "Joute, the task you propose is massive. To unify the country—"

"Is to heal it," she interjected gently, placing a hand on his arm as she leaned to pick up his porcelain coffee cup and add three teaspoons of sugar, gently stirring it with heightened sensuality as she looked deep into his eyes, knowing intimately that it was the way he enjoyed it. "You possess the acumen of a statesman, the heart of a patriot. Lead them not just as President of the South, but as a beacon for all people of Ayiti," she added as she extended the cup to him.

"I had many discussions on the subject of unification with Alexandre, before his death. He was against it as the North and the

South have different mindsets, different ideologies, a move that would certainly lead to another war and bloodshed" Boyer protested.

"And that is why he had to go," revealed Joute.

"What do you mean by 'he had to go'?" asked her lover. He studied her face, searching for a clue to the mystery that had eluded him for the past two-plus years. Did she have Alexandre poisoned?

"The ideas of Alexandre were to keep Ayiti torn apart. He was not in favor of challenging Christophe, but the man who named himself king is no longer an obstacle," she reasoned. The opportunity is now ours."

Boyer's heart pounded in his chest as he confronted Joute, "Did you have Alexandre poisoned, Joute?"

Joute's eyes widened in surprise, and she set down her cup with a clatter. She had hoped that Boyer would never ask about Alexandre's death, but now it seemed inevitable. She took a deep breath and looked into his intense gaze.

"Jean-Pierre, I know you loved him like a brother," she began carefully. "I loved him too. But you must understand that he was an obstacle to our plans for Ayiti's unification."

"What do you mean by 'our plans'?" Boyer asked, his voice trembling with emotion.

Joute reached out and took his hand in hers, giving it a reassuring squeeze. "I wanted to tell you sooner, but I knew how difficult it would be for you," she explained. "Alexandre was not poisoned by me, but I did suspect it was to blame for his demise."

Boyer felt the blood drain from his face as he processed her words. He had suspected this all along, but hearing it confirmed by Joute made the reality hit him harder than he anticipated.

"Why? Why did he have to die? Why didn't you warn him? Stop his senseless death" he asked, tears welling up in his eyes, as much for his friend Pétion as for the betrayal he felt from Joute.

Joute's expression softened as she stroked his hand gently. "There are powerful forces at work, some beyond our control. In part, also because we need a leader who is willing to bring our country together," she replied. "Alexandre was too stuck in the old ways, too afraid of change, too complacent."

Boyer pulled away from her touch and stood up, pacing around the room as he struggled to process everything. His mind was reeling with conflicting emotions – grief over losing his friend and anger towards Joute for manipulating the situation. Was she involved? How much did she know? Could Alexandre's death have been prevented? Was it of her doing, her coaxing? "You expect me to just accept this? To become your puppet?" he finally exclaimed.

Joute stood up as well and walked over to him, placing her hands on his shoulders and looking into his eyes with sincerity. "No, Jean-Pierre," she said firmly. "I expect you to lead Ayiti towards a brighter future and I will be alongside you."

Boyer's heart softened at her words, and he could see the sincerity in her brown eyes. She was irresistible. Irresistible to him, to Pétion who he had betrayed by his clandestine affair with her while he was still alive. Irresistible to many. He was still reeling, yet within him, a spark of determination was slowly being ignited. He looked at Joute with resolve, his cheekbones catching the soft candlelight.

"Joute, this nation has seen enough death, enough betrayal," he said, his voice strained. "I... I will lead us to unification, for the sake of our people's future. But know this..." His gaze hardened. "I do not condone your methods."

"They are not my methods," Joute pleaded with desperation in her voice. "It was the work of others, I swear. You know me, Jean-Pierre. I am a woman of principles."

But he could see the guilt in her eyes and knew there was much more she wasn't telling him. Yet, despite this, he still loved her and was willing to overlook her faults. He remembered the day his dear friend and mentor, Alexandre Pétion, had died. It had been just over two years ago, but the pain and shock were still fresh in his heart. He couldn't believe it when Jean-Baptiste Bayard Junior had suggested that Pétion's death may have been caused by poisoning. Jean-Pierre had refused to accept the possibility and had lost another friend that day when he stood his ground as Junior refused to shake his hand. Jean-Baptiste Junior always prided himself on being a man of integrity.

Since then, Junior had retired from the senate and returned to his hometown of Jérémie where he managed the family shipping business and expanded into hardware, general merchandise, and construction materials. He had even branched out to other towns in the Southern Peninsula; Les Cayes, Port Salute, and others, as well as Jacmel which he now called home. Jean-Pierre couldn't help but feel happy for him - finally out of politics, and of what had been rumored, awaiting on his parents, Jean and Marie, to join him in their retirement in Jacmel.

But now, as president of the country, Jean-Pierre knew he couldn't do it without Joute by his side. She had helped him consolidate power and they were in a good place thanks to her cunning strategies and manipulations. But now was not a time for reminiscing. "How do you propose we unite the country, Joute?" he asked, bringing them back to their pressing matter at hand. "Shall I march my army north and begin attacking while they are still in disarray after Christophe's death?

"No, that would be a grave mistake," Joute cautioned. "Aggression will only galvanize opposition towards us. We must be subtle, nuanced."

Jean-Pierre raised an eyebrow. "From the woman who suggested assassinating Christophe not but two years ago?"

Joute's face blanched but she recovered quickly. "I...we...were desperate then. It was a different time. A different landscape."

He considered her words, swirling the dark liquid in his porcelain cup pensively. The silence stretched between them, pregnant with unspoken thoughts and fears. Finally, he nodded. "We shall try your path of subtlety and nuance. Do you believe we can achieve this dream? Together?""

"More than ever," Joute affirmed, her gaze unwavering. "And I have already set matters in motion to ensure our success."

"Explain," Boyer commanded, the ruler within him rising to the fore.

"General Alain of Saint-Marc," she revealed, meeting his surprise with a knowing smile. "He commands respect among the Northern ranks. I've arranged for you to meet, to discuss the future of our nation."

"Without my knowledge?" Boyer's tone carried an edge, though it was tempered by curiosity.

"Sometimes, my love, the seeds of concord must be sown in secret to protect them from the ravages of doubt. I needed you to have plausible deniability in case it did not go as planned. It was safer for you not to know," Joute replied, her fingers tracing patterns of assurance along his skin. "Trust in me, as I trust in your vision for a united Ayiti."

Boyer nodded slowly, absorbing the gravity of her words. "When is this meeting?"

"Tonight," Joute answered. "Under the veil of darkness, where truth often finds its clearest voice."

"Very well," he acquiesced, a newfound determination lighting his features. "I will meet with General Alain. For the sake of Ayiti, for the hope that still flickers amidst our scars, we will speak of unity."

"Freedom is born from the resilience of those who dare to dream," Joute murmured, "And it is with such dreams that we shall build a future worthy of our collective sacrifices."

In the dim glow of a single oil lamp, the map sprawled across the mahogany table appeared as a battlefield itself, marked by lines and shaded territories that told stories of conflict and ambition. General Alain's finger traced the contours of Saint Marc, his touch lingering on the parchment as if to draw strength from the very land he had vowed to protect.

"Then it is agreed," President Boyer's voice resonated through the hush of the clandestine chamber, each syllable heavy with the weight of impending change. "You shall keep your ranks, your lands untouched."

Alain nodded, his stern features softening with relief. "And that includes all officers of the North. And in return, our swords will lay the foundation for unity, not division. We must convince the people of our sincerity."

"Words are seeds from which trust may bloom," Joute interjected, her gaze locked with Boyer's. The candlelight cast shadows upon her face, highlighting the resolve etched into her visage. She was the architect of this accord, the unseen hand guiding Ayiti toward a horizon brightened by the prospect of peace.

"Public support will sway the masses," Boyer agreed, his eyes reflecting a vision of a nation healed from its self-inflicted wounds. "The proclamation must be heartfelt, unequivocal."

"Let them not only hear but see our conviction," Alain said, standing tall, his posture as unyielding as the mountains that cradled the city. "The combined armies must march into Cap Henry together for the hope that rests within every Ayisyen heart."

Silence fell, and in that moment, the ghosts of the founding fathers of the nation; Louverture, Dessalines, Pétion, and Christophe seemed to whisper through the walls, their legacies the unspoken witnesses to history's inexorable march. "From now on there is no longer a Cap Henry, but simply *'Le Cap'*," Joute offered with a commanding voice.

The following evening, the president and his first consort—affectionately known to the people as Joute— had extended an invitation to Jean-Baptiste Bayard Junior and his wife for an opera night in Port Républicain. Joute believed it was essential to bridge the divide with this influential family of the Southern Penninsula while also showcasing unity with the young retired senate president.

Everyone knew that he had been a crucial ally of Alexandre Pétion, instrumental not only in securing Pétion's presidency for life but also in many of his notable achievements.

Yet, as Joute prepared for the evening, her mind drifted to the day of Pétion's death—a haunting memory that felt painfully fresh. She recalled Junior's barely concealed accusations that danced around her and Jean-Pierre Boyer like shadows, never fully naming their intended target. If only he had known then about the child she carried that day, a secret tethering her fate to both men, Alexandre and Jean-Pierre, would he have considered her guilty of murder?

Their daughter Azéma's birth was shrouded in swirling rumors among the populace. The month of October 1818 held a thick veil of mystery, as everyone speculated about who the child truly belonged to. Was it Pétion's, the late president's? Or did it belong to Boyer, the new leader? Joute knew the truth deep down in her heart - Jean-Pierre Boyer was Azéma's father. But there remained an unsettling doubt that gnawed at her conscience - could history ever forgive her?

Despite this doubt, Joute had stayed at the palace after Pétion's death at the invitation of the new president. It was gracious towards a grieving woman, thought the citizens. He was acting as a faithful mentee of Pétion everyone believed. Of course, he would allow the ex-president's mistress to remain at the palace. But in reality, she was now Boyer's mistress and new concubine, just as she had been to Pétion. When the child was born in October, Boyer claimed it as his own, putting on a grand gesture for the public. They all thought Joute had been consoled by Boyer after Pétion's death and had fallen in love with him post-death. However, the truth was that their love had blossomed before Pétion's passing, shrouding their relationship in secrecy and deception.

Port Républicain had long unseated Cap Henry as the new center of the arts since the ouster of French rule. Port Républicain was alive with culture, vibrant with music and dance, and bustling with artistic expression. It was a stark contrast to the North dominated by a chilly British influence and the strict codes of conduct under the Code

Henry. So as a result, writers, poets, artists, musicians, and others flocked to the Grand Sud for more freedom of expression.

The people of Port Républicain had embraced their newfound freedom with open arms, shedding their former colonial identities and embracing a new sense of national pride. And one of the ways they expressed this pride was through the arts.

The streets were lined with theaters and opera houses, each one vying for attention and patronage from the city's elite. It seemed that every week there was a new performance debuting in Port Républicain, drawing crowds from all corners of the country.

The majority of these performances were brought over directly from France, sometimes only a few months after their première in Paris or elsewhere. The people of Port Républicain eagerly awaited these productions, eager to experience French culture firsthand without having to travel across the Atlantic.

Not everyone was pleased with this influx of French influence. Some saw it as a threat to Ayisyen identity and culture. They argued that by constantly looking to France for artistic inspiration, Ayiti risked losing its unique voice and perspective.

However, many saw value in embracing both French and Ayisyen influences in their art. They saw it as a way to honor their past while forging ahead into a brighter future.

Additionally, a noteworthy number of literary works were written by locals living on the island, specifically in the South. One of the most intriguing aspects of these theatrical productions was the use of Creole parody. In these works, they would take inspiration from French literature but change the setting to modern-day Ayiti and incorporate local characters and Creole actors. The use of Ayisyen Creole in the dialogue to engage a wider audience was the custom and this sprouted new local acting companies and neighborhood theaters around the Grand Sud as well.

President Boyer, accompanied by Joute and their entourage of eight, including guest of honor Jean-Baptiste Bayard and his wife Marie Victoire, arrived at the Grand Opera House of Port Républicain to thunderous applause. The atmosphere was celebratory, fueled by news of the recent turmoil in the North. Joute couldn't help but feel awed by the opulence surrounding her. The theater was lavishly decorated with velvet drapes cascading from high ceilings adorned with glistening chandeliers.

Tonight's performance was to be a tribute to the Bayard's with the performance of the opera Le Chevalier Sans Peur et Sans Reproche Ou Les Amours de Bayard - *The Knight Without Fear and Without Reproach or The Loves of Bayard* – It was a tale of the loves of the French Knight, Pierre Terrail known famously as Chevalier de Bayard who had lived in the early 16th century. He was of no relation to Junior, but the name of the opera had given Joute an opening as a partial reason for the invitation, she had told Boyer.

She took her seat next to Boyer in their private box with their entourage of four other couples, surveying the audience below. There were familiar faces scattered among the crowd - prominent families, and other influential figures in Ayisyen society, which she waved to all.

The opera was written by Jacques-Marie Boutet de Monvel and the composer Marie-François-Stanislas Champein

The chatter of the crowd faded into a collective silence as the opera began. The soft strains of a violin filled the air, followed by the soaring voices of the opera singers and the rhythmic percussion of the orchestra. The sound was both enchanting and powerful, drawing the audience into the story.

The narrative of the opera was a profound reflection of love, heroism, and sacrifice. The protagonist, a gallant knight, embodied the virtues of bravery and honor. His sworn duty to protect the realm from enemies was juxtaposed with his passionate love for a damsel, whom he fought tirelessly to save. This intriguing tale stirred emotions in the audience who watched with bated breath as scenes of valor filled the stage.

As the opera unfolded, Jean-Baptiste Bayard was afflicted with an uncanny feeling of resonance. The knight's relentless pursuit of honor and the constant struggle to balance duty with love aligned too close with his own life. He felt his wife, Marie Victoire's hand tighten around his as she too felt the eerie parallelism, shedding tears as the performance continued.

Meanwhile, President Boyer observed the audience's rapt attention, understanding that well-executed theatre had always been a formidable means of swaying public opinion. He would use this art form during the upcoming walk towards unifying the country in the next few days. Art will meet diplomacy and he will leverage tonight's performance as a lesson of how to leverage the next several days of his own performances in the North to his advantage.

As the final act of the opera neared, a palpable sense of anticipation filled the room. The riveting story had gripped everyone's hearts so far - would it end in heartbreak or triumph? Unbeknownst to them, an echo of this uncertainty hung heavily over their own lives.

In a climactic scene, the knight faces a cruel choice between duty and love. With poignant resignation, he chose duty, leaving his beloved weeping at the loss of their shared dreams as the curtain closed for the final of four acts.

The audience erupted into thunderous applause as the curtain reopened for a final bow from the performers. Jean-Baptiste and Marie Victoire joined in, struck by the powerful emotions evoked by the opera's bittersweet ending, tears still visible at the corner of her eyes.

With a glass of champagne in hand and Joute by his side, Boyer later introduced them to new influential figures at the backstage reception and toasted his plans for unifying the country. Jean-Baptiste and Marie Victoire listened intently, impressed by Boyer's strategic vision for Ayiti's future. They had always been aware of his political prowess but seeing it in action at an opera was a new experience.

As they said their goodbyes and made their way back to their carriage destined for the Grand Hotel, Jean-Baptiste couldn't help but feel a sense of trepidation from the encounter. Joute and Boyer were very nice, too nice perhaps. Marie Victoire could sense her husband's thoughts and placed a reassuring hand on his arm. She knew that together, they would navigate whatever challenges lay ahead.

Three days hence, when the first rays of dawn broke over Port Républicain, the air was heavy with anticipation, tinged with the briny touch of the sea. As the sun rose above the horizon, its warmth spread across the island and awakened a sense of determination among the people.

The rumble of thousands of boot-clad feet echoed through the streets as the Grand Sud's army assembled, their steadfast expressions forming a tapestry of courage woven from the threads of six thousand souls.

Boyer rode to the central square with a crisp uniform adorned with medals and golden epaulets atop his powerful steed, a symbol of his authority and leadership. His face, chiseled like the rugged cliffs that hugged the coastline, reflected the resilience and strength of Ayiti's tempestuous history. Thoughts of Joute lingered in his mind, a silent tribute to her unwavering influence, mirroring the deep blue depths of the ocean that had carried so many to these shores in chains, now bearing witness to their descendants' rise.

In the central square, six brigades stood at attention, each led by a Brigadier General. As Boyer's arrival was announced, a hush fell over the crowd. He looked around him, struck by the significance of this moment in history - one that he would surely leave his mark on. The line of officers before him was impressive, with the highest ranking standing at the forefront followed by their subordinates until finally, the captains holding their divisional flags flapping in the wind brought up the rear. Behind them stretched an endless sea of soldiers at attention, ready to follow their leader into battle.

"My fellow officers and soldiers," Boyer began, his voice booming over the ranks like a tidal wave before it breaks. "The time has come for brothers and sisters to once again embrace. North and South will come together and unite this country as one. For far too long have we been divided by our differences. But today, the mighty armies of the South and West will join forces with those of the North and Northwest, and together we will triumphantly march towards Le Cap to assure our people that we are once again united. There will be no battles, only solidarity with our comrades."

The crowd erupted in cheers, their unified voices ringing out in unison as they too joined in on the call for unity. "Forward one and all, for unity! For peace! For prosperity! For Ayiti!" Boyer's words echoed throughout the square, carried by the wind like a rallying cry.

And as his powerful voice once again roared, L'Union Fait la Force! *Unity Creates Strength!"* the crowd picked up the resounding chant - "L'Union Fait la Force! L'Union Fait la Force! L'Union Fait la Force!" as the words continued to reverberate through the air, L'Union Fait la Force! It was a testament to the enduring spirit of Ayiti and its people. L'Union Fait la Force!

As the army began its march toward Le Cap, the earth beneath their boots quivered with the promise of change. Each step was a heartbeat, each breath a chorus, joined in a symphony of hope that resonated far beyond the confines of the island.

Through fields where sugarcane bowed beneath the burden of history, past villages where faces lined with stories of survival turned toward the procession as soldiers advanced. Their banners fluttered in the breeze—a vibrant declaration of intent—as they moved as one entity, bound by the shared dream of a future forged from the resilience of their collective spirit.

The following day, they sighted the demi-brigade of Colonel Poulin in the distance which was on the march towards Port Républicain to defect from the northern army. General Allain had intercepted them and assumed command, briefing the captain in charge of what was about to occur. Together, they rode towards Boyer with the divisional flag and stopped before him, and saluted as Boyer and the accompanying generals returned their salute. "General Boyer", General Allain stated. "The armies of the north stand with you. I present the Ninth Brigade and we submit to your command".

"General Allain, I welcome you. You will ride in the front ranks with me and our corps of generals. Captain, you will honorably lead your demi-brigade to join our ranks. We welcome you to the unified army of Ayiti!" This joining of the ranks continued with the fifth regiment, the eighth, and the seventh on the way to Le Cap, shortened to no longer be referred to as Cap Henry.

As the dust settled on the outskirts of Le Cap, the armies of the North and Northwest stood in silent vigil awaiting Boyer. The morning mist clung to their uniforms like a shroud, and the air was thick with the anticipation of what was to come. They had assembled not as adversaries but as compatriots, united by the gravity of the moment.

President Boyer rode at the vanguard of the combined forces of the South, West, Saint-Marc, and L'Artibonite, his steed a dark silhouette against the burgeoning daylight. Beside him, General Alain's eyes were steely reflections of resolve, his posture unwavering as they approached the northern ranks. He had sent his message and was assured of a positive receipt, however, he always was prepared for the unexpected. He, Boyer, and the generals of the southern armies rode towards the deceased king's once most staunches supporters; Generals Rouanez, Prévost, Dupuy, Besse, Magny, Pourcely, Romain, Daut, and Brave at the head of the combined armies of the north. Their hands rested on their sword pommels, trained and ready for a change of heart from their Northern adversaries. Would there be an attack of surprise, or an ambush? Or would they honor the agreement?

"Brothers!" Alain's voice cut through the hush, bridging the gap between the two forces. "Today, we stand on the precipice of a new dawn for Ayiti."

From the northern contingent, the generals rode forward, their expressions etched with the weight of history and stopped to salute Boyer and the other generals. Then the hands of the North met in

President Jean-Pierre Boyer, mounted at center, addresses the combined armies of the North and South on the outskirts of Le Cap before they enter the city in comradery.

solemn fraternity with the hands of the South, clasps that spoke louder than any proclamation could. It was a tableau of unity, each leader embodying the aspirations of a nation fragmented by strife yet bound by an indomitable spirit.

"Let us forge a future where our children can live under one flag," proclaimed Boyer with the agreement of the northern generals, his gaze sweeping over the sea of faces before him. The soldiers' eyes, some alight with fervor, others clouded by memories of discord, all turned toward the voices of their commanders.

"Unity is the bedrock upon which we shall rebuild this land," General Rouanez from the North affirmed, his tone imbued with a conviction that resonated within the hearts of all present. Murmurs of assent rippled through the ranks, a chorus of shared purpose blossoming amidst the scars of war and division.

The air was thick with the heady scent of hope and new beginnings, mingling with the earthy aroma of verdant fields. It was as though the very essence of possibility had been distilled into every breath they took. A sense of unity permeated the gathering, a convergence of spirits united under the banner of peace.

But as the sun rose higher in the sky, casting a brilliant golden light on the assembled masses, tinges of uncertainty began to creep in. This alliance marked not an end, but a beginning of a treacherous journey ahead. And yet, it also held immense opportunity.

Boyer's commanding voice cut through the tension, urging them forward. "Let us march to Le Cap," he declared, his words carrying both determination and caution. "But let us not be blinded by the brightness of this day. Our path is littered with remnants of colonialism and the lingering specters of division that still haunt our beloved country."

With steady strides, the combined armies started their procession toward the heart of the city, a living tapestry of resolve and apprehension. Each soldier carried within them echoes of past battles and whispers of unknown challenges yet to come. As they drew closer to their destination, residents emerged from their dwellings to bear witness to this historic moment - southern forces joined with those from the north.

A mile outside the city's border, thousands of civilians fought to push their way through the crowd, desperate to catch a glimpse of the prideful display marching towards them. The once quiet streets of Le Cap were now a cacophony of chaos, packed to the brim with a sea of bodies all clamoring for a glimpse of the approaching army. Twelve thousand soldiers marched towards them in perfect unison, their victorious strides echoing off the buildings like thunder. As they drew closer to the center of the city, the excitement and anticipation among the citizens grew to a fever pitch.

When Boyer and his army finally reached the city center, a massive stage stood before them, adorned with flags and banners of victory. As the generals dismounted from their horses and ascended the stairs together, General Allain's booming voice proclaimed Boyer as the president of Ayiti, soon to be once again united. The deafening cheers of the crowd drowned out any doubts or fears that may have lingered in Boyer's mind as he strode confidently to stand by Allain's side on the grand stage.

Boyer raised a hand, the gesture prompting an immediate hush over the crowd. He surveyed the sea of faces before him; men, women, children - all of them Ayisyen, all of them looking to him for guidance and leadership.

"My brothers and sisters," he began, his voice resonating in the still air. "We have been through a long and arduous journey. We have seen our people suffer, we have seen our land scarred by conflict, and we have seen heroes rise and fall." He paused, the weight of his words settling heavily among the crowd, and leveraged his lesson from the opera of the other night.

"But today... today we also see dawn breaking on a new era for our country. Today, we are no longer divided north and south but stand together as one Ayiti!" His words echoed off the cobbled streets and buildings around them. The crowd erupted into cheers again, their jubilation shaking the very ground beneath them.

Amidst a sea of red and blue flags fluttering proudly in the wind, Boyer stood tall and addressed his people. His deep voice carried over the crowd as he turned to face Allain and his fellow generals of the North. "These mighty generals, sons of Ayiti, defenders of our lands, protectors of you the people, we stand together as comrades" he proclaimed. The energy of the crowd grew as they awaited his next words. Suddenly, Boyer raised a 750-page book high above his head for all to see - the infamous Code Henry. An overwhelming chorus of boos erupted from the crowd as they expressed their disdain for this tyrannical law.

With a swift and dramatic gesture, Boyer threw the hefty book to the ground and brought his right boot down upon it with force. The sound echoed through the square as he shouted, "No more!" The crowd exploded into an extended cheer, their voices filled with hope and determination for a better future. It was clear that change was coming and they were ready to fight for it alongside their new leader.

As the crowd's cheers gradually subsided, Boyer again raised his hand for silence. "But even as we break the shackles of our past, let us remember the sacrifices made by those who have fallen," he admonished, his voice filled with a mix of sorrow and reverence. "Let us remember our late King Henry Christophe...a leader who in his way sought to bring order and prosperity to our land."

At the mention of Christophe's name, an uneasy silence fell over the crowd. Uncertainty lingered among the sea of faces; The King was a man who demanded respect but also spurred fear. His iron-fisted rule, his relentless drive for progress – it was all too fresh in their memory.

At that moment, Boyer could feel the nation's mixed emotions - relief at the end of Christophe's oppressive regime, a thread of respect for his unyielding spirit, and an echo of anxiety about what lay ahead. Boyer held those emotions, cradling them in the palm of his hand as he spoke again.

"Christophe's rule was harsh, yes. His methods were severe," he acknowledged, "And yet, we must recognize that beneath his stern exterior, he bore a deep love for this land and its people. His vision was a brighter future for Ayiti. A future built on strength, discipline, and order."

He paused as his gaze swept over the crowd - over the faces etched with hardship and resilience, over the hands roughened by work and war. He saw in their eyes the same determination that had fueled the revolution and inspired their relentless pursuit of freedom.

"But now," he said slowly, his voice heavy with sincerity, "it falls upon us to shape this future - not under the yoke of tyranny, but born from unity and understanding."

As the words washed over the crowd, a murmur of agreement began to ripple through them. It was like a gentle wind stirring the surface of a calm sea - unassuming at first, but gradually gaining strength. Their faces were hardened masks sculpted by years of struggle and uncertainty, but in their eyes, Boyer could see the sparks of hope kindling. He was speaking with those who loved their king and to those who despised him. A sense of appreciation and loathing for the man. He was a president for all the people and provided a path forward to those who hated the king and to those who loved him, together they would walk.

"King Henry's reign has ended, and with it, so has our division," he said, his gaze meeting those of the people one by one. "North or South, brothers against brothers, all will now unite as we are one Ayiti. One people, united by our shared past and our common future. As our great leader Toussaint Louverture once said; *'the roots are many and deep - they will shoot up again'*, and let us not forget Dessalines who cried out, *'L'union fait la force!'*, or my friend Alexandre Pétion who proclaimed *'In many we are one, united we are strong.'*"

The crowd responded with a unity of cheers and applause that ricocheted off the buildings lining the square. The discord that had plagued them for so many years was finally beginning to dissolve.

Jean-Pierre Boyer had been gone from Port Républicain for nearly three weeks now, organizing the new unification of the country that he declared on October 26th, 1820, nearly a week after first entering Le Cap. There was still much to do in the reorganization from a Kingdom into a unified country, but everything was going on track as Joute read the latest letter received. His correspondence would arrive by daily messenger, albeit a week later than written.

The last paragraph of each of Jean-Pierre's letters would contain rhapsodies of love and sensual innuendos that would make her blush, such as; *"Every sunset I see, mon amour, pales in comparison to your beauty... Every breeze that caresses my face is but a ghost of your tender touch... How I yearn for the warmth of your body, the taste of your lips... I count the days until I can hold you again, feel your heartbeat against mine..."*

Joute would blush at these words, a warm and sweet sensual sensation blooming within her like a blossoming orchid. But then followed the pangs of longing, the sharp pain of missing him so acutely that it took her breath away.

The days felt long and quiet without Jean-Pierre by her side, their house filled not with his charming laughter and passionate debates about Ayiti's future, but with an echoing silence that served as a bitter reminder of his absence. Still, Joute was proud of what they were doing for their country and knew that this unification was necessary for Ayiti to heal from its deep wounds.

The knock on the door was a soft but insistent rapping, almost like a gentle reminder of someone's presence. Joute's voice echoed against the walls of the study as she called out "Entre!" to the incoming secretary.

"He has arrived, Madame," the man quickly said.

"Show him in," Joute replied.

Juan Núñez Blanco strode into the room as an actor would stride onto an acting stage, his head held high and his posture exuding confidence. He was a man of many talents and skills, but above all, he was a master manipulator who had met his match with the likes of Joute.

Juan Blanco lived in the Spanish east and was well aware of powerful forces seeking to align themselves with Gran Colombia, whereas he preferred an alignment with the Republic of Ayiti as he felt he could better advance his career with Ayisyen governance as opposed to a government bowing to a far off country like Gran Colombia.

"Ah, my dear Joute," he said in his smooth, honeyed voice as he approached her with a charming smile. "It is always a pleasure to see you."

Joute felt a sense of unease settle in her stomach as she stood to greet him. She knew that Juan was not to be trusted, and Jean-Pierre had no clue that she was meeting with him. She could only hope that this meeting would yield positive results for the unification of Ayiti in the west with the Spanish portion in the east for a unified island of Hispaniola.

"Thank you for coming, Juan," Joute said politely, masking her reservations behind a pleasant smile.

"It is my pleasure," Juan replied smoothly, taking Joute's extended hand and kissing it lightly. "You know I am always at your service."

Joute resisted the urge to roll her eyes at his slick words and gestures instead motioned for them both to sit at the small table in the corner of the study.

"I trust you have read President Boyer's proposal for unification?" she asked, getting straight to business.

"Of course," Juan answered with a nod. "And while I agree with the idea in principle, I must say that there are certain details that need to be discussed."

Joute raised an eyebrow in curiosity. She knew that Juan would not agree to anything without some sort of personal gain for himself.

"What sort of details?" she asked cautiously.

Juan leaned forward with a sly smile, his eyes glinting with ambition. "As you and I both know, your president - your lover, eh?

He has no knowledge of these talks or this agreement. But Hispaniola has been divided for far too long. It is time for us, as Hispaniolans, to unite and lead our country towards prosperity. And who better to lead than someone like myself? A man with connections spanning the entire island, and with the best interests of our people at heart."

Joute listened to Juan's words with a growing sense of suspicion. She had always known that he harbored ambitions for power, but she never expected him to be so bold. "And how do you propose we deal with Núñez de Cáceres?" she interrupted, her voice laced with doubt. "He is the power broker in the Spanish East, even more powerful than your governor, and plans to break away from Spain and join forces with Gran Colombia. What plan do you have in mind?"

Juan's smile widened as his plan began to take shape. "I will lead a group of revolutionary fighters to attack San Luis Fortress," he explained confidently. "From there, we will expand our control to the Cibao region and establish a junta that will denounce Núñez de Cáceres and his Independent State. We will accuse him of being 'shapeless and antisocial' for not abolishing slavery and aligning himself with wealthy landowners who oppose emancipation."

Joute listened intently as Juan continued outlining his plan. "But how do you plan on gaining support from the Peninsulars - those born in Spain who refuse to renounce their citizenship?" she asked.

"That is where you come in," Juan replied smoothly. "We will gain the support of influential figures in towns west of Santo Domingo by convincing them to reject Núñez de Cáceres. With this accomplished, he will be isolated in Santo Domingo, despised by the Peninsulars, unable to control wealthy plantation owners who want to maintain slavery, and rejected by town notables who desire peace and stability. They will be at each other's throats. And that is when Boyer will make his move."

Joute's eyes sparkled with excitement as she pieced together the final step of their plan. "President Boyer will then write an open letter to Núñez de Cáceres that will be published in every newspaper promising the Spanish Hispaniolans everything they desire -

autonomy from Spain and Gran Colombia, freedom from slavery, increased commerce, and protection by the mighty Ayisyen military," she exclaimed. "We will make the letter public where he has no option but to accept or flee. It's a perfect strategy!"

"And I will be the one leading this movement," Juan declared confidently.

"Let's not get ahead of ourselves, Juan," Joute cautioned, her strategic mind continuously at work. "Jean-Pierre Boyer is still the president, and I know how best to present your petition. Leave it to me."

As Juan and Joute continued to work together to solidify their plan, Juan couldn't help but feel in awe of Joute's intelligence and strategic thinking. He had always prided himself on being a master manipulator, but he suddenly understood that while he thought he was the one pulling the strings, she had already bested him.

"You may go now Juan," stated Joute. "I will send word for you when we will meet next."

"But what of my assurance of a special role in all of this?" Juan asked, somewhat surprised by the sudden dismissal.

"You need not worry Juan. You have my commitment that you will play a major role. As I said, I will send word," she said with finality.

Juan left Joute's home, with a mixture of excitement and skepticism brewing within him. He had thought that he was the one leading this revolution, but now it seemed that Joute was the mastermind behind their plan. He couldn't deny her intelligence and cunning, but he also couldn't shake off the feeling of unease.

As Juan left the palace, Joute observed him getting into the carriage from behind the curtain of the large window. She turned and looked at the room. This was her government. This would be her planning. Yes, Juan would play a pivotal role, as would Jean-Pierre Boyer. But in the end, the conquest of the eastern part of the island and Santo Domingo would be hers to checkmate on the chessboard.

The room was silent, the lone sound being the gentle tick-tock of the mahogany clock against the wall. Joute walked over to the desk, her fingers gently tracing the smooth surface of the chessboard that lay upon it. Each piece has been meticulously placed in position by her, a silent testament to battles yet to unfold.

Under her touch, the pieces felt heavy with potential, each one representing a move in her grand design. Juan would be the knight, his charisma and ambition serving as vital tools in their revolution. His loyalty might lie elsewhere, but she would play on his blind ambition and his passionate desire for power.

The king was already beaten and gone. That was Henry Christophe. Pétion, the Rook was deceased and out of play. Boyer would be a bishop, his political prowess and diplomatic acumen guiding them from a distance. His presidency was not to be underestimated, for he held an undeniable sway over their people. However, even then, she knew when to use him, and when to sideline him for better prospects.

And herself? She was no mere pawn in this game of power. No, she was the woman, and the woman is naturally at the center. The Queen; commanding, calculating, a force to be reckoned with. Yet, she knew too well the dangers of hubris. She would not allow herself to be swept up in the intoxication of imminent power. There were still battles to be fought, alliances to be formed, and betrayals to ferment or guard against.

In the distance, she heard the rumble of thunder, a storm was approaching. The room darkened as clouds shrouded the sun casting an ominous shadow. She looked towards the window, her eyes drawn to the brewing turmoil in the leaden sky. It was a fitting reflection of the tumultuous times they lived in. She noted the irony with a bitter smile as she calculated the next chapter of the Republic of Ayiti, and her soon-unified Republic of Hispaniola.

To be continued

Subscribe for updates on future books in the saga.

www.TriumphToTragedy.com

Epilogue

Centuries later, school children will gaze admiringly before the weathered statues of Ayiti's four founding fathers, their gaze lingering on each bronze visage as if searching for understanding in this solemn garden of remembrance where history whispers through the leaves.

Toussaint Louverture's statue bares an expression of dignified resolve. A man of visionary ideals, Toussaint had been the cerebral architect of the revolution, his acumen unrivaled. His successes were myriad: the brilliant military campaigns that swelled with ingenuity, the social reforms that aimed to bind the wounds of slavery, and his desire for the colony to be the powerhouse in the trade business of the Americas. Yet, his failure was personal; a misplaced trust led to his capture, and ultimately, he perished in a frigid jail cell far from the tropical home to which he committed his life to.

A few paces away, the statue of Emperor Jean-Jacques Dessalines stared fiercely into the distance. His countenance was etched with the scars of battle, both literal and metaphorical, as a slave and as a military commander. A leader of indomitable spirit, Dessalines' dedication to independence was absolute. Though his methods were contentious, steeped in blood and iron, his triumphs cemented the foundation of the free nation. But the specter of his ruthlessness lingered, casting a shadow over his legacy until an assassin's bullet ended his reign.

Alexandre Pétion's likeness radiates charisma even in effigy. With a natural allure that drew men to his cause, Pétion was an artilleryman turned tactician who navigated the treacherous waters of politics with aplomb. He championed the rights of the blacks and the gens de couleur and sought to dismantle the vestiges of colonial hierarchy. Despite these noble endeavors, his tenure was marred by internal divisions and accusations of self-serving schemes.

The final statue, that of King Henry Christophe, loomed with regal austerity. Christophe, the indefatigable builder, had raised fortresses and palaces from the earth and forged the first kingdom in the new world. His reign brought education, structure, and pride to his people. However, his stringent codes and rigid governance chafed against the populace, breeding discontent that would ultimately lead to the tragic demise of his planned dynasty.

But where are the statues of Marie-Madeleine Lachenais, affectionately known as "Joute"? She was a woman who could sway the scales of power and easily guide influential leaders, such as Alexandre Pétion and Jean-Pierre Boyer, in the direction she deemed strategically necessary. This earned her the nickname of *"The President of Two Presidents"* among those who truly understood her impact and stepped away from her path.

And what about Queen Marie Louise Coidavid? She was the delicate balance between ruthless tyranny and rare moments of kindness within the kingdom her husband, King Henry Christophe, so aggressively sought to build.

And let us not forget Empress Marie-Claire Heureuse Félicitée Bonheur – the only person, man or woman, who could tame the ferocious nature of her husband, Jean-Jacques Dessalines, and his insatiable thirst for complete control through brutal means when he felt necessary.

Lastly, we must never forget Suzanne Simone Baptiste Louverture – the senior among these remarkable women. She stood by her husband, Governor General Toussaint Louverture, offering wise counsel and unwavering support to one of the most influential men of that time.

Triumph To Tragedy is a tale of great men, with their numerous achievements and personal flaws, all accompanied and balanced by the great women they wisely chose as their lifelong partners. The next installment of Triumph To Tragedy – Book Four, will feature additional larger-than-life figures that have been lost or overlooked in history, as Jean-Pierre Boyer strives to unite the island of Hispaniola into one Republic of Ayiti.

Coming in Fall 2025:
Triumph To Tragedy – Book Five

From Unification to Occupation

www.TriumphToTragedy.com

Daniel J.D. Bayard

NOTABLE CHARACTERS

FRANÇOIS DOMINIQUE TOUSSAINT GUINOU
DE BREDA LOUVERTURE

Also known as Toussaint L'Ouverture or Toussaint Bréda; (1743 – 1803) was the most prominent leader of the Ayisyen Revolution. During his life, Louverture first fought against the French, then for them, and then finally against France again for the cause of Ayisyen independence. As a revolutionary leader, Louverture displayed military and political acumen that helped transform the fledgling slave rebellion into a revolutionary movement. Louverture is now known as one of the "Founding Fathers of Ayiti".

In 1802, Toussaint was captured and deported to France on the 74-gun French ship the Créole. He warned his captors that the rebels would not repeat his mistake, *"In overthrowing me you have cut down in Saint-Domingue only the trunk of the tree of liberty; it will spring up again from the roots, for they are numerous, and they are deep."*

During his imprisonment at the frigid Fort-de-Joux in Doubs, France, Louverture, who was, after all, a French General, attempted to gain an audience with Napoleon who refused. He wrote a memoir and died in prison on April 7, 1803, at the age of 60.

SUZANNE SIMONE BAPTISTE LOUVERTURE

Suzanne Louverture (1742 – 1816) was the wife of Toussaint Louverture. When in 1801 the constitution appointed Toussaint as governor of Saint-Domingue, she received the title of "Dame-Consort."

In 1802, Charles Leclerc's troops captured her along with her husband and the rest of her immediate family and shipped them to France. Madame Louverture survived her husband, who died in a French prison the following year. She was the mother of three boys, the youngest of which, Saint-Jean, died in 1804 in Agen, France. She died in 1816, in the arms of her sons, Placide and Isaac in Agen as well.

JEAN-JACQUES DUCLOS-DESSALINES

Dessalines (1758-1806) was a leader of the Ayisyen Revolution and on January 1, 1804, became the first ruler of an independent Ayiti. He soon after enacted the 1805 constitution. Under Dessalines, Ayiti became the first country to permanently abolish slavery. Initially regarded as governor-general, Dessalines was later named Emperor of Ayiti as Jacques I (1804–1806) by generals of the Ayisyen Revolutionary Army and ruled in that capacity until being assassinated in October of 1806. He has been referred to as one of the founding fathers of the nation of Ayiti.

MARIE-CLAIRE HEUREUSE FÉLICITÉ BONHEUR DESSALINES

Félicité (1758 - 1858) became Empress of Ayiti (1804–1806) as the spouse of Jean-Jacquess Dessalines and they had seven children together. During the siege of Jacmel in 1800, she was applauded for her work with the wounded and starving. She managed to convince Dessalines, besieging the city, to allow roads to be opened for food, clothes, and medicine which she delivered.

She had the keen ability to curb the cruel excesses of her husband, Emperor Jean-Jacques Dessalines, and is credited with saving many French colonists during his rule.

HENRY CHRISTOPHE

Henry or Henri Christophe (1767 – 1820) began his military career as a slave drummer boy in the famed Chasseurs-Volontaires de Saint-Domingue during the American Revolution. Upon his return to Saint-Domingue, he reportedly worked at the Hôtel la Couronne, albeit for an unknown period, where he eventually earned enough money to buy his freedom. As an adult, he became a key leader in the Ayisyen Revolution and ascended to be a monarch of the Kingdom of Ayiti by proclaiming himself king. Christophe set out to improve all aspects of life in his Northern Kingdom, focusing on building defense mechanisms such as the famed Citadelle, erecting multiple opulent palaces, expanding agricultural production, and educating his people. However, his work codes and societal methods were deemed tyrannical and created unrest amongst his people. He suffered a stroke and fearing overthrow through revolution, committed suicide with a famed silver bullet.

MARIE-LOUISE COIDAVID CHRISTOPHE

Coidavid (1778 - 1851), was the Queen of the Kingdom of Ayiti from 1811–1820 as the spouse of Henri Christophe. She was born into a free family; her father was the owner of Hôtel de La Couronne in Cap-Français, Saint-Domingue. Henri Christophe was a slave purchased or leased by her father and he supposedly earned enough money in tips from his duties at the hotel that he was able to purchase his freedom before the Ayisyen Revolution.

They married in Cap-Francais in 1793, having had a relationship with him from the year prior. They had four children: François Ferdinand, Françoise-Améthyste, Athénaïs, and Victor-Henri. She was exiled for 30 years after Christophe's death. Shortly before her death, she wrote to Ayiti for permission to return, however, died in Italy.

ALEXANDRE SABES PÉTION

Pétion (1770 – 1818) was the first President of the Republic of Ayiti from 1807 until his death in 1818. He is acknowledged as one of Ayiti's founding fathers; a member of the revolutionary quartet that also includes Toussaint Louverture, Jean-Jacquess Dessalines, and his later rival Henry (Henri) Christophe.

Pétion distinguished himself as an esteemed military artillery officer and commander with experience leading both French and Ayisyen troops. The 1802 coalition formed by him, Dessalines, Christophe, and others against French forces led by Charles Leclerc would prove to be a watershed moment in the decade-long conflict, eventually culminating in the decisive Ayisyen victory at the Battle of Vertières in 1803.

JEAN-PIERRE BOYER

Boyer (1776 – July 1850) was one of the leaders of the Ayisyen Revolution, and President of Ayiti from 1818 to 1843. He reunited the north and south of the country into one unified Haiti. He then marched into the Spanish East of the island, the current day Dominican Republic, and brought all of Hispaniola under one Ayisyen (Haitian) government by 1822. Boyer managed to rule for the longest period of any of the revolutionary leaders of his generation from 1818 to 1843.

MARIE-MADELEINE "JOUTE" LACHENAIS

Joute (1778 – 1843), was a politically active and influential Haitian woman. She was the mistress and political advisor of both President Alexandre Pétion and President Jean-Pierre Boyer, exerting a significant influence over the affairs of state during their presidencies for a period of 36 years (1807–1843). She was called "The President of two Presidents," and regarded to have been the most politically powerful woman in the history of Haiti before the introduction of women's suffrage in 1950.

Joute was the daughter of Marie Thérèse Fabre and the French Colonel de Lachenais. She was the mistress and concubine of Alexandre Pétion, with whom she had two daughters, Cecile and Hersilie. In 1807, When Alexandre Petion became president, she acted as his adviser. Petion appointed Jean-Pierre Boyer as his successor with her support.

After the installation of Jean-Pierre Boyer in 1818, she functioned as mistress and political advisor to Boyer as well and had a daughter, Azema, with him. After Boyer lost power in 1843, Joute and her daughters, referred to as Boyers family, were escorted to a ship to follow Boyer into exile to Jamaica. She died shortly after her arrival in Jamaica.

JACQUES-VICTOR HENRY CHRISTOPHE

Jacques-Victor (March 1804 – October 1820) was Prince Royal of Haiti and heir apparent to the throne of the Kingdom of Haiti. He was the youngest child of Henri Christophe, then a general in the Haitian Army, by his wife Marie-Louise Coidavid. His father became President of the State of Haiti in 1807, and on March 28, 1811, he was proclaimed King of Haiti. The Prince Royal had an older brother who died at age 11 before the proclamation of the kingdom. Following the death of his father on October 8, 1820, the Prince Royal should have been proclaimed King Henry II of Haiti, but the country was already in turmoil and he never had a chance. Ten days later, he was murdered, either being bayoneted or shot, by revolutionaries at the Sans-Souci Palace.

BENOIT JOSEPH ANDRÉ RIGAUD

Rigaud (1761 – 1811) was the leading mulatto military leader in Saint Domingue during the civil war in the colony. His protégés were Alexandre Pétion and Jean-Pierre Boyer, both future presidents of Ayiti. He returned to Saint-Domingue in 1802 with the expedition of General Charles Leclerc to unseat Toussaint but was arrested for disobeying orders by French commanders and sent back, and imprisoned in the same fort as Toussaint Louverture. He later returned to Haiti after the revolution in 1811 in an attempt to once again gain power and rule the Southern Peninsula. A heavy drinker, he died six months after his return due to illness.

POMPÉE VALENTIN VASTEY

Vastey (1781 - 1820), or Baron de Vastey, was a Haitian writer, educator, and politician. Vastey was a "mulatto," born to a white French father and a black Haitian mother. He first served in the administration of Dessalines, then as secretary to King Henry Christophe, and tutor to Prince Victor Henri. Vastey may have fought in Toussaint's army and is said to have been the second cousin of the French novelist and playwright Alexandre Dumas. Vastey is best known for his essays on the history and contemporary circumstances of Haiti at the time. He was raised to the rank of baron and appointed secretary of the Legislative Commission responsible for preparing the Code Henry, a 750 page document outlining the laws of the land.

REAR ADMIRAL SIR HOME RIGGS POPHAM

Popham (1762 – 1820), was a Royal Navy commander who saw service against the French during the Revolutionary and Napoleonic Wars. He is remembered for his scientific accomplishments, particularly the development of a signal code that was adopted by the Royal Navy in 1803. He was promoted to rear admiral in 1814, appointed Knight Commander of the Order of the Bath in 1815. This was capped off with a personal gift from Prince Regent in the Knight Commander of the Royal Guelphic Order in 1818. He served as Commander-in-Chief, Jamaica Station from 1817 to 1820.

FRANÇOIS CAPOIS - CAPOIS LA MORT

Capois (1766 – 1806) military career began in 1793 after a visit with independence leader Toussaint Louverture. Capois is mostly known for his extraordinary courage and especially his herculean bravery at the Battle of Vertières in which the French general Viscount of Rochambeau, commander of Napoleon's army even called a brief cease-fire to congratulate him. He was nicknamed "Capois la Mort" *(Capois to the death)* for his numerous episodes of defying death during battles.

LAMOUR DESRANCES

Desrances (unknown birth – 1803) was born in Africa and brought to Saint-Domingue as a slave who shortly afterward escaped for the mountains to join the maroon bands. He had mixed loyalties throughout his lifetime. At the time of the Civil War of Knives, Desrances was loyal to André Rigaud in his battle against Toussaint Louverture and was one of the few black officers in the predominantly mulatto Rigaud-loyal army. After Rigaud's defeat by Louverture, Desrances accumulated power and mobilized the maroon warriors in the mountains surrounding Port-au-Prince and Saint Marc. After the French invasion in 1802 he later changed his loyalty to the French under Général Pampile de Lacroix to fight against Dessalines' forces, defeating Dessalines' army at the outskirts of Port-au-Prince and forcing his retreat, a victory that finally convinced Toussaint to surrender to the French and seek retirement before his arrest, deportation, imprisonment, and subsequent death in France. He was later hunted and killed by Dessalines' forces.

NAPOLEON BONAPARTE

Napoleon (1769 – 1821) was a French military officer and political leader who rose to prominence during the French Revolution. Together with his brother, they engineered a coup to seize power of the French government. He later was crowned emperor and was then known by his regnal name of Napoleon I, He led several successful campaigns during the Revolutionary Wars. He unsuccessfully attempted to re-enslave the most valuable of the French possessions, Saint-Domingue, from 1801 to 1803, almost bankrupted the country, and forced to sell many assets, including the Louisiana territories to the United States. This doubled the size of the young country overnight.

SIMÓN BOLÍVAR

Bolivar (July 1783 – 17 1830) was a Venezuelan statesman and military officer who led what are currently the countries of Colombia, Venezuela, Ecuador, Peru, Panama, and Bolivia to independence from the Spanish Empire. He is known colloquially as El Libertador or the Liberator of America.

During his climb to power, he was beaten and escaped to Jamaica, then to Haiti. In January 1816, he was introduced to Alexandre Pétion, President of the Republic of Haiti by a mutual friend. Bolívar and Pétion impressed and befriended each other and, after Bolívar pledged to free every slave in the areas he occupied, Pétion gave him money and military supplies.

After initial victories, he was once again beaten and returned to Haiti in early September of the same year, where Pétion again agreed to assist him with ships, soldiers, arms, money, and a printing press. He returned to South America and eventually was victorious.

U.S. PRESIDENTS JEFFERSON, MONROE, AND MADISON

Jefferson's refusal to recognize the independence of Haiti in 1804, then crippling the Haiti's economy with an embargo from 1806 to 1810, was emulated by Madison and Monroe, the Virginians who succeeded him. When, in the 1820's, the issue was again debated in the Senate, Southern senators refused to acknowledge a nation formed by black slaves who rebelled against white slaveholders. "Our policy with regard to Haiti is plain," insisted Senator Robert V. Hayne of South Carolina. "We never can acknowledge her independence." It was not until 1862, in the midst of the Civil War, that the Lincoln administration finally recognized Haiti.

Jefferson, in a letter to his successor, James Monroe, wrote "that too much contact might advance the contagion of freedom to the United States. We may expect black crews, super cargoes, and missionaries thence into the Southern states." It was an unwelcome prospect and, for Southern planters, disturbing, they insisted, and must be quarantined to the island country of Haiti.

MARIE SAINTE DÉDÉE BAZILE

Bazile (unk. birth-death), known as Défilée and Défilée-La-Folle *(the crazy),* is a figure of the Ayisyen Revolution. She is remembered for retrieving and burying the mutilated body of Emperor Dessalines after his assassination at Pont Rouge, at the northern entrance to Port-au-Prince. Dédée Bazile was born near Cap-Français to enslaved parents and made a living serving as a sutler to the army of Dessalines.

DR. EDWARD STEVENS

Stevens (1754 – 1834) was an American physician and diplomat. He was a close friend of Alexander Hamilton since early childhood in Danish St. Croix, now the US Virgin Islands. Stevens served as the United States consul-general in Saint-Domingue (later Ayiti) from 1799 to 1800. President John Adams sent Stevens to Ayiti with instructions to establish a relationship with Toussaint Louverture and express support for his regime. Following his arrival in April 1799, Stevens succeeded in accomplishing several of his objectives, including the suppression of privateers operating out of the colony, protection for American lives and property, and right of entry for American vessels. The convention, signed on June 13, 1799, continued an armistice among the three parties and gave protection to British and American ships to enter the colony and engage in free trade.

Inspiration and Collaboration from Jean-Bernard Bayard

"An incredible work of research. A profound, deep, and engaging look at Haiti's compound dichotomy. An excellent historical tool for my books"

...Daniel J.D. Bayard

In writing the Triumph To Tragedy Series, it was essential to match the stories with an accurate accounting of history, and most importantly that the actual sequence of events follow the correct timeline. This would ensure that the story be rendered as an authentic recording of history, albeit in a genre of storytelling that educates readers of the personalities, culture, foods, and ambiance of the period through enlightenment and entertainment.

To accomplish this goal, I needed an expert with whom I found in Jean-Bernard. He is not only my dear cousin, but on this journey, I have grown to respect and admire his knowledge and understanding of history. JB, as I affectionately call him, has been an incredible resource in Ayisyen/Haitian and world histories. He rattles off names, dates, and places like an efficient encyclopedia with a full understanding of the relevant characters.

If you are interested in a non-fictional, unfiltered account of the history of Haiti, I highly recommend his new book; In Search of An Identity. You won't be disappointed.

In Search
Of An
Identity

A Personal Introspective Look
By Jean-Bernard Bayard

Jean-Bernard felt compelled to write this book for a simple reason; he had always felt refuted, if not rejected, any time he introduced his nationality. From a young age in his country of birth, Haiti, he had to prove to people that he was Haitian. He used to be called "Ti Blanc" which means "Little White" or "The Outsider".

Today, as an American citizen, the situation had gotten worse. The Haitian community in the United States does not believe him when he tells them that he is a Haitian. The American community does not believe him when he tells them that he's American, because of my French/English accent. *"So what am I?"* he asks. He explores this in his book alongside the storied history of politics and the culture of Haiti.

He actually wrote the book longhand, and with the love and patience of his wife Patricia, who painstakingly typed the words into a document, he was he able to finally publish the work years later.

Jean-Bernard Bayard was born in Diquini, a suburb of Port-au-Prince, Haiti in 1947. He moved to New York in 1964. He returned to Haitii for fifteen days for one of his brother's wedding in 1969. He received great insights into his country of birth and of his family heritage from his father, a career military officer.

While assimilating into the foreign culture of his adopted country, he felt compelled to delve into his own culture to better understand himself. His multiethnic heritage of Taino, African, and European cultures has always been a mystery to him, which he explores in his book.

ABOUT THE AUTHOR
Daniel Jean-Dominique Bayard

Mr. Bayard is an award-winning author and magazine columnist for Haitian and Atlantic history. He was born in Port-au-Prince, Haiti, and raised in the United States when his parents fled to New York in 1958 from the brutal Duvalier dictatorship at the age of one. He returned to Haiti for the first time as a teenager of 17 and has been fascinated with Haiti's culture, people, and historical significance ever since. He lived and owned a business in Haiti for a short period and came to love it.

While researching his family's ancestors dating back to the 17th century, he became intrigued with the complexities and drama of Saint-Domingue, the colonial precursor of Haiti, or its indigenous name of Ayiti, and the revolution that gained its freedom and independence. In-depth research into all aspects of the period's history and colonial society led him to write these thrilling, enlightening, and entertaining novels of his family's story, and the nation's triumphs, and tragedies.

Mr. Bayard is married with 4 children, and blessed with 6 grandchildren.

Winner
International
Impact Book Award
2024

Ancestors of the Author

Philippe Bayard (Lille, France DOB 1689)
(Arrived in Saint-Domingue circa 1710)
Married Marie Debreuse

Jean-Philippe Bayard (Son) 1725
Married Jeanne Guillemette Bachelier

Jean-Baptiste Hyppolite Bayard (Son) 1750
Married Marie Jasmine

Jean-Baptiste Bayard (Son) 1775
Married Marie Victoire Georges

Achilles Othello Bayard (Son) 1823
Married Elizabeth Pressoir

Georges R. Bayard (Son) 1850
Married Marianne Clerie

Thomas Bayard (Son) 1879
Married Alzire Sansaricq 1881

Daniel Thomas Bayard (Son) 1912
Married Marcelle Elisabeth Oriol 1921

The Author:
Daniel Jean-Dominique Bayard (Son) 1957
Married Lily Anne Marie LaPlace 1957

THE REPUBLIC OF AYITI

Ayisyen Creole: Ayiti

The country of Ayiti is located in the Caribbean on the western third of the island of Hispaniola. It is bordered by the Dominican Republic to the east, the Caribbean Sea, and the Atlantic Ocean.

Ayiti's terrain consists mainly of rugged mountains interspersed with small coastal plains and river valleys. The government system is a republic; the chief of state is the president, and the head of government is the prime minister.

Ayiti has a largely traditional economic system in which most of the economy relies on subsistence farming, and government regulation is widely constrained. Ayiti is a member of the Caribbean Community (CARICOM)

In color, the flag of Ayiti's top section is Blue and the bottom section is Red. The inserted image in the center of the flag consists of cannons in Blue, Red and Green in a White background.

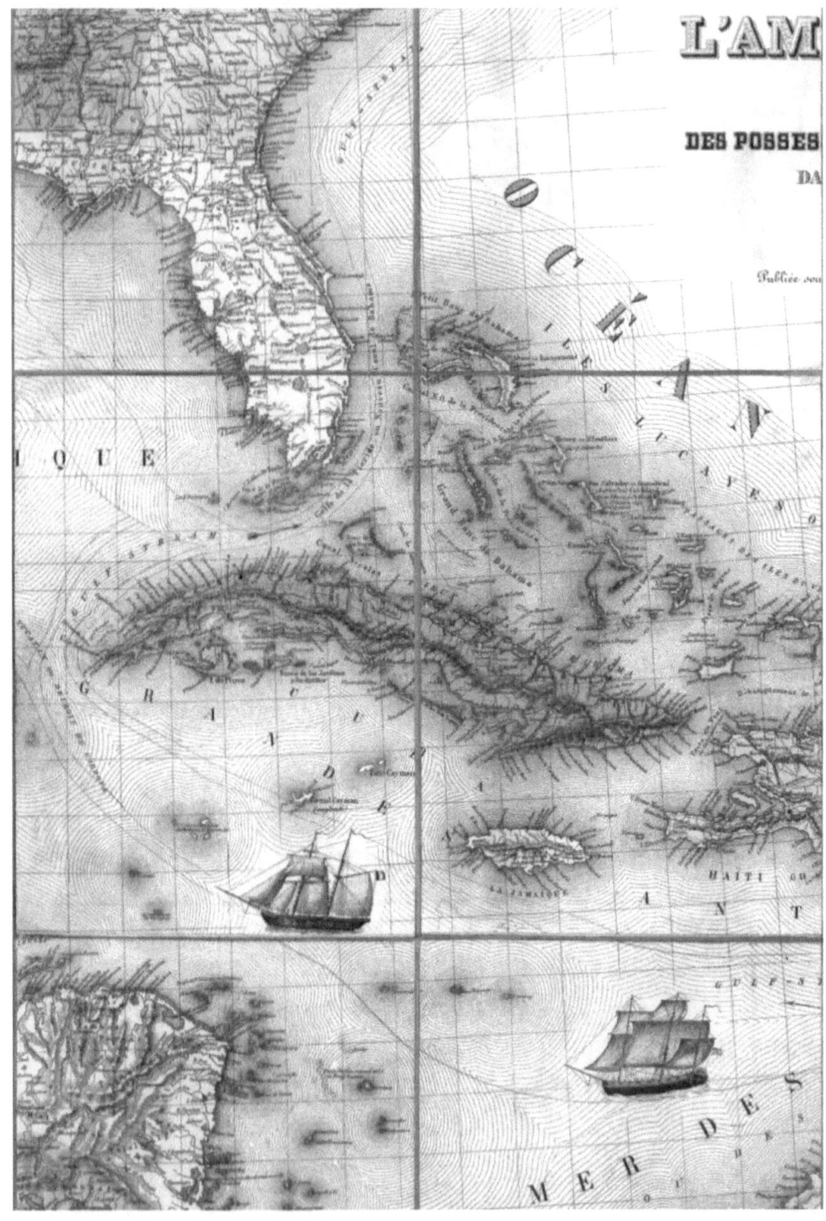

L'AM
DES POSSES
DA
Publiée sou
OCÉAN
ÎLES LUCAYES
GRANDES
HAÏTI ou
MER DES

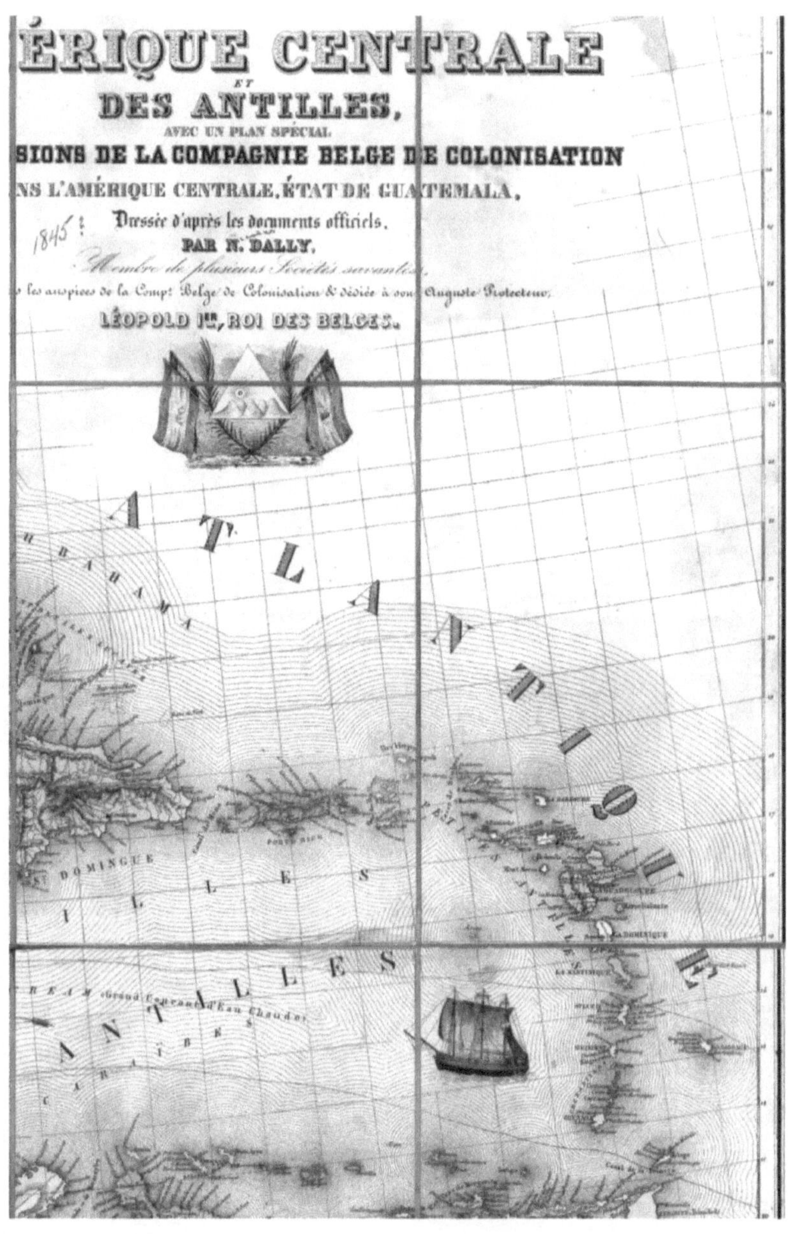
ÉRIQUE CENTRALE
ET
DES ANTILLES,
AVEC UN PLAN SPÉCIAL
SIONS DE LA COMPAGNIE BELGE DE COLONISATION
NS L'AMÉRIQUE CENTRALE, ÉTAT DE GUATEMALA,
Dressée d'après les documents officiels.
PAR N. DALLY,
Membre de plusieurs Sociétés savantes.
les auspices de la Comp. Belge de Colonisation & dédiée à son Auguste Protecteur,
LÉOPOLD Ier, ROI DES BELGES.
1845
ATLANTIQUE
BAHAMA
ST DOMINGUE
PORTO RICO
ANTILLES
ANTILLES
CARAIBES
Grand Courant d'Eau Chaude
LA MARTINIQUE
GUADELOUPE
LA DOMINIQUE